Lady & Boxer Investigators - Magnicide

Lady & Boxer Investigators, Volume 2

Marcel Pujol

Published by Plumas Uruguayas, 2024.

This is a work of fiction. Similarities to real people, places, or events are entirely coincidental.

LADY & BOXER INVESTIGATORS - MAGNICIDE

First edition. November 11, 2024.

Copyright © 2024 Marcel Pujol.

ISBN: 979-8227649973

Written by Marcel Pujol.

Table of Contents

Lady & Boxer Investigators - Magnicide 1
CHAPTER 1: WHO WATCHES THE WATCHER? 4
CHAPTER 2: THE CANDIDATE 16
CHAPTER 3: PRISONER 2746 31
CHAPTER 4: FIRST INTERVIEWS 40
CHAPTER 5: ANABEL PULANSKY 50
CHAPTER 6: EXECUTION IN BATTALION 14 63
CHAPTER 7: THE TRAITOR? 74
CHAPTER 8: PRESIDENT VALDEZ 88
CHAPTER 9: THAT WOMAN HAS TO DISAPPEAR 106
CHAPTER 10: PRESIDENT BORDERRAGUI 119
CHAPTER 11: SUSPECTS' STORM 141
CHAPTER 12: THE INCARNATE DEVIL 155
CHAPTER 13: POISON IN THE COFFEE 168
CHAPTER 14: HERE THEY ARE MADE, AND HERE THEY ARE PAID 182
CHAPTER 15: PRESIDENT DE LA RÚA 204
CHAPTER 16: TUPAMARO, POLITICIAN, MURDERER, AND TRAITOR? 217
CHAPTER 17: GENERAL MENINI RUIZ 238
CHAPTER 18: SIBLINGS 250
CHAPTER 19: NOT AGAIN 262
CHAPTER 20: COUNCIL BY THE FIRE 277
CHAPTER 21: MY DAD. MY AUNT 306
CHAPTER 22: FIRE... LIKE IN THE OLD SALOON . 329
CHAPTER 23: A DIFFICULT INTERROGATION 340
CHAPTER 24: THIS HAS TO END 360
CHAPTER 25: YOU SHALL NOT DRINK FROM THIS WATER 373

*To all those who have suffered and **continue** to suffer under dictatorial regimes in their countries, and yet have managed to maintain their sanity, refusing to follow the de facto leader of the moment.*

PROLOGUE: DEATH AT THE THERMAL BATHS

Arapey Thermal Baths, Salto, Uruguay, Saturday, July 18, 2009, 9:30 PM.

Lorenzo felt sorry for the only remaining guest at the Palm Pool, one of the few closed public pools, decorated inside with a variety of palms, giving an exotic and relaxing atmosphere to the bathers. However, he couldn't wait until his shift ended at 10 PM to go to the bathroom. Sometimes you can hold it, sometimes you can't.

He had been working as a full-time municipal employee in the lifeguard sector for three years at the Salto City Council. He needed to contribute to his parents' household while finishing his degree in Agricultural Engineering at the University Center of Salto. Naturally, this lifeguard position, during the low season in the middle of winter, involved *not only* monitoring for drowning but also additional tasks like collecting wet towels, mopping to prevent slips and falls, chatting casually with older patrons, and ensuring that some unruly grandchildren weren't splashing others, who generally came for relaxation and seeking the supposed healing properties of the thermal waters. Although these properties had never been scientifically proven (nor had anyone bothered to do so), this was the marketing pitch for tourism at the Arapey Thermal Baths.

The young lifeguard checked his wristwatch. He had been in the bathroom for only five minutes—nothing that could get him in trouble, even if a supervisor happened to pass by. However, when he tried to open the bathroom door, which swung outward, it was locked tight.

"What the hell...?" Lorenzo exclaimed. "The last thing I need is to be locked in the bathroom. Damn it! These doors only lock from the inside."

He pushed and pushed for several minutes, trying to get the door to budge from its frame, but there was no way.

"It must be the humidity; it got stuck. What the hell am I going to do now?" Panic set in, not from the fear of being trapped indefinitely but from worrying about who he could call to let him out, which took him away from his job of preventing drownings in the pool.

His first thought was to call his supervisor, but then he remembered it was Saturday and his supervisor didn't work at the Arapey Thermal Baths on weekends, especially not on a national holiday like July 18. He would be over an hour away by car in the city of Salto and he would also have to explain why he left his post to go to the bathroom. He decided to call Karen, his current girlfriend, who was working the night shift at the municipal Hotel Termas del Arapey.

"Hi, Karen, how are you? All good?"

"Lolo, what's up? Yes, I'm fine. I was just about to start my shift."

"Can you delay your start a bit? I think I'm in trouble."

"What happened?"

"I got locked in the bathroom at the Palm Pool, can you believe it?"

"What?!"

"Just what you heard. Can you come by and see if there's something blocking the other side, or... I don't know... check if there's someone from maintenance who can help me force it open?"

"Sure. I'll send a text to my supervisor and ask him to send someone from maintenance."

Countless minutes passed as the trapped municipal employee occasionally tried to force the door open and sent texts to Karen asking how long it would take. Finally, in one of the many attempts to push it open, the door gave way as if it had never been locked.

"Damn it! You could have opened earlier, couldn't you?" he monologued to the door.

He hurried back to the pool, glancing at his watch: 9:55 PM. "*Twenty-five minutes away from your post, you **idiot**, just because you couldn't hold it a little longer,*" he chastised himself.

Then he saw him: the only guest remaining in the Palm Pool was now floating face down... motionless.

"Shit-shit-shit-shit!" His adrenaline surged, and he dove in to bring the lifeless body of the septuagenarian to the edge.

He checked for a pulse. It was nonexistent. He began CPR, a skill he had learned in lifeguard training. This is how Karen and the municipal maintenance worker found him.

"Karen, call 911, please. Send an ambulance, now!"

CHAPTER 1: WHO WATCHES THE WATCHER?

C*ountry Club of the private neighborhood La Horqueta, Buenos Aires, Argentina, Sunday, July 19, 2009, 7:20 PM.*

Geraldine Goldman and Viktor Ielicov, private detectives—she Uruguayan and Jewish, he Russian and atheist, she a former head of Press for the Uruguayan National Police, he a former heavyweight boxer, all of this before they got together four years ago to dedicate themselves to private investigation-, had been in the same location for the last hour and a half. Inside the rented car, observing with their telephoto camera the subject of their current investigation: Natalie Ricci, a former top model and current actress, suspected by her husband, billionaire businessman Sergio Fávregas, of being unfaithful.

"How horrible if we ever got to this point, right, Vik?" Geraldine asked after a long moment of mutual silence.

"To suspect that the other is being unfaithful?" the colossus with an aquiline nose and feline eyes wanted to confirm.

"Yes, and to have to resort to private investigators like Fávregas did to follow his wife, to see if we can take pictures of her sleeping with another man, and that kind of thing."

"That's true," the retired boxer shrugged. "I mean, if at some point I get bored with our relationship, Gera, I'll just tell you, period. What's the need to hide, giving you a kiss in the morning after breakfast, and instead of going to work, I go sleep with someone out there?"

"Right? What's the need? Besides, at this point, it seems we're pulling the wool over our client's eyes. I mean: Natalie is an exemplary mom. She takes her kids to school, goes and films her scenes in the movie she's shooting, goes to events where she's invited, and we somehow sneak in, day in and day out. Without the glamour of red carpets and public exposure, she's the most *ordinary* person on the planet: she has a husband, three kids, works, then comes home and spends some time with her husband. What's suspicious about all that for her husband to think of hiring us?"

"Well... she's not *that* ordinary, we can agree on that, right? Look at the former top model and actress, up on a tree branch, dressed in black, watching through binoculars at her husband, our client, while he plays squash at the Country Club of the private neighborhood where they live."

"Clearly, distrust goes both ways, doesn't it?" Ielicov raised a suggestive eyebrow.

"Totally! But since our schedule is currently empty, having been following her for 10 days, we'll continue for another 10. After all, Fávregas has no shortage of money, which brings to mind that we're going to have to start investigating our clients *before* taking a case."

"What do you mean?"

"Our fees are pocket change for this millionaire."

"Hey, it's not like $400 a day plus expenses is chump change, my love."

"But we could have charged him *double*."

"And he also could have chosen *not* to hire us if we raised our published rate on our website and in the classifieds."

"You make a good point there," conceded the Communication graduate from ORT University, and more recently with a license issued by the Argentine Federal Police as a private investigator, despite being Uruguayan. "Do you remember what you charged when I hired you, four years ago?" she smiled.

"Well! But are you ever going to stop bullying me about that?" the muscular man showed annoyance. "What did I know about how much my work was worth? For me, $50 was fine, and it kept me at the top of the filters from cheapest to most expensive. Remember, I had only taken 3 cases after getting my detective license when you called me to solve the case of the first serial killer in Uruguay."

"Oh, no. Don't pin that blame on me. I had given the details of the case in the email I sent to your sister, and she didn't read to the end because it was too long," shrugged the curly-haired brunette.

It's worth clarifying at this point that referring to "you", or "tú" in Spanish, in Geraldine's case, despite the fact that in the Río de la Plata it is much more common to use "vos," was due to her upbringing in a cultured family, and her desire, when she was still engaged to Julián Sterenstein, to preserve the proper use of language and to pass that custom on to children she would never have. In Ielicov's case, he learned Spanish from his Chilean mother.

Geraldine's cellphone rang at that moment.

"What's this?" she was astonished. "Is it a new case?" she answered the Nokia N97. "LNB Investigations, how can I help you?"

"Geraldine?" an elderly voice sounded on the other end of the line.

"Yes. This is she. Who am I speaking with?"

"This is Cortez."

"Secretary Cortez?" the former head of Press for the Uruguayan National Police wanted to confirm.

"The same. I hope I'm not catching you at a bad time."

"No, not at all. We're currently in an ongoing investigation, as that's what I'm doing now with my partner, but we're just in surveillance, nothing more."

"*Precisely* for that reason I was calling you. I need to hire you, if you're available."

"Please tell me the details of the case," she said very seriously and professionally, but her expression towards Ielicov was one of pure excitement and anticipation.

"Last night, the body of Francisco 'Pancho' Mojica was found dead in a pool at the Termas del Arapey."

"Wait. Are we talking about the politician, the former *Tupamaro*?"

"That one, yes. The one who was running for president in October for the Progressive Front and was leading in voter intention."

"Oh my god. And I suppose that if you need us on the case, it's because he didn't die of natural causes, correct?"

"Absolutely not. That is: the initial forensic report listed the cause of death as a heart attack, but... new reports indicate he had very little chance of having one."

"I understand. And will the Secretary of the Interior pay our fees this time? Because last time you still owed us," Geraldine reproached.

"What?!"

"Don't you remember? In the case of the Decorator. I went to your office with the proposal to hire an international detective, one who would give an external view of the case, you approved the expense... only *verbally*... and then it turned out that three 'advisers' appeared like paratroopers - and I'm making air quotes with my fingers - from the FBI, and you discarded my idea when I had *already paid* Ielicov's fees and his travel and accommodation expenses out of my own pocket."

"Aaaahhhh, yes. *Now* I remember. But tell me how much I owe you, and I'll write you a check. That's the least of it. And going back to your earlier question, it's not the Secretary of the Interior that will cover the costs of hiring you. Look, Goldman... I think you and I have always had a very sincere dialogue, right? I would hate to burst any illusion you may have, like thinking that Santa Claus or the Three Kings exist, but nowadays, political parties have at most a 5 or 10% influence over the decisions that affect a country. The rest are rules of the international market, and in large part, the real decision-makers in politics are the sponsors of electoral campaigns."

"The lobbyists. Right. Are they the ones who will pay us?"

"Yes. So, if you want to raise the fee a bit, that's up to you. I was tasked with finding the best possible solution to this predicament, and my recommendation was to hire the two of you."

"Well... thank you, I suppose," Geraldine didn't know how to react, "but why *us* in particular?"

"Were you or were you not the ones who caught the Decorator?"

"Yes, we were... And now that I remember: the Uruguayan state *never* gave us official recognition."

"It wasn't even necessary! That friend of yours, the writer, published the whole story in his book."

"And who could deny that he was within his rights? On one hand, he was involved in solving the case, and on the other, he took a bullet that almost sent him to the other side."

"Well then, Goldman. I would need your response as soon as possible. Are you going to take the case?"

"Yes, as soon as we finish this one, of course. We don't usually leave cases unfinished. Vik"—he asked his partner, who had been listening on the Argentine side of the conversation, since the Nokia

N97 didn't have a hands-free feature—"how long do you think until we can wrap this up here?"

"In 15 or 20 minutes, give or take. But you have to hurry. In 1 minute, we'll lose the window of opportunity," the detective assured, keeping his gaze fixed on the camera's telephoto lens.

"Did you hear that?"

"Yes."

"Good. As soon as we finish here, we'll grab our things at the hotel and take the first flight to Uruguay. Is it to Termas del Arapey we need to go? Add 5 or 6 more hours to that."

"Forget the commercial flight. Let me know when you leave the hotel for Aeroparque Airport, and we'll send the presidential helicopter to pick you up."

"Understood. We'll do that," she ended the call.

"Shall we go?"—Ielicov urged, and both got out of the rental car.

Natalie Ricci, born in Uruguay, had built her career from the ground up all by herself, without anyone's help. Not even her parents. They wanted her to be a doctor or an engineer, but from the young age of 14 and at just 1.60 meters tall, her calling was the runway. Modeling, traveling, appearing in advertising campaigns... Her first TV spot was at 15, and over the years and decades, the ad became increasingly uncomfortable for both her and those who saw or remembered it. She walked with very short shorts down a sidewalk in a neighborhood, walking her little dog, and there was a group of guys on her path. She stopped, and a commercial voice said, "Relax. You're with BO." Then Natalie continued walking, very confidently. This is how a well-known tampon brand advertised that it was not only normal and understandable for men to look at a minor's backside but that the only thing the victim of street harassment—how it would later be legally defined in serious countries around the world—had to take into account was that when they looked at her butt and shouted lewd things, there shouldn't be a blood stain on her tiny shorts.

Anyway, that simple and outdated ad had earned her countless calls for campaign after campaign across the river, in the city of Buenos Aires, which led her to move there, even as a minor, to forge her career. How she had gone from those promising beginnings in the modeling and showbiz world to lying on a tree branch, the bark digging into her torso, glued to the binoculars, waiting to see if her husband really was as regular as he seemed at the squash club, or if it was all a sham and he was off with someone else, was a path she couldn't decipher.

Two strangers approached her husband as he was leaving the Country Club with his bag in hand, heading for his Mercedes. For a moment, she feared they were robbers who had somehow bypassed the private security of the high-end mansion complex, or even kidnappers. Whatever had happened between them in recent years, with the marital tensions and distance, he was still her husband and the father of her children. It was *healthy and natural* that she still worried about his physical safety.

However, Sergio seemed to know the individuals who had approached him quickly. There was a burly man, the kind you'd expect to see as a security guard, and a rather tall and thin woman with curly dark hair tied back in a ponytail.

"What the hell is this?"—she whispered to herself, still following the conversation between her husband and the strangers.

However, her panic grew when all three seemed to be heading *directly* toward the tree she was perched in. "What do I do now?" she thought, but quickly dismissed the idea of descending hastily. Ricci was in great shape given her job, but the climb had already been challenging, and the branch she was on was at least 5 meters above the ground; to get down, she needed to carefully watch where she stepped, which branches could support her weight and which couldn't...

Finally, they were under her, at ground level.

"Can you come down by yourself, Natalie, or do we need to help you?"—the burly man, looking like Hercules, asked with a smile.

"Come on, Ricci. There's nothing to fear"—assured the other stranger.

"Who are these two, Sergio?"—the actress and former model still didn't trust them.

"They're private detectives. I hired them, Nati. Can you please come down so we can talk civilly?"

The three at ground level waited patiently for Ricci to descend without breaking her neck. But as soon as she touched the ground, she turned toward the trio with fire in her eyes.

"So now you have private detectives following me?"—she shot at her husband.

"The dead woman said to the beheaded one,"—Geraldine added, pointing at the high branch where Natalie had been spying on her husband.

"Well, they both distrust each other,"—wanted to be the mediator, the former heavyweight boxer—"let's start from that basis. First, let's clarify that for 10 days and 10 nights we followed you everywhere, Ricci, and we've already assured Fávregas that you're clean."

"Of course I'm clean! Newsflash!"—the Uruguayan, who had been living in Argentina since she was 15, scoffed. "It's *him* who always runs off."

"I'm heading out 'there'"—he made air quotes with her fingers too—"for work. Except when I'm here, releasing the day's tensions through sports. But at least I don't work with my ex-boyfriend," the businessman threw down the gauntlet.

"Oh, is this all about Lucas?"—she pointed at the detectives with a wide gesture.

"Who is Lucas?"—Geraldine intervened.

"Lucas is Nati's ex-boyfriend," explained the one who had issued the challenge. "They were the media couple of the moment before she started dating me."

"Are you an idiot?!"—the actress fumed. "I *already* explained that putting him as the director in the movie we're filming is a media move by the production company to generate press and anticipation *before* the premiere."

"Alright. Time out. I think I've got it," Ielicov intentionally shifted the topic.

"What do you mean?"—the couple exclaimed in unison.

"What's happening to you two. And I'm going to be very clear and blunt, although I'll do my best *not* to be rude. Can I?"—he waited for them to nod. "What's happening to you two is that you're *not* having sex, or at least not with the frequency and intensity that you used to. How far off was my basketball shot from the hoop?"

"Having sex? What's that?"—the Uruguayan rolled her eyes, her ivory face with delicate features showing disbelief.

"I'm afraid you're right, Ielicov," admitted Fávregas.

"Then we're on the right track. What you two don't need is to climb trees or hire detectives. What you two need is couples therapy"—he waited for his words to sink in among the spouses. "Now, if you want, I can give you a preview, okay?"

"Are you a psychologist as well as a detective?"—Ricci asked, genuinely intrigued.

"No, but... I manage as a negotiator in these matters,"—*before* Geraldine, Ielicov had led a dissipated life with women, and many of his dates were married, and after making love, they would tell him all their complaints about their husbands. "First question,

Sergio: I need you to remember something nice from when you weren't dating yet and you were courting her."

"Okay"—the accused swallowed hard. "What can I say about when I met Nati in person? She was... I mean: she was on all the magazine covers. She was a goddess! But when I started to insert myself through connections into all her events and fashion shows..."

"I almost filed a restraining order against you, idiot,"—the Uruguayan smiled.

"I remember, yes,"—he smiled back. "That's when I started to notice that all the media attention and exposure hadn't gone to her head. And that's what made me fall in love."

"Your turn"—this time Viktor addressed the contractor's wife.

"Well... what can I say? I saw him there, looking at me during the fashion shows and events, and of course it scared me a little, but I started asking around, and it turned out Sergio was a multimillionaire, and yet, can you believe the guy didn't have enough self-confidence to approach me and say hello? That vulnerability in him, which you wouldn't expect from someone who has it all, seduced me."

"We're still on the right track,"—the boxer praised. "Now I'm going to ask you both the same question, and I want you to answer from the heart, okay? Sergio, do you still desire Natalia? I mean, do you want to be intimate with her?"

"She's the sexiest woman I've ever met in my life. The most beautiful woman on the planet,"—the businessman stated sincerely. "If only she weren't in a bad mood all the time, treating me badly..."—he changed to a tone of reproach.

"Time-time-time,"—the boxer called for a timeout, like in basketball. "When I used to box, at least you had to wait for the bell to ring before throwing punches"—he noticed it made both of them smile. "Now it's your turn, Natalie: do you desire your husband?"

"I *melt* every time he touches me. I get a shiver, but the good kind, if you know what I mean, from head to toe. But of course, for him to touch me, he'd have to take a moment away from his computer and his little phone..."

"Ricci. No low blows,"—Ielicov warned, like a boxing referee. "Now then. Last question for both of you: do you or do you *not* have enough money to live comfortably for yourselves, your children, and your grandchildren?"

"We're doing well, yes,"—the multimillionaire admitted.

"Nothing to complain about,"—his wife agreed.

"So, guys,"—Ielicov smiled widely—"what's the point of breaking your backs trying to accumulate more and more? Yes, I know. You're going to tell me you do it so your three beautiful children, who from what we've seen are very well-mannered, cheerful, and friendly, and who surely worry you about their future, have everything they need and more, but... what difference will it make to them when you pass on your fortune, that is... when you make peace with God and move on to the next level, to put it in video game terms, whether you leave them 10, 20, or *30* million dollars? If you raise them well and with love, surely when they grow up they'll be able to make good use of what they inherit and generate much more"—he paused significantly while the spouses' eyes glistened. "Enjoy yourselves, here and now. You, Sergio, learn to delegate, man. Surely you have a CEO who can handle a good part of what you do, and you, Natalie, if instead of going to three events a week you go to just one, how much less will you earn? And how much more will you be able to enjoy your husband and your children?"

"I love you, you idiot"—Sergio said to his wife, hugging her and kissing her lovingly, tears of reconciliation in their eyes.

"And I love you"—she replied. "And I love you."

"Do you think we should leave the car here and walk home?"—he suggested.

"Sure"—she agreed.

"Ielicov, Goldman"—the businessman shook the hands of the detectives alternately—"thank you. Thank you *very much* for your services."

"Don't mention it, Fávregas"—Geraldine waved it off. "Even marriage counseling is included in our fee. Should we send you the invoice along with our banking details for the transfer?"

"Yes, please do."

"And don't forget to include the banking fees to be covered by the sender," added the raven-haired detective.

"I'll keep that in mind."

Ricci and Fávregas were already far away when the detective said to his partner:

"Wow! And that hidden talent for negotiating in couple conflicts? You kept that well-hidden, huh? Where did you learn it?"

"Trust me, you *don't* want to know,"—he replied tersely, aware that discussing the dozens of women he had been with before his current partner was not exactly a conversation topic Geraldine enjoyed, quite the opposite.

"I can imagine, look"—she rolled her eyes—"well, shall we take a helicopter to Uruguay to solve a high-profile murder?"

"Ladies first."

CHAPTER 2: THE CANDIDATE

S*alto International Airport, 70 kilometers from the Termas del Arapey, Sunday, July 19, 2009, 10:15 PM.*

As soon as the Bell Hu-1 war helicopter, commonly known as the Huey, which had last seen real combat in Vietnam in '74 and had been donated by the United States to Uruguay three years prior, in 2006, was put at the service of the President of the Republic, landed at the helipad, Viktor and Geraldine descended with their bags, instinctively holding their heads despite not wearing hats, perhaps just out of a cinematic or televised reflex from having seen it so many times in movies, while the still-rotating blades ruffled their hair.

"Corporal Fernández, Mechanized Cavalry Regiment No. 4 'General Artigas'!" shouted a young Latino in military uniform. "I'm your liaison with the Armed Forces. Please follow me to complete the immigration process." He pointed to a desk inside a hangar where an officer from that agency awaited them, heavily bundled up due to the low temperatures.

"Passports, please," requested the immigration officer, waiting for the documents to be handed over, stamped them, and simply said, "Welcome to Salto," after which he stood up and left.

"Just like that, without checking our bags?" Ielicov was surprised.

"From what I've been told, time is of the essence," Fernández answered the rhetorical question. "Please follow me to the car."

An hour later, having exchanged only trivialities among the three of them, they arrived via a winding, semi-paved, bumpy road at the Arapey Termal, the most luxurious complex in the Termas del Arapey. In the restaurant, which now housed only a few guests, Fernández directed them to a table where three gentlemen awaited them, two in suits and another in just a jacket with the top button of his shirt undone. One was familiar to both of them; he was the one who had summoned them, Secretary of the Interior Aníbal Cortez. The other, a man with a mustache and the top button of his shirt undone, was familiar to Ielicov from his involvement in the Decorator case, and *painfully* familiar to Goldman. She addressed him before even greeting anyone else.

"What are you doing here, Toro?" she shot him a furious look.

"Hey, calm down, I don't bite," joked the burly man with the mustache.

"He's the current Chief of Homicides of the National Police," Cortez interjected.

"And why so much resentment toward me, if I may ask?" asked "Toro," as everyone knew him in the force.

"You remember the last time we talked, right? Let me refresh your memory: you were interrogating me as a suspect in my father's death."

"Ooooohhh, right," the veteran man recalled. "But that was *ages* ago, and I was doing my job, you know: following the leads we had."

"Yes, the leads that my brother, who turned out to be the Decorator, *planted* to frame me."

"Geraldine, listen: did I hold you that time? No. Should I have even called you to testify at Central Headquarters? Maybe. If I have to apologize every time I follow leads that could potentially lead to solving a case and it turns out that it's not like that..." he shrugged.

"Geral... partner..." Viktor attempted to mediate the conflict. "We both know your brother played us all: you, me, the press, the entire National Police, the Judiciary... Toro acted in line with his position, okay?"

The mentioned woman took a tense moment to calm down. The Chief of Homicides noticed and extended his hand.

"Past is past?" offered Gervasio "Toro" Villa.

"Past is past," she accepted.

"Well, now that we're all calmer," Cortez began, "let me introduce you to Detective Ariel Di Lorenzo," he pointed to the third member that neither Viktor nor Geraldine knew. "He's the detective in charge of the case."

"A pleasure, Ariel," Ielicov extended his hand to shake the newly introduced man's hand. He couldn't be over thirty, tall and barely athletic, leaning more towards thin.

"The pleasure is mine. Geraldine," the young man offered his hand to the private detective.

The five of them took their seats at the table.

"Alright, let's get down to business," Goldman proposed professionally. "Cortez summoned us because the police don't believe that the initial cause of death identified by the forensics—a myocardial infarction—was the *actual* cause of death, am I right?"

"There are two indications that point in the opposite direction," began Toro in his deep voice. "Number one: Mojica was the favorite candidate to become president in October, and as such, he had an electoral strategy behind him, advisory groups, support from the Progressive Front, and so on. One of the requirements was to undergo a full medical examination twice a year. The last one, which he had last month, indicated he had only a 2% chance of having a heart attack. In short: the guy had iron-clad heart health."

"And that brings us to the second indication," Di Lorenzo chimed in, "the lifeguard."

"What about the lifeguard?" Ielicov inquired.

"At the time of his death, however it happened," the young National Police detective dismissed with a gesture, "Mojica was alone in the pool. There was a lifeguard with him. It's the policy of the Intendancy of Salto that there's always one present at public pools. The issue is that around 9:30 PM yesterday, according to the official's account, he felt the urgent need to go to the bathroom, a need that couldn't wait, if you know what I mean, and he went. But when he tried to leave the bathroom and opened the door, which opens outward, he couldn't get it open. He said he struggled and struggled, but it was as if a wall had suddenly been built behind it."

"We verified that the door in question has no external latch, and it opens and closes without a hitch," Toro continued. "The lifeguard was trapped there for 25 minutes. He panicked and called his girlfriend; we've interrogated her too, and she corroborated it. He called her for help and to bring someone from maintenance with a crowbar to help him get out, and around 9:55, the door opened without problems. He rushed to the pool and found Mojica floating face down, lifeless."

"He pulled him to the shore," Di Lorenzo continued, "tried to revive him, his girlfriend and the maintenance guy arrived, they called an ambulance, but it was no use."

"*Of course*, the lifeguard is the prime suspect on the list, right?" Goldman wanted to confirm.

"We know," Toro confirmed. "We have him in custody while we investigate his background, but still... whether it was him or something or someone prevented him from leaving the bathroom... the hypothesis of a heart attack from an old but healthy guy... I wouldn't bet all my chips on natural causes as the reason for death."

"Alright," the former Russian boxer stroked his chin, his typical gesture of thinking. "Still, there's something I want to clarify with you, although I suspect I already have the answer: Why involve external help?" he pointed to himself and his partner. "The police must have around 30,000 officers, give or take, am I remembering the figure correctly? What are my partner and I doing here?"

"Now it seems there's another one with amnesia, besides Toro," Cortez mocked. "Do you remember how the Decorator case was handled, the scandal it caused, how the National Police was left looking ridiculous, the infiltrators from that sun-worshipping sect among our ranks?"

"The ones at this table are the only ones who have all the details, Vik," his partner smiled at him. "No one else knows that Senator and presidential candidate Francisco 'Pancho' Mojica may have died from something *other* than a heart attack."

"What I suspected," confirmed the ex-boxer.

Gym and Equipment Room at the Arapey Termal Hotel, Termas del Arapey, Monday, July 20, 2009, 8:20 AM.

Geraldine watched in fascination, as usual, the impossible amounts of weight being lifted by the current detective and former heavyweight boxer from Vladivostok.

"Do you realize you're lifting *twice* my weight, bench pressing?"

"Yes," the muscular man confirmed with effort. "The price of staying in shape."

By that time in the morning, as was the routine for the detective duo, it didn't matter where they were working; they had already gone for a run for an hour, and then each had been on their respective machines and weights for another 45 minutes in the gym. Viktor finally set the barbell with 120 kilos on its supports.

"That's enough for today," he declared.

"Let's shower and change," she suggested. "We have a meeting with our client at 9, and I don't know about you, but I *intend* to have had breakfast by then."

"Are you sure we don't have time for a quickie?" he smiled mischievously.

"Let's see."

By 9 AM, they had indeed finished breakfast, and were showered and dressed in their usual attire: he in a navy suit, white shirt, and gray tie, she in a navy suit, white shirt, and no tie. They immediately noticed that the newcomer in the hotel restaurant was the lobbyist they were expecting.

"Wait: an Afro-descendant?" she whispered to her partner.

"What? Isn't that common in Uruguay for a lobbyist?" Ielicov was surprised, also in a low voice, but stood up in time to greet the newcomer, who was well over six feet tall and clearly familiar with the gym and weights, judging by his suit and overcoat. "You must be the representative of the corporation that hired us, right?"

he extended his hand to shake with the newcomer. Viktor Ielicov, private detective."

"Geraldine Goldman," his partner did the same.

"Iván Reno," the newcomer introduced himself after the formal greetings. "What a cold day, huh?" he remarked, and as if he owned the place, called the waitress who promptly arrived. "Good morning. I'd appreciate a hot chocolate and two croissants. If they're sweet, even better; if not, the savory ones will do."

The waitress from Arapey Termal left with the order.

"A pleasure to meet you, Iván," Geraldine began the conversation. "This time, we're supposed to be working not directly for the Secretary of the Interior, but for the business group you represent, which was behind Senator Mojica's presidential campaign. Am I correct?"

"Absolutely, Detective Goldman," Iván smiled widely, showcasing a perfect smile. "You see, I don't want to bore you with the details, but the CSA Group is very interested in understanding the *exact* circumstances of the candidate's death that we supported. We went with Secretary Cortez, and he recommended you based on your background, so the CSA Group would be hiring you to find out what caused Mojica's death, and especially: *who and why he was killed.*"

"I understand," the Russian chose to be cynical. "Administering justice in a possible homicide case takes a backseat to figuring out what it means for your investment in a candidate, doesn't it?"

"Don't misunderstand me, Detective Ielicov," he paused to receive his order from the waitress. "Thank you, dear. Democracy and institutional stability are *key* for the normal development of our business, but if any rival corporation ordered his murder, or if some foreign group did it, we need to be informed firsthand to know how to navigate our commercial interests."

"Alright," Geraldine accepted, more interested in taking the case than in being champions of justice. "You understand this isn't an ordinary case. I mean: if confirmed, it's a high-profile homicide, and considering the polls that almost confirmed him as the next president of the republic, we'd be talking about something close to a political assassination, wouldn't we?"

"Are you negotiating with me, Geraldine?" Iván smiled broadly, dipping the tip of his croissant in the chocolate for a few seconds before eating it, noticing that he had left the curly-haired, pale-skinned woman somewhat speechless. "Yes, *you are* negotiating with me," he laughed, revealing his perfect teeth. "Oh, come on. You have nothing to be ashamed of, detective. I'm the commercial representative for a group that encompasses dozens of companies across various sectors, with exports in almost every country. Feel free to be direct with me; don't hold back," he winked.

"Well, getting to the point," she tried to regain her dignity, as if it had fallen to the floor or been left in her purse, "our published daily fees on our website and in the classifieds state $400 plus expenses, but for a complex and delicate case like this one... you'll understand that we'd want to charge a bit more. Do you have the authority to negotiate on behalf of the CSA Group?"

"Broad authority," Mr. Reno replied after another bite of his croissant, which he had also dipped in the hot chocolate.

"Good. We'll set our fees at $600 per day plus expenses. Generally, we require an advance of five days, that is, $3,000 at the start, and in cash or bearer's check, whether we resolve it or not, and our clients usually give us an envelope with cash for expenses or a debit or credit card that we'll use at our discretion for accommodation, travel, bribes..."

"I see no problem with that," he accepted, finishing his first croissant. The tall, muscular Afro-descendant pulled out a checkbook from his briefcase, quickly wrote a check for $3,000, and handed it to them along with a Master Gold credit card. "Please be prudent with expenses, and keep the receipts, because I have to report back to my bosses later. The PIN for the ATM is 1373."

"Alright, and for this case, since we understand that speed is crucial, we'll set a bonus of $5,000 if we solve it before the police, and within a week, meaning by next Monday at this same time. The uncertainty of who may have killed Mojica, or even just the speculation, can impact the markets, the interests of Uruguayan bonds, and even the dollar exchange rate, not to mention investor confidence. In other words: CSA's business could be affected if this drags on."

"Oh, wow. I hadn't thought of it that way, but yes, you're right, Goldman. Uruguay has always been well regarded internationally for its institutional and economic stability. International banks and governments *know* what to expect from Uruguay, to put it simply. I accept the bonus, but let's raise the stakes and make it more interesting: let's bump it up to $10,000 if you solve it in the first four days, that is, by Friday morning."

"That sounds good on our end," the detective shrugged.

"Now, getting to the matter at hand," Ielicov changed the subject once his partner had finished discussing financial matters, which he wasn't great at, "who could be at the top of the list of those who would benefit from the winning horse dying before October?"

"The list is long, Ielicov. Let's start with the opposition, since Mojica was from the currently governing party. The strongest opposing candidate is Luis Alberto De La Rúa, from the Conservative Party. We could also consider Economist Daniel Arturi, who was Mojica's running mate after losing to him in his party's primaries. A pretty bland guy, I admit, low-profile, but with an exceptionally high intelligence, capable of orchestrating the death of his ticket mate to take the presidency for himself. Of course, under these unfortunate circumstances, the Progressive Front will have to call a party convention to designate a new ticket, but I can't think of anyone who could replace the political weight and voter support Mojica had other than Arturi. And it's not that he has a significant political weight of his own. In fact, I think his list received about 7 or 8% of the total votes in the Progressive Front primaries, but he's a consummate strategist, able to make alliances with other sectors, and you can bet that as soon as he heard about Mojica's death, he started calling *every* leader in his party to ask: 'Mojica is dead. Will you support my candidacy for president?'"

"I see. Alright. Let's continue with his electoral platform. What promises did Mojica make during the campaign, should he become president, that could have alarmed someone or some group?" Ielicov pressed on.

"I can't think of any," the lobbyist seemed puzzled. "I mean: he had the profile of a man of the people, concerned for the well-being of his fellow citizens, with a high populist profile. Let's see... he promised quality education for everyone, regardless of social strata, state reform, and greater citizen participation, transparency in public management..."

"Did that transparency include *serious* investigations into the forced disappearances during the dictatorship?" Geraldine interjected, feeling she had regained some of her lost dignity from earlier.

"Well," Iván shrugged. "You surely know the story of 'Pancho' Mojica: he was a Tupamaro, fought armed against the democratically elected government, which his group deemed fascist, attempting to establish a more communist regime, so to speak, like Cuba. He lost, was captured, and then the military dictatorship that began in '73 imprisoned him in a solitary cell for 12 years under inhumane conditions... They didn't kill him in particular, but they did kill many of his comrades. It's normal for him to want to know what happened to those who weren't as lucky as he was to survive the military government, and yes, it was on his political agenda to investigate what happened to the 130 men and women who the military disappeared."

"*That's* a motive," Viktor commented to his partner. "Now, let's move on to more mundane matters. Was Mojica married? Did he have children? Who would inherit his estate when he died?"

"Are you referring to the farm where he lives, and the yellow Volkswagen Beetle?" the lobbyist dismissed with a gesture. "Sorry. Maybe since you come from abroad, you don't have much context. 'Pancho' lived with just the clothes on his back, little more. He was married to Laura Pulansky, from his same group, the Popular Movement, and they had no children. By party policy, both donated 70% of their salary as senators to the party, so I don't think you can pull a thread from there."

"Alright," accepted the one who had asked. "Let's draw up a list of our first interviews then."

Viktor took a small notebook and a pen from the inside pocket of his jacket.

"Don't worry, detective. We prepared it for you in advance."

Opening his briefcase, Ivan took out a sheet with an Excel spreadsheet printed on it, detailing by columns name, relationship (with the deceased), phone number, and email address.

"Uh-huh," Geraldine examined. "Luis Alberto De La Rúa, Daniel Arturi, Laura Pulansky... Javier Bravetto, president of the Progressive Front?"

"Yes, it's just a titular position," Reno dismissed with a gesture. "But he might be the one most aware of the electoral engineering to replace Mojica, and who is supposed to succeed Mojica in the formula."

"The president Tabaré Valdez?!" Viktor was surprised. "Does that mean that if we dial this number, the president of the Oriental Republic of Uruguay will answer in person?"

"The CSA Group supported Valdez when he won the elections in 2004 as we did now with Mojica in 2009. Believe me, Dr. Valdez is the *most* interested in ensuring that his party's country project continues into a second term. Valdez will provide all the logistical support you need, including the police and the army, if necessary."

"Oh, yes, that. Before I forget," Viktor remembered. "One of the first expenses we're going to make on the corporate card you just gave us is to rent a car. It was very nice that an army car picked us up at the airport last night, but we work independently."

"As you see fit," accepted the expert negotiator.

"Alan Douglas, campaign advisor," Geraldine continued with the list.

"He doesn't leave his side," Ivan affirmed. "He manages his schedule and writes his speeches for public appearances. You should talk to him."

"Gabriela Vilariño," Viktor read. "Personal secretary. She and Douglas are staying at this hotel, along with Mojica."

"Jorge Larrán and Pedro Méndez, leaders of the Conservative Party and Independent Party senate caucuses, respectively," Geraldine continued with the list. "And what role do they play?"

"Oh, yes, it was a somewhat sensitive topic to leave it printed," Reno switched to a confidential tone, having finished his breakfast, with just a bit of chocolate left in his cup. "You see... I understand that you are Uruguayan, Goldman."

"That's right."

"Well, it won't be unknown to you that between '73 and '85 there was a civic-military dictatorship here in Uruguay, and that the return to democracy was guaranteed by the vote at the polls in '83, but *also* by the Naval Club pact in '84, where the conservative parties agreed with the de facto regime *not* to prosecute those who had committed crimes against humanity during the dictatorship."

"I'm familiar with that part of history, yes," Geraldine assured.

"Well, then, in '86, already in the framework of the return to democratic life, the law of expiration of the punitive claim of the state was promulgated, more familiarly called the Expiry Law, to ensure that repressors and human rights violators were not prosecuted."

"And then in '89, a referendum was attempted to repeal it, right?" the detective recalled, who at the time was 14 years old, enough to be aware and understand the political life of her country.

"The green vote and the yellow vote, that's right. The initiative to repeal it lost, but for these October elections, the Progressive Front, with Mojica at the head, supported a *new* initiative to repeal that law."

"Oh, I didn't know that part. I've been living in Buenos Aires for 4 years. Besides, our work takes us a bit around the globe, you can imagine."

"Yes, of course. It's no shame *not* to be aware of the day-to-day political issues of a country where one does not live. The point is that those who most promote the non-repeal of this law are senators Larrán for the Conservative Party and Méndez for the Independent Party."

"Oh, wow!" Ielicov connected the dots. "Does that mean that if the repeal promoted by Mojica is approved at the polls, the generals and torturers could start being prosecuted and sent to jail?"

"Precisely. But not only that. Former president Borderragui himself could be prosecuted and imprisoned for his collaboration with the '73 coup and for enabling the establishment of the de facto regime."

"Wow. There's a thread to pull, Vik. Imagine, being a torturer enjoying the millions you stole from Uruguayans, in your retirement in your mansion, with the prospect that one day the police will knock on your door and take you away to be prosecuted, to very likely *die* behind bars."

"Something doesn't add up," the former Russian boxer stroked his chin. "And be careful, it's not that back home I come from a super democratic and free regime. But 24 years after the dictatorship, that is, in a democratic regime, with elections and all that... crimes committed during the dictatorship still *haven't* been investigated?"

"The Expiry Law provided, yes, to 'investigate,'" the lobbyist made air quotes, "what had happened to the detained-disappeared, but..."

"Not very enthusiastically, right?" the Russian understood.

"Not at all. Borderragui is on the list," Geraldine confirmed.

"That's right. Also, with this referendum move, and considering that Mojica was imprisoned by the military for 13 years, kept in a hole, it is expected that, if approved by the citizens, the repeal I mean, he will go all out to prosecute and condemn the former coup plotters, if he had reached the presidency."

"What a time for one to have an unlikely heart attack, right?" the private detective ironized. "And this other name sounds familiar too, but I don't remember from where: Amadeo Píriz. Collaborator, it says in the relationship with Mojica. A bit ambiguous, isn't it?"

"*Purposeful*, ambiguous, and double-edged, too. Píriz is a sworn enemy of Mojica. They hate each other... a lot. Both were Tupamaros in the sixties, and when they were caught, Amadeo Píriz decided to collaborate with the de facto government, betraying his comrades, *including* Mojica. This was recently called into question when Píriz returned to Uruguay after more than 20 years in exile in Spain. He even wrote a book, (Word of Amadeo), where he tells *his* version of events, claiming that he didn't betray anyone or collaborate with the military in any way, raising suspicion that he was framed by the other Tupamaros—Mojica, Huidó, Pulansky, Zabala—who pointed to him as the infiltrator. I can already tell you that Píriz is having a hard time here in Uruguay. People insult him and spit at him in the street, and he receives death threats..."

"What a disaster if he *wasn't* the informant, right?"—Geraldine understood. "Or that, after all, there hadn't been a snitch in the first place."

"I suppose we'll never know for sure,"—shrugged the burly lobbyist. "It's Amadeo's word against that of the other Tupamaros."

"And why did they include two former secretaries of Mojica on the list?"—Viktor wondered.

"Who knows a politician's life better than their personal secretaries?"—the Afro-descendant replied with another question.

"Makes sense,"—agreed Ielicov. "I suppose in that same vein, we should include the one who, by last name, could be Mojica's sister-in-law, Anabel Pulansky."

"Yes, she's Laura's twin, also a former Tupamaro, and you have her close by. Well... *relatively* close. She lives on a ranch in Paysandú with her husband and son."

"Let it not be said that the CSA Group doesn't do its homework,"—Geraldine raised an eyebrow.

"Whatever you need from our side, detectives, and I mean *whatever*, call me at any hour. I never turn off my cell phone. I'll tell you more: most politicians will be found today at 7 PM in the Legislative Palace. Mojica's wake will be in the hall of lost steps, and all the politicians will be there: De La Rúa, Larrán, Méndez, Pulansky, President Valdez... My flight leaves from Salto Airport at 5. If you can make it, I'll take you."

CHAPTER 3: PRISONER 2746

Punta Carretas Prison, Montevideo, Uruguay, July 18, 1971, 12:10 PM.

The mayor Falcone was eating rotisserie chicken with his hands when prisoner 2746 was brought in. If there was anything he liked about his job, it was making prisoners feel bad. Keeping them poorly dressed in winter, locking up those who misbehaved in metal cells under the sun for hours, ensuring that the food was irrevocably cold, and that any act of disrespect or disapproving glance towards him or any of his subordinates was punished with no less than 2 months in solitary confinement without visits, of course—the only mental escape valve in any prison where one learns as an inmate what's happening outside, how their family is doing, and gets to know their new grandchildren or nephews...

In his mind, the director of Punta Carretas Prison believed that if they committed crimes and had a good time in prison, they would return to committing offenses once released. Meanwhile, and not out of pure sadism but from personal conviction, the career police officer made the prison experience as harsh and horrific as possible to prevent recidivism.

Prisoner 2746, in particular, was supposedly one of the most dangerous they had in the facility. He had been part of the National Liberation Movement—Tupamaros, from its inception years ago until the dissolution of the urban guerrilla group that sought to establish a socialist state in the style of Cuba through bombings, kidnappings, and robberies. Only, as Ernesto 'Che' Guevara himself said in a talk at the University of the Republic a decade earlier, on

March 8, 1961, 'here in Uruguay, you can't do the same as in Cuba because you don't have jungles or mountains.'"

And how right Guevara was, since while it made noise and alarmed the population, by 1971, the MLN was already dissolved, and all its members were imprisoned in Punta Carretas. Therefore, and out of pure prudence, even though 2746 was brought in handcuffed, it would have suited Director Falcone to have armed guards in his office if there was a guerrilla man on the other side of the desk with the potential to kill anyone who thought differently than him.

However, for quite a while, all he did was eat his rotisserie chicken in front of the inmate, washing it down with a liter of Coca-Cola. When he finished eating, he gestured for the prison guard to leave and let them be alone.

"I apologize for not offering you any, 2746, but as you can see, half a chicken was barely enough for me."

"Why did you call me, Falcone?"

"To make you a proposal. That's how generous I feel today."

"Proposal for what?"—the inmate was puzzled.

"You see,"—he wiped his lips and hands with a cloth napkin—"you leftist murderers did us a great service in the sixties. The work you did was *impressive* for advancing our goals in the country. We are *infinitely* grateful, from the bottom of our hearts, for having opened the door for the Implementation of Urgent Security Measures four years ago, which are still in effect. Now repression against crime is something else entirely, and justice can be administered with an iron fist. And all those great advances, we owe to you."

"Ha. You're welcome,"—said the Tupamaro, somewhat ironically, understanding that the ideological end of his movement was exactly the *opposite* of what resulted.

"But here we have you, 2746, and all the Bolsheviks in your group, and now good people can walk peacefully down the streets, and the truth... the truth is that we need you out there, why lie?"

"What?!"—the inmate was taken aback. "Are you saying you're going to set us free, just like that?"

"Mmm... something like that. Look, 2746. If you were chosen to have this conversation, it's because we *know* you are a very intelligent and charismatic person. After all, you are one of the leaders of that gang of common criminals with delusions of being the great liberators of the homeland that the Tupamaros are. And as your leader, we're going to ask you to betray them."

"But... but... how could I betray my own? Who do you think you are talking to?!" he got agitated, deviating from the line that, in any other situation, would have earned him 2 to 6 months of solitary confinement. But this was *not* any other situation.

"I think I'm talking to a very intelligent man, as I said, who yes, might have his crazy revolutionary delusions and stupid Bolshevik idealisms... but who also knows what's good for him. Do you see where I'm going?" he raised a suggestive eyebrow.

"A coup is coming, isn't it?" he expressed what not only the Tupamaros but the general population had known for years: the most likely response to the revolutionary and socialist advance in Latin America was the establishment of a de facto regime, supported, of course, by the United States.

"Do you see why we chose you, among all your group of idiots?"

"And what would a coup imply for the conditions of incarceration?"

"Oh, my friend. Then we will have *complete* freedom to do whatever we want with the prisoners"

"Then you have everything planned, don't you?"

"Not us. This comes from o*ut*side Uruguay, and you know it, 2746. Now, are you with us, or would you prefer that when the military takes power, we torture you indefinitely? Think about the benefits of being on our side. We will have to hold you, of course, after the escape, and you'll point out all your buddies like a good hunting dog, but let's take a very simple example. Today I ordered half a rotisserie chicken. If you join us, maybe next time I'll order a *whole* chicken. Half for me, half for you. Do you like wine?"

"I prefer cane liquor."

"Well, a bottle of Velho Barreiro to go with the chicken. Or would you rather suffer, endure, and be mistreated for the next 10 or 20 years for a plan that will never succeed?"

"Tell me a bit more about how we're going to get out of this prison," said the inmate, smiling slyly.

Pool of Las Palmas, Termas del Arapey, Uruguay, Monday, July 20, 2009, 10 a.m.

The current Head of Homicides of the National Police, Captain Gervasio "Toro" Villa, and Detective Di Lorenzo were waiting for the duo of detectives outside the pool, smoking.

"Good morning, Toro"—greeted Geraldine upon arrival, shaking hands with the mustached Indian—"Di Lorenzo"—she did the same with the young detective.

After the formal handshakes among the four, they entered the enclosed pool. The heat and steam were comforting compared to the 5 degrees Celsius outside. Several bathers, averaging around 65 years old, were using the municipal facilities, including what appeared to be the grandchildren of the elderly. The presence of the two police officers and the two private detectives—who clearly weren't there to immerse themselves in the thermal pool surrounded by palm trees—caught attention, but the four ignored it.

"Well, this is where the body of Senator Mojica was found," Di Lorenzo pointed out. "According to the lifeguard's account, around 9:30 p.m. last Saturday, July 18, he was on duty and Mojica was the only guest in the pool, but at that hour, he testified that he had to go to the bathroom urgently. If you would follow me, please," he indicated the way. "This is the bathroom. According to the municipal lifeguard, when he tried to leave, five minutes after being inside, the door was locked tight. I love that expression: locked tight," the homicide detective in charge of the case smiled.

"Alright, time for a little test," proposed Ielicov, after checking several times that the bathroom door opened and closed easily. "Di Lorenzo, please step into the bathroom, and when I tell you, try to get out."

"Let's go!" the young detective replied enthusiastically, and after the Russian detective gave him the signal, he tried to open it.

"I can't. It won't even budge from the frame," he announced. "It's like it's nailed shut."

"Try with all your strength. Slam against it with your arm," requested the former boxer.

"Same result," Di Lorenzo confirmed. "It still won't give."

"Thanks, detective," Ielicov smiled as he opened the door.

"If I didn't know you as well as I do, Toro, I'd say that's a look of surprise," joked Geraldine.

"I'm stunned," replied the giant descendant of indigenous peoples, his well-groomed mustache twitching. "I can't believe it. We're going to have to release the lifeguard."

"I don't understand anything," the one who had been locked in the bathroom said. "What happened? How did you manage to lock me in if there's no latch on the outside?"

"I leaned against the door that opens outward and pushed," Ielicov shrugged.

"There are some more modern devices," Goldman added. "We saw them at a convention in Denver, I think it was last year. They're two metal plates that slide into the slot and open like a hydraulic jack, applying pressure to the frame and the door, preventing it from opening."

"Yeah, but that would have left marks on the paint and the wood," his partner examined.

"That's right. And the version with a rubber coating wouldn't have worked in this case." -she nodded-. "Not enough space".

"So, a guy pushed the door from the outside while... what? Another one killed Mojica?" Villa continued the reasoning.

"It could have been the same person," Geraldine hypothesized. "Viktor, despite being six feet tall, weighs 120 kilos, and I can assure you it's all muscle," she smiled, patting the boxer's sturdy arm. "How long could it have taken someone of his physique to hold Mojica's head underwater until he drowned and come back to block the door? Two... three minutes?"

"The time it would normally take the lifeguard to do his business in the bathroom, and that's if he was hurrying," continued the Russian private detective.

"What the killer or killers had to avoid was the lifeguard arriving in time to revive him; I assume CPR is part of basic lifeguard training," the tall, slender detective with curly black hair made an eloquent gesture. "In any case, 25 minutes seems like *a lot*. After 2 minutes without oxygen, 8 minutes—if we're exaggerating—if they can revive someone through CPR, the brain is already irretrievable. They'd be reviving a vegetable."

"Maybe the killer wanted to make sure," speculated Di Lorenzo.

"There are no cameras in this place, right?" asked Ielicov.

"In a thermal pool? Why would there be?" Gervasio "Toro" Villa showed his annoyance.

"And is the toxicology report from the Forensic Technical Institute conclusive? Was there *no presence* of toxins in the body?" Geraldine inquired, for whom, in the four years she had been in her new profession as a private detective alongside Viktor, this was not the first time they had been hired to solve a homicide.

Anyway, it's worth clarifying. Goldman was *never* an action-oriented woman, not even someone who took sports seriously as part of necessary health care. Before meeting Viktor, she thought that maintaining a light and balanced diet was enough. However, when she met the former boxer in extreme situations, during the Decorator case, her life changed forever.

What had never changed was her passion for studying as a way of life. By 2005, she was a Penta lingual, with three of the languages she spoke almost without an accent, and any book that fell into her hands—almost never fiction, but rather theses and essays on various topics—was devoured and assimilated. When she joined forces with her current partner on private investigations, she had fervently dedicated herself to engaging with themes related to her new profession, and it could be said that, while homicide cases didn't account for more than one in ten, perhaps, she knew *everything* there was to know about topics as diverse as toxicology, knives, firearms, well-known cases of serial killers, and exotic subjects like venomous spiders or plastic explosives. All in theory, of course.

"There was no presence of toxins," Villa recalled. "But Dr. Lía Regueiro mentioned a primary analysis (one done here in Uruguay, let's say), and a second blood sample that was sent to a lab in Argentina, one that has bigger or better machines; I couldn't say..."

"Is Lía Regueiro still at the ITF?!" Geraldine exclaimed in surprise.

"Yes, she's the head now," confirmed the descendant of indigenous peoples, shrugging.

"Yeah. It was probably because they almost blew her up when the Decorator's henchmen blew up the ITF facilities. Where are they now?"

"In an annex of the Faculty of Sciences, in Malvín Norte."

"Ah, yes. I know it. Let's get back to the myocardial infarction," Geraldine closed the topic. "If Lía performed the autopsy, we can confirm that it *was* the cause of death. But if Mojica had a full check-up not long ago, it only showed a 2% chance of having one... how could he have had a heart attack?"

"Are you referring to the fact that a muscular guy held his head underwater until he drowned?" raised an eyebrow the head of Homicides of the National Police.

"I see where you're going, Geral," Viktor sided with his partner. "If a scare could trigger a heart attack, there would be more heart attack victims in traffic accidents than people who were lightly or severely traumatized."

"Exactly! There *must have been* an accelerant in combination with the scare. Without looking at our previous case notes, I can think of cocaine, anabolic steroids, excessive nitroglycerin, fentanyl..."

"There are going to be two key factors here," Di Lorenzo wanted to add: "blood tests and testimonies from his close ones to know what Mojica ate or drank before coming to the pool."

"Don't forget the glass and the whiskey bottle," Gervasio "Toro" Villa also contributed.

"Was Mojica *really* allowed to come with a whiskey bottle to drink at the pool?" Ielicov wanted to confirm.

"It was 'Pancho' Mojica," Villa shrugged. "That's why he came at this hour. During the day, he was always walking around with his mate, but at night he really hit the Mac Pay hard."

"*Mac Pay*? He drank *that* on a senator's salary?" Geraldine almost grimaced at hearing the cheapest brand of the cheapest on the market.

"To each their own," shrugged the mustached man.

"Well, I think we're done here. Right, Geral?" Ielicov asked.

"I think so. We have *millions* of interviews ahead of us," she confirmed. "I propose we finally use Corporal Fernández's services as a driver and try to track down the lifeguard locked up in Salto and Mojica's sister-in-law at the estate outside Paysandú, and then see if we can make it in time for Mr. Reno to give us a lift to Montevideo in his plane."

"Let's roll, partner!" Viktor smiled at her.

CHAPTER 4: FIRST INTERVIEWS

Hotel Arapey Termal Restaurant, Monday, July 20, 2009, 10:30 AM

Gabriela Vilariño patiently waited, sipping a lemon tea, for the detectives who had summoned her. She had her suitcase with wheels and her briefcase next to her. Despite being over 40 years old for some time now, the late candidate's secretary looked well-groomed, made-up, formally and properly dressed in a light brown two-piece suit, and a generous neckline. She gestured to the detectives when she saw them enter, so they would come closer.

"Graciela Vilariño, I assume," Geraldine extended her hand to shake the secretary's.

"Indeed. It's a pleasure to meet you."

"Geraldine Goldman. Viktor Ielicov."

"The pleasure is ours. May we?" the detective pointed to the empty seats.

"Please," accepted the woman with a smile, who seemed to have been naturally blonde but now, at her age, was surely frequently assisted by dye.

"You were expecting us, correct?" wanted to confirm Ielicov, as they had not yet had the chance to call anyone.

"Iván Reno informed me that you would probably want to speak with me while we were all at the hotel."

"Ah. I see," Geraldine tried to hide her suspicion caused by this. "Well, how about we start with what Mojica was like?"

"As a person or as a boss? Because you understand that with the number of years I was his secretary and the number of hours a day we went everywhere together, I knew both aspects: the public and the private of how he was."

"Start wherever you like," Viktor requested.

"Alright. As a person then. Pancho was a *disgusting* human being. He smelled bad; it seemed he was scared of soap. We had to cover his odor with *a lot* of perfume, sometimes, especially in the summer. He was unpleasant when eating, and as a human being, he was misogynistic, macho; that is, he had a very poor concept of women, and was in love with his reflection in the mirror. For him, everything he said was *great and brilliant*, and anything that sounded different was because the other person was an idiot and a right-wing radical."

Both detectives were petrified for a moment by such an aggressive and succinct description.

"I see. It seems you didn't like him much, then," Ielicov ironized.

"Not at all," dismissed the interviewee with a gesture. "Nor did I need to like him either. He was my boss, after all. Ours was an almost purely professional relationship."

"Why 'almost'?" Geraldine was intrigued by the use of that word.

"I was his lover," the secretary answered bluntly, taking a sip of her tea. "And before you judge me, I know he was married, but I doubt he wanted to touch Laura Pulansky more than to move her when she snored at night. Besides, there were no feelings involved, just sex. I took it as part of my job. When he was stressed by what had happened during the day, or had drunk too much, he came to my room, and I already *knew* what for. I made it easy for him, pretended I was interested in the idea, faked it for 5 or 6 minutes, then faked an orgasm, and he put on his pants and went to his room. I went to the shower to get... well, you know, and also to get rid of the stench of that being, and then on to the next thing."

"But you let yourself be treated like that?" Ielicov didn't understand at all, for whom, although he had lived a dissolute life regarding women before meeting Geraldine, he understood that relationships were mutually consensual by definition, and any deviation was an aberration.

"Dear... do you know how much I earned as your private secretary? Well, I *used* to earn it, now that he's gone. We'll see what the Progressive Front wants to do with me, but I seriously doubt they'll offer me a post as a senator or deputy. Only in that rare event, which I don't believe will happen, would I earn more than I do now."

"So, you let yourself be used... for money, basically," Goldman wanted to confirm.

"Nothing more, nothing less, and for the perks: hotels, free meals, trips... Listen: every job has its things you like to do more and things you like to do less. At least I have a great salary, and the party hasn't taken me out of my position yet. I guess it's so I can help you two with whatever you need in your investigation, because after that, I'll surely meet the same fate as Alan. They called him this morning to inform him that his services were no longer required."

"Alan Douglas, the campaign advisor?" Ielicov recalled from the list handed to them by the CSA Group lobbyist a few hours earlier.

"Yes. There he is if you want to interview him before he leaves." She pointed to a young man in his 30s, impeccably dressed, carrying a laptop backpack and a wheeled suitcase at the reception desk, surely checking out of the hotel.

"I suppose we can track him down later, if necessary," Geraldine considered.

"Poor Alan," lamented the blonde in her mid-forties. "He's contracted, which is why they can dismiss him just like that. I'm not. I am from the party. I was a councilor in Canelones until they proposed I become Mojica's secretary. What a shame we won't be able to sleep with Alan as often as we used to. You see? With him, I actually *enjoyed* having relationships. So handsome... so clean... so dedicated... And I don't feel like a cradle snatcher for being twelve years older. Not at all! Where were we?" The woman in the light brown two-piece suit snapped out of her daydream.

"As a boss, strictly in work matters, what was Mojica like?" Geraldine asked. Except for some specific detail, like a phone number or an address, the two rarely took notes during an interview because they were 100% focused on the person they were speaking to, and if one of them happened to overlook something, the other would surely remember it.

"As a boss, well: another technological dinosaur, like all politicians his age. Believe me, I tried *countless* times to get him to at least learn how to turn on the computer and check his emails, but it was no use. I filtered and classified them, and read him the ones I thought were relevant. I answered most of them in his name. Then I passed him calls, organized his schedule because Alan and I were in sync on that: he arranged public appearances and events, and I added things like appointments with the hairdresser, or his work hours and interviews in the Senate."

"I understand. And as a politician, what was he like?" Viktor inquired. "Reno hinted that he was more of a populist type."

"*Very much* so! He built his political career selling a character. And he sold it well! Everyone sees him as a humble guy, close to the people, down-to-earth, who spoke like ordinary folks, not like lawyers or other professionals who become congressmen or senators, and that's how he won the electorate's sympathy. He *crushed* Arturi, who is an economist, in the party's primaries, not to mention he even had the luxury of saying on camera—listen to this because you'll hear it repeatedly during this investigation—'Daniel doesn't have sex appeal.'" She laughed at her own imitation of her boss. "You see? Even in that, Alan advised him, or coached him, as they say now, on how to speak to sound more 'authentic.'" She made air quotes with his fingers.

"Let's talk about Arturi. Reno mentioned he could be behind Mojica's murder," Ielicov got to the point.

"Daniel?" She pondered for a moment. "It makes sense: he stands to gain the most if Mojica is out of the picture. But I *seriously* doubt the party convention would allow him to run for president in October. In that, at least, I have to agree with my former boss: economist Arturi doesn't connect with the people. The advantage we had over De La Rúa would surely be reversed if we put him as a candidate. Bravetto could best tell you what's going on with that electoral strategy, or Dr. Valdez himself."

"The president of the Progressive Front and of Uruguay, respectively, right?" Ielicov recalled.

"The same."

"Any other enemies Mojica might have had who could have sent someone to kill him?" Goldman asked.

"Well, the military for sure." Vilariño emphasized gesturally. "Anyone who tortured, killed, disappeared, or ordered it during the dictatorship must be, and pardon my French, waiting with bated breath to see whether the repeal of the amnesty law goes through. I know that what gets voted on in the plebiscite that will be held simultaneously with the presidential and legislative elections didn't strictly *depend* on Mojica, but he was the biggest proponent and the loudest voice for repealing that law. I suppose one of those dictators could have hired a hitman to kill him. Then there's Amadeo Píriz. I'm sure Iván spoke to you about him."

"He did, yes. A complex case, right?" The Russian detective wanted to encourage her to spill more.

"Isn't it? What's worse than a traitor who goes and tells the military where his comrades in arms, the revolutionaries, are, and then, when the dictatorship ends, takes off to Spain, only to return and claim in a book that it wasn't him? Mojica *hated* him."

"And do you believe Mojica's version and that of the other Tupamaros, who claim he was the traitor?"

"At this point, I don't know what to believe about it," said the secretary, shrugging. "But one thing was certain: both Píriz and Mojica spoke ill of each other to anyone who would lend them a microphone."

"I see." Geraldine mentally reviewed if she had another worthwhile question to ask the secretary/mistress to ensure she wouldn't lose a great salary, according to Villarino's words. "I think that's all for now. Vik?" She consulted her partner.

"I can't think of anything else. Just this: since you took care of Mojica's calendar, would you be so kind as to pass us the last... I don't know... two months? Sometimes in cases like this, there are people or events that may have triggered the order to assassinate the victim. Our email is on the card." The former boxer handed her a business card.

"No problem. Can I give it to you this afternoon? I have everything packed, and the official car is waiting to take me to Montevideo. As if the years I had to put up with the idiot I got stuck with as a boss weren't enough, I still have to go to the Hall of Lost Steps at the Legislative Palace, put on a serious face, and maybe bring an onion or a lemon to rub on my eye, to see if I can squeeze out a crocodile tear, so I don't stick out like a sore thumb with the theme of the event, which is a wake."

"Yes, of course," confirmed Viktor. "Whenever you have time."

Salto Prison, Salto City, Uruguay, Monday, July 20, 2009, 11:40 AM

While Villa and Di Lorenzo were completing the necessary paperwork before the judge to have the poor lifeguard, who had been unable to save Mojica after being locked in the bathroom of the Piscina de las Palmas for 25 minutes, released from preventive custody, they had secured a room where the private detectives could speak with the temporary inmate.

"Good afternoon. My name is Geraldine Goldman, and this is my partner, Viktor Ielicov. We are investigating the circumstances surrounding the death of Senator and presidential candidate Francisco 'Pancho' Mojica."

"Poor Pancho," expressed the athletic municipal officer. "I couldn't save him. I was going to vote for him in October."

"We want to ask you some questions about that night," began Ielicov. "How long have you been a lifeguard for the Salto municipality?"

"Two years... almost three."

"And had you seen Mojica at the pool before?"

"Yes, of course. Every time he came to the thermal baths, he came in the late afternoon to the Piscina de las Palmas. He usually showed up around 6 or 7 PM, alone, generally with his backpack and thermos, and he would stay there until it closed. This time, luckily, I was able to talk to him. It must have been two or three days before... well... what happened happened. He told me he was coming to enjoy his last free time until the elections in October, and that the pool reminded him of his parents because they used to bring him there when he was a kid."

"And what did he do for those 3 or 4 hours in the closed pool?" Geraldine inquired.

"He thought."

"He thought?" Ielicov asked again, clearly wanting him to expand a bit on the information.

"Yes, Pancho, unless he was forced to, like if another swimmer approached him and started talking, invading his space, let's say, alternated between swimming for a long while, always against the edge, and putting on his robe to sit and drink mate, and you could see him lost in thought, like he was contemplating something. Who knows what, but for a guy who went through what he had to go through…" The current inmate at Salto Prison shrugged.

"Are you referring to the years he spent locked up during the military dictatorship?"

"Locked up? I wish he had *only* been locked up. Those bastards put him in a cistern for *12 years*," a mix of admiration for his political leader and hatred for the fascists was evident in the athletic young man's gaze. "Who knows what they did to him there, because it's clear that there are things that can't be told, not even for the one they announced would be his official biography, which is set to be published next year."

"Let's go to your account of what happened on Saturday night," Geraldine pretended to have read the statement, as she hadn't had access to it, only to Villa and Di Lorenzo's account at the pool. "You state that you were locked in the bathroom between 9:30 PM and 9:55 PM last Saturday, July 18. Is that correct?"

"Yes, the door got stuck. It was the strangest thing. And after all that time, when I called my girlfriend who also works at a hotel in Termas del Arapey, I went to jiggle the door one more time, and it opened like nothing."

"Is it common for you to go to the bathroom during your work shift?" Ielicov pressed.

"No, not at all. Look: I cover the shift from 2 PM to 10 PM at that pool, generally five days a week, with rotating days. Sometimes it's from Tuesday to Saturday, like last week, sometimes from

Monday to Friday, and so on. My break is from 5:30 to 6 PM, when the morning lifeguard is still there. During that half hour, I go to the staff room, heat up whatever I brought in my tupperware for dinner, eat, brush my teeth, do what I need to do in the bathroom, and then from 6 to 10, that is, until the pool closes, I'm at my post. That day, I don't know what happened to me, maybe it was the lentil stew I ate during my break, I don't know... I *had* to go to... you know, or I would have an accident."

The private detectives exchanged a significant glance, trying to reveal as little as possible of what they both were understanding.

"Tell me, Lorenzo: in the staff room, do they have lockers with locks to store the food they brought?" Geraldine asked.

"Not at all! It's kept in the fridge, but there has never been any problem with colleagues eating each other's food," the lifeguard clearly had no idea of the context behind the question.

"And where does the Mac Pay whiskey fit into all this?" Ielicov changed the angle of the conversation, a strategy he often used with his partner when they didn't want the interviewee to catch on to where their line of questioning was headed.

"Oh, yes, that!" the lifeguard smiled. "I told you Pancho brought his thermos and backpack. In the backpack, the sly guy brought a bottle of Mac Pay and a glass for when the last swimmer left, which wasn't him. He would ask me if I minded if he poured himself a little whiskey and set it down by the pool—just like the personal secretary of the deceased, Gabriela Villariño, predicted, the lifeguard mimicked the way the former Tupamaro and very possibly future president of Uruguay spoke, only moving the left side of his lips—and I told him it didn't bother me, of course. Who could deny that right to a guy who did everything Pancho did for the country?"

Once outside Salto Prison, and before getting into the car driven by Corporal Fernández, Viktor whispered to Geraldine, "It's clear that the accelerant you mentioned to provoke the heart attack was in the whiskey, right?"

"Absolutely! And that tupper of lentil stew had a laxative someone slipped in to get the lifeguard out of the scene."

"How much planning went into this, my love. I think Arturi is our first person of interest, right?"

"Yes, but first we have the sister-in-law who lives on the ranch in Paysandú."

"Rolling, rolling, rolling, rolling my life," Ielicov hummed.

"And how do you know that song by Fito Páez?" Goldman asked, surprised.

"Seriously? Haven't we been living in Argentina for four years already? How could I *not* know that song by heart?"

"Look at me asking questions too," smiled the now not-so-orthodox Jewish woman.

CHAPTER 5: ANABEL PULANSKY

Chacra "La Redención," outskirts of Quebracho, Paysandú Department, Uruguay, Monday, July 20, 2009, 2:25 PM

Corporal Fernández stopped the army's official vehicle near the entrance of the modest ranch house. An elderly woman of indeterminate age with completely gray hair was waiting on the porch. She clearly wasn't expecting them since they hadn't been able to communicate their arrival in advance; the Excel spreadsheet that Mr. Reno had given the detectives only listed the address and directions on how to get there.

The detectives approached the elderly woman, who got up from her rocking chair upon seeing them arrive.

"Good morning," Ielicov greeted. "We're looking for Anabel Pulansky."

"Good day, young man. It seems you found her," the homeowner smiled.

"Geraldine Goldman," the detective introduced herself, and they shook hands.

"Why are you coming in a military car?" she shot back, pointing to the vehicle that had brought them to this place, next to which Corporal Fernández was lighting a cigarette.

"It's just transportation," Ielicov assured her. "We have *nothing* to do with the Armed Forces of this country or any other," he gestured dismissively. "We are detectives, and we've been asked to find out everything we can about Francisco Mojica's death."

"Oh, yes. I heard on the radio that he died. It was about time for that son of a bitch."

Geraldine turned to see someone in the distance who hadn't stopped chopping wood with a double-handed axe since they arrived.

"That's my son, Facundo, but he doesn't like people. So don't be surprised if he doesn't come to greet you," the elderly woman smiled. "Would you like to take a seat?"

"If it's not too much trouble," the former boxer smiled in response.

Once all three were seated on the porch of the ranch house, where for a moment in winter, at this hour, the sun was shining, warming the cold air, Geraldine was the one to bring up the topic.

"I understand from what you said that you didn't get along with your brother-in-law, is that correct?"

"Dear," the elderly woman smiled at her. "I don't get along with the vegetable vendor at the market who, if I don't choose the fruits and vegetables myself and let him pick, offers me the ones that are more spoiled. I haven't seen Francisco since the return to democracy. Well, of course: I went to the wedding when he married Laura, but just that. Let's put it this way: if Francisco were being burned at the stake in front of me, I would bring a little grill, some ribs, and take advantage of the coals."

"Really *that* much?" the Russian was astonished.

"Worse. He was a *despicable* being in every way. A consummate son of a bitch! An egotist and a manipulator who only cared about himself, himself, and in last place, also himself."

"I see," Geraldine accepted the extreme frankness. "Let's go back to the 60s and 70s when you both were part of the MLN-Tupamaros."

"What times," reminisced the septuagenarian with super-clear eyes, whether from genetics, cataracts, or a combination of both. "I mean: before we lost the guerrilla and they locked us all up, right? Because after that, things got *tough* for us. Laura and I came from a middle-to-upper-class family. Francisco did not. Francisco grew up in the countryside, but we were all tempted by the story of urban guerrilla warfare, and how it had succeeded in Cuba, and the redistribution of wealth and all that jazz. So, we ended up belonging to the same cell as Francisco. Oh, if you had known him back then..."

"Was he handsome?" Ielicov guessed.

"It was meant to be a give and take, as they say around here in the countryside. He was broad-shouldered, had a perfect smile, very manly, with light eyes and slicked-back hair... Anyway, at first, he went out with me for a while"—and something clearly clouded her gaze as it shifted from dreamy nostalgia to deep bitterness, but she waved it away with a hand gesture, as if swatting away a fly—"The thing is, Laura won him over afterward, and I, well... I ended up with the second most handsome guy. Francisco was super charming with people. He'd start talking to you and you'd be mesmerized, like he was hypnotizing you. That's why he got to where he did in politics after the dictatorship. But then I started to see through his deceptions. The guy didn't give a damn about the Tupamaro guerrilla, nor social justice, nor Cuba, nor equitable wealth redistribution... What he was, was a cult leader gathering his followers to flatter him. It wouldn't have mattered to him whether it was the Tupamaro movement, a Pentecostal church, a neo-Nazi sect, or the metalworkers' union. I might seem silly, but I've read a lot," the very elderly woman smiled. "All cult leaders have a pattern. There was Charles Manson, for example, or that guy with sunglasses from the seventies, what was his name?"

"James Jones, I think. The one from the Jonestown massacre," Geraldine chimed in from her wealth of random knowledge accumulated from a lifetime of studying.

"That's the one, from Guyana! Well, Francisco was the same, but in a local, downgraded version. Yes, he attracted people to his entourage, he made you believe he was the best being on earth, but then, when you looked at the results of all his grand urban guerrilla efforts, what was there? Going out to kill the first police officer seen on the street, kidnapping someone from the Ministry of Economy and making him live in the People's Prison on what a minimum-wage earner makes... I mean, what was that? It was nothing! We were dazzled by the example of Cuba, and by how blind Mojica made us all, but in reality, we were 100 or 200 Tupamaros against *an entire country* with established democratic institutions and repressive forces backed by the United States. To put it bluntly, kids: we were *fools* for believing it, to tell the truth. But Francisco *thrived* on that, and that's why I can't stand him."

There was a long moment of respectful silence among the three, while only the sounds of the countryside and the interviewee's son chopping wood could be heard in the background.

"Tell us about Amadeo Píriz," Ielicov broke the silence.

"I barely knew him. He was from another cell of the Movement. What's up with him?"

"We've heard he returned to the country recently, and that he and Mojica hated each other."

"Oh, yes. All that story about him being the one who betrayed us all and pointed us out to get recaptured after the escape from Punta Carretas Prison, right?"

"That's right."

"Look, I can't tell you yes or no whether it was him. What I can tell you is that the Tupamaros *never* had a chance of winning. Whether there was or wasn't an infiltrator, a snitch, it's one person's word against another's, but the fact is that the repressors *never* needed one."

"I understand, Mrs. Pulansky, and we are infinitely grateful for your hospitality. We will continue investigating, but in case we want to contact you, besides coming to your house, how would we reach you?" Geraldine tried to wrap up the interview.

"Are you talking about by phone?"

"Yes, if you could give us one..."

"And why would I want a phone?" the septuagenarian raised an eyebrow. "I'm from another era, my dear. If someone has something interesting to tell me, they'll come all the way here to visit me, and if I have something interesting to share with someone, I'll go into town to tell them. My husband does have a cell phone because he's always out on delivery runs. You can tell him anything, and if he's not with me, he'll pass the message along. Do you want me to write it down for you?"

"Yes, I'll note it down in my phone," Goldman said, taking out her Nokia N97. "Go ahead," she requested, writing down the number the elderly woman dictated.

"Did you know my husband is a retired military officer?"

"What?!" was the detectives' simultaneous expression of astonishment.

"What? A Tupamaro can't fall in love with one of the soldiers who had us locked up?"

"No, of course," Geraldine stammered.

"Horacio wasn't like the others. In fact, there were few in the army who were involved in torture and disappearances. Most were just ordinary soldiers doing their service in the barracks, mowing the lawn, feeding prisoners like me, and things like that. It's one of the reasons, I think, why they still haven't found any of the 130 disappeared: the ones who knew everything were few, and they *obviously* didn't go around telling people they were committing crimes against humanity. And it's not like the torturers introduced themselves when they came with their ski masks to torture or rape us and said, 'Nice to meet you, my name is Walter Pérez, I'm a lieutenant here in the battalion, and I'm going to torture you for a couple of hours,' if you see what I mean."

"So you married your guard?" Viktor smiled. "Wow! What an atypical love story, right?"

"It's just... I was very pretty back then," the septuagenarian recalled nostalgically, "and there were several who made advances toward me in the barracks, but Horacio did it respectfully. That poor guy had to *really* work hard just to get me to talk to him! But he finally won me over by making sure my food was served hot, and occasionally, whenever he could sneak it in, he'd pass me a little glass of wine to enjoy," she winked.

"I'm glad you found happiness together, despite the extreme circumstances under which you met," Goldman smiled at her.

"Love is like that, dear. And you two, besides investigating together, are you a couple?"

"Is it *that* obvious?" Ielicov was surprised.

"Oh, my dear. You know what they say: The Devil knows more because he's old than because he's the Devil."

Joanicó between Cipriano Miró and Larravide, La Unión, Montevideo, Sunday, November 28, 1971, 12:15 AM.

Three heavily armed police officers waited in the Indio truck alongside the tupamaro who had agreed to inform on his comrades to the authorities in exchange for better prison conditions while he was at Punta Carretas. Following the "spectacular" escape he coordinated with them from that prison, he was to receive preferential treatment in every sense, even though he had to remain incarcerated to maintain appearances.

"What a damn heat!" one of the officers complained. "Are you sure you have the right address, prisoner 2746?"

"Yes, of course. It's here, at the shoe factory, where they used to gather. At least, before they caught me again," he joked. "Look, that one coming is Olavarría. The 'Vasco' José Olavarría."

"Attention all units. We have the first tupamaro entering. Hold your positions until we give the order."

"Received," crackled through the radio.

"And that one seems to be Zabala," the traitor pointed out.

They continued like this for another five minutes until it seemed all the guests at the party had arrived.

"What's it like inside?" the chief of the operation, who had initially made the deal with the tupamaro in Punta Carretas, wanted to confirm.

"It's a shoe factory. When you enter, there's a 10 or 15-meter hallway with doors to the offices on the left side. At the end of the hallway is the production area, with the machines and shelves, and on the other side of the offices, there's a staircase going down. What can I say? Only two people can go down at a time. It's quite steep. It leads to the basement, where they have the material storage. They must be gathered there."

The operation chief relayed the layout to all units, and at the order to attack, the officers in the Indio truck sprang into action, while police vehicles and an army truck arrived from both corners.

"Oh, it's nice to see the boys doing their job," the former director of Punta Carretas prison lit a cigarette. "See, 2746? Things should always be like this. I mean, we get paid for this, right? To maintain order in the country. You tupas cause trouble, kill, kidnap, and rob? We lock you up. Then we let you out to catch you again, and the simple worker who gets up early, makes his mate, and goes to work in the factory knows he can walk peacefully on the streets. It's a win-win situation, 2746. The common citizen wins, sleeping peacefully with the door open, you win, enjoying your benefits even while locked up, I win as I climb the police hierarchy, and companies win because they have a stable country to set up in... We all win!"

Salto International Airport, 70 kilometers from the Termas del Arapey, Monday, July 20, 2009, 4:45 PM.

Geraldine and Viktor thanked Cabo Fernández for his services and made their way with their bags toward the Gulfstream G550, which bore the logo and name of Grupo CSA on its tail.

"What are the people who hired us doing back?" the Russian commented. "Selling drugs, right?"

"Oh, don't be prejudiced, my love. It's just a private jet. Companies use them all the time because time is money," the not-so-orthodox Jewish woman rolled her eyes.

"Yeah, and they're expanding the hole in the ozone layer with every trip," Ielicov scoffed, visibly annoyed. "All so their executives don't have to endure the grueling 5 or 6-hour drive to Montevideo and can arrive in a comfortable 30 minutes."

"Do you want to get on or not?" asked the curly-haired woman.

"Will they have vodka on board?" the boxer smiled as he greeted Iván Reno, who was coming down to meet them at the jet's stairs. "Mr. Reno. Thank you for waiting for us."

"Just Iván is fine," the Afro-descendant waved dismissively. "But if you arrive 15 minutes before departure time, Ielicov, there's no need for apologies. Come on. Can I help you with your bags?"

"No, I think we're fine," she declined.

Once they settled into the comfortable reclining seats of the aircraft, a flight attendant came to take their orders. The Grupo CSA lobbyist ordered a martini with two olives. The detectives preferred coffee.

"So, how's the investigation going?" the lobbyist who had hired them on behalf of the business group wanted to know.

"Well, we already know how he died," Geraldine started.

"That fast?"

"Yes. We have little to no doubt that something was put in the whiskey he usually drank by the pool at Las Palmas on Saturday, and that the lifeguard was also poisoned, but with a delayed-action laxative that someone slipped into his tupperware meal he had between 5:30 and 6 PM, during his break. This caused him to need to go to the bathroom when he normally wouldn't, and then someone entered the pool, drowned Mojica, and the stress from feeling close to death triggered a myocardial infarction. The same person who drowned Mojica, or someone else—we're not sure—pressed against the door with their body to keep the lifeguard trapped in the bathroom for 25 minutes, ensuring that he couldn't resuscitate the presidential candidate."

"Wow!" Reno expressed, surprised. "And you figured this out within the first 24 hours of taking the case?"

"That's how good we are," Ielicov smiled. "What's going to be more complicated is figuring out who killed him because it seems Mojica had many enemies in his political career, and personally as well. Plus, we're intrigued by the different perceptions people had of the victim, depending on who you ask."

"And what's that about?"

"The victim's secretary—" Goldman interjected, "for instance, received repeated sexual harassment from Mojica. She accepted it as part of her job, but how many times are *too many* to decide to kill the harasser? Just because she didn't reject his advances doesn't mean she didn't suffer. Then there's the lifeguard, who idolized Mojica, 100%. The victim's sister-in-law, on the other hand, despises him to the point of not caring and even *applauding* that someone ended his life. We couldn't interview Alan Douglas, his campaign advisor, but I doubt he had motives to see him dead. I mean, with Mojica dead, he's out of a job."

"Sure, but he'll find another one. He's *excellent* at what he does, Douglas. And regarding how others perceived him... let's just say Mojica had a very eccentric lifestyle and way of doing politics. Part of it was Douglas's creation, of course, but he could easily irritate people. That same eccentricity, however, was what attracted the masses, the voters. It's normal that if you ask a Uruguayan about Mojica, you won't find lukewarm comments. They'll either be radical on one side or the other."

"We're ready for takeoff," announced the flight attendant.

"Yes, that's fine," the Grupo CSA executive approved with a gesture.

"And what can we expect at the wake, in the Pasos Perdidos hall?" Ielicov inquired.

"A mix, honestly. Many will be there because they *have to* be there. The entire political spectrum will attend, along with some family and friends outside of politics, although he had few. His own wife, Laura Pulansky, is a senator. More than a wake, it's going to be a protocol event, really. The president, Valdez, may say a few words, as well as the widow. Perhaps some other leader from the Progressive Front, I couldn't say. I wasn't involved in organizing this event. But don't be fooled by the sad faces of some. They preferred Mojica dead rather than alive, which doesn't mean they killed or ordered his murder. But still... that brings to mind that you won't be able to freely say you're private detectives investigating the possible homicide of Mojica. You'll need to come up with some story for the interviewees."

"Insurance investigators?" Geraldine suggested.

"That's not a bad idea," Iván thought. "Have you done that before, like, making up a story for your cases?"

"Many times!" Viktor exaggerated, knowing he wasn't good at subterfuge but aware that Geraldine, in her previous role as head of press for the National Police, was an *expert* at hiding and lying. Basically, she was a performer.

"Don't worry, Iván. No one will notice," assured her partner. "When did Mojica marry Pulansky?"

"In 2005, I believe," the mentioned replied.

"Well, let's say that when they got married, and given his advanced age, Mojica thought it prudent to take out a life insurance policy—" the detective continued, "without telling his wife, to leave her 'something' in case he died. He paid the premium every month in secret. The insurer accepted the policy because he was basically a healthy individual, with unbreakable health despite being 70 years old".

"What the insurance doesn't cover is if the cause of death was suicide, and that's what we're investigating. Of course, we'll appreciate every interviewee keeping the topic of conversation confidential," Ielicov added. "How are we doing with the façade?" he asked his contractor.

"Magnificent!" Reno rewarded with a wide, perfect smile that stood out even more against his dark skin.

"Who knows there's an open case investigating a homicide?" Goldman wanted to know. "Let's say: who will laugh in our faces if we go with the insurance company story?"

"Good point. There's Secretary of Interior Cortez, of course, President Valdez knows, then the two homicide detectives who interviewed them at the baths, but no one else in the police, Mojica's secretary knows, and the director of the Forensic Technical Institute, Dr. Lía Regueiro... I can't think of anyone else."

"The widow doesn't know?!" Ielicov was surprised.

"Oh, right. I forgot. Pulansky *never* believed he died of a heart attack. I mean, she wasn't just Mojica's colleague in the Senate; she was also his wife. They practically had a 24/7 relationship. She insisted and pulled strings until they had to tell her. Moreover, she had to authorize that the body not be buried today but remain at the ITF until the investigations are completed."

"Are they going to bury an empty coffin today?" Geraldine's large black eyes widened.

"Yes, from the ITF. The body will go to the Pasos Perdidos hall, where it will be in an open coffin, and after the memorial service, they will change vehicles. The one that the caravan takes to the family mausoleum in the Central Cemetery will carry an empty coffin. The car with the coffin containing the body returns to the ITF."

"That makes sense," the former press chief pinched her lower lip with her thumb and index finger. "If days pass and there's no burial, the press would start to speculate—rightly so—that Mojica didn't die of a heart attack, as reported to the public, but that he was murdered. That would lead to all kinds of social disorder and protests."

"Exactly," Iván approved of the reasoning, as it was the same one followed by the corporation he represented. "If it were to become known that the leading candidate from the ruling party in the polls was murdered... the country would *explode*, even economically. We trust in your discretion and cleverness to prevent this from happening, detectives."

CHAPTER 6: EXECUTION IN BATTALION 14

Parachutists' Battalion No. 14, Toledo, Uruguay, Wednesday, December 8, 1971, 3:30 a.m.

Prisoner 2746 had been taken from his cell in the middle of the night without being told why. He was led to the inner courtyard between the supply shed and the covered garage where the gardening equipment was kept. It was raining, but he was not offered an umbrella.

When he turned the last corner and saw another prisoner on his knees with a hood on, his hands tied behind his back, and next to him the General who led the battalion and the former director of the Punta Carretas prison and current head of the anti-subversive brigade standing next to the prisoner, the former Tupamaro and current collaborator of the law enforcement forces felt his heart sink.

He feared the worst, and he was right to fear it: the dictatorship had already begun, and the police and the army had officially gone from just arresting subversives... to killing them... to executing them without trial.

"Oh, hello, 2746" –the police officer greeted him, smoking a cigarette, he did so under an umbrella.

"What... what is this?" - the prisoner wanted to know, who was only called by the number he wore on his uniform, from when he was legally locked up in the Punta Carretas Jail.

"Look, the other day in the shoe store operation, not *everything* went perfectly. There was a mistake that we have to correct here and now. This colleague of yours" -he pointed to the prisoner kneeling in the mud and with his hood up- "recognized you inside the Indio truck when they were about to load him into the army truck with the other Tupas. Of course he didn't confess it during the initial interrogation, but we put all of those we caught in individual cells, uncommunicated, and little by little we began to... physically pressure them to get better answers."

"You *tortured* them" - the traitor removed the euphemism.

"Torture is not allowed in a democracy, for now we call it physical pressure. The thing is that this son of a bitch confessed to us that he saw you, 2746, and that goes against our interests, I don't know if you understand what I mean. *No one* can know that you are with us, that you are informing us, do you see what I'm getting at?"

"Are you going to kill him?"

"No" - he put out his cigarette in the mud - "*You* are the one who is going to kill him."

"But... but..." - stammered the ex-guerrilla who had made a deal with the devil to save himself.

"No buts, 2746. Take my gun" – Falcone offered it to him, after making sure that the soldiers on guard had taken their own automatics, in case the prisoner tried something –. "Things are very clear here: either you are *with* us, or you are *against* us. And you already *know* the conditions of confinement for those who are against us. Do you understand me, 2746? Now I'm going to take off this bastard's hood, and you're going to shoot him in the head, OK? Looking him in the eyes, like a man. Are you with us, or are you against us? Make up your mind!" - he took off the prisoner's hood.

The traitor to his cause of libertarian urban guerrilla and to his comrades in arms recognized, despite his face deformed by the blows, José "El Vasco" Olavarría.

I'm sorry, brother" - prisoner 2746 only said so that the one who was going to be executed could hear him, since the head of the anti-subversive struggle and the general in charge of the 14th Parachutists' Battalion in Toledo had taken a few meters away, no doubt to avoid being splashed with blood and brains - "but it was you, or it was me" - he pointed with a trembling hand at the head of his former companion and friend.

A flash illuminated them, and then another.

"What the hell is this?!" - the prisoner was surprised with the weapon in his hand.

After he was able to stop laughing out loud, the head of the anti-subversive struggle made signs to the former Tupamaro to approach the roofed space where the gardening machinery was kept. There was a woman in military clothes, with "something" in her hand that looked like a camera.

"And Nancy? Did it come out okay?" - the police chief asked the photographer.

"Wait, they must dry" - the soldier answered, waving the instant photos from the Polaroid camera.

Once the images became clear, prisoner 2746 could be seen clearly pointing at the head of José "el Vasco" Olavarría, on his knees.

"What a marvel this new technology is" - the former Director of the Punta Carretas Prison appreciated -. "You take the photo, and it appears developed in seconds. Good job, Corporal."

"Thank you, sir" - the army officer answered, and left.

"I don't understand anything" - confessed the one who still had the weapon in his hand.

"Give me that weapon, it wasn't even loaded" - he waited for the other to return the service weapon to him -. "We *already* knew that your loyalty was with us, but we needed a guarantee that, in the future, you would not turn around and confess everything. So now you are *officially* one of us, and if you get the bad idea of betraying our pact, because... a traitor is *always* a traitor, and you may well betray your new allies... this photo of you pointing at the head of someone known in the media is published" - the police chief shrugged his shoulders - "and you are *lynched*, 2746. As easy as that: you are lynched."

Hall of the Lost Steps, Legislative Palace, Montevideo, Uruguay, Monday, July 20, 2009, 7 pm.

The CSA Group lobbyist quietly pointed out to the hired detectives who were the people in the room that they would have to interview to continue investigating who had killed the senator and presidential candidate Francisco "Pancho" Mojica.

"And the one taking the microphone now is President Valdez" - finished the tall and strong Afro-descendant.

The pair of detectives was attentive during the speeches that followed the reactions of the participants in that posthumous tribute. President Valdez was followed by the words of Mojica's widow, Laura Pulansky, who was interrupted several times by the emotion that did not let her continue, but due to her job as a senator, she somehow managed to finish what she had to say to the audience. Then, a master of ceremonies invited those present to follow the caravan that would soon leave for the central cemetery, and there were many who headed towards the exit on Avenida de las Leyes, but there were two who went in the opposite direction, towards the inside of the building. It was those whom Ielicov and Goldman decided to approach.

"Excuse us, senators. If you had a moment" - Geraldine called their attention.

The two legislators, one from the Conservative Party and the other from the Independent Party, turned to see who was calling their attention.

"Goldman?" - the one with the most powerful physique recognized the detective with curly jet-black hair -. "What a pleasure, long time no see!"

Geraldine had to submit out of courtesy to a tight hug from the former mayor of Paysandú and current senator, since they had known each other for a long time, from when she was press chief of the National Police.

"How have you been, Larrán?" - she returned the greeting-. "Let me introduce you to my partner, Viktor Ielicov" – she introduced his partner and partner.

"Nice to meet you," the Russian detective formally greeted both senators.

"As you may know, or may not, four years ago I left my position as the head of press for the National Police, and now I work in private investigations. Here, take my card—she offered one to each senator-. "We are currently investigating the death of Senator Mojica for the insurance company British Royal Star Alliance."

"Oh, I see," the imposing senator from the Conservative Party clearly didn't find this relevant.

"We would need to speak with both of you for a moment, if you could give us some time," Viktor continued, "in private."

"Our clients this time, British Royal Star Alliance, want to ensure that Mojica's death falls under the causes of death for which they need to pay the amount to the beneficiary, Mojica's widow, before making the payment."

"Of course," the Independent Party senator, Pedro Méndez, participated for the first time in the conversation. "I'm not going to the cemetery with the caravan. Are you, Jorge?"

"Not a chance," laughed the large Conservative senator. "One thing is protocol, and another is the cemetery. Only the closest to the deceased go there. Your office or mine, Pedro?"

"Mine is closer," decided the lean senator with a goatee.

Once the four were comfortably settled in the luxurious, old-fashioned office of the Independent Party senator Pedro Méndez, it was Larrán, whose imposing physique intimidated like a Kingpin from Spiderman comics, but *with* hair, who resumed the conversation.

"So now you're into private investigations?" he asked Geraldine.

"Yes. Since I met this wonderful human being and better investigator," she pointed to her partner and boyfriend, "a new world of possibilities opened up for me to grow as a professional and as a human being," she smiled, thinking she had closed the subject of previous conversations. "The truth is that Mojica had taken out a life insurance policy with the company that hired us this time, and we were tasked with determining with *100% certainty* the cause of death."

"But didn't he die of a heart attack?" the host of the occasion, Senator Méndez, asked with genuine surprise, perhaps his hosting skills were a bit rusty since he hadn't even offered them a glass of water.

"That's what was officially reported," intervened Ielicov, "but if the insurer hired us, it's because they have grounds to believe that it may not have been a natural death. And we are not implying that he was murdered, not at all," the former boxer was emphatic even in his gestures, "but we also need to rule out other possible causes of death, like self-harm."

"You understand, senators, that everything we discuss here must be kept under the strictest confidentiality, right?" Geraldine wanted to confirm.

"Of course!" the legislators replied in unison.

"Good," she began. "Having clarified this, tell me: what was Mojica like as a senator?"

There was a comedic pause among the duet of senators, who could easily have been Laurel and Hardy, or "el Gordo y el Flaco", as they are known in Latin America, as they tried to determine who would start. It was the living representation of Oliver Hardy (the fat one, or Senator Jorge Larrán from the Conservative Party) who began, in his deep, gravelly voice:

"Well, I'll start. Mojica was a *great* opponent. There's no doubt about that!" he emphasized gesturally. "I mean, right now we are the opposition in this period, but you know what I mean. Since I dealt with him, Mojica was on one side, and I was on the opposite side, no matter which party was in power."

"Understood."

"He was a hard guy to convince, to be honest. If he was stubborn about saying this was red"—he placed his hand on the brown desk—"he would keep insisting it was red, no matter the arguments you put in front of him. And while the Front was in the minority in the chambers, you'd listen to him, pretend to pay attention to his arguments, but at the end of the session, when it came to the vote, and we were the majority, the law came out stating that this desk was brown, you see what I mean?"

"Clearly. A stubborn person."

"Stubborn is putting it *mildly*, Goldman," Méndez joined in. "Being a parliamentarian means being flexible. Sure, you push your own ideas forward, but you also need to be open to debate and the ideas of others. With Mojica, that was *impossible*," he declared from his five-foot-six height, which was noticeable even while sitting.

"I don't know about you, Pedro, but I don't recall ever changing his mind on a *single* law during this period."

"Neither do I."

"I'll tell you more: on one hand, it was a relief for me, personally, that he was leading the polls and that, if the pollsters were correct, he was going to become our next president, to get him *out* of the Senate once and for all."

"Besides, Mojica was one of the few in the Senate without a university law degree," Méndez added.

"But you don't need to be a lawyer to be a senator, do you?" Geraldine questioned.

"It's not... and it is," Larrán nuanced. "You see, what do we do here in the legislative palace? We draft and approve *laws*, right? Most are passed almost without discussion among political parties because it's *obvious* they need to be implemented, but there's maybe about 20 or 30% that deserve a higher level of discussion. And the laws are written in legal language. To raise your hand for or against, you need to *understand* what the law implies and what the consequences of its implementation are."

"Mojica clearly didn't understand them," Méndez concluded. "He voted one way because his party told him what to vote, but sometimes he did it out of emotion, nothing more, without caring about the implications for the reality of Uruguayans that the laws he was voting for would have."

"Like the IRPF law in 2006," recalled the imposing senator from the Conservative Party. "What a disaster that was!"

"What are you referring to?" asked Geraldine, who, although she was Uruguayan, had not been in the country since 2005.

"Of course, you weren't here," Larrán recalled. "The Left never governed until 2005, and one of the first laws they enacted was the one that replaced the Income Tax and the Payroll Tax with the Personal Income Tax, the IRPF. From then on, basically, it penalizes doing well in life based on your work," the hefty legislator shrugged.

"How so?"

"Before that law, those who didn't work as employees, the employers, contributed part of their earnings from rents, benefits from company shares, and such, as Income Tax, while dependent workers contributed a percentage of their salaries as Payroll Tax," explained Méndez.

"Starting from that law enacted by the Progressive Front, those taxes were replaced by a scalable percentage based on how much one earns from salaries, the IRPF. There's a segment of the population that was relieved of having to pay the Payroll Tax, those who earn the least, but once you surpass $600 or $700 a month, the state starts to withhold 10% of what you earn, then 15, 20, 25, and even up to *30%* of your income."

"Pure and simple wealth redistribution, socialist style," the Russian understood.

"Yes, that's how they sold it to the people," Senator Méndez leaned back in his chair. "But do you think that affects those who have more? Not at all! The ones who *really* have money here in Uruguay aren't workers who earn a salary and have between 10% to 30% of their income taken to contribute to state coffers. The *real* powerful ones, own farms, companies, meatpacking plants, and for $2,000 or $3,000 a month, they have accountants who help them avoid paying taxes through the most unbelievable loopholes, limited liability companies, offshore accounts, front men, etc., and they *avoid* paying tens of thousands of dollars in taxes, which is what they should be contributing."

"The ones who suffer from the IRPF are the workers who strive to advance in their jobs," Larrán added, "and who could earn more based on hard work, and suddenly see that those who put in less effort to progress in life get taxed less, while those who work harder get taxed more. That's why I said at the beginning: that law penalizes those who put in the most effort."

"I understand," Ielicov pondered. "Why should I bother to put in effort if in the end, I'm financing those who do less, right? A bit like the regime back home, because I'm from Vladivostok."

"Oh, look at that. No one would have guessed. You don't even speak with an accent," smiled the Kingpin of the Conservative Party.

"It's because my mother is Chilean, and at home we always spoke a mix of Russian and Spanish... or Chilean," the former boxer smiled back. "And what do you think about the plebiscite for the repeal of the Expiry Law?" The detective went straight to the point, as that was where the lobbyist from Group CSA had indicated

Senators Larrán and Méndez as the biggest opponents to Mojica on this issue.

"*Another* disaster waiting to happen if they get the votes!" Jorge Larrán emphasized. "Why stir up the muck of the past? What's done is done, that's what I think. Mojica put it in his electoral platform to gain votes, I'm *sure* of it."

"But doesn't it make sense that if a country supported terrorism from the state, with the disappearance of opponents and subversives, it should investigate what happened to those opponents?" the not-so-orthodox Jewish woman having chosen an atheist as her partner in life and in business, continued her incisive questioning.

"But that's *already* covered in the Expiry Law!" exclaimed Senator Larrán with grand gestures. "If the Progressive Front didn't use that article in the Expiry Law that allowed them to investigate what happened to the disappeared during the dictatorship, that's *their* problem. It was President Juan Batlle himself, in his previous term from 2000 to 2005, who started to *seriously* investigate what happened to the victims of state terrorism. What does it add to incarcerate 6 or 7 elderly former repressors to justice in a geriatric prison?"

"It's textbook populism, detectives," Senator Méndez concluded very seriously. "Mojica supported the repeal to gain votes, nothing more."

CHAPTER 7: THE TRAITOR?

M*editerranean Sea and Antarctic Sea, Punta Gorda, Montevideo, Uruguay, Friday, October 26, 1979, 9:50 p.m.*

Loud knocks on the door interrupted the chess game that Magdalena Schebor and her son, the sole occupants of the two-story house plus an underground garage, used to have after dinner. Mother and son looked at each other. Although the boy was only 10 years old, he knew, because his mother had told him, that they were in a dictatorship, and such insistent knocks on the door at that time of night could not mean *anything* good.

"Hide in your room, Fer, I'll take care of it."

"OK, but *shout* if something bad happens" - the boy answered.

"Who is it?" - asked the lady of the house, when she was sure that her son had left the living room covered with well-polished parquet.

"It's me, Magdalena! Open!" - demanded the male voice from the outside of the door.

"Go away. I don't want to know *anything* more about you!"

"Look, Magdalena. You have my son in there. Today I came alone. If you don't open, I'm going to come with the boys, and I'm sure you don't want that, do you?"

"What the *hell* do you want with me?! - the owner of the house snapped in her face, when she decided to open the door.

"Where's Fernando?" - demanded the arrogant man to whom she had opened the door of the house that didn't belong to him.

"And what the hell do you care about Fernando, son of a bitch and collaborator of the military?!" - the owner of the house confronted.

A resounding slap was Schebor's response, one that knocked her to the floor, her long red hair curling on the parquet floor.

"Sorry, Magui. I didn't mean to..." - the intruder stammered - "Fer is my son, and I only want to take care of him, contribute to his livelihood. If only you would let me give you a check from time to time, once a month..."

"Go back where you came from, son of a bitch! We don't need *anything* from you. Fernando is *not* your son. You planted the seed to provide the genetic material from which a human being was built that has *nothing* to do with you, collaborating son of a bitch!"

The intruder's new blow, this time to the belly, was more than the 10-year-old boy they were referring to could bear. The two adults in the living-dining room with polished parquet floors, looked, both amazed and frightened, at the child in question in the conversation, holding a .38 revolver in his hands, pointing at the torso of the man who had interrupted the mother-son game.

"You're *not* going to hit my mother!" said the boy with the gun.

"Son, please put down the gun," asked his mother.

"No. You're leaving," said the boy with the .38 to the intruder, "and I'll put down the gun."

"Okay. Okay. I'm leaving," raised his hands in a sign of surrender, the man with broad shoulders, clear eyes, greased hair who had broken into the peace of a private home, "but *know* that you're my son, and I'm going to get you back," added the stranger as a warning before leaving.

"Fer, listen to me" –Magdalena took her son's face in her hands when the intruder left-. "We have to get out of here. This place is no longer safe. Pack a bag with only the essentials and we'll get the hell out of this country, is that clear?"

"Yes, mom. I'm coming. But... are *you* okay?" -her son wanted to know the essentials.

"I'll *always* be okay with you, my love" –the mother kissed her son's forehead-. "Now hurry up, this son of a bitch will surely be here with fascist reinforcements as soon as he can."

Canelones 2036, address of Amalia Píriz, Cordón, Montevideo, Uruguay, Monday, July 20, 2009, 8:30 p.m.

The owner of the house opened the door before the detectives had to ring the bell a second time.

"Good night" –she greeted them–. "You must be the insurance company detectives who want to talk to my brother, right?"

"Goldman and Ielicov" – Geraldine introduced themselves– "Thank you for opening the door so late."

"Yes, yes" – the sixty-year-old in her dressing gown and slippers downplayed her – "Come in, come in. Amadeo is waiting for you by the fireplace."

The disorder of the house could only be compared to that of a drug addict in an eternal cycle of recovery and relapse: everything was out of place, dust covered everything, there were cobwebs where there should have been corners, there were huge empty spaces where volleyball could be played, and then there was a pile of clothes on coat racks and chairs. Clearly, there was a lack of warmth in the huge, high-ceilinged house. Clearly, too, the detectives would not have been surprised if they had found rats running around freely.

A septuagenarian in a bathrobe and slippers, with sports gear visible underneath and a wool cap on his head, stared into the fire with his clear eyes, his mind lost in the flames, seemingly unaware of the newcomers. A three-quarters-empty bottle of White Horse whiskey and a half-full glass rested on a small table next to his armchair. It was only when the tall, slender lady and the burly former heavyweight boxer sat down beside him that he lifted his gaze.

"Good evening," he greeted them.

"Amadeo Píriz, it's a pleasure to meet you," Geraldine said, extending her hand to grasp his soft, flaccid one. She waited for her partner and companion to reciprocate the formal greeting before they both settled next to the old man.

"Amalia told me you were coming to talk to me about Mojica, right?" the former Tupamaro replied, straight to the point, as if he was sedated in some way—whether by alcohol, marijuana, prescription barbiturates, or some combination of all three. "What do you want to know about that son of a bitch?"

"What led you to hate him the way you *clearly* do?" Ielicov pressed.

"Ha. Do you think being pointed out as the traitor among the Tupamaros is nothing?" the wrinkled septuagenarian shot back. "I've carried that cross my *whole* life, a cross that doesn't belong to me."

"We understand that it wasn't just Mojica who pointed you out as the traitor in the Tupamaro ranks," Goldman interjected sharply. "Huidó, Zabala, Pulansky as well..."

"Laura Pulansky, right? Mojica's wife," Píriz raised an eyebrow. "What's a wife going to say that differs from what Mojica said? Ha. And the others conspired against me to make me the scapegoat. But it's all in my book. Why don't you read it?"

"It's possible we will," Geraldine replied. "And why would they point you out if you weren't the one?"

"It's crystal clear, my dear. Why else? One of them was the traitor, and they got together to cover it up. I was just their scapegoat. That's why I had to get the hell out of this country as soon as the military released me from prison. Ask Vasco Olavarría who shot him in the head, even *before* the dictatorship was officially declared."

"Vasco Olavarría?" Ielicov asked, since that name had not come up in their ongoing investigation.

"José 'the Vasco' Olavarría. He was with us in Punta Carretas Prison when we escaped... it would be... September '71, I think.

Over a hundred Tupamaros and members of other guerrilla groups escaped through a tunnel we dug for two months. And then the bastards started picking us off one by one, sometimes several at a time, but this time they didn't send us to the normal prisons. No. They locked us up in dungeons at military barracks. And that's when they started to torture us. To give us *catanga*"

"Excuse me. What does it mean to give us 'catanga' mean?" asked the Russian detective, as, although his Spanish could be considered almost native, some terms from the Río de la Plata slang eluded him.

"It refers to physical abuse," his partner explained.

"Torture. Why call it anything else?" the former Tupamaro, marked as a traitor by his peers, shrugged. "They say"—he made a clear gesture that what he was about to say could be taken as hearsay—"they say... that Olavarría saw the face of the traitor when he was recaptured during the raid at the shoe store, that he confessed under torture, that he had seen his face, and that's why they shot him, even while democracy was in place. So, he wouldn't reveal the secret of the pact between the military and the traitor in our ranks. I heard the shot. I remember it as if it were today"—his gaze drifted again, lost in the fire—"in the middle of the night, a night pouring rain. Much later, when they started bringing us together with those from Don Mateo's shoe store, Olavarría was no longer with us. You do the math and see if it adds up differently."

A moment later, the detectives were on the sidewalk, getting into the rental car. Píriz had answered the rest of their questions willingly, and the old man's account had all the internal coherence one could expect given his blood alcohol level and the distance of his memories from the pre-dictatorship and dictatorship period.

"What a smell of alcohol that man had!" Geraldine complained, starting the engine. "I think it's going to be stuck in my clothes," she sniffed the blue jacket of her suit, as they both wore dark blue suits that matched, except when they were on surveillance or undercover.

"But how well he articulated, considering all the alcohol he had consumed. It reminded me of my parents. They drank as if there was no tomorrow, but you never saw them incoherent or slurring their words."

"Must be habit," the curly-haired brunette shrugged. "I think we're done for today, right?"

"To the hotel, agreed, but first let's grab a bite, shall we?"

"I'm *starving*. I'm sure there's something open on 18 de Julio, even on a Monday night. What do you think?" she asked, turning left onto Pablo de María, toward the main avenue in downtown Montevideo.

"For me, it's clear that Píriz *firmly* believes in his account."

"Yesss," the driver stretched. "That doesn't mean we should take his words as facts."

"Of course not. We'll need to verify with other sources."

"I went to high school right here," she pointed to a three-story building on her left as they cruised down 18 de Julio Avenue.

"Lycée Français," the former boxer read with a strong foreign accent. "Yeah, I remember you telling me."

"Wow! I can't believe 'La Paponita' is still open," she parked on the north sidewalk of the wide avenue.

"Open at this hour, you say?"

"Open in the first decade of the 21st century. It's such a 20th-century bar, you'll see. You're going to *love* it. How many times did we have lunch there with my high school classmates? What a time!"

Avenida Italia and Propios, La Blanqueada, Montevideo, Uruguay, Monday, July 20, 2009, 9:15 PM.

The car was parked just where they left it on Av. 18 de Julio, as both had accompanied their dinner in a bar in the capital with some alcohol. They still had a task to complete that day, and they stopped a taxi. Geraldine couldn't wait to be alone with Viktor and needed to get something off her chest, so she chose to speak in Russian (the fifth language she had learned and the one she spoke with the most accent and imprecision) to tell her partner something without the taxi driver catching on to the topic of their conversation.

"Everything Píriz said is so strange, isn't it?"

"So, it seems there was indeed a traitor among the Tupamaros," agreed the former heavyweight boxer from Vladivostok. "Different from what Anabel Pulansky thought."

"It seems so. All of this should be checked against the historical records from the dictatorship period in Uruguay and the prior era, under the governments of Pacheco Arévalo and Borderragui, when the first prime measures were implemented."

"It's called 'security measures,' not 'prime,'" the man with the aquiline nose corrected her with a smile.

"Oh, right: 'security measures.'"

"Do you think President Valdez can give us access?"

"If he can't, I don't know who can," she shrugged.

"Forget it, kids," surprised both of them the taxi driver, an elderly veteran nearing sixty, speaking to them in Russian. "President Valdez won't be able to give you access to the information you need. I'd suggest going for the former repressors of the time. Borderragui, for instance."

"Wait: do you speak Russian?" Goldman switched to Spanish.

"My mom was a Russian immigrant, and my dad was an Italian immigrant. I only know how to say 'buona sera' in Italian and little more than that. Not sure if that gives you a hint of who wore the pants at home. Ha."

"Sorry. That was a lapse on our part, sir..."

"Vitali. Sergei Vitali."

"Mr. Vitali," Ielicov said. "You'll understand if we ask you to be discreet about what you just heard."

"Yes, my son. No problem. It sounds nice to hear and speak Russian. Ever since my mom went off to play balalaikas with the Lord, I hardly have anyone to talk to, except when I go to Máximo Gorki for the meals they hold, with the presentation of the Russian folk-dance troupe."

"And why couldn't the president have access to the historical files on state repression?" Viktor wondered.

"For the same reason no dictator has ever been locked up," the taxi driver shrugged. "Because in the naval club pact, and later with the Law of Expiration, it was agreed that the *bastards* would remain unpunished for the crimes they committed. And remaining unpunished means: if we did something wrong, just keep going, said the football referee. Besides, I can't imagine a torturer filling out an A934 form with the name of the Tupamaro and the cause of death: bullet to the head. Bury it, hide it, cover it with dirt on the battalion's grounds."

"Sounds logical. We have Borderragui's contact number, but whether he wants to give us an interview is another matter," Geraldine told the taxi driver.

"If you manage to interview him, please give him a kick in the ass for me. My mom, being Russian, narrowly escaped the military, and that's because when the coup came, at Máximo Gorki, the Russian cultural and social center, they had the foresight to burn the membership records, because if not..." he left the conclusion hanging in the air. "Well, we've arrived. It's 275 pesos."

"Here's 300, that'll be fine," Geraldine handed him the bills through the tray connecting the driver's compartment to the passengers via the armored partition. "But I would ask you for a receipt, if it's not too much trouble."

"Yes, of course."

"What a mess we made" – Viktor ran his hand through his curly hair, when they got out of the taxi and were in front of the new facilities of the Forensic Technical Institute.

"I couldn't agree with you more, partner, but, seen in perspective: what a source of information the taxi drivers are!"

"Always!" - they gave each other a romantic kiss before entering.

The concierge showed them how to get to the morgue. Dr. Lía Regueiro, clearly, with whom they had collaborated during the Decorator case in 2005, had left the message at the door that the detectives would arrive, when they previously called her on her cell phone to ask if they could come and visit her.

"Geraldine, how nice to see you again!" - the forensic doctor in her lab coat hugged the newcomer -. "Viko dear!" - she did the same with the detective.

"Thank you for receiving us at this time, Lía" - thanked the boxer.

"Oh, it's nothing" - dismissed the petite, mouse-like doctor with a gesture - "I had to wait for the chilly buddy to be brought back anyway."

"Chilly buddy" - Geraldine laughed - "I suppose some things don't change."

"Do you want to see it?"

"If it wouldn't be too much trouble" - Ielicov asked.

It wasn't very common in their cases that they had to deal with a homicide, and even less common was that they had the full backing of the state to do so, but it was necessary to have that talk with the coroner in charge of the post-mortem investigations of what, at this point, seemed to be a clear homicide.

"I present to you Francisco "Pancho" Mojica" - the coroner opened the refrigerator chamber, and pulled the corpse onto the platform mounted on wheels - "Cause of death: myocardial infarction. No presence of toxins in the blood. Previously unbreakable health, according to the medical check-ups presented by his office. I don't know what else to tell you," The brunette shrugged.

"Is it okay if we talk in front of him?" - Ielicov pointed to a redhead with messy curls and glasses in an adjoining office.

"Yes, no problem. It's Franco, our new chief toxicologist. He's Argentine. He's been working here for... two years, maybe. Franco!" - she shouted at him -. "Since when have you been working at the ITF?"

"Since October 16, 2007, doctor" - the man in question answered, after taking off his headphones. He put them back on.

"He's almost deaf when he puts on headphones to work. He says the noise of typing bothers him. Anyway... we all have our issues, right? So, they hired you two from among the *thousands* or tens of thousands of private investigators there are. Congratulations, guys!" - she smiled widely.

"Thanks, Lía. I suppose it had something to do with how we performed in the Decorator case" –Ielicov was very serious-. "How have you been? Wait. Is Aníbal still working for the ITF?"

"Me? I was *reborn* that day, Viko. And about Aníbal, what can I tell you? He went like most people to safer places than a state job where the Sun Orators can blow up the building" –she shrugged her shoulders-. "Well: what else do you need to know about the little chilly buddy?" -she pointed to the corpse of the presidential candidate with the Y-shaped incision in the chest between them.

"We *strongly* suspect that he was given heart rate accelerators to cause the heart attack" –Geraldine answered-. "Amphetamines, cocaine, nitroglycerin..."

"Hmm. Let's see. It would have come out in the toxicology test, right? Franco! Do you dare to bring me the primary toxicology test of the little chilly buddy number 6?"

"I'm coming, Doctor," the voice came from the office, and soon she was with the requested report, then he retired to the office, put his headphones back on and continued working on the computer.

"He's a sweetheart, Franco. Two years working with me and he still doesn't call me by my first name" - smiled Doctor Regueiro in charge of the Forensic Technical Institute -. "Difficult to say" - she studied the three-page-long analysis -. "He had high cholesterol. Well: *all* the high cholesterols, but it's normal based on what was known to be his food: fried food, breaded cutlets with French fries, above all. Shit! How much had this Christian drunk before he died? 4.5 degrees of alcohol in the blood! I would have been *amazed* if he could even walk back to his hotel. He would have been zig-zagging, at best."

"Witnesses agree that he was a heavy drinker at night" - Ielicov added.

"There's no doubt about that!" -the coroner finished reading the analysis-. "I regret to inform you that, if something had been given to speed up his heart, that would *not* appear in this primary report. We would need the more complete analysis that we sent to Buenos Aires."

"And when would those results be available?" -Geraldine erred on the side of anxiety.

"Ugh. A week, usually" -Regueiro rolled her eyes-. "But I understand that the Homicide department took the bottle of Mac Pay and the glass found next to the pool. Maybe they can have a quicker response, with the the scientist."

"We will consult them, of course, but tomorrow. Today is too late. We need to check something else with you, Lía" - Viktor pointed at the refrigerated corpse, or "chilly buddy" as the coroner referred to her clients - "If Mojica had been in the pool, drinking a whiskey, and someone had come in and drowned him, increasing his heart rate by doing so, and that under the premise under which we are working, that is, that they had added some heart rate accelerator to cause a heart attack... where could he have marks?"

"Well, let's see. It would be on the back of the neck, or on the head. What muscle strength are we talking about?"

"Like mine, or even stronger."

"Wow! I didn't know there could be *anyone* stronger than you, Viko," the doctor smiled, on the verge of triggering jealousy in Geraldine, but then returned to a professional tone. "Can you help me turn him face down?"

In a moment, the three of them managed to place Mojica face down. Lía brought over a floor lamp to look for bruises.

"No. There don't seem to be any marks on the neck. Well, we'll need to shave the back of his head," she said, and, putting action to her words, she brought over a basin of water, an electric razor, and a manual one. Carefully, she shaved the deceased until the back of his head was bald. She positioned the special lamp closer again. "Damn it!" —on the back of the presidential candidate's head now appeared marks, small bruises, as if a hand had forcibly submerged Mojica's head—. "This maneuver must correlate with one of the wrists," she said, illuminating the wrist of the deceased with the lamp designed to detect bruises not visible under normal light. Marks from a struggle were also visible there. "Viko, a little demonstration?" asked the director of the ITF.

"Of course," the detective agreed.

"Put your right hand behind my head, and with your left hand, grab my left wrist. I'm going to try to struggle and break free, and you're going to try to stop me."

"When you're ready, Lía," confirmed the former boxer when he was in position.

Lía had her torso at a 45-degree angle to the vertical of her legs, as the candidate would have been if he had been standing on the bottom of the thermal pool. Lía struggled with all her strength, but she couldn't regain the vertical position.

"Ready. Ready. I give up," she said between gasps.

"So, it seems there's forensic evidence that Mojica was *indeed* murdered, despite the official cause of death being a heart attack, right?" Geraldine raised a suggestive eyebrow.

"How do you two do it, guys?" the doctor asked again.

"We think rotten," confirmed Viktor Ielicov. "And unfortunately, we usually hit the mark."

CHAPTER 8: PRESIDENT VALDEZ

Executive Tower, seat of the Presidency of the Republic, Independence Square, Montevideo, Uruguay, Tuesday, July 21, 2009, 8:55 AM.

Viktor and Geraldine underwent the usual scan at the security portal, plus a manual scan, had their photos taken, and their right thumbprints recorded when they were granted access and given their visitor badges, being told that they would find the president's office on the 14th floor.

"Do you think these security measures will be standard, or are they heightened after Mojica's assassination?" Ielicov asked his partner in the elevator.

"Hard to say, partner. I left this country four years ago, but when I was the press chief for the National Police, I could almost walk through security just waving my hand."

When the elevator doors opened on the 14th floor, a man in his 60s, with sparse, fine hair slicked back and a bulky build, was waiting for them.

"Gonzalo Hernández, secretary to President Valdez," he introduced himself seriously, extending his hand. "You must be the investigators hired by Group CSA."

"Geraldine Goldman. This is my partner Viktor Ielicov."

"Nice to meet you, Mr. Hernández."

"The pleasure is mine. Please, follow me."

The newcomers to the presidential building followed the serious man in the light gray suit to a double door made of fine wood, which he opened without knocking.

"President, your nine o'clock appointment," Hernández announced.

A man in his sixties stood to receive them, dressed in a pristine dark blue suit, white shirt, and red tie, representing the colors of his political party, although now he represented all Uruguayans. A pin on his lapel displayed the national flag. His gray hair likely required a good half-hour of daily maintenance, and his smile was perfect.

"Thank you very much for coming, detectives," he said, shaking both their hands.

"The pleasure is ours, Mr. President, for giving us a moment of your time."

"Gonzalo, I think you'll have to miss this meeting," he said very seriously to his secretary.

"I'll be at my desk if you need me."

"Alright," the oncologist and first president elected by the Progressive Front in Uruguay's history immediately got to the point, as soon as his secretary left through the double doors. "I don't have much time, but whatever I can share with you, I'm all yours," offered the president of all Uruguayans. "What's the status of the investigation into Mojica?"

"He was murdered," Ielicov affirmed without a doubt.

"We have physical evidence of whoever killed him, or at least one of those who killed him," the private detective was always meticulous about the correct use of language. "Muscular, with above-average physical strength, even *much* above average. To give you an idea, similar to my partner," Geraldine pointed to the former boxer.

"Wow!" President Valdez exclaimed. "I see Minister Cortez was right when he pointed you out as the best for this case."

"And we're cheap, just imagine," Ielicov joked. "As for the murder weapon, we have little doubt it was a cardiac stimulant in the whiskey he usually drank at night, along with the muscular guy who held his head underwater until he heart attacked. Last night, we were at the Forensic Technical Institute, and Dr. Regueiro confirmed that our hypothesis was valid, based on the bruises on the back of the victim's head and on his left wrist. This was long premeditated, President Valdez. They studied the victim's habits, followed him, looked for the right moment to intoxicate him with a cardiac stimulant like cocaine, amphetamines, ephedrine, or nitroglycerin, waited for it to take effect, and then attacked when Mojica was alone in the palm pool, pushing his head underwater. Panic did the rest, and he died of a myocardial infarction while a muscular man blocked the swimmer's door, who was also poisoned by being given a laxative in the lunch he brought in his Tupperware for his 5:30 to 6 PM lunch break, so he would have to go to the bathroom, giving the assassins the opportunity to strike."

"Gonzalo," the president of the republic pressed an intercom. "Clear whatever you have in the next 15 minutes."

"Understood, Mr. President. But at 9:30, the Chinese delegation arrives."

"No problem. I think 15 minutes will be fine. Detectives... where did you come from?" Only admiration shone in the eyes of the oncologist, who would lead the Executive Power of a nation of three and a half million souls and a Gross Domestic Product of $45 billion until March 1 of next year.

"Well... we appreciate your comments," Geraldine blushed, "but we still haven't told you the bad part. There are two details, if you can call them that, where we haven't made much progress: who and why?"

"There are *many* individuals and groups that would benefit from Mojica's death," Ielicov added.

"The Conservative Party, for starters," Valdez scoffed.

"Indeed. We understand that their candidate, Dr. De La Rúa, was trailing Mojica in the voting intention polls. The repressors of the dictatorship that the State would have the authority to judge and imprison if the repeal of the Expiration Law were passed, Amadeo Píriz, who has a *deep-seated* hatred for Mojica..."

"Is he *not* going to have one?" Valdez shrugged. "The judicial system exonerated Amadeo Píriz of all charges."

"And that?" the Russian was surprised.

"There was a criminal complaint against him for collaborating with the dictatorship by pointing out his fellow Tupamaros, but Píriz was clever," the president smiled. "He hired a good lawyer, and it turned out that the accusations, if there were any—this is still pending definition—were against violators of the laws, people who committed kidnappings, thefts, and murders during a democratic period, that is: *before* the dictatorship. It would have been a civilian providing information to the police to catch common criminals."

"So, the key point here, whether Píriz was the one who denounced his comrades, was never clarified," interpreted the former press chief of the national police.

"Exactly! Look, detectives: you have a *very delicate* issue on your hands. So delicate that I would say it could shake the foundations of democratic institutions," the impeccably groomed president said seriously.

"Is it *that* serious?" Geraldine was astonished.

"The issue is this," Valdez said, bringing his fingers together. "And I want you to put yourselves in *my* shoes. If Mojica died of natural causes," he shrugged. "These things happen. No one is exempt, and no one knows that better than I do as an oncologist. If he was killed for personal reasons, let's say, for example, that his wife found him in bed with another woman and hired someone to kill him... maybe that's *not* the best example because his wife is a senator, but do you understand what I mean?"

"Of course!" Goldman confirmed for both of them.

"Such things *also* happen. They are springs of each person's private life. Now then... if your investigations reveal that it was Dr. De La Rúa who ordered the hit, or even the Conservative Party... that would be almost a coup d'état! Assassinating the candidate who is leading in the polls? It's the most twisted and nefarious way to rig an election. What if it were the military, wanting to prevent the repeal of the Expiration Law? If that gets confirmed, I ask you to inform me *before* anyone else, because I'll leave my resignation on my desk and take the presidential helicopter to drop me off in Argentina, Brazil, or Paraguay, because what's to follow will be mass protests outside the military barracks, with the military defending their installations and the police intervening... I don't want to be in charge if that happens."

"We understand your predicament, Mr. President," Ielicov was empathetic. "But we need your help, and perhaps the Minister of Defense, to gain access to the military files on the state repression against the Tupamaros and the general population during the dictatorship, to clarify this matter."

"Ha! The famous dictatorship files," Valdez rolled his eyes. "We *never* had access to them, if they ever existed," he shrugged. "And believe me, my Minister of Defense, José Bayardiz, and I have traveled this country far and wide, asking battalion by battalion, barrack by barrack, 'General, do you happen to have any documentary records of the disappearances and clandestine arrests during the dictatorship?' The answer was always the same: 'You're free to open our files and look.' The best option you have, detectives, if you want to continue that line of investigation, is to talk to the living actors of that period, starting with former President Borderragui, of course."

"He's on our list of interviews," Ielicov assured.

"I'm glad. Borderragui not only rolled out the red carpet for the military. During his presidency, emergency security measures were also used to arrest and interrogate civilians based on nothing at all. Oops. Look at the time," the president checked his watch. "9:27. The Chinese delegation arrives in 3 minutes, and I need to go to the bathroom first, so if you'll excuse me," he stood up to formally shake their hands.

"We appreciate your time, Mr. President," the former heavyweight boxer shook the outstretched hand.

"If you need *anything* from me, just call Gonzalo, and he'll relay it to me," the president of Uruguay let the detectives find their way out as he headed to the private bathroom adjoining his office.

"What intensity this man has, huh?" Viktor asked his partner, once they were outside the Executive Tower.

"He has a country to lead, what can I say? Let's be grateful he gave us 30 minutes of his time. What's next? Borderragui?"

"Seems like the next mandatory interview," Ielicov confirmed.

Geraldine looked up the number of the former president, the last one before the period of facto, from the list Mr. Reno had printed and dialed it on her mobile.

"Good morning, Mr. President. This is Geraldine Goldman from LNB PI detective agency. How are you this morning?"

"Who is this?" came the rough voice of an elderly man on the other end.

"Geraldine Goldman. I don't know if you remember me. I was the press chief for the National Police for many years. You've probably seen me on TV numerous times."

"Oh, yes. That rings a bell."

"Well, Mr. President, we need to talk to you for a moment about Mojica's death," the detective got straight to the point.

"And what do *I* have to do with Mojica?"

"You dealt with him, we understand, during your presidency when he was an active member of the guerrilla group National Liberation Movement—Tupamaros."

"Those sons of bitches...! They wanted to take the country by force, and we defeated them and locked them up. Then they escaped again, and we locked them up again. Over my *dead body* would they create another Cuba here."

"Precisely, Mr. President. We were hired to investigate his life, Mojica's, and provide the insurance company that contracted us with complete certainty about the cause of death."

"But didn't that son of a bitch die of a heart attack?"

"It might be. That's what we're investigating, and your input, if you could grant us an interview today, would be *crucial* for us to get a sense of what Mojica was like at that time. If it turns out he died of natural causes, well, the insurance company pays the life insurance amount to his wife..."

"WHAT?!" Borderragui interrupted. "Is all of this to benefit that other con artist, Laura Pulansky, that leftist daughter of a thousand whores? *No way* I'm going to collaborate!" he added angrily, and then, further from the phone, he could be heard saying, "Ha. Goldman. She had to be *Jewish*."

After that, there was no response from the other side. Geraldine's stomach churned, and her eyes filled with tears from rage. Viktor had pressed his ear to the mobile receiver to listen, since the Nokia N97 still didn't have the option for hands-free calls. The boxer looked at his partner with concern.

"Calm down, my love," he gently stroked her arm. "It's just another decrepit anti-Semite fascist."

"No... No... He's *not* going to win this so easily," she said, searching her phone's contacts for the number of the Head of the Homicide Department of the National Police, Gervasio "the Bull"

Villa, with whom she had a long-standing relationship. "Hello, Toro. Am I catching you at a bad time, or can you talk?"

"Hello, Geraldine. You can talk, no problem. I was just doing some office work."

"Thanks, Toro. Tell me, how feasible is it to force a witness who might have valuable information for the case to testify if they refuse to answer our questions voluntarily?"

"Whoa! And I thought they stopped torturing people on the rack," joked the descendant of indigenous peoples. "Let me see if we have any cattle prods or materials for dry and liquid submarines from the dictatorship era in the basement."

"Come on, you're being ridiculous. I mean, at least, I don't know... *summon* him to headquarters, to scare him a bit, or have both of you present to apply some pressure."

"Well, it can be done. A summons is requested from the judge, it's issued, and he will have to appear to testify."

"And what if he doesn't?"

"They bring him in by force to testify, but *nobody* does that. They know it's in their best interest to come voluntarily when we call them."

"Alright, could it be organized for some time today?"

"Wow! That's a bit rushed, but given the circumstances..."—he left unspoken the understanding that clarifying the murder of Francisco "Pancho" Mojica was almost a national priority at that moment.

"It *is* necessary, Toro."

"Then... let me see... Judge Omar Friade would surely issue an order within five minutes of our calling him."

"Gervasio, are you *serious*?"

"I was just kidding, Geraldine"—laughed the burly police inspector with a very retro mustache, reminiscent of Harley Davidson, after mentioning one of the many fatalities from 2005 during the Decorator case, one who, incredibly, had died in an accident in the bathroom—"Let's see... I have Judge Leguizamo noted down as being on duty, even though we're in judicial recess. I'll hang up and call him to issue the summons. Are you guys in Montevideo?"

"We're almost certainly here today and tomorrow."

"Perfect! Who are we summoning to testify?"

"Former President Juan María Borderragui."

"Wow! Let it *not* be said you two aren't aiming high. You're really going for it, my girl. I'll let you know when we have him here at Central Headquarters."

Chacra of Francisco "Pancho" Mojica and Laura Pulansky, Rincón del Cerro, Montevideo, Tuesday, July 21, 2009, 10:45 AM.

"It's freezing as hell here!"—the boxer complained as they got out of the Chevrolet Corsa they had rented using the corporate card from Grupo CSA (always keeping receipts for every expense).

"Ah, yes, that's what the countryside is like"—she inhaled the cold winter air as he drove them there—"Just like in the city, only here the air moves."

The detectives were confronted at the front gate of the farm by a dog weighing about 15 kilos, a mixed breed, with only three legs, barking furiously at them.

"Calm down, Manuela, calm down, these are the visitors we were expecting,"—her human, the house's matron, scolded her—"Excuse her. She's always like this with people she doesn't know." She stroked the dog's head to let it know the detectives were not a threat to the property. "And I think she senses why Pancho hasn't returned,"—the bitterness in the widow's voice was palpable, her face all wrinkled, but the strokes on the dog's head seemed to calm her a bit—"Come in, come in"—she opened the door, which creaked on its hinges.

"Our deepest condolences,"—the muscular detective extended his hand—"Viktor Ielicov, private detective."

"Geraldine Goldman"—the slender, pale-skinned brunette did the same—"We share in your sorrow."

"Laura Pulansky, young people,"—the elderly senator from the Popular Movement attempted a smile—"Come, let's have some mate on the terrace; it's somewhat sheltered from the wind because it's blowing from the west today." Once they were all seated in plastic chairs, the former Tupamaro got straight to the point—"So? Do you already know who killed Pancho?"

Only her eyes resembled those of her twin sister, Anabel, extremely light, almost translucent, whether due to genetics, cataracts, or a combination of both. Aside from that, no one would have guessed they were even sisters. Anabel was broad-shouldered and tanned, surely a result of working in the fields. Laura was more compact and thin, pale-skinned. Anabel had long, brown hair with abundant gray strands, disheveled. The senator's hair was short, neat, and completely gray.

"Not yet, Senator…"—Viktor began.

"Laura, my son. Laura"—the senator dismissed the formality with a gesture—"All Uruguayans know us by our first names. Why bother with formalities?"

"We already have a pretty clear idea of how he was killed, though,"—Geraldine tried to be optimistic.

"Oh, really?"

"We have almost no doubt that they gave him a cardiac stimulant mixed in with the whiskey he used to drink at night."

"Ha! Pancho drank and drank when he wasn't working,"—the widow reminisced nostalgically.

"And then they waited for the lifeguard at the Pool of Las Palmas to be forced to go to the bathroom, leaving Mojica alone in the pool. They definitely used a laxative on the lifeguard, mixed with whatever he had for lunch between 5:30 and 6, when he took his break. When the lifeguard was in the bathroom, which had a door that opened outward, a muscular guy held the door shut so he couldn't get out for more than 20 minutes. In the meantime, or just before this, someone shoved Mojica's head underwater, and between the cardiac stimulant and the logical fear of drowning, it caused him a heart attack, which was the initially determined cause of death."

"Shit! So, this was well planned,"—the widow concluded, although she brewed a mate and finished it while still lost in thought—"This looks like it was the military who don't want the

Expiry Law to be repealed..."—the former Tupamaro left the thought hanging in the air.

"They're among the suspects, Laura,"—Ielicov approved very seriously—"but at this point, it would help us if you could provide more information about your husband. What was he like? What was your activity together when you were Tupamaros?"

"Well, look, my son. What can I say? Pancho was *always* a dreamer, and that was what we admired most about him back in the guerrilla days. He envisioned Uruguay following the example of our Cuban comrades. He saw social programs, wealth redistribution, and freedom from imperialist influences... But besides that, he could convince you of *anything* when he spoke, because he spoke from the heart, you know? And he had... he had a way with words that *hypnotized* us all. We'd have fallen at his feet."

"Like that?"—the Uruguayan detective raised her eyebrows, the only one in the duo who understood the River Plate slang indicating that all the women wanted to be with him.

"Oh yes. And Pancho was a catalogue handsome young man as the good-looking guys of the time, like Gary Cooper or Cary Grant. He was very attractive, but luckily I was the one who got him,"—the elderly woman smiled mischievously.

"Some people have told us he also had an affair with his twin sister, Anabel"—Geraldine went straight to the point.

"Oh, yes, but that was before he started going out with me"—the former Tupamaro waved her hand dismissively—"And it ended badly,"—she shook her head—"But I talked to my sister about it, and she gave me the green light to start courting Pancho."

"What do you mean by 'badly'?"—the former press chief of the National Police asked again.

"Neither of them ever told me, so I suppose it must have been serious,"—the hostess shrugged—"but what I know is that after they broke up, they never spoke again. Anyway, Pancho was free, I did things right, I talked to my sister, and she said something like, 'I don't want anything more to do with him, so if you want, he's all yours.' That's roughly what she told me."

"I understand"—Viktor thought carefully about how to phrase the next question—"We were talking with Amadeo Píriz..."

"That son of a bitch!"—the homeowner cursed.

"He claims, and in fact published a book about it, that if there was a traitor among the Tupamaros, it wasn't him,"—the private detective pressed on incisively.

"How could it *not* be him?"—the old woman was getting angrier, and Manuela, the three-legged dog, growled at the detectives in support of her human.

"Laura"—Geraldine attempted to mediate—"What real evidence do those who point to him as such have, that he, and not anyone else, was the traitor among your ranks who collaborated with the authorities to capture you after the escape from Punta Carretas prison? And we ask you to reason this out as the legislator you are, one who deals with crafting laws every day, including criminal laws."

The daughter of a well-off family from Malvín, who was tempted in her youth to join a revolutionary force that sought to overthrow the institutions to establish a Cuban-style regime, was later imprisoned, repeatedly raped, systematically tortured for almost 15 years, only to be released when democracy returned in 1985, at 41 years old since she had left her mother's womb, but already looking 65 at that time, she thought about it for a *long* moment, which the detectives respected.

"Look, Geraldine" - the ex-Tupamaran was very serious - "Pancho and Ñato told us that it had been him, that it had been that son of a bitch Píriz who had handed us over to the military. Why wouldn't we believe them?"

"Who is Ñato?" - asked the only person not born in Uruguay in the conversation.

"Huidó" - the Uruguayan detective of the duo answered for the interviewee - "They were both held captive together during the dictatorship, weren't they?"

"They were thrown into a well for 13 years!" - the former Tupamaro pointed out, as if indicating a cistern into which the military had thrown her partner in struggle and life, and Mojica's best friend and partner in arms and struggle, "Ñato" Huidó. - "Are you insinuating that the two of them invented Píriz's betrayal?" - Manuela, the 3-legged dog, growled again, accompanying her human's mood.

"We are *not* insinuating anything" –the former heavyweight boxer from Vladivostok wanted to be emphatic even in his gestures-, "but we need to know all the facts, ask the right questions to the right people who will bring us closer to the truth of what happened to your husband."

"Well" –the Uruguayan parliamentarian tried to be open-minded-. "As for evidence that one can see and touch... we don't have it. If you look at it in terms of what a judge can hear, it's Pancho and Ñato on one side saying that it was Amadeo Píriz, and Píriz saying that it wasn't him."

"So, the plan could very well have been concocted by him, right?" -Goldman opened the possibility, needing to have some clue of who had killed Mojica.

"Nnnoooo" -the former Tupamaro stretched out, thinking about it, however-. "I don't think it was him. Píriz was always a coward. He would never do anything but rant against Pancho, may he rest in peace. To give you an example, when we were active with the Tupamaros, in the sixties, when we planned a job, he would not touch a weapon even if they came cutting throats. He preferred to stay behind and watch over the crowd."

"Of course. I understand" - the pale-skinned brunette with prominent cheekbones accepted the defeat of the possibility -. "And what about Dr. De La Rúa? We understand that, with her husband dead, he is the one who leads the possibilities of being elected president in October."

"The Progressive Front is *stronger* than one person, my dear" - the old woman smiled confidently -. "My husband fell, but another will take the party flag and in October the citizens *will* re-elect us as government, you will see."

"But your husband had a very particular appeal to the masses" - tried to refute the arguments of legislator Ielicov.

"He had it. That's true, but his fighting spirit will not be extinguished because he is *no longer* with us. He will surely infect every politician of my party at every event, and Pancho's spirit will put us in government again. Now, returning to your question" - the senator was more than used to answering questions from the press, and to taking up a pending issue if she so wished - "if De La Rúa has the motives and the means... he *has* them, I can assure you of that. He was already president, from 1991 to 1995, and during his presidency there were corruption scandals throughout the administration. Somehow, he always managed to stay clean from the mess, but don't doubt that he got rich handsomely during that period, and he is surely very tempted to repeat the experience. But we are *not* going to let him, rest assured. The Front is going to win these elections, and if it is not in the first round, it will be in the runoff, then. We just have to find the candidate to succeed him at the convention we're going to have this coming Saturday."

"It's interesting, because we were going to ask you exactly about that" - Geraldine got straight to the point again - "Who is the candidate who would replace Mojica on the presidential ticket? Will Arturi become the presidential candidate for the Progressive Front? What do you think?"

"It seems like you're a journalist, my daughter" - laughed the Tupamara.

"I'm going to ask you *not* to insult me" - continued the one who had asked jokingly – I" don't know if you remember me, but I dealt with journalists on a daily basis when I was head of the press for the National Police."

"I remember you, yes" - smiled the lady of the house - "What a handling of the press you had, that you threw it away. No, I don't think Daniel will be the presidential candidate this Saturday" - she shook her head - "They'll choose someone else. Who knows. Maybe *I* could even be a candidate" –she shrugged her shoulders-. "It's not for nothing that the Popular Movement was the list with the most votes in the last elections within the Progressive Front, and those who, according to the polls, captured more than 40% of the voting intentions of our party. But if with that question they were looking for a suspect" –she was suspicious-, "Daniel is *far* from planning a murder, not even by hiring hitmen. He is an intellectual, a fool in every sense, he must have a very high IQ, for sure, but he is a real docile. He opposed Pancho in the primaries and lost but... *abysmally*, but he took it with soda, and accepted to be vice president. Anything for the party. And if you see *me* as suspicious, buy glasses, guys" –she smiled at them-. "Pancho and I were life partners, and partners in struggle. A *whole life* together, imagine" –the smile this time of the ex-Tupamara was bitter-. "Look, how I possibly get him killed?" - she dismissed with a gesture.

"Was he faithful to you?" - this time it was Viktor who was incisive, bringing up without telling the interviewee that Mojica's secretary had confessed to being the deceased's involuntary lover.

"How would I know if he was faithful to me or not?"! -reacted the old woman with almost transparent eyes-. "Look what you ask me! And, besides, what the hell would it matter to me? You can imagine that at our age we didn't have a very passionate relationship, right? And if he was in the mood and found someone, of course I wouldn't have liked to find out, but as long as he didn't bring diseases home, I... out of sight, out of mind" -the veteran shrugged her shoulders-. "If he had brought diseases home... Ha. That's when he would find out!"

Moments later, the private investigators were in the comfort of the rental car, and its heating, above all, heading to the urban center of the city of Montevideo.

!Do you believe all the nonsense about poverty, and the humility with which they live?! -Viktor commented to his partner and life-sharing in a low voice, already on the way to the car.

"Not for a second! That sweatshirt the woman was wearing, which looked so warm, for example, is from Manos del Uruguay. It must be worth 700 or 800 dollars, but that's about it, just like that. The salary for a month of a half-time bricklayer in this country."

"It could have been a gift, perhaps."

"But even so..." - she left the thought hanging in the air.

"What cold blood, this woman" - commented the ex-boxer, this time at the wheel, as they were accustomed to doing in their cases, one time one drove, another time the other.

"She's a politician, Vik, what can I say?" - shrugged her shoulders her partner and life-sharing- "Believe half of what you see, and none of what you hear, as Lou Reed says in his song. Which one is it?"

"I don't remember, but I think I remember that it's a quote attributed to Edgar Allan Poe."

"How cultured, my love!"

"You know: boxers *also* read, when we're not hitting someone or a bag."

"Funny" - she smiled at him - "Well" - she took her cell phone to see the list of interviews they had left - "You choose. We still have De La Rúa, Arturi, Bravetto and stopping by my old office. Ooorrr..." - the curly-haired brunette stretched suggestively, seeing that it's almost noon-, "we could stop somewhere downtown for lunch and then continue."

"Are you hungry already? But we had breakfast 4 hours ago!"

"All doctors recommend not fasting for very long periods of time."

"Yes, well... whatever you want. I don't understand where you fit all that food in that sexy emergency body of yours" - he was gallant.

"Metabolism, I suppose" – she interrupted herself to see who was calling her cell phone – "Toro Villa" – she told her partner, seeing the captor – "I suppose lunch will have to wait."

CHAPTER 9: THAT WOMAN HAS TO DISAPPEAR

SIDE Headquarters, 25 de Mayo Street, number 11, Buenos Aires, Capital Federal, Argentina, December 10, 1980, 9:15 AM.

The dark-gestured veteran, who many people were afraid of just looking at, even if they didn't recognize him as the former director of the Punta Carretas Prison, or the current director of anti-subversive struggle of the Uruguayan National Police, hadn't been in the waiting room outside the office of the director of the Argentine Army Intelligence Secretariat for long, when the director himself opened the wide double oak doors of his office, and let his visitor in with a formal greeting.

- "Carlitos, dear" – the greeting from the high-ranking military officer (he was six feet three inches tall, and high in the hierarchy of the armed forces) would have seemed affectionate to anyone who saw it, except that his thin lips did not move from the straight line, that is to say: he did *not* smile – "Nice to see you here."

"The pleasure is mine, as always, Oscar" – the Uruguayan pronounced the name correctly, with the accent on the "a", even though in Uruguay they had them on the "O", even though it was an acute proper name, undoubtedly a cultural contamination from the Oscars, from the academy.

"Come in, come in" – the Argentine military man invited with a gesture and closed the double doors of his office behind his guest – "I can offer you a whiskey, do you want?"

"Yes, thank you, but just a medium one, I came driving."

"Aha" – the owner of the office proceeded to serve two glasses of Johnny Black Label, one stronger than the other. He invited the Uruguayan to sit down, did the same, and after clinking glasses, made the usual joke between the two: "Until victory... always!" - a phrase attributed to Ernesto 'Che' Guevara, the Argentine revolutionary, participant and totemic figure of the Cuban revolution, defeated and his corpse displayed before the cameras and the villagers in Bolivia. The nature of the joke between repressors of subversion was clear: they were quoting one of the many Bolsheviks, communists and hippies they had defeated in their careers, with the double meaning that *they* had been the ones who had emerged victorious.

"You can imagine that I didn't come to visit you for our usual monthly meeting, right?" - asked rhetorically the Uruguayan.

"And, no. That's the 15th of every month" - he referred the Argentinean about the monthly meeting in which they coordinated the anti-subversive "efforts" between the allied nations, that is to say: I have these prisoners there in Uruguay that we have already decided to stop extracting more information from through systematic torture, and we need you to "disappear" them in Argentina, and the director of the SIDE gave the Uruguayan the files of the Argentines who needed to be disappeared in another country, to cover the tracks of each dictatorship. Anyone who saw those meetings from outside, and did not understand the sordid and criminal nature of what was being discussed, could have mistaken them for schoolchildren exchanging stickers from the fashion album in the school playground. "Also, you came driving, which is unusual for you when you visit me, so I deduce that it is something important and classified that you want to talk to me about. Well... *more* classified than what we talk about every month. That's as far as my intelligence training at the SIDE goes. You'll have to tell me the rest. Although... maybe it has something to do with the fact that they lost the plebiscite, right?"

The top leader of Argentine military intelligence was of course referring to the referendum to establish the legal and constitutional bases for the civil-military power to continue governing for 15 more years, and for 15 more, and so on, at the discretion of the military leadership. Since the vote in Uruguay is secret, the response from the polls was a resounding: There's no way we'd approve this! In other words: the dictatorial government's initiative did not prosper, giving them an indication that perhaps they were *not* as popular as they had estimated, nevertheless, it took them another five years to cede power to democracy.

"Something, yes, but it's not just because of that. I mean, with this plebiscite: the citizens don't want us. So what? We're the ones who have the weapons, and we're going to leave whenever we damn please. Look, Oscar... do you remember that I told you about our star informant in the late sixties and early seventies?"

"Prisoner 2746? Of course! A gold mine, I think I remember, and what a son of a bitch you are" – *now* the Argentine soldier was smiling – "to have kept the way you called him, 2746, or prisoner 2746, for a *whole* decade, depriving him of hearing his name or surname."

"Fuck him for being a jerk."

"Do they still have him in the barracks?"

"Yes, of course. We can't let him go because the others would notice, but he eats with the officers in the barracks, has access to a hot shower and all that. And we also give him temporary releases, so he can go to the brothel in Pando or do whatever he wants, on the weekends, and money so he can have fun. He may or may not go back to the barracks to sleep, but on Sunday nights he has to be back until the following Friday. Sometimes, from time to time, we have to give him a little tap, so he can show the other Tupas that they are also "torturing" him" - the Uruguayan repressor made the air quotes.

"Of course. Everything is to conceal that there is an agreement with 2746."

"Exactly. If something works... why touch it? But look what I found out, and it was the infiltrator himself who told me: we had finished dinner in the officers' lounge of the barracks with 2746 and the other officers, we went out to smoke a cigarette together, he had had too much to drink that time, and he goes and confesses to me that he had had a son before we caught him."

"And you didn't *already* know that?" - the Argentine raised an eyebrow, indicating his disagreement with such an omission in the investigation.

"Can you believe it?" - the Uruguayan shrugged his shoulders. "It had nothing to do with the anti-subversive struggle, whether he had one, ten or no children with a woman or a harem. Or so we thought at the time."

"But you see that the anti-personnel mine that was kept hidden for so long now exploded in your faces, or you wouldn't be here. Or am I wrong?"

"And yes. You can imagine that when he told me that all the alarms went off, but I pretended not to, and I think I said "ah, look," so he would continue talking. And can you believe that the *idiot* goes and tells me everything? The name of the mother, the name of the kid, where they lived at the time in Punta Gorda, that she never let him get close to the kid, and that he used his temporary outings to harass the mother of his son, basically, to bother her at home, claiming paternal rights over the kid."

"He knew that the poor woman wouldn't be able to call the police, right?"

"Of course not. Anyway, to make a long story short, it turns out that the woman endured and endured for years, until she left Uruguay with the kid."

"She settled in Argentina, right?" - understood the Director of the Army Intelligence Secretariat.

"It's most likely. He thinks that. Also, at that time, it was at the end of last year, I think, when he realized that she had escaped, he told me that he had found out that he had heard that a Tupas sympathizer had escaped from the general arrests at the beginning of the seventies, and he made us believe that his ex-wife was a communist. Of course, we deployed the police apparatus and in a few days, we found out that she had crossed the Concordia bridge to Argentina at the end of October last year. The woman had family in Argentina, in Córdoba. The thing is that 2746 asked me a few days ago to speak with my contacts in Argentina - he pointed to his local counterpart -, to be able to locate this woman, and her son."

"You laughed in his face, I imagine."

"And yes. Look if *I* was going to waste resources in finding his son. But then I asked him a key question, a moment's inspiration, I always pretended. I asked him why they had separated. The guy turned pale, idiot, and then I knew that "something" he had told the mother of his son about his dealings with us, and I decided to move the interrogation to something more "motivating" so he would tell the whole truth."

"I imagine. I would have done the same. So? What had he told her?"

"Everything! His dealings with us to point us out to the other Tupamaros, the clandestine burials, the torture, my name, that of many of the officers..."

"Does he know anything about me?"

"No, I *never* told him about you, you can imagine. The thing is that the chick clearly broke up with him, when the kid was still a baby, but one day 2746 went to knock on her door to harass her, probably drunk, and claim his right as a father to see his son, and the house was empty."

"She hit the road and now we have a civilian with information that could screw up all of our lives" - the Argentine military leader understood the seriousness of the matter, stroking his well-shaven chin -. "Well, it affects you more on the Uruguayan side than us here, but by transitive, knowing the details affects us all, apart from us sending subversives to bury them there. That woman *has* to be found, wherever she is."

"And yes, Oscar. I wouldn't worry about 2746. We can keep him alive and in the conditions he is in now, but restricting his temporary outings a little, or following him, because we already saw that he makes a mess when he goes out there. In addition, we have his silence guaranteed. In local terms, we have him by the balls."

"Oh, really?"

"Yes, look" - he took something from his inside pocket and showed it to his Argentine counterpart - "it's a Polaroid photo we took of him in 1971."

The photo was in a transparent nylon bag, but the Director of the SIDE took it out of the bag anyway to see it better.

"Wait, wait, wait. What do you mean, you had Polaroid cameras in 1971? They're just *now* becoming popular here."

"Oh, you see? The advantages of being one of the favorite forces within the National Police. The money came from the United States, and in the distribution, we could *always* choose first, and they didn't control us so much in what we spent."

"Here in Argentina, up until 1976, when we took power, the budget was a pittance. Let's see..." - he took a moment to analyze the color snapshot - "The one standing, holding the gun, is prisoner 2746, did I understand correctly?"

"Yes."

"And who is the other one?"

"Vasco" Olavarría, another Tupamaro. 2746 pointed out a shoe store where the Tupamaros met, we organized a raid that ended in 10 points, but when they were loading Olavarría onto the military truck, the guy turned his head and saw 2746 next to me. You can imagine that we couldn't leave him alive with that information."

"And no. Of course" - the Argentine dismissed it, as if it were the most obvious thing in the world - "So 2746 killed him just like that."

"The gun wasn't even loaded, dude, but you see that photo, and what do you see?"

"Yes, it's clear. If this photo is made public, 2746 will be lynched in the public square. Forget what the Italians did to Mussolini. If this comes to light, what Mussolini received from the crowd will seem like a *caress* compared to what they would do to this son of a bitch."

"That's why I was telling you: we have our collaborator under control. His ex-wife, on the other hand, is a latent risk."

"Isn't it going to be? Because if we have to hand over power to democracy, you, me, and all of us who act in the anti-subversive repression will know how to keep quiet and not betray ourselves or our comrades in arms. But the civilians, on the other hand..." -he left the thought hanging in the air-. "You stay calm. You give me all the information you have and we will find that son of a bitch and kill her."

"And don't forget the son. He must be about 11 years old by now."

"Yeah, sure. Don't worry. My boys won't hesitate when the time comes" - he smiled grimly -. "Hey, speaking of nothing to do, I heard that you built yourself a little house in Camboriú. Your stuff is going well, man!"

"It's true. And your informants are doing well too, Oscar. Two floors, three rooms, on the beach, wonderful. I invite you to spend a few days there, if you want. I'll take all of January and go there with my wife. When you can and want, come over, you're my guest."

"It's very likely that I'll accept your invitation, I assure you. Here in Capital Federal in January you can't breathe, because of the heat. But first I'm going to have to take care of this bitch and her son. You *know* you owe me one, right?"

"Of course! You can collect it whenever you want, Oscar."

Access to Montevideo, going under the Carlos María Ramírez bridge, Montevideo, Tuesday, July 21, 2009, 11:40 AM.

"Toro, tell me, what happened?" -Geraldine answered the call.

"We have former president Juan María Borderragui here at Central Headquarters."

"So soon?!"

"See? Sometimes it seems like you underestimate us, Geral. The thing is, I don't know how much longer I can hold him. He came with his son, who, oh surprise, is none other than Senator Borderragui."

"What?! A former dictator has a son who is a Senator of the Republic? That's crazy! How could I know? Remember, I haven't lived in Uruguay for four years."

"Yes, he's a Senator and also a lawyer, but the guys tell me he's a corporate lawyer, so he has no influence in criminal matters. Listen to me: how long until you get here?"

"It depends. If they fine us for speeding or reckless driving, will you help us get them removed?"

"Of course!"

"I estimate about 20 minutes."

"Perfect! I'll let the entrance know to direct them where we are. In fact, I'll send Di Lorenzo to make the entry process smoother."

"See you there, Toro."

"What happened?" -the driver wanted to know.

"Step on the gas, Vik! I'll tell you the fastest way to get to Central Headquarters."

Not in 20, but in 18 minutes, they arrived at the six-story building, the headquarters of the Uruguayan National Police, and also the central prison, where VIP prisoners were held, so to speak, those who had committed minor offenses or received such short sentences that it wasn't worth mixing them with the general prison population, who would emerge retrained to commit much more serious and violent crimes, as well as criminals who have committed *very* serious offenses. But everyone suspected that the families of these las ones had paid a lot of money for them to serve their sentences there.

Pablo Goncalvez was one of these latter cases: the first multiple killer who raped and murdered three young women in the late '90s and was sentenced in 2001 to the maximum penalty in Uruguay—30 years without the possibility of reduction. It was said that the young man's family had paid and continued to pay a fortune for Goncalvez to stay there, in a model prison located in the city center, making it easy and convenient for his relatives to visit him, unlike other prisons that were located on the outskirts of the city of one and a half million inhabitants, or directly in the interior of the country.

The multiple killer was the most violent police case in Uruguay until the emergence of the Decorator, the first serial killer in 2005, in which Viktor and Geraldine were the main characters (and also the main resolvers), a recognition that was never officially given to them until Geraldine's former high school classmate, aspiring writer Aklmer Lupoj, published his first bestseller "The Decorator – the Hidden Truth" in 2007, detailing all the sordid aspects that the police and the government at the time tried to conceal.

Some political scientists claimed during the time of the killings perpetrated by The Decorator and his acolytes, the Speakers of the Sun, in that 2005, an election year, that it dealt a death blow to the traditional parties, paving the way for the first leftist government in the history of Uruguay, the Progressive Front, which placed President Valdez at the helm of the executive branch. The scandal, during Valdez's presidency, in 2007, with the publication of Lupoj's book, which illustrated in great detail the corruption and inefficiency of the National Police under the previous conservative government, somehow cleared the way for Mojica to become the second leftist president... if he had made it to the elections alive.

Even before arriving at the homicide department, the angry shouts of Borderragui's son could be heard, nearing 50, with a height and physical build that were intimidating in themselves. Next to him was a rather tall old man, trying to look dignified in his expensive suit but of thin and rather frail build, undoubtedly over 80 years old: the former president Juan María Borderragui, who had also been the last "democratically" elected president before the dictatorship, although there were reasonable doubts about the reliability of the vote count in the elections that put him in office, a position he held from '73 to '76, when the ruling military junta replaced him with his vice president, Álvaro Demichelli, who asked fewer questions and wanted less involvement in the dictatorial decisions.

All 20 desks in the homicide detectives' office were empty, likely so that the subordinates wouldn't have to witness the embarrassing (and verbally violent) spectacle. Ielicov and Goldman saw the corporate lawyer gesticulating and shouting at the very stoic Gervasio "Toro" Villa, head of the homicide department, and the Secretary of the Interior, Aníbal Cortez, who had summoned the duo to investigate Mojica's murder, which had quickly shifted from being a possibility to "we just need the toxicology report sent to Buenos Aires to confirm it."

"May I speak now?" -Toro Villa raised his hand with a smile, as if he was in school, but the insolence of his gesture achieved the desired effect: the ranting legislator fell silent. "Good, I know that your area is corporate law, and voting on laws in parliament and those things, so I will explain to you one last time, I hope, the difference between a *witness* and a *suspect*. The suspect is basically someone suspected of having committed a crime. They can be forcibly brought in, if necessary, for the initial interrogation, and the suspect *does have* the right to a prior conversation with their defense lawyer, or a public defender if they can't afford one, which is obviously *not* the case for your father. The lawyer can also be present during the initial police interrogation. On the other hand, a witness is summoned... *invited*, if you want to call it that, to provide information in an ongoing investigation. The witness *does not have* the right to have a lawyer present during the police's initial interrogation, but if at any point during their testimony there are indications that they might move from being a witness to a suspect, everything stops, the judge is notified, and *only then* do they gain the right to have their legal representative present. Doctor?" -he asked Secretary Cortez. "You who *did* study criminal law, even if you haven't practiced as a criminal lawyer since becoming Secretary of the Interior. Did I get the definitions and legal rights of witnesses and suspects right?"

"Word for word, Chief Villa," -Cortez replied with a smile.

"Oh, and one more thing I know about criminal law, due to my work, don't misunderstand me, because otherwise, I would be an illiterate fool: do you know why I didn't restrain you, handcuff you, and throw you in a cell as soon as you started shouting and pushing me, waiting for the prosecutor's charge for contempt of authority?"

"Because of my parliamentary immunity?" -the senator responded haughtily.

"Exactly!" -the mustachioed man replied, with features of indigenous descent. "To lift your immunity so you can be investigated and prosecuted for any crime, three-quarters of the general assembly must vote in favor, and, to put it bluntly, it's not worth my time to initiate that process over a loud, arrogant brat. So, now, if you don't mind, we need to talk to your dad for a while, okay? Can you clear the area for me?" -he gestured with his hands as if sweeping away dust. "Or should I call the guys to escort you out?"

"Go on, son," -the former president patted him on the arm. "Everything will be fine."

"You two," -the senator pointed a finger at Cortez and Villa- "you'll see! Your careers end *here and now*!" -he threatened, turning to leave, angry. "I'm *immediately* calling an urgent meeting of my party's caucus."

"Good luck with that!" -the head of homicide replied sarcastically. "With the three senators you have, you could just as well meet in a bathroom—10% of the electorate! Ha! Oh, well," -he added, as Pedro Borderragui stormed out of the detective room, slamming the door. "If we count the 15 deputies, then you're going to need a slightly larger meeting room."

"Yes, that disparity was due to the strong presence of the liberal party in the interior," -Cortez added.

"Well, Mr. Borderragui. Shall we move to an interrogation room? Ielicov, Goldman, Di Lorenzo, would you please join us?" -Villa invited, maintaining a steady gaze on the legislator, while out of the corner of his eye, he saw the private detectives and his subordinate arriving.

"Do you need me here for anything, Villa?" -Cortez asked.

"No, go ahead, Secretary. We've got it under control now that the loudmouth is gone."

"Great, then. I'll be in my office. Let me know if you need anything."

CHAPTER 10: PRESIDENT BORDERRAGUI

Rural house on the outskirts of Pirané, Province of Formosa, northeastern Argentina, November 11, 1982, 11:10 PM.

The strangers who got out of the Falcon wearing ski masks and armed had been examining the property for a while with their flashlights, probing the closed doors, the darkened lights, the shut windows, and the poorly nailed boards acting as bars to prevent opportunistic thieves from entering.

"I think we got bad intel, boss," one of the strangers in civilian clothes said to another, tucking his gun into his waistband.

"Looks like it," the one who seemed to be the leader of the group pulled off his ski mask. "Damn it. They slipped away again. Damn it!" He kicked the Falcon.

"Nothing in the shed," announced another who had come from the back of the house.

"Alright. Let's go. It's your turn, Gómez, to inform central command tomorrow that either we got false intel, or for whatever magic, they had a crystal ball and knew we were coming."

"And why me? What is this, a joke from God?" Gómez protested, now also with his ski mask pushed up on his forehead.

"Because it was the SIDE that gave us this tip, right? And who's from SIDE here?" He gestured widely with a smile.

"Okay, fine. I'll report tomorrow. Still... who are these two sons of bitches that always slip away from us? They don't even tell me why their arrest is a priority."

"What do I know, Gómez?" the operation leader shrugged. "If they don't tell you, who can imagine they'd tell me? I'm just following orders. Alright. Let's head back to the barracks. The 29th of cavalry is treating for beers tonight, boys."

"Yay!" Gómez scoffed as all four anti-subversive forces got back into the Falcon. "You know we have several theories among the officers about why we've been looking for these two for two years, right?"

"Let's hear it, because we have some hypotheses at the barracks too."

"For me, this has *nothing* to do with the anti-subversive struggle, or crime repression, or fighting communism, or whatever."

"Oh, really?"

"No. I think this bitch is the rebellious daughter of some general who ran off with the general's grandson, and that's why they're putting so much effort into finding them."

"Oh, really, Gómez? Then why the order to eliminate and disappear?"

"There's a good point," the operative contributed, pondering for a bit. "Maybe she had a huge fight with her father before leaving, called him a damn fascist or something, or maybe she stole important plans, or has evidence that could incriminate the general in some illicit fund movement... What do I know?"

"See, Gómez? That's why we talk about it among the officers at the barracks, but just to pass the time. Orders come from above, and that's it. End of story. What does it matter what that bitch and her kid did?"

Meanwhile, inside the seemingly abandoned rural house on the outskirts of the town of Pirané, population 7,000, in the province of Formosa, several minutes after the sound of the six-cylinder, 4.1-liter engine of the Ford Falcon had faded into the solitude of the countryside—a true assault on the ozone layer and a significant contributor of greenhouse gases—Magdalena Schebor finally relaxed her grip on the barrel of the Argentine-made Bersa double-barreled shotgun and took her right index finger off the trigger. She set the weapon aside and began to cry uncontrollably, huddled in a corner, away from the windows.

Her almost 14-year-old son, also huddled in another corner of the dilapidated property, set down the revolver on the floor and went to comfort his mother, but soon they were both crying and embracing each other for a long while.

"I can't take it anymore, Bicho!" Magdalena finally exclaimed, calling her son by his affectionate nickname, Bicho (Bug). "I can't take it anymore!" Her blue-eyed pupils were all red from crying. "Are you okay?" she stroked her son's hair.

"Yes, Mom. I'm okay, but how much longer are we going to keep hiding and running?"

"I've *already* talked to you about this, Bicho: until the military leaves power. Only *then* will we have some breathing room."

"But why *us*, Mom? What did we do? You're not even a communist or anything."

"You heard them, my love, before they got in the car: even they, who have been chasing us for the last two years, have *no idea* why they're looking for us," she tried to sound convincing, although she had a pretty clear idea of why.

"Then why don't we flee to Paraguay or Brazil?"

"Bicho, take me seriously for once in your life when I explain the current political context, okay?" The slender woman, whose nearly 14-year-old son had already outgrown her, was firm. "Uruguay, Brazil, Paraguay, Chile: all dictatorships. Intelligence collaboration among the de facto governments and everything I've told you. So basically, it doesn't matter whether we stay in Argentina or flee by land. And don't even think about showing our pretty faces at an airport, no matter how small. No. Our best strategy is to keep moving and relocating."

"I think the best option is to go to Buenos Aires."

"Are you crazy, Bicho?!" the adult exclaimed in the rural house. "How are we going to walk into the wolf's mouth?"

"Think about it for a second, Mom: if we stick with the metaphor of the wolf's mouth, it's a *gigantic* mouth, with 15 million inhabitants. We could blend in with the crowd. And besides, they'd never think we'd go towards *them*, when for the last two years they've been coming towards *us*, into the interior of Argentina."

"Mmm... that makes sense, I'll admit. But first, let's pack our bags and get the hell out of this place. It's not safe anymore. I'll pack the bags, you go get the bike from the reeds, and we'll leave with the lights off; there's still some moonlight."

"Okay. I love you, Mom," he hugged her.

"And I love you, Bicho. And I love you."

Central Headquarters, at the intersection of San José and Yi, interrogation room number two of the Homicide Department, Tuesday, July 21, 2009, 12:50 PM.

When Villa finished the formal introductions and everyone was seated (although Villa introduced Goldman and Ielicov with a vague "special advisors on the case"), it was the head of homicide who got down to business.

"Well, Borderragui. I'm going to explain what this interrogation is about, at least as much as we can share, because this is an ongoing investigation."

"Yes, of course," the interrogated man accepted. "And I apologize if my son got upset a moment ago. It's just... what was said in the citation..."

"What part?" asked the mustached officer.

"That if he didn't show up to testify voluntarily, I would be *brought in* to testify in two days, meaning... they would force me to testify."

"Yeah," Villa shrugged. "That's how things work. But don't worry, it's nothing personal against you. The citations for testimony from judges are all the same. It's a Word document that's already prepared; the only thing that changes is the name of the court case..."

"Which in this case said 'Classified,' if I recall correctly," interrupted the octogenarian.

"Yeah, well, you understand that sometimes that's necessary," the giant, who descended from Native Americans, dismissed. "Then the field for the summoned party is filled in, the date, the days they have to appear voluntarily before being brought in, and that's about it: the judge's secretary prints it, the judge signs it, and we enforce it. It's a matter of routine."

"I understand, I understand," Borderragui nodded. "And what questions do you have for me?" The tone of the wealthy rural producer and former president was one of absolute cooperation.

"Now we'll get into that. Our special advisors, Goldman and Ielicov, will ask you the questions, but first I'd like Di Lorenzo, who is the detective handling the details of the case, to explain the guidelines for this, which is an informal interrogation."

"Of course," the subordinate accepted. "In informal interrogations, Borderragui, we don't film, transcribe, or record *anything* that's discussed here. Not even notes are taken. Okay? It's just us asking you questions, and you responding to the best of your ability, do we have an agreement?" If Di Lorenzo's words veiled a threat for the interrogated, suggesting that the guarantees of personal integrity for the former president could be compromised, and that, if they wanted to, they could put a plastic bag over his head to suffocate him while the others held him, as long as they didn't leave physical marks, it remained open to interpretation by the interrogated.

"Sure, no problem," the old man swallowed hard. "It must be for the confidentiality of the testimony, right?"

"Of course it is," Di Lorenzo shot a sly smile at his boss.

"Now then," the hulking head of homicide smiled in turn, "with the grounds of this informal interrogation clarified, I'll hand the floor over to our special advisors."

"Thank you, chief," Geraldine began. "Please tell us, Mr. Borderragui, we'd like you to explain how you became president in '72." The question was decidedly tangential to what they really wanted to know, but it brought the interviewee closer to that time.

"Oh, what can I tell you, my daughter? Wait. Would you mind calling me President?"

"I see no problem with that," the Jewish woman shrugged. "You were President, and the last one legitimately elected at the polls before the dictatorship, so I can call you that. How did your rise to the presidency happen? Because I'm Uruguayan. My partner isn't. And I believe I recall that before being president, your name had *never* been associated with politics, am I correct?"

"Yes, of course. I was just a rural producer. I had my fields, my ranches, I did my business... Until one fine day, I received a call from the Liberal Party, which I'm affiliated with, and they asked me to come to the party's headquarters, close to here, on Martínez Trueba Street, because they had something to discuss with me."

"And just like that, they suggested you run for president?" she asked, knowing from their experience who would be asking which questions based on the area of interrogation they were covering with her partner. "Is that how it happened?"

"Exactly like that. That's what they proposed to me in the meeting I had with the leadership of the Liberal Party. I remember telling them," -the wrinkled old man smiled-, "and what does it mean to be president? I know about farming, livestock, and rural business. They explained to me that being the president of a country is somewhat like being the president of a company, just on a larger scale: managing resources, overseeing purchases, expenses, and sales, personnel to direct, imports, exports... A lot of it didn't make sense to me regarding why they wanted me as a candidate, but then they appealed to my liberal heart and told me they needed me, that they needed a candidate with my profile."

"In what sense?"

"In the sense that we were coming from a government from my party, yes, but where the president died halfway through his term, and the vice president, Jorge Paredes Arezzo, 'Bocha' Paredes, as everyone called him, took over. What can I say about that guy? He was a boxer in his youth, a very tough, rigid, and overbearing person... *Nobody* liked him much as president within the party, but according to the constitution, if the president died, the vice had to take over," he shrugged. "It was a period of great fear among the citizens, fear of the Tupamaros, of course, who began to rob, kidnap, and kill. But there was also fear of the excessive presence and repression by the police and military because 'Bocha' didn't hesitate to call in the military to patrol the streets to ensure order."

"The famous Security Emergency Measures, right?"

"Exactly. I mean, they're in the constitution too, but if you ask me, they should only be invoked in *extremely* dire situations, like civil war."

"And weren't those the conditions under which you assumed office?"

"No way! The Tupamaros and the other smaller guerrilla groups were already locked up. They escaped from Punta Carretas, yes, but they were gradually recaptured."

"I understand. In that sense, you offered a less rigid, more approachable profile as a candidate..."

"Yes, and remember, I came from a rural background. The Liberal Party had been losing ground in the interior of the country, votes that had gone to the Conservative Party, and we had become more urban, the liberals."

"So, your candidacy closed the proposal to regain votes in the countryside, did I understand correctly?"

"You understood perfectly, my daughter. And one fine day, I was giving speeches, and then I was wearing the presidential sash at the Suárez and Reyes residence. What can I say?"

"But the Security Emergency Measures *continued* under your government, didn't they?" Viktor interjected for the first time.

"Yes, they continued, yes," the old man rubbed his wrinkled forehead before continuing. "Look, the only ones who really know what it's like to be president are those who have *actually* been in the position. People think that you make tons of important decisions as president, but we hardly decide anything. It's the advisors and the ministers who draft the decrees, and the presidency's secretariat that sets up your meetings, schedules your visits and trips... It's a lot of work being president, but in terms of decisions that you *truly* take on your own initiative, it's little to none. Maintaining the Security Emergency Measures, I mean, during the start of my presidency, was a clear example of something I couldn't revoke. I could manage to do it, after much insistence, but they were lifted a few months before the coup, which... provided little consolation to the population, of course."

"What was the saddest part of living under a permanent state of siege, Mr. President, during the time of the Security Emergency Measures?" Geraldine asked.

"For the population: everything. Being subjected to 'routine' controls, freedom of association cut off, especially unions, closed, not being able to gather with more than four people on the streets..."

"That was, as I understand it, to cut protests down to zero, right?"

"Not to mention—" the old man agreed.

"And how did that affect you personally?"

"Censorship of the freedom of the press, if I'm being honest. I like talking to people, even *arguing* with them, with reasons, and I'm not afraid of any questions a journalist might ask me. But during my presidency, and in the campaign leading up to it... all the journalists asked condescending questions to the government. There was no opposition media. I remember one time a journalist asked me... I can't recall the media now... but it was definitely leftist. He asked why the Tupamaros had been locked up in the barracks for years without a sentence."

"And what did you answer that journalist?" Finally, the interviewer arrived at the point Geraldine wanted to make after so much detour.

"I didn't get the chance, can you believe it?" the former president shrugged. "As soon as he asked me that question, two security officers came and took him away, protesting. The next day, his newspaper, or weekly, was shut down."

"What a topic the Tupamaros are, right? But to be frank, that journalist had a point with his question."

"*Of course* he had. How could it be justified that *years* after being locked up, there was still no firm judicial sentence to keep them imprisoned? And not in ordinary prisons, but in cells in the barracks."

"And could that be done during the democratic part of your mandate?" Ielicov pressed. "I mean, could it *legally* be done?"

"Can you believe it, young man? It was enough for them to be considered enemies of the state, subversives, people who wanted to overthrow the government by force."

"Enemies of the state in wartime?" Geraldine made a gesture of disbelief. "I find it hard to see the Tupamaros as a serious threat to the institutions."

"Well... my thinking at the time was similar to yours, Goldman. I was less bothered by the armed threat, because there wasn't one, than by the long-term consequences of keeping them imprisoned *without* a judicial cause, which they *certainly* deserved."

"Causes like..." the interviewer let the witness complete the thought.

"Everything! Theft, looting, kidnapping, murder... And none of this could be judged, because the status of enemy in wartime came *before* that. The gold from the Maillot family, from the tobacco companies, they stole to finance their movement. A common and simple robbery, and they couldn't be judged for that. The murder of Aníbal Moyano, a month after I took office... what can I say? Aníbal and I were very good friends, and we had business together as well. I was a rural producer and he was a transporter.

One day those sons of bitches from the Tupamaros kidnapped him, asking for 200,000 dollars for his release. That's not chump change. Somehow, between his company and mine, we paid those bastards, and he turned up dead days later. How do you explain that, in the middle of democracy, a Tupamaro like Mojica was about to become president? A *murderer?*" Now the once-calm old man looked agitated.

"I suppose there were reprehensible actions from both sides, or else the law of expiration wouldn't exist, would it?" Ielicov raised an eyebrow.

"Wouldn't that be ironic? Ha. That Mojica would have been elected in the upcoming elections as president, that... that... *being*, and that the repeal of the Expiration Law would also have been approved, and in the ceremony where Valdez hands the presidential sash to Mojica, the police come and arrested him as a suspect to interrogate him about his involvement as a material author or as an ideologist in the kidnapping and subsequent murder of Aníbal Moyano in '72."

"But isn't it true that common crimes expire after 25 years in this country?" pointed out Viktor, who since they had taken the case had shown continuous interest, consulting his partner, a Uruguayan, about local laws and norms, and had an exceptional retention ability for data, especially regarding the case they were following. My calculations tell me that if your friend Aníbal Moyano was killed in '72, that crime expired in '97, 12 years ago."

"On top of that!" Borderragui was indignant. "It was just to provide an example, nothing more, one that hit close to home."

"I understand," the former heavyweight boxer wanted to sound empathetic before laying out the facts. "The crimes against humanity, on the other hand, *do not* expire, and if the repeal is approved, they *will* be investigated."

"Crimes against humanity. Ha. As if they ever existed in this country. Do me a favor!" the witness continued down the path of anger. "All this talk about torture, clandestine murders, disappearances, and death flights... Do you know what that is? Just pure lies from the left, orchestrated from the Soviet Union, trying to take control of Latin America! Of course: since they couldn't do it by force, now they do it through the ballot box. Look how leftist governments are blooming all over South America: Uruguay, Argentina, Bolivia, and don't even get me started on Venezuela! All with lies dictated from the USSR that here puppets like Valdez repeat like parrots."

"Excuse me for interrupting the special advisors' interrogation for a moment," Villa said with his cavernous voice, but evidently touched in his deepest fiber by the witness's words, putting forth all the self-control he could muster. "I was 14 years old, so I remember *vividly* when four big guys kicked in the door of my aunt's house, Ayelén Velázquez, with assault rifles and ski masks, and they took her away by force while one of the intruders subdued me and put a boot on my neck while pointing a war rifle at me. And that was in '74, Borderragui, when *you* were president. I never saw my aunt again. And do you know what my aunt was until '68, when your party's urgent security measures were imposed, which among other things banned the unions? She was a union representative, from the leather workers' union. I *never* saw my aunt again. Tell me, am I or am I *not* within my legitimate right to ask what happened to her?"

"And are you sure that your aunt wasn't kidnapped by the Tupamaros, since as we've been discussing, that was their modus operandi—kidnapping and killing?" the former president replied with arrogance.

"Chief Villa, please!" Geraldine pleaded for clemency for the hardline right-winger in front of them, anticipating that the situation might get out of hand.

"Yeah, take it easy, Geral," the giant said, rising to leave, panting. "I'm going to smoke a cigarette outside and see if that calms me down. Good luck when they come looking for you as a suspect in crimes against humanity, grandpa," he patted the witness on the shoulder with his massive hand. "I hope it's me who gets sent to look for you at your mansion in Carrasco," he said, and without another word, left the interrogation room, leaving Di Lorenzo as the only institutional representative of the police.

The air was thick enough to cut with scissors; the atmosphere in the room had become so tense, with the witness on one side of the table and three detectives on the other—two of whom were introduced as "special advisors," and the third was a real policeman.

"Well. Picking up where we left off..." the very pale and freckled brunette tried to regain control of the situation.

"Wait. Are you investigating me for crimes against humanity here?"

"But no, man!" Viktor was emphatic. "If you were called as a witness, you are just a witness, nothing more. Not a suspect. But you must understand that some comments one makes can sometimes hurt feelings, as was the case with Chief Villa," he smiled, only after a measured pause asking, "Are you worried about the repeal of the Expiration Law being approved, Mr. President? I mean, what plans do you have for November 1st of this year, in case the repeal is approved at the polls?"

"Me? I suppose it will be a Monday, because they always vote on Sundays," the wealthy man in his expensive suit downplayed. "Are you trying to ask me, in plain terms, if I'm scared of what justice might do to me? I have a clear conscience and clean hands, young man," he showed his wrinkled palms to the detective. "Do you know what this repeal of the Expiration Law is really about, Mojica, Valdez, and the whole shebang? It's a maneuver by the USSR to establish communist regimes throughout Latin America..."

"Excuse me for making a clarification, Mr. President," Ielicov raised a finger, "but when I left Russia in 2005, it was still called Russia. The USSR died in 1989, with Gorbachev, Perestroika, and Glasnost."

"Oh, really, kid? And what democratic guarantees have there been since that time of clean and democratic elections, of freedom of expression, of not being on a perpetual merry-go-round of candidates anointed by the single party? Huh?"

"Oh no, I think you misunderstood me. I wasn't trying to say that there is freedom of expression in Russia or that there is even a democratic opposition. I was just making a clarification about the name of the country," he shrugged.

"Oh, yes, they changed their business name, so to speak," the former Uruguayan president smiled maliciously.

"So to speak," the Russian detective conceded.

"Well, clarified this matter, do you know what this is? The final victory of Russia," he looked at Ielicov to see if he approved of the term, "over the United States. Look how well these leftists did it. First, they forged the naval club pact, which led to the Expiration Law of the State's Punitive Claim. Perfect up to that point. The Tupamaros are neither investigated nor condemned for their crimes, nor are civilians and military personnel for *alleged* crimes committed during the period of military re-institutionalization."

"Are you talking about the dictatorship?" Geraldine pretended to clarify.

"It's the same thing. Then 24 years pass since that gentlemen's pact at the naval club, meaning today, 2009, let's say the

Uruguayans approve the repeal of the Expiration Law in October, and the next day Mojica and all those *sons of bitches*—murderers, kidnappers, and *worse* that the Tupamaros are—no longer have amnesty in their favor, but... oh, what a coincidence! 25 years have *already* passed since their crimes, and on the other hand, the statesmen who do think about the country and its institutions come to ask us if we know where so-and-so the unionist is, or so-and-so the communist party leader, and we say: what do I know? Have you looked in Sweden, where it's *known* that those who disagreed with the regime emigrated, because they're within their rights, and opened supermarkets and are making a ton of money, and they're laughing at what people say about them here in Uruguay? Nothing at all is going to happen on November 1st of this year. But the left will have gained votes in this whole democratic process, they will have gained power in Latin America, guided like puppets from Moscow."

A prolonged silence followed the quasi-fascist speech of the former Uruguayan president.

"Wow," Geraldine finally broke the silence. "Let no one blame you for your imagination not being grounded to distort reality at will, Borderragui. But don't misunderstand me: I believe everyone should be able to express their feelings and political tendencies in whatever way they see fit."

"Same here, my daughter," the former president returned to his well-rehearsed role as a good-natured, conciliatory old man.

"I still want to revisit a key point for the investigation: tell us what your relationship was with Francisco Mojica, recently deceased," the Jewish member of the detective duo plunged the dagger into the heart.

"WHAT?! What relationship are you talking about with that filthy, vile, common criminal, forever unpunished by ordinary justice?!"

"My partner is very precise with the use of the Spanish language, as you've seen, Mr. President," Ielicov smiled. "She said 'relationship,' she didn't say 'friendship.' A relationship can be of enemies or just acquaintances."

"Oh, I see. You want to know if I got to know him? If I dealt with him during that time?"

"Precisely," Geraldine confirmed.

"Yes, I did deal with him, mostly during prison visits. By tradition, the Uruguayan president makes a tour of the prisons every year to see firsthand how the prisoners are doing. The prisoners elect delegates to speak on behalf of all and meet with the president, making their requests, the improvements in prison conditions they would like, and one sees what is within one's power to grant them, like buying mattresses or blankets."

"*All* the prisons?" the private investigator asked suspiciously.

"Yes, sir. All the prisons. In my time, it also included the cells in the barracks. It was... I wouldn't know how to describe it. To give you an equivalent of what is known or seen in World War II movies and documentaries... The prisons in our country were like war prisoners' camps, protected by the Geneva Convention, in theory. The places where they kept the Tupamaros were like Auschwitz."

Hearing the name of one of the worst concentration camps where the Nazis disposed of the "Jewish threat" struck hard with the detective. Viktor knew that for a moment that would throw her off balance, so he decided to take control of the interrogation.

"Can you describe what you saw during those visits?"

"They had no beds, no mattresses, no blankets, no warm clothing. They only had a shirt and thin pants, with no socks or shoes, and that was all year round, even in winter. They were in two-by-two cells, and the solitary ones were dark prisons, without light, without water, not even a toilet. They were barely fed, that was clear; you could see their ribs through the pajamas they wore, and they could hardly stand, they were so weak," he clicked his tongue. "Yes, it's true: they attacked democracy, they attempted an armed uprising to overthrow the institutions, but one thing is one thing, and another thing is another thing."

"And you couldn't do anything to change that, as president?"

"I already explained it to you, my son," Borderragui got angry again. "A president has little to no decision-making margin in a full democracy... much less in a government run by the Armed Forces. But then more and more radical decrees started coming for me to sign, increasingly restrictive of individual freedoms, and there came a point when I could no longer sign any more," he shrugged, his eyes filled with sadness at the memories, whether sincere or carefully rehearsed. "Censorship of authors, for example. Bermúdez, for instance. I *loved* what Emilio Bermúdez wrote. In fact, I love what that author continues to write. And he wasn't even a communist. But since his plots involved people challenging the system, whatever it was, that of the time... censored. 'War and Peace' is one of my all-time favorite works, but of course, since it was written by a Russian, it was banned, and so it went with everything..."

"We understand your predicament at that time," the Jewish detective recovered from the shock that hearing Auschwitz had caused her. "Would you say there was a breaking point for you, where you could no longer sign decrees coming from the military hierarchy, or was it more of a process?"

"There was one, yes. They sent me to sign the dismissal and preventive imprisonment of a high school teacher who had the bad idea of including the emergence of democracy in Greece in the curriculum. Can you imagine?"

"What audacity, right?" Ielicov was ironic.

"That's when I said: enough. I won't sign any more of this crap, and that's when they came to notify me at the presidential residence in Suárez and Reyes that I was no longer president, and that Demichelli was going to succeed me. I remember it as if it were today. It was around midnight. 'The Tiger' Falcone and his henchmen came, and they gave me an hour to pack my bags and leave the presidential house."

"Wait. We didn't have that name. Tell us a bit about 'The Tiger' Falcone."

"Yes, of course. Carlos 'The Tiger' Falcone was the director of the Punta Carretas prison when the Tupamaros escaped, but instead of punishing him for that escape, he somehow got promoted higher and higher in the police hierarchy under Paredes Arezzo's administration, and then mine, until he became the chief within the Political and Social Order Command Police (COPS). Can you believe that American-sounding name the military invented? COPS, like police in English. They were the anti-subversive body by excellence during my presidency and even more so during the re-institutionalization. They had no scruples. They had no legal limits. And they had a big budget."

"Interesting character," Goldman thought out loud. "If, within our investigation, it was relevant to find that person, where could we track him down?"

"*Outside* of Uruguay, that's for sure. He was one of the first to flee abroad, even before the return to democracy."

"Any hints about where he might have fled?"

"Some say he went to live in Brazil, but who can guarantee that?" the octogenarian shrugged. "He was very well connected, both within the de facto government and with the allied re-institutionalizations in the region."

"Interesting," Geraldine carefully considered her next question. "Let's go back to Mojica, as unpleasant as that person may be to you. Surely, as president, you had access to the complete file on one of the most prominent Tupamaro leaders of the time, right?"

"I did, yes. What do you need to know about him?"

"How he was. Not as a threat to democracy, which you made very clear you saw him as, but as a person, in his life, let's say."

"Mojica was just a run-of-the-mill lost hippie. A bohemian. One of those who doesn't like to work, who finds it hard to pick up a shovel, so to speak, who prefers to go drink wine and get high on a corner rather than pick up a book. He barely finished high school, but then he didn't finish his Agricultural Engineering degree because he was seduced by all those tales of making a new Cuba in Uruguay and all that; later he wanted to wage war on the country with two crapped-out AK-47 Kalashnikovs they sent him from the USSR. Ah, I see you're not correcting me this time, young man," he smiled at the Russian ex-boxer.

"For the time, it *was* the USSR; we can agree on that," the addressed replied.

"And what about women? How much detail did the file you were given on the prisoner contain, and I see you retain very well in your memory, despite the time that has passed?" Geraldine commented.

"He was a wastrel. A *promiscuous* one. To put it bluntly, and I apologize to the lady present..."

"Go ahead, Mr. President," Geraldine authorized, eager to hear the details and armored in her detective career against any vulgarities she might hear.

"Mojica slept with *everyone*. Every critter that walks ends up on the grill, as the saying goes. Or in other terms: any female creature that walked, he would take to bed."

"We understand the reference, of course, and we appreciate your time testifying in this case we are advising on. Viktor, do you have any other questions for the witness?"

"Nothing for now," his partner replied, and since it was clear the interrogation had ended, they all stood up to exchange formal handshakes.

"Just one more thing, if you don't mind, Mr. President," Geraldine pretended to remember when the octogenarian had already turned his back to leave.

"Tell me."

"Earlier today, I called you pretending to be an insurance investigator who wanted to ask you some questions about Francisco Mojica's death, regarding a policy he took out that benefited his widow, Laura Pulansky..."

"*You* were the one?!" Borderragui couldn't believe it.

"Research resources," Geraldine shrugged it off. "I also recall you were reluctant to meet with us, which is why we had to resort to the mechanisms of the Uruguayan legal system to speak with you as we have. In light of our conversation, do you think it was in an acceptable tone of respect and cooperation?"

"Well..." the former Uruguayan president didn't know how to react. "Yes, of course it was. It was quite civilized."

"I agree," she smiled tightly. "That's why it *grates* on me, and I would like you to tell me why, before hanging up, you said: 'It had to be a Jew.' Do you have something against the Jewish people?"

Geraldine relished every second as Juan María Borderragui, rural producer, former president, perhaps the main person responsible for handing power to the military during the past dictatorship that lasted from '73 to '85, struggled to formulate his next words.

"It was..." he began to stammer. "I have *nothing* against the Jewish community. In fact, I have Jewish friends. It was just that... it caught me at a bad moment, and you were talking about people I despise, Mojica and Pulansky. If I offended you with my words, I sincerely apologize."

"Apologies accepted, Mr. President. Shall we go, Vik?"

"Juan María Borderragui, thank you again for appearing before the summons. You are free to leave," Di Lorenzo informed the witness.

Moments later, the private detectives found a stoic Gervasio "El Toro" Villa smoking on the facade of the Central Headquarters that faced Yi Street.

"Toro, can you pass me a cigarette, please?" Geraldine asked.

"And one for me, if it's not too much trouble," Viktor requested.

"Don't you already earn enough to buy your own cigarettes?" the mustachioed giant feigned annoyance, but still handed each of them a cylindrical killer and offered them a light.

"It's not that, Toro," Viktor clarified. "We don't smoke. Not at all," he dismissed with a gesture.

"It's just that when we have such a fruitful and well-rounded interrogation like this, the spirit of John Hannibal Smith from The A-Team rises in us, and we'd love to smoke a cigar, but in the absence of one, a cigarette of any brand will suffice."

"Did you get what you wanted from him?" the chief of national police homicide wanted to know.

"And more!" the one with sparkling jet-black eyes smiled.

"President Valdez was right," Ielicov supported. "If you want to know what happened during the dictatorship and in the pre-dictatorial period, talk to the protagonists who were there, and Borderragui was one of the main ones."

"Then, did he order Mojica to be killed?" the mustachioed chief of homicide investigations wanted to confirm the essentials again.

"No, but he gave us some very interesting leads to follow," replied the former head of the National Police press office enigmatically. "And your performance up there deserves an Oscar, Toro," she patted the muscular back of her longtime acquaintance.

"Thank you. Thank you. Two thousand thanks. All for getting to the truth of the matter."

"By the way, how's your cousin, Ayelén Velázquez? She was a theater actress, right?" Geraldine made an effort to remember.

"No, listen. It seems a new gig has opened up for what she does. Now they call themselves stand-up comedians. They're actors who go and tell jokes in bars, and apparently, she's doing well, or at least that's what she tells me. They pay her between 6,000 and 8,000 pesos for each performance in a bar, weddings, birthdays, or bat mitzvahs, telling rehearsed jokes. Ayelén is thinking about moving out of her parents' house, that says it all."

"Congratulations to your cousin, Toro!" she patted the back of the sturdy descendant of indigenous peoples. "Now, Vik: it's either lunch or I can't guarantee my actions or mental coherence," the stylish detective kindly threatened.

"After you, partner," the ex-heavyweight from Vladivostok made a gallant gesture.

CHAPTER 11: SUSPECTS' STORM

Small town 'El Zanjón' main and only square, Province of Santiago del Estero, Argentine Republic, December 10, 1983.

News had been circulating for several months that the dictatorship was coming to an end in Argentina, that the military was going to hand over power to democratically elected authorities, which meant the end of the long ordeal for Magdalena Schebor and her only son, affectionately nicknamed Bicho (Bug), through towns with fewer than five thousand inhabitants, like El Zanjón, always using different names, always renting for a year when they actually planned to stay only a month, changing used cars periodically, using only cash, carrying a dozen IDs that they had made with a forger... always fleeing the repressive apparatus that was searching for them.

The bar "Macondo," one of only two bars in the town, was overflowing with people that morning in December, which promised to be scorching, although perhaps only a tenth of those present had actually gone there to consume something. The rest were expectant for the speech of Ricardo Alfonsín, the first president elected at the polls after seven years of military dictatorship.

If a fly had flown, its wings would have been audible during the pauses that President Alfonsín left in his emotional speech. Emotional, yes, but not radical, as was to be expected, with the armed forces observing the transition to democracy, ironically despite having been elected by the Unión Radical (Radical Union), which had defeated the candidate Ítalo Ludera from the Peronist Party.

There were two people in the audience, a woman in her forties, with coppery hair prematurely streaked with gray and very bright blue eyes, undoubtedly below one meter sixty in height, and a young boy who at fifteen had already surpassed one meter seventy in height. They saw something *more* than the general hope of the patrons at the bar "Macondo" for the return to democracy, respect for human rights, the end of persecutions for holding divergent ideas from the established order, the end of clandestine raids, the end of disappearances... What mother and son saw was that they could finally resume their lives... settle somewhere... return to high school (for the young man), reapply for a job (for the mother).

One phrase resonated from Alfonsín's emotional speech, and undoubtedly any Argentine of sound mind at the time etched it in their memory: "With democracy, you eat, you educate, and you heal." And indeed, there were wounds to heal in the South American nation! To begin with, if in Uruguay, with a population ten times smaller, there were 130 disappeared during the military dictatorship, in Argentina there were not 1,300, as the arithmetic would suggest, but *30,000* disappeared. The mothers and grandmothers of Plaza de Mayo began their silent protest with their headscarves, walking in circles around the obelisk in Plaza de Mayo in 1977, during the height of the military dictatorship. Even British musician and activist Sting dedicated a song to them: "They Dance Alone."

What were they demanding? That the dictatorship end and democratic institutions return? That the repressors were judged for crimes against humanity? Nothing as risky as that. What the mothers and grandmothers of the disappeared sought was an answer to a question so genuine and human that even the bloody apparatus of state repression in Argentina could not stop it:

"Where are they? Where have our sons and grandchildren been taken?"

But democracy returned on that scorching afternoon; Alfonsín's speech was broadcast nationwide. People celebrated and embraced, but just as there was a Law of Expiration of the State's Punitive Claim in Uruguay, there was an equivalent in Argentina, the Law of Due Obedience, in 1989, which blocked justice from investigating crimes against humanity and kept the repressors safe and sound, enjoying the billions of pesos stolen from Argentines until 2003, when it was repealed at the polls.

And then there was the wound of the Falklands War. To maintain their grip on power, the military leadership had attempted to reclaim the 'Islas Malvinas' by force in 1982 (if one took the Argentine name for the archipelago in the Atlantic Ocean, it was indeed closer to the Argentine coast than to the distant British Isles), or the Falkland Islands (if one aligned with the government of Margaret Thatcher, the Iron Lady).

As always, the bill for the "military conflict" was paid by the least fortunate. On the Argentine side, young men who were required to serve a year of military service, known in Argentina as "colimbas," were prematurely drafted to go reclaim the islands that the de facto government claimed were Argentine. On the British side, they hardly sent English, Welsh, Irish, or Scottish soldiers; instead, they filled the Royal Navy ships with Nepalese mercenaries, the Gurkhas, to ensure the enclave remained under the British crown.

649 Argentine soldiers died in the conflict, equipped with inferior weapons, aircraft, ships, and military training compared to their opponent, but the greatest scourge for the populace was the young men who returned mutilated, with promising lives cut short, lives to rebuild, their comrades' brains and blood splattered on their faces in nightmares.

All of that was *also* part of what the president promised to heal with the return to democracy. But it was by no means easy. The Carapintadas, a group of army officers led by Aldo Roca, rose up in arms in December 1987 and in January 1988, reaching a negotiated surrender to make it clear to Argentine democratic wills that they were *still* there and *still* armed.

But for Magdalena and her son, that was the end. They cried *rivers* like everyone else present at the bar "Macondo," but on their way to the tent they had set up in the nearby bushes by a creek, in the Volkswagen "Fusca" that was their escape vehicle at the moment, the driver said to her son:

"Now it's *really* over, Bicho. We're going back to our lives," the adult at the wheel decided. "You're going back to high school and graduating in whatever you want, and I'll look for a job, because in the end, the sale of the Punta Gorda house isn't going to last us a lifetime."

"We beat them, Mom. We beat the bastards."

"Yes, that remains to be seen, son. Alfonsín's speech didn't sound like a show of strength to me, what do you want me to say? I want to see us settle somewhere, let a year pass, and not have someone come to kick our door down."

"Positive spirit, Oldie."

"Old, the rags!"

"I love you, Mom."

"And I love you, Bicho. And I love you."

Bar Facal, 18 de Julio and Yi, Montevideo, Tuesday, July 21, 2009, 1:55 PM.

Geraldine and Viktor had ordered a Napolitan milanesa to share, a Diet Coke for her and a sparkling mineral water for him.

"So, I'm going to try a typical dish from Uruguayan bars, which basically consists of what would take a week of training to burn off. Did I get that right?" smiled the former heavyweight boxer at his partner.

"Look, if you fill up on a third and leave the other two thirds for me, with my morning routine and a bit of metabolism I thank Jehovah for, I won't gain weight," she replied.

"Fine. We'll see when it arrives. Who killed Mojica?"

"It could have been several people," they shifted from casual banter to the case as if nothing had changed. "The military back then couldn't do it themselves, as we saw at the hot springs, but they surely know of some fat arms in the barracks who think it's fine to lean left in Uruguay or who idolize their superiors who will end up in jail if the repeal of the law of expiration goes through."

"I'm going with Arturi. Even without having interviewed him yet, everyone has described him as a super-intelligent schemer, and someone who embarrassingly lost in the primaries, relegated to being a backup in the next term."

"Pulansky might have personal reasons we don't know about. We both got the feeling that there was something she was hiding, didn't we?" she confirmed.

"That something could very well be that he was a macho and a violent man at home, and Pulansky saw the double opportunity to get rid of her husband and pull the strings internally in her party to be the one the congress chooses for the presidency this coming Saturday. Did you notice how she emphasized that their list, from the Popular Movement, captured more than 40% of their party's votes?" he hypothesized.

"Could be. I'd rule out Borderragui, based on what we just talked about with him."

"Why?"

"He feels very secure about *not* being affected by the repeal of the law of expiration, as if he's shielded in some way."

"But he's the exact opposite, ideologically speaking, of what Mojica was and represented, and he hates him," Ielicov interjected in the storm of suspects.

"True, but you've seen how much he enjoyed debating, right? I see a character prepared for statements, for the press, even for criminal justice if he were to be judged: 'I did what I thought was best for my country. If there were crimes against humanity in my government, I wasn't informed. I defend freedom of thought, even if it opposes mine,' and all that."

"That facade fell when we took him down the right path," pointed out Ielicov. "Okay: Borderragui off the list. I'd rule out Píriz too. He reminds me of my grandfather Iván, my dad's dad. He fought in the Second World War, was in the Battle of Stalingrad. He saw the *worst of the worst*, and you always saw him with a distant look in his eyes, like he was gone from this world. It was hard to get him to connect one thought to the next, trapped in an infinite loop of slaughter and hell. I can't imagine him devising a plan to kill Mojica, hiring hitmen, thinking about an alibi..."

"Agreed, Vik. Thanks," interrupted Geraldine when the waitress brought their plates. It's worth mentioning that this conversation was taking place in Russian, a language that Ielicov spoke as a native, and Goldman as an advanced student, just in case the bar staff or customers caught any part of their conversation. It was unlikely anyone other than the taxi driver would speak Russian at Bar Facal. "The motivations of the secretary and the campaign advisor seem too little to see Mojica dead: he lost his job instantly, and she, despite the sexual harassment, seemed to see it as part of her well-paid job."

"What about De La Rúa?" Viktor began to cut the 25-centimeter diameter milanesa in half, covered with tomato sauce, ham, and mozzarella, carefully leaving a fried egg on top of each half, along with the Russian salad, made of boiled potatoes and carrots, peas with a generous amount of mayonnaise, fries, and lettuce and tomato salad—at least as much as could fit on the plates, because a good amount of fries and Russian salad remained on the platter, simply because it couldn't fit on the plate. "Enjoy your meal, my love," he threw her an air kiss.

"Enjoy, Vik. Everyone points to him as corrupt, claiming that during his presidency from 1991 to 1995 there were corruption scandals in his government, but none ever implicated him. That speaks to a puppet master power over his surroundings to see himself as the biggest beneficiary of returning to the presidency, and Mojica seemed to be his biggest obstacle to that."

"What time is our interview with him today?"

"At 7 PM, at his mansion in Carrasco. I'd rule out senators Larrán and Méndez too. They'd be capable of debating Mojica in parliament to the death, defending their ideas, but in that regard, they're just like Borderragui: very sure of themselves and their convictions. They'd campaign to ensure the repeal of the law of expiration doesn't win at the polls, but they wouldn't assassinate him."

"Mmm... yes. Agreed on that point. Larrán and Méndez are off the list."

"I don't think I'll manage with just a third, Geral," Viktor appreciated another bite. "This is amazing, although calling this Russian salad could certainly qualify as cultural appropriation."

"Could you believe this side dish is *indeed* based on a 19th-century Russian salad, the Olivier salad?"

"You're joking, right? No offense, but what does *this* have to do with Olivier salad? They took out the chicken, the shrimp, and the hard-boiled eggs."

"What sense would it make to keep those as side dishes, with all that protein?" she raised an eyebrow.

"True. In a country with three heads of cattle per person, beef is the queen, don't you think?"

"Exactly! I think we should visit Anahí after lunch."

"Your former deputy press chief when you were in charge?"

"Now she's in charge of the department. I keep up with her life and work through WhatsApp, and although Reno didn't mention her and didn't include her in the contact list, it's hard for me to believe that Minister Cortez has kept her out of what's *really* going on with the investigation into the near-magnicide."

"After the media bombshells in the case of the Decorator exploding one after another in Cortez's face, it would be at least reckless to leave his Press Chief out of the loop", Ielicov agreed.

"Given how organized and detail-oriented she is, she probably already has a contingency plan, and a contingency plan for the contingency plan, in case it leaks to the press that Mojica didn't die of a myocardial infarction, as was publicly stated."

"We'd do well to visit her, yes. You know? I feel a bit guilty about the calorie bomb I'm eating."

"Oh, Vik, but if you can't finish it, I'll take care of the leftovers, right? We're not going to waste food," she smiled at him.

"Feeling guilty and not being able to finish my half of this delight are two separate things," he said seriously. "While we're at it, I was thinking about when we could use our wildcard."

"I thought about her too, Vik," since they both knew who they referring to, "but we don't have anything concrete yet. We have too many suspects; we still don't know what the murder weapon was, whatever comes from the analysis sent to Buenos Aires... I'd wait until we have something more solid that she could give her expert opinion on."

"Maybe... We'll see," he partially agreed. "Let's finish in order: first with this Napolitan milanesa for two, then the interviews, in order, with Anahí, Bravetto, Arturi, and De La Rúa, and we'll talk about it again at dinner, what do you think?"

"I couldn't agree more," Geraldine said, spearing two fries, dipping them in the runny yolk of the fried egg, cutting a piece of the milanesa covered in sauce, ham, and mozzarella, and sending it to her mouth.

San José 1620, National Police Press Department Office, directly across the street to the Police Central Headquarters, Montevideo, Tuesday, July 21, 2009, 2:22 PM.

A new face, as Geraldine noticed, had been put in charge of the reception desk. He asked them seriously, while trying to be cordial, what brought them there.

"We came to talk for a moment with Anahí, your boss," Geraldine smiled. "You're new here, aren't you, Matías?" she read from the badge the officer wore on his lapel.

"Quite a bit, yes. I've been working here for 6 months. Who should I say is looking for her?"

"Let them through, Mati, the office isn't that big!" they heard a voice call from a distance.

"Right this way, please," the police press officer courteously showed the newcomers in.

When Viktor and Geraldine arrived at an office that, by its characteristics, seemed to be the main one, they found a rather petite woman dressed in a light blue suit, perfectly made up, painting her nails.

"Come in, come in," the owner of the office invited them, "I'm almost done." The newcomers patiently waited for the new Press Chief of the National Police to finish either her grooming or something she considered crucial for her role as the visible face of the National Police in any contingency. She admired the result of her nails and blew on them carefully. "Viko! Geral! What a pleasure to see you here," she stood up to affectionately hug them both, being careful not to smudge her still-drying polish on the navy blue suits of the detective duo. "So, without being detectives or anything like that, like you two, I can get an idea of why you've come to visit me," she winked. "Please, have a seat."

"I see my old office treats you well," the private detective smiled at her longtime friend and successor in the role. "Not much work at this hour?"

"For now," the head of the police press office shrugged. "Mojica died of a myocardial infarction; there's a forensic report confirming it. Toro and Di Lorenzo maintain secrecy around the case in the homicide department. They hired the best private investigators in the world," she indicated to her guests, "to ensure that everything stays behind the scenes... what could possibly go wrong?"

"Well... not exactly the best..." Ielicov blushed, dismissing the idea with a gesture.

"Were you or were you *not* the ones who finally caught the Decorator?" the thin thirty-something woman asked again.

"And no one knows better than *you* how *hard* that was," the Russian said seriously.

"Nothing out of this world, Viko," she dismissed with a gesture. "The .32 caliber bullet entered here"—she pointed above her right ear—"exited here"—now pointing near her left temple—"yes, it *did* stain the floor of my basement in Cerro with my brain and bits of skull, but the sound of the shot alerted the neighbors, who called 911, and a few months of coma and a *lot* of reconstructive surgery later, plus a metal plate where my skull used to be"—she tapped a surgical prosthesis that sounded like metal—"plus a year of physical therapy retraining my brain in the most basic motor functions, and here I am: alive and kicking, doing my best to make sure this Mojica case doesn't turn into anything even remotely resembling the Decorator case."

"How do you do it, my friend?" Geraldine asked, getting emotional to the point of tears. "I mean, moving on after what happened to you in that case... partly because of me."

"And *you*, Geral?" the owner of the office replied very seriously. "You lost your father, you lost your brother, you found out your brother killed your mother when you were kids... You saw your fiancé, whom you swore faithful love to, but who was actually a hardened serial traitor, fall out of a window from the tenth floor to the asphalt. You were accused of murder, and yet you found your way to reinvent yourself into the woman you are now, a professional private investigator. You tell me how *you* did it, and I'll tell you how *I* did it."

For a long and intense moment, the long-time professional collaborators, one the mentor of the other, but both sharing a common traumatic experience, looked into each other's eyes and nodded to say together:

"Resilience, my friend!"

The three laughed together at the coincidence of two women who had last seen each other four years ago, with Geraldine having shaped the role of Press Chief that previously didn't exist in the Uruguayan police, and Anahí as her successor in that position.

"How have you been all this time, Anahí?"

"Well, you see..."

"I see you've kept your love for classical Spanish, after all," the woman with the curly raven hair smiled at her former subordinate.

"Oh, yes, well. It kind of stuck with me, we could say," she shrugged. "The recovery was complex. I went to therapy for a long period, and I think I might hold the world record for MRIs for the plate I have where my left skull should be. But according to the doctors—or at least what I understood," she made a significant gesture to clarify that she didn't fully grasp everything she was recounting, "the bullet passed cleanly through my head, and my brain seems to have *reorganized* itself somehow to not affect my higher cognitive functions or my ability to communicate. So, when I was able to return to work, it turned out I had your position and your salary, Geral. What can I say? A great benefit legitimately earned or a bit of institutional guilt. You choose," the diminutive woman shrugged, especially compared to the 120 kilos of muscle of the heavyweight ex-boxer, or the former Press Chief turned private detective, who stood at a height of one meter seventy, with a slender build and a deep female voice. "But needless to say, I didn't refuse, and here I am, four years later, running the place, with the peace of mind that everything is prepared for *any* scenarios that might arise: whether Mojica was killed by former repressors, or by the opposition's De La Rúa, or by the Bolivian cocaine mafia that plans to use Uruguay as a landing and transit point for their product to more lucrative destinations like Europe, Australia, or Japan. You choose, my friend: give me the scenario and I have a media contingency plan for whatever might come."

"And what if Mojica was killed by ghosts from his past?" Viktor suddenly considered.

"Be more specific, my love," this time it was Geraldine who asked him.

"I mean, just throwing it out there..." the mentioned one replied. He was evidently lost in his own thoughts. "We're looking at the motives to want to see the candidate who was leading in the presidential race dead from a traditional standpoint, meaning: who would benefit the most if he died, who his political rivals were, his biggest detractors, what benefit someone could get from him being dead instead of alive, but... what if... this wasn't more than a crime of passion... I'm just tossing an inspiration onto the table... what if this had to do with something or someone affected by Mojica's past actions?"

"Like the wife or a child of one of the victims of the Tupamaros, you mean?" his partner wanted to follow his reasoning.

"Exactly! Or that, in his dissolute life... what was that saying Borderragui used?"

"Every critter that walks ends up on the grill."

"That one, yes! If, as former president Borderragui recounted, he was that disorganized and varied in his romantic life, and had left someone pregnant... He was also a highly effective manipulator. Remember, Pulansky also remembered him as a very attractive young man whom all the women wanted to be with."

"Later, at that time, he wouldn't have recognized himself as the father of the child, and this would have brought the mother shame and social exclusion. Maybe she would have had to give the child up for adoption and go abroad. So, was that your line of reasoning?"

"Something like that, yes. Sometimes, when there's a public figure involved, we forget they're also human beings who, bluntly speaking, eat, poop, have ovarian or head pain... and they can also be murdered for reasons just like everyone else."

"How graphic, Viko!" Anahí smiled.

"But you have a point there, Vik," Goldman approved. "Perhaps in the interviews that remain, we should probe into Mojica's personal life before the dictatorship."

CHAPTER 12: THE INCARNATE DEVIL

Güemes Sanatorium, Güemes Street 1200, Buenos Aires, Federal Capital, April 12, 1991, 4:20 PM.

The rhythmic beep of the electrodes connected to his mother's chest, prematurely aged, transmitted to the heart monitor, was what kept him not only awake but focused on the medical texts he had to study for the upcoming exam, having previously evaded the Argentine dictatorship, and now a third-year medical student, while his mother, Magdalena Schebor, was kept alive by a combination of nutrients injected into the IV bag that was changed periodically. Nutrients and morphine, in increasingly higher doses to alleviate the pain.

The young adult born in Uruguay had suspended his studies for three years, or at 22 he could have been in his final year of the basic medical program at the University of Buenos Aires. Three years during which they had been fleeing from the death squads of the military repression, without a clue as to *why* they were being hunted. If his mother managed to wake up, that would be the first question he would ask: "Mom, did you know at that moment *why* they were after us?"

Magdalena had *never* found happiness since the return of the dictatorship. She tried not to be a bitter woman but focused on being a functional and practical adult for her son. Did she have to work and endure a terrible boss to put food on the table? That was done. Did she need to pressure her son appropriately to complete his suspended studies, which left him three years behind his high school classmates? She guided him along the right path. Did she have to walk a lot and look for deals on anything, from meat to potatoes or clothing? What was the problem?

But the woman went through her forties smiling only *very* occasionally, and she was *never* heard laughing. Many times, her son found her with a distant gaze, her face clearly troubled, undoubtedly reliving traumatic events from the past, and the young man who was becoming an adult suspected it had something to do with him, or more specifically, with who his father was.

Magdalena was always evasive about it, maintaining her story that his father had been a Chilean backpacker passing through Uruguay and that, broadly speaking, he was a child of the golden era of hippies in the '60s and '70s. In any case, the constant anguish had degenerated into cancer because the body *suffers* from the deep pains of the soul, needless to say... the unbearable burdens one cannot or does not want to share with anyone else.

That morning, the treating oncologist had again offered the medical student to increase his mother's morphine dose "a little more," known in the jargon of countries where euthanasia is not legal as "taking her to the other side," or in medical terms, giving a narcotic trip to a terminal patient with advanced metastasis who was not responding favorably to chemotherapy or radiation therapy. Accelerating an inevitable process from a medical standpoint.

That morning, the young man reminded the oncologist once more that euthanasia was only legal in a few countries in the world, among which Argentina was *not* included, and asked for the exact opposite: to withdraw the morphine. Eventually, the absence of the narcotic derived from the opium poppy in the patient's bloodstream would wake her up due to the pain that the morphine had also anesthetized, and that moment came around 6 PM.

"Bug" —the woman, nearing fifty, weak from chemotherapy, gaunt, and as they say colloquially in the Río de la Plata: at her last breath, weakly recognized.

"Mom" —he put down his medical text and took both of his mother's hands in his.

"Is it morning or afternoon?"

"Afternoon, 'Ma. It's April 12 today."

"Did they have me doped for so long? I must be about to kick the bucket, I suppose," —the pragmatic woman attempted a smile despite the pains slowly coming over her as the opiate left her bloodstream.

"Don't say that, Mom. As long as there's life, there's hope."

"Bug" —she was very serious—. "What do the doctors say?"

The medical student swallowed hard. He knew he couldn't hide anything from his mother, nor paint her a rosy picture. It wouldn't have been fair to the patient either.

"That you have weeks... maybe just days left to live. But you have to *fight*, Mom. You have to get out of here."

"No, Bug. One knows when their time has come, and I've achieved everything I aspired to in my life, which was to see you become the adult you are now."

"And don't you want to meet your grandchildren?"

"What? Have you already left someone pregnant?"

"No... I mean... as a hypothesis."

"Tell my story to your children, if you ever have them, and tell it well," —she warned him.

"Mom. Who was my father really?" —the young man asked bluntly.

"Maybe it's time I tell you, right?" —she took an understandable pause to gather her courage before what she was about to say—. "He wasn't a Chilean backpacker passing through. If I made up that story, like parents do with the tooth fairy or Santa

Claus, it was so you wouldn't grow up to be a resentful young man, a person who hates..."

"Was he really that bad?"

"He was the *devil incarnate*, Bug, but I didn't find out until it was too late."

"Until I was born, you mean," —sarcastically replied the son of the cancer patient in stage 4.

"No, Bug, *never* think that about yourself. You were a wanted child, and a loved child. Look, here's how it was. I met your father in college. We fell in love, we moved in together, and that's when you were born. The thing is, it was a difficult time. You've probably read something about the pre-dictatorial period and the dictatorship in Uruguay."

"Yeah, of course."

"And of the Tupamaros Movement."

"Also that. Little by little, things are starting to come to light."

"Well. Your father became a Tupamaro, and I... I didn't really *approve* those things, but he told me he didn't participate in the more violent crimes, in the kidnappings and murders, and I believed him... at the time. Then he was imprisoned in Punta Carretas prison. By that point, I was already pregnant with you, and later he escaped with the rest of the Tupamaros, an escape that became famous."

"Yes, I read about that too, of course."

"The thing is, your father and I saw each other very rarely, you can imagine, clandestinely, but luckily, they never connected his name with mine, or they would have come to interrogate me too. And your father began to tell me that there was a traitor among the Tupamaros, someone who collaborated with the repression, who pointed out his comrades during raids, and he also told me about intelligence information that was starting to reach their guerrilla movement, about the tortures in the barracks, the kidnappings and disappearances, the executions and clandestine burials in Battalion 14 of parachutists over in Toledo... About the collaboration between the head of the repression, the former director of Punta Carretas prison in Uruguay, and the director of the SIDE here in Argentina... In Uruguay, we were *already* under dictatorship, but here the military were gradually setting things up. He even told me that the director on the Uruguayan side, Carlos... something, I think his name was, was already sending death flights for those they wanted to disappear in Uruguay, like the case of Vasco Olavarría, the first Tupamaro disappeared by the military, so they could dispose of the bodies here in Argentina... Oh, how it hurts" —the terminal patient complained as the calming effects of the morphine continued to fade.

"And didn't you suspect how all that information was getting to my dad?" —his son asked suspiciously.

"Love makes you foolish, Bug, what can I say? Besides, everything in me refused to suspect that the traitor among the Tupamaros was him. Anyway. Until one day I saw him. I saw him having coffee with that son of a bitch, Carlos... —she struggled to remember—, well, with him, the head of Uruguayan repression, the one most responsible for the disappearances, the tortures, the executions... I wanted to deny reality, and reality hit me hard in the face. It was in the Michigan bar. I remember it as if it was today. The weather was nice, and I took you out for a walk in your stroller, and suddenly I see from the sidewalk that son of a bitch, Carlos something, whom I recognized from the pictures in the newspapers and on television, sitting there with your father, having coffee. I'm sure he didn't see me, your father, I mean, but from that day on, I told him it was over between us. I made up a story. He didn't believe me much, I think, but I was firm and inflexible in my decision. I told him I didn't want him to *ever* see you again. That he should forget about you, Bug."

"I can imagine" —the young man, now 22, couldn't believe what he was hearing, something his mother had kept to herself all her life—. "Did he accept it?"

"What do you think?! He used to come to the house sometimes, always on weekends, and the scene repeated itself *every* time. I'd ask you to go to your room, I'd open the door because I knew he wouldn't take no for an answer, that if I didn't, he'd call his military friends, we'd have a big argument, he always came drunk... *always*. And then he'd leave. Sometimes he'd get violent, sometimes he'd hit me... sometimes he'd rape me too, Bug."

"I can't believe that son of a bitch!" —the young man exclaimed, tears of anger and impotence filling his eyes.

"He had the impunity of the collaborators of the military regime, what do you want me to say? Until one day during one of his visits, you didn't listen to me; that is, you didn't stay in your room, and you grabbed my revolver and pointed it at him, demanding that he leaved and that leaved me alone for good."

"Yes, I remember that day. I was about 10 years old, right?"

"Yes. 10 years old and pointing a revolver. *That* was my breaking point. I couldn't tolerate that environment and that situation for you."

"And the next day, we packed our bags, you put the house up for sale, and we came to Argentina."

"I *knew* he only came on weekends, so we left on a Monday..." —she left the sentence unfinished. Her eyes rolled back.

"Mom. Mom! MOM!" —the third-year medical student tried to make her react, but Magdalena Schebor didn't respond. He ran to the door and shouted at the top of his lungs—. "A DOCTOR!! A DOCTOR!!!"

Colonia 1771, Central Headquarters of the Progressive Front, Montevideo, Tuesday, July 21, 2009, 2:22 PM.

A secretary in her fifties announced and ushered the detectives into the office of the leader of the political party as soon as they arrived. Professor Bravetto was a tall, elderly man in his eighties with a friendly demeanor who maintained his fitness and looked elegant yet practical in a simple suit. After the formal introductions and the usual offering of tea, coffee, or water (the detectives *clearly* preferred water: they had been talking to one person or another all morning), they got down to business... very much in the Uruguayan style, with some preamble first.

"So, how long have you been involved with the Progressive Front?" —Geraldine asked.

"From moment *zero*," —he emphasized, making the number with his hand. You could see the sparkle in his eyes from the pride it brought him—. "On February 5, 1971, our party was founded, and I was there among the founders. Yes, I know what you're going to say, that I don't look *that* old," —he joked, waving his hand dismissively, "but the truth is I've been involved since the start, and I was one of the seven deputies we managed to get elected in the late '71 elections."

"Look at that," —the former boxer acknowledged.

"Yes, that's how it was. I sat between Larrán and baby Sendic; I remember. Wow. Those two were *fierce* in parliamentary debates. Next to them, *I* was a baby."

"Excuse me. Are you referring to the current Senator Jorge Larrán of the Conservative Party?" —the detective asked, surprised.

"Yes, of course! We've always been very close friends with Jorge. We *still* are, even though he switched to the Conservative Party in the '89 elections."

"Got it."

"Look, detectives. Here in Uruguay, politics are like this: we can have different ideas; in fact, that's what *enriches* democracy. But at the end of the day, we're just people defending our ideas and the ideas of those who voted for us, so why hold grudges?"

"And Larrán lost in the primaries of his party against De La Rúa, as far as I understand, right?" —Geraldine asked—. "We've been based in Argentina for four years now, but since I'm Uruguayan, I always try to keep up with what's happening in my country."

"He lost, yes. And it was a rough primary for him, to be honest," —he clicked his tongue—. "But I talked to him about it. I said, 'Buddy, you're a strange one in the Conservative Party.'"

"Because he represents the more left-leaning wing?" —the former head of the Uruguayan national police press office wanted to confirm.

"Exactly! And the Conservative Party, in the Uruguayan political landscape, is as far to the right as we get. Even the Liberal Party is more centrist than they are."

"And in its early days, in '71, did you have dealings with Francisco 'Pancho' Mojica?" —the Russian cut to the chase.

"No, I never dealt with Mojica back then. He was locked up with the other Tupamaros in Punta Carretas prison, and then there was that famous escape from that prison, and they returned to clandestinity. He didn't formally join politics and the Progressive Front until the return to democracy in '85."

"And in your opinion, how was Mojica as a politician?" —Goldman asked.

"As a politician?" —the octogenarian scratched his forehead—. "He was very tough. He was in line with baby Sendic, defending the interests of the most humble, of the rural people... He was very approachable, you could talk to him about all kinds of topics; in fact, he was never arrogant or anything with me, even as he gained more weight within the party each year. But with the government, when we were in opposition, he didn't let them get away with anything. He was *always* ready to pounce, whether the Conservatives or the Liberals were in power."

"And then, in the term that's now ending, he was Minister of Livestock, Agriculture, and Fisheries, am I correct?" —the Uruguayan woman asked again.

"Yes, he was... a bit of a political strategy within the party. We had won the first presidential election with Tabaré, and we placed key senators in ministries who were positioned as possible successors to Valdez in the elections coming up now in October. Mojica was the strongest candidate in that regard."

"And the *second* strongest?" —the Russian asked suspiciously, narrowing his eyes.

"Arturi, of course," —Bravetto assured—. "But don't think that just because he was Minister of Economy in this government and ran in the primaries, the party is going to promote him as the new presidential candidate."

"But he was running as Vice, right?"

"Yes, but the presidential figure and the vice president are *not* the same. The vice president only presides over the chambers, nothing more," —the elderly man waved dismissively—. "The president leads the entire executive, especially in a country like Uruguay, which is highly presidentialist. If you ask me," —he made a gesture to excuse himself, warning that what he was about to say was purely personal opinion—, "Senator Pulansky has *much stronger* chances of becoming the presidential candidate."

"Yes, but then... she's a woman, right?" —the Uruguayan in the duo raised an eyebrow—. "Is Uruguay *ready* to have its first female president in history?"

"What do I know?" —the president of the Progressive Front shrugged—. "We leave those calculations to the political consulting firm we've been hiring for years. And we pay them well," —he opened his eyes wide—. "So they better advise us properly. The margins with the Conservative Party in the polls aren't *that* comfortable to win by absolute majority in the first round, and any variation we make now in the presidential formula might not sit well with the electorate, and we lose, or it might appeal to the voters, and we win."

"What firm advises you on electoral matters?" —Viktor asked.

"Crispiani. Do you want the contact?" —he offered.

"I don't think it's necessary at the moment," —the one who had asked shook his head—. "It was just to know. If we need it, we'll consult Mr. Reno later."

"Ha. Reno. What a character. But the CSA supported us and continues to support us strongly in this campaign, so if they ask us to collaborate with you, *of course* we will," —he smiled.

"And aside from Arturi and Pulansky, who else do you think would be on the list of possible presidential candidates?" —the pale-skinned woman with freckles asked.

"Well... it could be any of the senators from the Popular Movement. They carry over 40% of the electoral will of our party. It could be Huidó, Zabala..."

"We'd be interested in speaking with Senator Huidó, if possible," —Viktor thought aloud—. "And with Zabala too. We understand both were with Mojica in the National Liberation Movement Tupamaros. Am I correct?"

"Yes, of course. Let me check the schedule and I'll note down their cell numbers for you," —he proceeded to do so on his personal card—. "But if you want to take advantage, the entire political leadership of the party is meeting here at 3:30 PM, in the meeting room. We need to start discussing what formula is going to be proposed this Saturday in the assembly."

"Wonderful idea!" —the now less orthodox Jewish woman smiled, recalling her former engagement to the also Jewish Captain Julián Sterenstein before she met Viktor and before the tragic events of the Decorator in 2005 that claimed so many lives, including that of the captain and chief of the homicide brigade of the National Police—. "Do you think you could resolve it today?"

"No way!" —Bravetto laughed heartily—. "This will take long, daily meetings, I can assure you. There's a *lot* to discuss because in politics, one always has to think in two scenarios: either you win the presidency or you lose. If you lose, that's the simpler scenario: the elected senators take their seats in the Senate, the deputies the same, and we're opposition for the next five years. Now... if you win..." —he clicked his tongue—. "That's when things change, because many elected senators will resign their seats to be appointed as Ministers, and since Ministers have a lot of public exposure, they will be the ones heading the options to run in the party primaries for the next election, as happened this period that is ending with Mojica, who was Minister of Livestock, Agriculture, and Fisheries, and Arturi, who was Minister of Economy. And also, we have to re-check if the eventual substitutes for those senators, who would become the titular ones, will represent our party's interests well in Parliament... But then there's the free will of the assembly members," —the former parliamentarian opened his eyes wide and raised his eyebrows.

"How so?" —Viktor asked—. "I know my accent doesn't give it away, but I'm Russian, and back home things work differently, let's say."

"Oh, you're Russian? Yes, of course. Ielicov. Look, I'm also asking what I need to know," —the literature professor smiled—. "The ones who are meeting here today, at the party headquarters, are the leaders of each sector of the Progressive Front. The goal of these meeting*s*," —he emphasized the "*s*"— "is to reach a consensus on what formula we'll propose at the party's general assembly this Saturday at the Platense Patín Club. But then the assembly members, who number 494, may or *may not* agree with what we decide here, and if we leave these meetings without a consensus, but with two presidential formulas, then hold on tight because we'll be arguing for *hours* at the assembly."

"And all this for the death of a single person," —the private detective reflected aloud.

"And all this for the death of a single person," —Bravetto repeated, reflecting himself—. "Let's see: Mojica was a vote-gathering machine. With him, we were *sure* to win this election. Besides being a comrade, with his death, we also lost a leadership position."

"I understand," —Viktor simply said—. "Do you remember what the results were in the last primaries for your party?"

"Yes, of course: Mojica won with 47% of the votes, and Arturi came in second with 43%."

"I don't understand," —the Russian stroked his chin, both he and his partner had an almost photographic memory for what witnesses and interrogated individuals stated during a case—. "Why did Vilariño, Mojica's secretary, tell us that Mojica *crushed* Arturi in the primaries? Those were her words, right, Geral?" —he confirmed with his partner—. "The margins seem a bit tight: 47 to 43."

"Well, maybe a bit of bias for her boss, what do I know? Perhaps, and only perhaps (you can check with her, of course), she was referring to how Mojica started very far behind in the pollsters' surveys. The first measurement before the primaries gave 52% to Arturi and 43% to Mojica."

"And in one or two months, Mojica made an epic comeback, as they say in football, right?" —the only Uruguayan in the detective duo wanted to confirm.

"More or less," —the president of the leftist coalition agreed.

CHAPTER 13: POISON IN THE COFFEE

Café del Prado, Madrid, March 19, 1995, 9:25 AM. One of the many customers at that hour in the emblematic café in Madrid, a man in his fifties born in Uruguay, was watching people pass by while sitting at a table, sipping his coffee with croissants, when one of the waiters sat down at his table without asking for permission.

"Nice day, isn't it?" —the waiter asked, stretching.

"Yes, of course. Go ahead and sit down," —the ex-Tupamaro said ironically—. "It's a free country, Spain, after all, right?"

"Yes, free from Francoism and dictatorships. A bit like Uruguay, don't you think, Amadeo?" —the one serving at Café del Prado fixed his deep, angry gaze into the light eyes of the man in his fifties.

"Who are you?" —the man on guard, who everyone in Uruguay pointed to as the one who had betrayed the National Liberation Movement—Tupamaros and had pointed out his comrades to the authorities so they could be captured, tortured, killed, and disappeared— asked.

"I'm the one who poisoned your coffee and who's here to ask you some questions in exchange for the antidote," —he patted his shirt pocket—. "You might not start feeling the symptoms for a couple of hours, but when they find out what I poisoned you with at the hospital, it'll already be too late because the m-mm-mmm-mm—" —he omitted the name with a triumphant smile—, "it's undetectable. Basically, if one doesn't know what they're looking for, as a doctor, they won't know how to counteract it in time. And they say the agony before death is ter-ri-ble."

"What do you want? I don't have any money. I only have what I'm wearing and a little more."

"The Tupamaros didn't practice listening to others back in Uruguay in the 60s and 70s, did they? I told you I came to ask you some questions in exchange for your life. Look at what it boils down to: getting through to midnight alive or not," —he pulled out a test tube with a stopper from his shirt pocket. The liquid looked yellow and viscous—. "Just 10 milliliters of happiness, and you'll make it to midnight alive. You refuse to tell me the truth, or I detect that you're lying, and goodbye Amadeo Píriz. A pleasure (or displeasure) having had you in this world, depending on the side. See you in the next life, if there is one."

"If you came to ask me something, then *ask*. What the hell!" —the veteran snapped.

"But no tricks, okay? Because I can get nervous too and drop the antidote," —suddenly he dropped the test tube, causing complete shock and terror in the ex-Tupamaro, only to catch it 20 centimeters lower with his other hand—. "No tricks, Píriz," —he waited for the other to nod, still trying not to have a heart attack at seeing how the antidote that separated his life from his death almost shattered on the floor—. "Tell me: how did you know Magdalena Schebor?"

"Who?" —the man in his fifties was surprised.

The young, impudent waiter and blackmailer fixed his gaze on him for a moment, trying to gauge whether the Uruguayan born in '43 was trying to deceive him. Píriz genuinely seemed *not* to know who Magdalena Schebor was, but his son, who had lost her four years earlier and since then had dedicated his life *obsessively* to finding the one responsible—his father—and to learning undetectable ways to kill (and in medicine too, a bit of both went hand in hand, as one can easily imagine), decided to keep pressing.

"Magdalena Schebor. Copper, straight hair, very sparkling green eyes, lived in Punta Gorda."

"I think you have the wrong person, son," —by habit, the ex-Tupamaro was about to take another sip of his coffee, but then remembered that the one in front of him had poisoned it—. "Did you poison the croissant too?"

"No. Not the croissant. You can eat that safely," —the waiter dismissed with a gesture and paused for a moment, lost in thought watching the people passing by outside—. "But if it wasn't you, then who was it?"

"Who did what, kid?"

"She confessed to me on her deathbed that the one who betrayed the Tupamaros, the one who sold them out to the military, was the... the one responsible for her death."

"Aaaahhhh," —Píriz stretched. "So the one you're looking for is the supposed 'traitor'—" —he made air quotes, being the older of the two seated at the café table— "*not* me."

"Everyone points to you, Píriz, as the traitor," —the twenty-something pressed again.

"'Everyone' is a lot of people, and forgive me for still treating you as 'you', but you're too young for me to treat you otherwise," —he took another bite of his croissant—. "*Mojica and Huidó* started that rumor that I was the traitor within the Tupamaro ranks, and when I got out of jail after 12 years, I could no longer walk the streets of my country. People insulted me when they saw me, spat at me, wouldn't serve me in shops... they even beat me," —the exiled man's eyes misted over—. "I had to get the hell out of there, what could I do?"

"But if it wasn't you, why did they point to you as the traitor?" —the pretended waiter wanted to be open-minded.

"Oh, you see! That's a good point. Do you like detective novels, kid?" —he took another bite of the croissant, knowing he wouldn't have anything to wash it down with since the coffee was poisoned.

"Not much. I prefer treatises on poisons and cures," —the young man displayed a rather morbid sense of humor.

"Well, tell me out of pure common sense, then: what's the *second* thing someone who has committed a horrible crime wants after not getting caught for what they've done? Or, to put it another way: what's the oldest, sneakiest tactic in the world to evade a crime?"

"Blame someone else," —the graduate from the University of Buenos Aires School of Medicine suddenly understood.

"You see? If there ever was a traitor among the Tupamaros... it was those two *bastards* who pointed to me as the traitor."

"What do you mean 'if there ever was'? I don't understand."

"Let me see how I can put this in terms a guy your age can understand." —he thought for a moment. Then he remembered that as part of the service, there was also a small glass of water. He took a sip to help down the solid part of his breakfast—. "You're young now, and you think you can take the world by storm, that you can poison an old bastard like me and get away with it, not getting caught and all that. Well, we, the Tupamaros, at your age, *also* thought we could take the world by storm and that with two crappy assault rifles, a few shotguns, and some little pistols, we could wage war against a country and win. And you know what? You *can't* win against a country with so few weapons and so few people. We bet, in our young and stupid heads—" —he tapped his temple with his index finger— "that the entire country would rise up in arms with us, and you know what the country did? First, they had no weapons because Uruguay *isn't* the United States, with the Second Amendment and everything, where one in every two Americans has a shotgun at home. And also, Uruguayans don't-want-problems—" —he separated the words. "They don't-want-problems, *period*! Uruguayans want to live their lives peacefully, start families, go to the stadium on Sundays, and have barbecues with friends. So, we were a hundred and some fanatical idiots against a country of 3.5 million people, trying to make a leftist revolution. It was **obvious** we were going to lose like we did. That's why I tell you: if you ask me—" —he pointed to his chest with his hand— "there was *never* a traitor, but if there was, you'll have to ask Mojica or Huidó if it wasn't one of them... or *both*."

"I think I will have to ask them," —the twenty-something, born in Uruguay and emigrated to Argentina with his mother at the early age of 10, thought seriously.

"Still, I'll give you some advice, kid: you won't get the truth out of those two by poisoning their coffee. Those two would prefer to be martyrs for the cause than grow old and end up senile, shitting and pissing in geriatric diapers."

"And why is that?"

"Do you know what Mick Jagger is supposed to have said once, live fast, die young, and you'll have a good-looking corpse? Look at Mick Jagger from the Rolling Stones, at 50 years old. Seems like that formula of living fast and dying young didn't work out too well for him. I'm sure he's eating healthy now and putting in an hour on the treadmill every day. Well, that's how those two were. They were *total idols* of the Tupamaro movement. They had the girls they wanted, they were total *rockstars*. And what happened when democracy returned? People carried them on their shoulders like *war heroes* because, poor things, what they had to suffer in military dungeons—" —the fifty-something's tone turned mocking— "having to endure 12 years of systematic torture in a cistern. Come on! Less wolves, Little Red Riding Hood!" —he dismissed with a gesture—. "Pure *bullshit*, if you ask me. Look, the thing was this: the army, whether right or wrong, had the mission to save the country from armed communist revolution, that is, us—" —the ex-Tupamaro raised his hand—. "And yes, I won't deny that if you insisted on singing the praises of Cuba, the glory of Che Guevara, that we were going to have another socialist revolution here in Uruguay, they'd give you a beating, I won't deny that. Did some get killed for not being able to 'reform' them, to put it one way? That's *also* true. I lost *many* friends who wouldn't back down and were still standing up to the military. But you know what? If you backed down and admitted you had lost, they left you in peace, and you were just another political prisoner. And Mojica and Huidó were like that. Sometimes you'd see them chatting away with the army in the battalion courtyard, or smoking a cigarette together. I did too, mind you. When I admitted I was a fool and that I had lost, I remember telling them: you know what? You won, brother. I lost. Now, how does this continue? Tell me, kid, that traitor among our ranks you said killed your mother?"

"I *never* said Magdalena Schebor was my mother."

"Come on, man, we're few and we know each other," —Píriz winked, finishing off the remains of his croissant.

"Well... it was indirectly, but he was responsible for her dying of cancer before turning 50."

"I'm really sorry, kid. Listen: I'll give you free advice, okay? If you want to know who the traitor among the Tupamaros was, don't ask Mojica or Huidó. Ask the repressors."

"Maybe I will," —the poisoner considered—. "Do you have a name you could give me?"

"I'd start with Carlos Falcone," —the veteran Uruguayan took a sip of water—. "He was the director of Punta Carretas Prison when we 'escaped' in '71, and because of such a colossal security error, he was appointed head of the Political Order Commission, COP, like police in English, the strongest repressive body of the national police, but it's known they didn't work alone. They collaborated with the Argentine SIDE to make people disappear who still insisted that the leftist revolution would be carried out in Uruguay. Now, you said I have until tonight for you to give me the antidote. Am I bothering you too much if I ask for it now? Or was that just an unfounded threat to make me tell you what I knew?"

"No. No-no. The poison was real. Take the antidote. You earned it, Píriz." —he passed the test tube with a cork stopper, which the fifty-something drank in one gulp—. "Well, I think it's time to resign from the job I got with false documentation and go back to South America to locate Falcone. Oh, by the way. What I put in your coffee is called ethylene glycol, and it causes metabolic acidosis after a few hours. It starts with abdominal pain, and by tonight, you'd be in a coma. The antidote might work and save you, but if I were you, I'd consult a doctor."

Colonia 1771, headquarters of the Progressive Front, Montevideo, Tuesday, July 21, 2009, 3:05 PM.

The private detectives, one Russian and the other Uruguayan, waited sitting next to the receptionist, who had been instructed to discreetly signal when Senator Eleuterio Hernando Huidó, nicknamed "Ñato" among the progressive ranks, entered the party's house while they sipped coffee from a vending machine. Finally, the fifty-something party official gestured discreetly as their next interviewee ascended the marble stairs.

"Senator Huidó, good afternoon," —Geraldine approached him, her hand extended to greet the genial-looking sixty-something with a prominent abdomen, light gray suit, and a balding head that threatened to be completely bald soon—. "Geraldine Goldman. It's a pleasure."

"Viktor Ielicov," —the boxer reciprocated—. "We're the investigators hired by the CSA Group to look into the circumstances of Mojica's death."

"Oh, how nerve-wracking. I thought you were journalists sneaking in," —he pointed to the sidewalk where vehicles from all TV channels and print media were gathered, waiting for any statements from party leaders who wanted to remain in power despite the unexpected death of their presidential candidate—. "Gabriela Vilariño told me you might contact me for some questions. I recognize *you* from somewhere," —the former Tupamaro indicated towards the tall, slender detective.

"Maybe from the police press office. You might have seen me on TV, but I've been a detective for several years now."

"Ah, yes, of course!" —the legislator remembered—. "From that whole episode with the Decorator and all that. How could I forget? What a moment that was for our government, just starting the first term in the history of our party!" —he smiled and widened his eyes.

"Yes, it was a complicated time," —Goldman only mentioned, thinking internally: *dozens* of people died at the hands of the Decorator and his sect, including my father and brother, and the only thing you remember is that your party's government was momentarily humiliated? Ha. Politicians.

"Would you like to step into an office to talk more quietly?" —he pointed to one at the side of the main hall of the party house—. "We don't have much time anyway," —he checked his wristwatch—. "Because if you're late to a meeting with Arturi, he gets *really* mad—" —the senator stretched—. "Like a dog when you touch its food bowl while it's eating. He foams at the mouth, Daniel. But if we can't do it now, we can continue later."

Soon, the three were seated in an office with a fairly extensive library behind the progressive senator.

"Why 'Ñato'? I've always wanted to know where the nickname comes from," —Geraldine broke the ice, detecting that all the affability of the nearly totally bald man only hid how tense the duo had made him with their unexpected visit.

"It's from when I was young. I was a boxer, you know?"

"No kidding!" —Viktor exclaimed, surprised—. "I was also a boxer not too long ago, four years and a bit." —The Russian detective understood where his partner's question was headed and continued the line of relaxation.

"With that build, you must have been a heavyweight," —the former Tupamaro joked now more relaxed, waiting for his visitor, who couldn't hide his 120 kg of muscle under a suit, to nod—. "I was welterweight. I even boxed professionally and all that. What times—" —he recalled nostalgically—. "That's where the nickname comes from, because most boxers get their noses broken in some fight and they end up like this," —he pointed to his nose—. "But not you, I see—" —he addressed Viktor—. "Looks like you were *good* at boxing."

"I held my own pretty well," —the eagle-nosed man smiled.

"Well, tell me, what would you like to know about Pancho? I suppose it won't be the usual stuff, right? That we were Tupamaros together, got caught, were put in Punta Carretas, escaped from there, and then got caught again and were held in barracks, being beaten like laundry for 12 long years, right?"

"No, of course. *Everyone* knows that part," —the interviewer dismissed with a gesture, deciding not to waste time on something that could be found in any other source, yet some interviewees had denied it, like Borderragui, for example—. "We'd like to know what you were like when you were young, what your relationship with Mojica was like on a daily basis. Did you go out dancing together, for instance?"

"Uuuhhhh, girl. Did we go out? We *owned* the night, let me tell you. We wore the dance floor down to the ground."

For a long moment, the detectives were subjected to a series of anecdotes about dance clubs they frequented, the music that was played and danced to back then, stories of outings together, and everything that people over fifty remember with romanticism and nostalgia about their youth, along with what any serious investigator can consider a foundation that over 80% of it is outright lies, most self-deceptions—that is, the one recalling it had filtered the truth to keep only the best and prettiest parts while overlooking everything else.

"So, you and Mojica were popular with the ladies, I'd say," —the boxer smiled.

"We did well, truth be told," —the senator returned a cheeky grin—. "More him than me, mind you. I was pretty ordinary. Yes, I was in great shape from boxing and all, but Pancho was a Hollywood heartthrob, with his strong jaw, sparkling light eyes, and perfect teeth. I'll tell you more: sometimes I felt like those little fish that swim on the back of a shark; I don't remember their name.

Those that the shark doesn't eat because they're faster than it or because the shark isn't interested since they're small or something like that, but they still get to enjoy the leftovers from what the shark eats."

"Remora fish," —Viktor supplied.

"Those ones," —the former welterweight boxer approved.

"But surely it wasn't all wine and roses in that aspect, right?" —the dark-eyed woman slightly shifted the direction of the conversation—. "There must have been some ugly moments with women." —She noticed the interviewee beginning to feel uncomfortable, which only encouraged her to continue down that line of questioning—. "We understand, for example, that Mojica dated Anabel Pulansky for a while, the twin sister of his current widow, Senator Laura Pulansky, and that ended very *badly*."

The current senator's face contorted, his features shifting from friendly to tense, even irate in an instant. Evidently, they had *touched* a sensitive point.

"If you don't mind, I'd prefer to change the subject."

"Yes, of course," —Ielicov accepted—. "We're also interested in delving deeper into your captivity in military barracks. We need to get a complete picture of that time for our investigation. Tell us: if we had to talk to the military who served at the barracks where you were held, who should we talk to?"

"Ha. Good point, kid. Yes, of course. I don't have a problem giving you some names. Because not *all* military personnel were bad, you know? There were bad soldiers and good soldiers, just like anywhere else. Like in Nazi Germany, for example. Not *all* Germans followed Hitler and his ideas. There were those who disagreed with the Führer and got the hell out, like Einstein, and others who endured and stayed in Germany until the wave of madness and destruction passed. Let's see..." —he thought for a moment—. "I think you need to talk to General Guido Menini

Ruiz. If Pancho had won in October, I would have taken the position of Minister of Defense, and Menini Ruiz would have been the commander-in-chief of the armed forces."

"Excuse me..." —Geraldine didn't understand—. "Didn't you have enough of the military and barracks to take on the role of Minister of Defense?"

"It was a strong political gesture, what was intended."

"Right, to reconcile with your former enemy to send a message of peace and to build a country together," —now it clicked for the former head of the Uruguayan National Police Press Office.

"Exactly!" —the progressive senator approved.

"But the referendum to repeal the Expiration Law that your party supports could be said to be going in the opposite direction, right?" —the Russian was suspicious.

"Yes... and no," —Huidó was ambiguous—. "Wounds *must* be healed; if not, they remain open and continue to hurt." —The interviewee's expression turned bitter.

"And was Menini Ruiz one of the good soldiers?" —Viktor asked.

"No," —the Uruguayan senator was categorical—. "*Precisely* because of that, we wanted him as commander-in-chief of the Armed Forces."

"*Another* strong political gesture," —Geraldine understood—. "Trusting someone who will most likely see his former military superiors fall one by one into prison for crimes against humanity sends the signal that democratic opening is *serious* and that the military is aligned with the government."

"Are you sure you don't want to be an electoral advisor?" —the former Tupamaro emerged from the dark place his mind had been in—. "Because these Crispiani folks charge us a *fortune* to advise us on something you understand so easily."

"I studied international relations and communication, what can I say?" —she shrugged.

"Wow, look at the time," —the interviewee checked his wristwatch—. "I have only six minutes left for the meeting, and I still need to get ready with my mate and hit the bathroom. Here, take my card, kids. If you need anything, call my secretary, and we'll schedule a meeting for another time. Gloria at the reception can give you General Menini Ruiz's phone number. Tell him you're going from me (to the general, I mean). It was a pleasure talking to you."

Back in the central hall, they saw the current Minister of Economy and presidential candidate, the very gray-haired economist Daniel Arturi, enter. It was Geraldine who recognized him and intercepted him.

"Minister Arturi. We are Goldman and Ielicov," —she introduced herself and her partner. The surprised progressive minister had no choice but to shake their hands, as they *literally* blocked his path—. "The CSA Group hired us..."

"Yes, *I already* know who you are," —the very gray man with a prominent nose and glasses said grumpily—. "But now is *not* the time," —he pointed to his wristwatch—. "I have a meeting, so if you want to talk to me, you'll have to call my secretary and schedule an interview. Now, if you'll excuse me..." —he gestured for them to step aside and let him pass.

"Who are you calling?" —Viktor whispered to his partner, barely containing her anger as he watched her pull out a Nokia N97 mobile.

"I have a better idea than calling his secretary to talk to him. Hi, Ivan. Do you have a moment to talk? Uh-huh. You see, we're at the headquarters of the Progressive Front, and a meeting of the leadership has just started. We still need to interview Arturi, but I'm afraid he's been a bit evasive about it. He told us to call his secretary to schedule a meeting, just like that. Is it possible for you to get us that meeting, but for *today*? Great, perfect. And... as soon as this meeting is over would be ideal. We'll be nearby, but it can't be after 6, because we must be in Carrasco at 7 to talk to De La Rúa. Excellent. Thanks for everything, Ivan."

"And?"

"He'll *get us* that interview, no matter what."

CHAPTER 14: HERE THEY ARE MADE, AND HERE THEY ARE PAID

O*utside Wollerau, Switzerland, residence of Oscar Newell, Sunday, April 19, 1998, 11:45 AM.*

The retired General of the Argentine Army was enjoying the pleasant spring day in his two-story house, with views of the mountains from the backyard. He was about to light one of his many River Plate-style barbecues in the circular charcoal grill when the doorbell rang.

"Who the hell is bothering me at this hour on a Sunday?" he exclaimed angrily, determined to ignore the bell.

He had been living alone since becoming a widower, and his children were all grown up, with families of their own, and none of them lived in Switzerland. It could be said with complete accuracy that the retired Argentine general was a solitary man. In fact, he only socialized with his friends and clients from the shooting club he managed not far from his home.

But the doorbell rang again.

"Whoever is coming to bother me can go to hell. It better is something important, or else..." The seventy-year-old Argentine left his book, "The Right in Argentina: From Peronism to the New Right" by Rodolfo Pinedo, open face down next to his wine glass and went to answer the door. Through the peephole, he saw it was a DHL messenger. "How strange, delivering on a Sunday at this hour," he muttered to himself, but he opened the door anyway.

"Good day. Are you Oscar Weller?" asked the young cadet in German.

Two things caught Weller's attention: first, that the messenger was wearing a surgical mask, and second, that there was no DHL vehicle in sight. "*What a moron, thinking everything has germs,*" he thought, arriving at this conclusion not only because of the mask but also due to the leather gloves, even though it was a pleasant 22 degrees Celsius. "*He must have parked his van at another house where he had a delivery, and to avoid greenhouse gases, he preferred to walk. Damn environmentalists!*"

"Yes, that's me," he confirmed, also in German.

"I have this urgent delivery for you," he said, handing over a package. "Please sign here." The messenger placed the form on the package before Weller could read who it was from. "Signature, printed name, and ID, please," he added, placing a pen on the form.

The former repressor was about to sign when suddenly the DHL cadet said in Spanish:

"And this delivery too."

The next thing the seventy-year-old Oscar Weller knew was that he was inhaling a gas that the stranger had sprayed in his face, an odorless gas that burned his nostrils as it traveled to his lungs.

"What... what did you spray on me?" the main figure responsible for anti-subversive repression in Argentina during the last dictatorship wanted to know.

"It's Novichok, you great son of a bitch. Does it ring a bell from your time in the SIDE? Oh... yes, it does. So you know you have 3 minutes before you start feeling the effects, two more minutes during which you'll be *begging* for death to relieve the pain you're about to feel, and after that, there's no cure or treatment that can save you from dying unless I inject you with this syringe," he pulled a fine 5-milliliter hypodermic needle from his pocket, "with Atropine, and this one," he took out a 10-milliliter syringe, "with

Pralidoxime. So, are you going to let me in, or are we going to have this unpleasant conversation right here at the door?"

"Come in. Come in. Hurry up!" urged the octogenarian.

However, the young false cadet wandered around the spacious living room of Newell's house for nearly a minute, admiring the paintings, the decorations...

"It's nice living off the money stolen from Argentines, huh?"

"What do you want from me?"

"Nothing from you, jerk. It took me *3 years* to find you, but see: I finally found you. What I want you to tell me is where the hell the other son of a bitch is hiding, your Uruguayan counterpart in anti-subversive repression. I'm talking about Carlos Falcone, of course."

"He lives in Chile. That's all I know. I swear!"

"In Chile?" the false messenger from the international logistics and transportation company raised an eyebrow. "But the last thing we heard about his whereabouts was that he was living in Camboriú, right?"

"Yes, he went to Camboriú when the re institutionalization in Uruguay ended."

"It's called a *dictatorship*, Oscar," the young man corrected, emphasizing on the "a" as they do in Argentina.

"Whatever it is. He built a house there, in Camboriú, on the beach..." Suddenly, he clutched his chest with his right fist.

"Oh, right," the twenty-something indifferently checked his wristwatch. "I told you the effects start in three minutes. Finish the story, and I'll give you the injections."

"But they found him there, and he had to move to Chile. I don't have his address, but I do have his phone number. The international code shows it's from Chile," he pointed to a notebook next to the landline.

"Okay. I suppose I can locate him from there. What do you know about the traitorous Tupamaro, the one who sold out his movement? Falcone must have told you something."

"Only that he called him prisoner 2746, or just 2746, by his prisoner number in Punta Carretas prison, and that this Tupamaro had a bastard son, whom Falcone had me track down all over Argentina, his son and ex-wife, but we never found them."

"Hello," the young man greeted with a smile and a wave. "I'm *that* bastard son you never caught because my mom was smarter than all of you fascist bastards combined. Oh, and this"—he pulled out a very fine syringe, removed the needle with its cap, and poured its contents into his mouth—"is orange juice. A bit too sweet for my taste. I prefer low-calorie."

The former repressor's horrified face, having fallen from the three-seat white leather couch to the floor, writhing in intense pain, was a *delight* for the one who had dealt the fatal blow, even though he was still breathing... for not much longer.

"My mom always said something, and how right she was! Here they are made, and here they are paid," he shot a furious glance at the dying man. "You're not going to reincarnate as a cow turd, as would befit Hindu tradition. And unfortunately, you're not going to hell, as it would be in the Christian tradition. You made many people suffer in *this* life, and now what you are receiving is the suffering of all those people together. I'm going to stay here, watching you die, then I'm going to take the recordings from the security cameras and they're going to find you in a few days, because your neighbors won't bear the smell of death that's going to come out of here, and you're going to be all swollen, green... disgusting. Oh, are you dead already?" -he confirmed when Weller had already remained still, and his chest was not moving-. "How little endurance you fucking fascists have, I tell you..."

Exit in front of Colonia 1771 street of the central headquarters of the Progressive Front, Montevideo, Tuesday July 21, 2009, 3:50 p.m.

Viktor and Geraldine waited a prudent moment for the mass of journalists that occupied the entire sidewalk to disperse before leaving. Clearly, until the meeting of the ruling party leadership was over, the journalists, their cameramen and their photographers had nothing better to do than wait, ask to go to the bathroom in some bar, buy biscuits and eat them, check their cell phone, or smoke. However, there was one journalist who recognized Geraldine when she left.

"Geraldine Goldman, former Press Chief of the police" -he walked towards her quickly, not before gesturing to his photographer to come closer- "I don't know if you remember me. Figueroa, from El Despertador" -he put out his hand to shake hers.

"Yes, I remember you, Figueroa" - she greeted.

"And you are that Russian detective, the one from Entrevero Square, the one from the chase and the shootings, right?" -he greeted the former professional boxer from Vladivostok in turn.

"Yes, I'm *that* detective" -he was very brief.

"I don't know if you remember me, I was there that day, in the Entrevero Square..."

"Get to it, Figueroa" -urged Geraldine, who knew the modus operandi, because it couldn't be called anything else (some call it editorial criteria, but that's up to them) of El Despertador, the second largest-circulation morning paper in Uruguay, of focusing its notes on scandalous articles that revealed, in each issue, corruption in both governmental *and* private spheres-, "we're in a hurry. And turn off the recording on your cell phone, for the love of all the saints!"

"Okay, okay. I'll turn it off. This is off-the-record."

"Friend" -warned the corpulent Russian to the photographer, who kept taking pictures of them.

"That's OK, Wilmer,"—Figueroa agreed. Only then did the photographer stopped snapping pictures—"So, what does the Progressive Front owe for the honor of having such distinguished visitors when they're about to elect a new presidential candidate? Any comments?"—he raised an eyebrow.

"I'm a press advisor now."

"Uh-huh. Press advisor,"—the journalist repeated—"Look, Geraldine, I've been at El Despertador for four years, and for us journalists in the street..."

"Wait: do you work for El Despertador or are you on the street?"

"Oh, that?"—the young man smiled, a few hairs on his beard and looking somewhat disheveled: the perks of not having to appear on live camera, since his was a written medium—"That's what a comedian on the radio calls us, I don't know if you know him, Darwin Desbocatti: journalists in the street. He calls us that about the reporters because basically our work is out in the open. Sometimes we're lucky enough to be let into a press room in the Executive Tower or at the police station itself, but if not, we're at the mercy of the elements, getting soaked, freezing, or burning up. As I was saying, for us reporters, it's very difficult to get an exclusive, because all the media go everywhere we're supposed to be, but I see my colleagues from other channels, newspapers, and radios didn't recognize you. I did,"—he looked at her maliciously—"both of you. So, tell me: what kind of press advisory is it that you came to do for the Progressive Front after the death of their presidential candidate and having to meet urgently to present a new formula heading into the elections in October?"

"No comments, Figueroa,"—Geraldine replied tersely, dodging the journalist to move away, with Viktor following her.

Unlike television media, which depend on cables, microphones, and cameramen, reporters from written press can freely follow those they want to interview, and Figueroa did just that, accompanied by his photographer.

"It's not really necessary for you to do that, Goldman, because we can easily fill in the gaps ourselves. Let's see... you're investigating the opposition candidates, taking compromising photos that can leave them exposed to the press... those photos are worth money. Let's say it's De La Rúa dancing a mambo naked and drunk, or picking up a transvestite in Parque Batlle. Any comments?"

"Fill in as you wish, Figueroa,"—Geraldine kept walking—"and tomorrow I'll buy a copy of your rag to laugh at how far off you were from reality." Suddenly, she noticed out of the corner of her eye that they were no longer being followed. "Can you believe this guy, Vik?"

"He's just doing his job,"—the muscular man shrugged—"not a very dignified one, but a job nonetheless. No one knows them better than you."

"That's true. Do you remember how this fool got hired by El Despertador? They say he found some photos from the case of The Decorator that the police didn't want to make public, but The Decorator himself *did want* the homicide on Andes Street to be known as his work."

"Was it him? What a scandal that was, but it seems the police and Minister Cortez learned to hide things better this time, didn't they?"

"That's true. If something leaks, it won't be from us."

"Where are you taking me, darling?"—the Russian asked, since aside from his involvement in the case in 2005 when he met Geraldine, he was unfamiliar with the city. Then he recognized the municipal building. Only then did he get his bearings—"Are we headed to the Central Headquarters of the Police?"

"No, sweetheart, I'm taking you to a bookstore."

"What do you have in mind, Geral?"

"You see: although we haven't talked about it among ourselves, it's *clear* we touched on a very sensitive point with Huidó when we got to the issue of problems with women, both his and Mojica's, in his youth, right?"

"If you were blunter, you'd say we put our finger in ass hole, in a way, but I agree. We *need* to follow that lead."

"Then it occurred to me,"—the detective managed to articulate after finishing her laugh at the crude remark—"that we know little to nothing about Mojica. Personally, I always voted for the Liberal Party, and to me, Mojica was that dirty progressive that the common people love because he slurs his 's' when he talks and conjugates verbs in a countryside style. For that reason, besides knowing what everyone knows, that he was a member of the Tupamaro guerrilla and later served 12 years in military battalions, I don't know much. I think it's time, since it seems we have a few hours before we can meet with Arturi, to buy a biography of our subject of study and read it."

"Sounds like a plan. But I'd also like to hear the other side."

"Are you talking about any book that some repressor might have published?"—she asked.

"No, and I don't think they would have sold many copies if they had published one. Amadeo Píriz mentioned he wrote a book himself, telling *his* version. I'd like to hear his account too, of what happened in those years. You know, this whole issue of Mojica and Huidó pointing to him as the traitor among the Tupamaros, and him saying he wasn't... smells very bad to me."

"Are you saying they pointed him out to exonerate themselves from being the traitors?"—the not-so-orthodox Jewish woman understood.

"It wouldn't be the first time someone farts in an elevator and immediately asks: Who was? Who was the disgusting one who farted?"

"Oh, Viktor. You *kill me* when you're so crude in your speech,"—she laughed heartily.

"I know. It's part of my charm repertoire,"—they stopped walking in front of the bookstore to kiss tenderly.

An hour and a bit later, they were each engrossed in their books. She was reading "Pancho Mojica: A Life in Times of Crisis" by Jorge Lanzari, while he devoured "The Time of Heroes" by Amadeo Píriz. Both were sipping smoothies, sitting on a bench in the municipal square, absorbed in their reading and reflections. Occasionally, they would comment on their findings or, at other times, the lack thereof.

"*Zero* comments about love relationships,"—Geraldine let slip.

"Same here. All the more reason to suspect something *murky* happened in that regard, or Huidó wouldn't have reacted the way he did when we touched on the subject."

They continued for a while focused on their respective readings, attentive to their phones when suddenly Viktor found something.

"Píriz resigned to the Tupamaro guerrilla in '71. Here it says that Píriz began to question the effectiveness of armed struggle and the growing violence within the group. He also felt uncomfortable with the lack of internal debate and the rigidity of the organization."

"He basically put a target on his own back to be labeled the traitor among his ranks!"—Geraldine understood.

"And what are two good-looking private detectives doing in my city investigating who killed Francisco 'Pancho' Mojica?"—a deep male voice sounded from behind them, surprising and alerting the detective duo. "Don't shoot. It's just me,"—the thirty-something man raised his hands in surrender, noticing that each surprised individual had instinctively reached for the holster where they kept their weapons.

"Lobo!"—Goldman reacted from her initial shock and stopped to greet her former high school classmate with a tight hug, the same person who had put into black type on white pages what had *really* happened in the events of The Decorator, in which all three had been key players. "How have you been?"

"I'm good. Viktor, my dear! Aren't you ever going to take my advice and grow out your beard? It looks so good on you!"—the writer embraced the Russian detective with an enthusiasm more typical of the Río de la Plata than Europe, with hearty pats on his solid back.

"You know, Lobo, in my line of work, a beard looks bad. It raises suspicion,"—the former boxer smiled.

"Don't tell me you now speak Russian,"—Geraldine asked, surprised, since the comments they made to each other in a public square were, of course, in that language.

"No, not at all,"—the writer dismissed with a gesture—"I *wish* I could speak the language of my ancestors through my maternal line. It was enough to see the books you were reading, one a biography of Mojica, and the other written by Amadeo Píriz, to put two and two together. Besides, since the news of Mojica's death in Termas del Arapey broke, my mind... you know how we writers are... I left the book project I was working on and started writing a horror and mystery story for my book 'Just in Case You Thought You Could Sleep, Volume 3,' where I develop a conspiracy theory in which Mojica didn't die from a myocardial infarction, as was officially reported, but was murdered. The story is called 'Magnicide,' because Mojica was leading in the polls for voting intention, so if someone killed him, they could have murdered the next president of Uruguay. Do you follow me?"—he saw his friends and collaborators in the book recounting the raw and *real* details of The Decorator case looking at each other and then at him, but not wanting to confirm the writer's supposedly outrageous hypothesis.

"Come on, guys,"—he scolded them with a gesture—"You don't have to deny or confirm anything. Mojica dies. Two private detectives I care *a lot* about return to Montevideo after the tragic events of The Decorator, Mojica dies in a thermal pool from a 'supposed' myocardial infarction, and one of you is reading a biography of Mojica while the other reads a book by the *supposed* traitor of the Tupamaro movement in the '70s. Tell me if two plus two has ever equaled anything other than four."

"Listen, Lobo,"—Geraldine, though she knew his real name from when they called the roll at the French High School, accepted that her former friend and would-be suitor preferred not to use it, due to how unpronounceable it sounded—"I don't need to remind you that what Viktor and I are investigating deserves the *utmost* confidentiality and anonymity, right?"

"Of course, Geral. Of course. Now tell me: are you coming over for dinner with Mica and me when you have a free moment? Maybe we can invite Lía from the ITF too, and we'll form the original quintet that solved the The Decorator case. Sound like a plan?"—He handed them a business card—"*Clearly*, I moved after my house was reduced to rubble that day. Call me if you want to have a campfire council like that time. Have a good day, guys."

They hadn't been back to their reading for two minutes after the Uruguayan writer friend of both had left when a WhatsApp notification rang on Goldman's phone. It was from a contact she had saved.

Iván Reno

"I've arranged an interview with Arturi in his office at the Ministry of Economy in 15 minutes. Are you at reach? Because if not, the next available slot would be tomorrow at 9:30, also at the ministry."

The detective showed the message to her partner, and they consulted each other with a glance after seeing what time it was.

Geraldine Goldman
"We'll be there, no problem. Better today than tomorrow. Thanks for your efforts, Iván."

Iván Reno
"Anytime. If you need anything else, just let me know."

"Are we?"—the boxer wanted to make sure.

"Yes, it's 8 blocks from here. It's not worth lifting the car. What would be prudent is to add more parking time, or we could get towed,"—joining action to words, she proceeded to extend the parking time by sending a text with the rental car's license plate and the minutes. "Done."

They arrived with a 5-minute buffer at the government building on Mercedes Street, at the corner with Avenida del Libertador. Something stopped them: the stampede of what sounded like a gunshot in the distance.

"Was that what I think it was?"—Geraldine asked her Russian partner.

"I can't think of anything else it could be. But it sounded distant,"—the former boxer considered.

At the *exact* time, not a second before or after, Economist Daniel Arturi opened the door to his office and let the detectives in.

"Economist Arturi, thank you for meeting with us," said Goldman after shaking hands and the progressive minister gestured for them to take a seat.

"Yes, as if I had an alternative. Ha!"

"And why wouldn't you have an interest in helping clarify the circumstances surrounding the death of your running mate?" Ielicov went straight to the point. "So far, of all those interviewed in this case, only former President Borderragui has shown reluctance to be interviewed. I wonder why that is."

"Because Mojica and I had *nothing* to do with each other. *Zero* points of contact other than belonging to the same political party. Is that what you wanted to hear?"

"If it's the plain truth..." the ex-boxer shrugged.

"It is. You see, the Progressive Front is *not* a political party, though we would *never* admit it in public. It's a coalition of parties. There are far-left sectors, like the Popular Movement of Mojica and Pulansky, and then there's my sector, which is center. Not even center-left. Just center. Mojica planned to take the country on a path of good intentions, populist gestures, and few or nonexistent economic results. If God wills, and the assembly votes for me this coming Saturday, I will guide the direction based on economic indicators."

"That's to be expected, being an economist," Goldman agreed.

"Precisely. It's as simple as this: if a Uruguayan doesn't have a decent job that allows him or her to put food on the table, they're not going to give *a damn* about the 5,000 pesos a month that the Ministry of Development gives them, or the free meals served in public schools. Any assistance the state provides will be insufficient, and it will increase the fiscal deficit, which will hurt our investment rating. But of course, good luck explaining this to the masses," the Minister of Economy scoffed.

"I'm not surprised Mojica said about you in the campaign that 'you have no sex appeal,'" the detective cited the words of the deceased's secretary, who had been sexually and professionally harassed by her boss for years, trying to hit a nerve.

"Do you know what's the funniest thing? He was absolutely right about that," he admitted regretfully. "That's why my campaign team advises me to appear more but speak less. Everything I'm saying to you doesn't make it into the speeches they write for me."

"So, was there consensus in the meeting at your party's headquarters regarding the ticket?" asked the Russian detective. "Will you be running as president and someone else as vice?"

"Not at all! Everything *but* consensus. In two hours, you can't decide something so important for our party. We agreed to continue tomorrow at 10:30 AM, but it's likely we'll be there all day. For now, there are three options on the table: me as president and Pulansky as vice, Huidó as president and me as vice, and Pulansky as president and me as vice."

"We're happy for you, Arturi. At least you're still in the running for all options," Viktor smiled.

"Yes, and someone from the Popular Movement is in all of them as well," the economist said bitterly. "The economy governs *everything*, even crime rates. If a father or mother, let's say the breadwinner of a household, doesn't have money to feed their children, it's *obvious* they're going to turn to theft or prostitution. And if those kids depend solely on the meal provided once a day at school, because there's no food at home, they'll perform worse academically, and we'll have fewer quality professionals to lead the country in the next generation. I don't know what else there is to clarify," he shrugged. "Anyway, the next ticket for the Progressive Front won't be decided by us, the leadership; it will be decided by the communists, as always."

"How is that?" Ielicov asked.

"It's a... *flawed* system, but it's in the constitution, so we have to follow it. You see, the assembly is composed proportionally by the number of affiliates in each sector, and the communists have always had more militants than the other sectors. They're the ones who establish and lead the base committees in each neighborhood, which translates into more affiliates, resulting in more assembly members. So, even though they represented 10% of our party's votes in the last elections, they have the right to 45% of the assembly members. If it were up to me," he gestured with both hands, "I would propose a constitutional reform where representation is proportional to the latest legislative vote. You, Communist Party, had 10% of the votes; you have the right to 10% of the assembly members. The Popular Movement obtained 43% of the votes; you get 43% of those deciding the new ticket, and so on."

"Sure. That would be a much more reasonable system, right?" the pale-skinned detective agreed.

"Reason is what voters lack. Votes are based on *feeling*, not reason, and the Popular Movement has always been *experts* at connecting with people."

"Have you done well financially in life?" Ielicov surprised him with a sudden shift.

"If you boxed as well as you interrogate now, Ielicov, you must have done quite well in the ring." He gave an intelligent glance behind his glasses. "I think I see where your question is coming from, but I'll answer it as if I didn't. Have I done well? Yes, I have nothing to complain about. I've always done well professionally, and I'm a financially stable man. I own a house valued at $300,000, another vacation home in Solís worth $200,000, my own car, and bank deposits of $120,000—all based on my own efforts and my wife's, who is an architect. And since I've been in public office, I can assure you she earns quite a bit more than I do as a senator or Minister of Economy. Everything is publicly registered in the asset statement that we both have to present annually, since I'm a high-level public official. And we don't do the foolishness that the Popular Movement does by donating three-quarters of their salary to the party. If I'm going to work and drain myself for a period of five years, rejecting better-paying independent opportunities, I have the right to earn 100% of my salary and do with it what I please, don't you think? Now, if your question, Ielicov, was whether

I have enough money to hire a hitman to have Mojica killed, *of course* I do!"

"I never said that was the reason for my question, but thank you for clarifying, Mr. Minister."

"*Former* minister," the interviewee corrected. "I had to resign a few weeks ago when it was officially announced that I would be part of the ticket for the upcoming presidential elections. They still lend me this office," he gestured broadly around them, "out of courtesy, I suppose. And also, because my substitute occupies the one that should belong to me in the Legislative Palace."

"Why July 18, I wonder?" the Uruguayan in the duo thought aloud. "I mean, it's an important date for our country, isn't it?"

"Wow. *Another* turn in the conversation that doesn't catch me off guard," the ex-minister smiled maliciously. "Speculating, we could speculate *ad infinitum*, Goldman: you, Tupamaro, want to lock us up—former generals and commanders who repressed during the re institutionalization that the constitution allowed us to enact by abolishing the law of expiration? We kill you on the day the constitution is sworn in. Or... if we're talking about De La Rúa, the constitutional reform that enabled the runoff and gave the traditional parties only *one* presidential victory, before allowing the left to take over in the current period, and everything indicated that it would continue in the next, I kill your candidate to see if they can still use the constitutional reform to their advantage. Oh, and let's not forget that it was the Tupamaros who kidnapped and killed De La Rúa's father."

"What?!" the detectives exclaimed in unison, surprised.

"Yes. Just as you heard. It's not often mentioned, as you can imagine, but it's a documented historical fact. The Tupamaros were engaging in extortionate kidnappings in the late '60s and early '70s, until they dismantled the guerrilla movement. Most kidnappings were for money to finance their guerrilla efforts, like in the case of Luis Alberto De La Rúa's father, but something went wrong, because he turned up with a bullet in his head in a vacant lot. And that's despite the family paying the ransom. So don't ask me to embrace the former Tupamaros. I tolerate them in the party because I have to. And also, because they bring votes. But agreeing with their ideology? Nothing could be further from my being. I'm also a suspect in killing my rival on the day we celebrate the swearing-in of the first constitution. As I mentioned a moment ago, the way the presidential ticket is defined according to the constitution is *wrong*... period."

"We didn't know about De La Rúa's father," the boxer stroked his chin.

"Honestly, neither did I, being Uruguayan," Geraldine admitted.

"Such things eventually come to light. You can fool some people, some time, but you can't fool all the people, all the time."

"Touché!" Viktor smiled. "I didn't picture you quoting Bob Marley."

"What can I say?" the only confirmed member of the ruling presidential ticket shrugged. "One likes the music one likes."

"Were you among the founding members of the Progressive Front?" Geraldine asked.

"Yes, of course. I've *always* been progressive, not like Mojica, who was Conservative before," he made a dismissive gesture.

"Did you know Mojica back then, when he was a Tupamaro and you were trying to steer the country left through politics?" the investigator probed suspiciously. "Just because your sector is center doesn't mean your party as a whole can't be identified as the most leftist option in Uruguay."

"Do you know you're mistaken there, Goldman? The Progressive Front is *not* the most leftist option. There's the Workers' Party, but they rarely manage to get even one deputy, let alone a senator. To return to your original question, if I didn't know him, it was because he was in hiding and I was not. I was a public figure. However, not having seen him doesn't mean I didn't hear all kinds of rumors about him. In fact, back then, there were party members who *did have regular* contact with the Tupamaro guerrilla, so some of the rumors might have been accurate."

"Any in particular you wish to share with us?"

"That he was quite a charmer. A ladies' man, I mean, who could win over *any* woman he wanted, which is why he didn't settle down with any, though some of those flings ended badly," the economist shot them a mischievous look. "If you've done your job well as private investigators so far, I think you know who I'm talking about, right?"

"We think we do, but we'd like to hear your version as well," Ielicov continued with an air of mystery.

"The rumors back then said that if Mojica dated Anabel Pulansky for a few months and they broke up on bad terms to the point of never speaking again, it was because Mojica got Pulansky (I mean Anabel) pregnant and didn't want to take responsibility for the child. In fact, the rumors said he asked her to have an abortion, and she refused. Ask Anabel who the father of her only child is: her current husband, who registered him in the civil registry as his own, or Francisco Mojica."

"That leaves me speechless, if that rumor is indeed true," the ex-boxer said after a few seconds of astonishment, before his partner and girlfriend did.

"That would be a motive not only electoral or constitutional but 100% personal, of course: to find out at 30-something years old that your biological father wanted you aborted and another man, the one who raised you, had to take care of you out of love for your mother. Besides, I understand that Facundo, that's the name of Anabel Pulansky's son, is a man of *great* physical strength."

"And how is the '*great* physical strength' relevant?" the former Press Chief was on the verge of losing her temper at what was clearly a violation of the secrecy surrounding the ongoing police investigation.

"Perhaps it's not relevant at all, but compare photos of Mojica and González, Anabel's husband, from that time: Mojica was rather tall, broad-shouldered, and well-muscled, while González was very short and rather skinny. If you put their photos side by side, who would you point to as Facundo's father, considering how well-built the boy is?"

"I think that's all, Arturi," Geraldine stood up furiously, to the point of not even shaking hands with the economist, and stormed off toward the elevator.

"We'll contact you if we need to ask more questions," the investigator was a bit more cordial, but still left without shaking hands with the gray-haired man in glasses. "Geraldine, listen to me," he tried to calm her once they were inside the elevator. "It's possible that Arturi didn't come across that information from the police investigation to get that detail about a muscular guy blocking the way for the lifeguard, or that he held Mojica's head underwater until he drowned, as we recreated in the ITF. Think about it, the leak could have come from the new forensic report Lia had to draft after our visit."

"Yes, but it's less likely that it came from the judicial sphere than from the police. Damn! It seems they don't understand why investigations need to remain closed until someone is formally charged—gossips, just gossips. But with two calls, we'll find out. Can you drive? Because I can't in this state."

"Sure. Taxi," Viktor requested since the rental car was fifteen blocks away, and they were short on time to get to Carrasco by 7.

"Hello, Mr. Hernández," Geraldine greeted the Presidential Secretary as soon as they were in the rental car, clearly aware that the calls she needed to make couldn't be overheard by a random taxi driver. "I need to ask you a question and request that you keep it between us. Thank you. Which political sector does Minister Cortez currently belong to? Because I believe I recall that when I was Head of Police Press, he responded to the Popular Movement, but you know how it is: alliances change over time. Uh-huh. He's still in that sector. I understand. Now I'm going to make a request because President Valdez told us that if we needed *anything* from the Executive Power, we should let you know. Thank you. What are the chances of making the presidential helicopter available to us tomorrow morning? The exact time? I couldn't tell you, but definitely before noon. Destination? Confidential, but it's about 400 or 500 kilometers from the capital. Can we inform the pilot when we board the helicopter, so he or she can communicate the flight plan to the tower? Oh! Who would've thought? It's the 21st century and there are still no female pilots in the Air Force? Seems like an opportunity for growth in the rights agenda, don't you think? Yes, of course: some changes take time. Thank you very much for your help, Mr. Hernández," she ended the call. "Sorry," she suddenly realized how many unilateral decisions she had made since storming out of the Ministry of Economy. "Sorry, sorry, sorry—*two thousand* apologies for what I just did, for making decisions without consensus. Will you forgive me?"

"It's not a big deal, Geral," the driver dismissed with a gesture. "Which way now?" They were ending Río Negro street, heading towards the waterfront, and they could turn left, right, or break through the wall to the beach.

"Oh, yes. Left. All straight for about 10 kilometers, and once we're closer to the area in Carrasco, I'll guide you to De La Rúa's house."

Besides, it was obvious that, regardless of how Arturi found out about Anabel Pulansky's son, the investigation, and that Facundo

González might be Mojica's unrecognized biological son, they would have to re-interview the elderly woman who doesn't use cell phones or landlines, and driving back and forth to Paysandú would take a day.

"Next call to Toro. I'm going to push him to see if the information leaked from Homicides."

"Okay. Ask him if he and Di Lorenzo can join us tomorrow in Paysandú while you're at it."

"Why?"

"You know how Toro impresses during an interrogation. Plus, in the hypothetical event that Arturi gave us solid information and not just speculation or unfounded rumors, we'll land a military helicopter on a suspect in a homicide case. That could bring problems."

"In the hypothetical case. Sure: better safe than sorry. Should I ask for bulletproof vests for us?"

"Hey, don't exaggerate, my love," Viktor smiled. "Just landing a military helicopter will be a pretty strong impact for that family; adding bulletproof vests would only amplify it."

"Okay. Calling Toro. Hi, Toro, how have you been? We're following leads and interviewing a ton of people. My throat is dry from talking, that says it all," the former Press Chief continued in a casual tone. "Tell me, Toro, was it you or Di Lorenzo who leaked details of the investigation into Mojica's homicide to Arturi? Uh-huh. Yes, of course. You sound *super* calm. Only Minister Cortez, you, and Di Lorenzo have access to the case file. I see. And what about the digital records? Ah. There aren't any... because they can be hacked," she repeated to her partner, as the Nokia N97 didn't have a speakerphone function. "They keep them in a safe that only you and Cortez can access. What information leaked? Let me see... Oh, yes. I just remembered: Arturi *knows* and threw it in our faces that the homicide suspect Francisco Mojica is someone with great physical strength! Tell me: how on earth did he find out if it wasn't through the police? Because we haven't talked to anyone except you two. Uh-huh. Wait a second. And why did a police officer from Salto interrogate the lifeguard before you guys got there? Yes, I get it, but doesn't the police have a helicopter to have arrived sooner? Well, Toro. I think it's time to ask for one, don't you think? Speaking of helicopters, we invite you and Di Lorenzo to travel with us to Paysandú to re-interview Anabel Pulansky. No way. No bulletproof vests, please. It could just be a rumor. Thanks for everything, Toro. We'll let you know tomorrow when we head to the airstrip so you can join us. You too."

"So the Salto police interviewed the lifeguard *before* the homicide unit?"

"It seems that way. But don't say it doesn't infuriate you to be hired for a top-secret investigation and suddenly have a key piece of information you discovered become public knowledge."

"If anything, the interview with Arturi showed us that he's someone to be reckoned with. Politicians of his caliber obviously have a team of investigators and intelligence to know more than their political rivals and to know how to dirty their opponents. He could easily have other Goldmans and Ielicovs at his disposal."

"No. I don't think so. There's no one like us. Gotta keep that self-esteem high, right?"—she fist-bumped the driver.

"*Always* high."

"Still, now that I think about it, the point Toro made is valid."

"What did he say?"

"Why would Arturi direct us towards that possible lead if not to *redirect* attention towards himself as a potential culprit?"

CHAPTER 15: PRESIDENT DE LA RÚA

Sheraton Hotel, Caracas, Tuesday, December 7, 1999, 9:25 AM.

Carlos stared at the beach and the bathers with a distant look. He pondered as he usually did when he was alone, which was most of his life. Especially for a septuagenarian, these introspections in a Caribbean paradise often involved reviewing his past. He had his daiquiri half-finished, with a little umbrella in the glass, and there was also an umbrella over his lounge chair, given how strong the sun was even at that early hour of the morning.

One of the beach waiters approached him with another daiquiri on a tray.

"I didn't order another drink," the septuagenarian in sunglasses snapped.

"Don't worry. This one's on the house. It turns out that the one you were drinking was poisoned, and the Sheraton is offering you another drink for free that isn't. But first, let me swap that glass with cyanide for this one that doesn't have it." The stranger took advantage of the old man's shock to make the switch, carefully picking up the glass he left behind with a cloth napkin.

"What the hell are you talking about?!"

"That drink you were having, sir, I accidentally—or maybe not—poured a lethal dose of potassium cyanide into it. Now, I have here," he pulled out a test tube from his hotel uniform pocket, "blue methylene, effective against potassium cyanide poisoning."

"Give me that!" The septuagenarian tried to snatch the tube, but clearly, the reflexes of the twenty-something were quicker. "Who the hell are you?!"

"I'm the son of Magdalena Schebor. Does my mother's name ring a bell?"

The eyes of the former repressors, architect of countless tortures and disappearances during the previous Uruguayan dictatorship, were the picture of sheer terror.

"Yes, it rings a bell, doesn't it? I had the misfortune of meeting your counterpart from the SIDE who lived in Switzerland, in a little town far from civilization. You haven't called him recently, have you? No, he didn't answer my questions. He preferred military pride over life. Now, I'm giving *you* the chance to live, Carlos Falcone, former director of Punta Carretas Prison, former director of the Political and Social Order Commission (COPS). How original with the initials, right? Like police in English. Who was prisoner 2746?"

"My chest hurts," the septuagenarian instinctively brought a clenched fist to it.

"That's because you're starting to have a heart attack, Mr. Falcone. It's one of the expected consequences of having ingested cyanide," he pointed to the half-finished daiquiri now on his tray with his eyes. "But I'm going to ask you to focus on a couple more questions before I give you the antidote," said the one holding the blue test tube calmly. "Who was prisoner 2746?"

"I added the 2746 to our informants on July 18, 1971, when he was imprisoned in Punta Carretas. I offered him an escape plan for him and all the other damn Tupamaros in exchange for him telling me where they were hiding. He was the first of the informants."

"And why did you let them escape only to catch them later?" The conversation was escalating in speed as one of the two (the one in the robe) was beginning to have a heart attack due to potassium cyanide poisoning.

"It was a strategy to prolong the emergency measures until re institutionalization began... GIVE ME THE DAMN ANTIDOTE, FOR GOD'S SAKE!"

"God? God must not have wanted my mother to flee with me for so many years, pursued by the Army Intelligence Service in Argentina, and for the anguish of keeping that secret to herself to have killed her from cancer later. Look, Falcone, last question and I'll give you the antidote: I have reasons to believe that Francisco Mojica is my father."

"Francisco Mojica had only one son, as far as I know, and he had him with Anab..." The former repressor's eyes rolled back in his head, on the brink of death.

"No. No. No," the twenty-something repeated with the test tube in hand. "The son of a bitch, you son of a bitch!" the doctor yelled, once again breaking his Hippocratic oath, using the knowledge he gained at the University of Buenos Aires to kill the second repressor in his life, without having heard from his victim's lips the name and surname of his biological father (in case it wasn't Mojica, which was also among the possibilities, though the dying man didn't know it). "A doctor! A DOCTOR!! I think he's having a heart attack!!" he howled to the four winds towards the five-star hotel.

Another guest at the Sheraton, a veteran of the Indochina War, a former naval fusilier of the French Navy, now 54 years old, instinctively heard the waiter's cry for help from the deck where she was flirting with a charming Italian of her age, perhaps stoking the coals below the grill, as would be staged on the Río de la Plata for a reconciliation evening with an intimate enemy.

Instinctively, she searched for her daughter among the tables of the deck, and both ran toward the lounge chair the waiter was pointing at. Edith lifted the eyelid of the dying man and saw that he was unresponsive. She followed the first aid steps from the Red Cross and opened the airway. She checked for a pulse by applying her ring and middle fingers to the septuagenarian's neck. There was none. She checked his breathing by placing her cheek over the nostrils of the hotel guest in the robe. No reaction.

"Laet. Get a defibrillator," she asked her daughter. "Starting CPR." The former naval fusilier interlaced her hands, found the space above the second rib, and began chest compressions. "One thousand, two thousand, three thousand, four thousand, five thousand"—she paused to breathe into the old man's mouth—"one thousand, two thousand, three thousand, four thousand, five thousand..."

Fructuoso Pittalluga 6412, Tuesday, July 21, 2009, 6:55 PM

"In the end, we arrived just fine, and we didn't have to exceed the speed limit"—Viktor turned off the rental car in front of the mansion that couldn't cost less than a million and a half dollars. "Wow, wow," he stopped to contemplate the facade. "When I grow up, I want to be president of Uruguay," he joked with his partner.

"Don't kid yourself. Here in Uruguay, a president earns around 8 to 10 thousand dollars a month, which is fine, but it doesn't buy houses like these. The De La Rúa family has been patrician and landowner since the days when we were a colony of the Spanish crown. Shall we announce ourselves?"

"Ladies first."

They were greeted by the butler and a sturdy private security guard. The former announced that De La Rúa hadn't finished his previous meeting yet, and the latter made them leave their weapons on a shelf and scanned them with a portable metal detector. At the appointed hour, the double doors of the former Uruguayan president's study opened, and the newly arrived detectives saw a tall, muscular man with honey-colored eyes and a natural redhead with blue eyes, both dressed in suits and of a similar age to the newcomers.

"Dana, Roger," an elderly voice called from inside, and the tall man and the redhead turned to look. "Be careful. Don't expose yourselves unnecessarily, or your parents will kill me."

"Don't worry. We know where to go and where not to," the slender thirty-something woman smiled as they left.

"Come in, guys," De La Rúa invited with a hand gesture, still seated, jotting something down in his planner. Only when they got closer to his desk did he stand up to reveal a short, stocky sixty-something man with a prominent belly, dark circles under his eyes, and a pronounced double chin. "So, I have the honor of receiving in my home the detectives who solved the Decorator case four years ago," he smiled broadly.

"The pleasure is ours, Mr. President," Geraldine shook his hand.

"Oh, please," he dismissed with a gesture. "Here in my house, you can call me Luis Alberto, or Cuco, as everyone calls me."

"Thank you for making time to assist us with our investigation," the former boxer shook hands.

"What a grip, man! Ouch!" the former president of Uruguay from 1991 to 1995 joked. "Please, have a seat. Would you like a whisky? I was just about to pour myself one."

"Thank you, Luis Alberto," she declined for both, "but we're fine as is."

"Of course, how silly of me. You're working, and I'm not. You're my last interview, and then it's time to eat and sleep because tomorrow will be a tough day." He paused to pour himself a generous glass from a bottle with a glass stopper and cork. "Tell me, how can I help you?"

"Well, as we mentioned over the phone, we were privately hired to investigate the circumstances surrounding Francisco Mojica's death."

"Well, I didn't kill him, that's the first thing I can tell you," he said very seriously, taking a sip of whisky and savoring it like a connoisseur. "I was at a political meeting of my sector, Ruísm, in Soriano, on Saturday night. And if your second question is whether I have the means to hire a hitman to have killed Mojica, yes, I do, but I still have no reason to do so."

"Wow," Goldman was taken aback by such an abrupt start to the interview with the opposition candidate who was leading in the polls among opposition sectors, though his 31% was well below Mojica's 48% in voting intention, "but no one said anyone killed Mojica."

"Yeah, sure, and I'm Tinker Bell. Let me flutter a bit and sprinkle some magic dust to see if you fly too. Come on, kids! No one hires private investigators to look into the 'circumstances' of a myocardial infarction, as the progressive government made public, and as the Forensic Technical Institute confirmed. Is there reason to suspect someone killed Mojica? Sure, but let's be honest with each other, okay?" he insisted more than asked. "And I ask this as the main interested party because the Decorator was the first case of a serial killer in Uruguay, and he was following a pattern, with the ultimate goal of establishing a far-right dictatorship. If the pattern of who killed Mojica is to eliminate the leading presidential candidate to destabilize democracy, now I'm that candidate," he pointed to himself, "especially after what just happened with Huidó. Or why do you think I had to hire a private bodyguard, the one who scanned you with the metal detector when you entered, when I *never* needed or had one, except when I was president? But in Uruguay, the president's bodyguards aren't like in the United States or other countries where they're constantly protecting the life of the leader. Here, bodyguards are mainly to clear a path for the president so he can circulate. When I was president, sometimes everyone would rush up to greet me, shake my hand, take a picture with me... And that was all very nice, but sometimes I had to be somewhere else in 30 minutes, and at one point, the security had to start clearing a path to the car. Or there were times when an unpopular measure had to be implemented because being president is *also* that, and security had to prevent people from rushing me to insult and spit at me. One time, someone even threw a small plastic bottle at me, fortunately."

"We understand your concerns, Luis Alberto," Viktor wanted to be empathetic, who, although it was hard to understand given his solid musculature, was the one who came off best in the duo, "but you don't need to be defensive with us. No one has pointed you out as the prime suspect in Mojica's death."

"Let's say," the conservative candidate exhaled heavily, "but I'm one of those who has the most to gain from Mojica's death, right?"

"One of the," Geraldine pointed out.

"Yeah, of course. When you live a life like Mojica did, enemies spring up like geysers in a park."

"Something like that we've heard from several sources. Wait: you just mentioned 'what just happened with Huidó.' What did you mean by that?"

"Oh, didn't you hear?" the ex-president widened his eyes. "They tried to assassinate him a couple of hours ago when he was arriving at the Legislative Palace after the meeting at the Progressive Front's house."

"No, we honestly haven't heard," the Russian verified. "Could it have been that shot we heard when we were entering the building for our previous interview?" he asked his partner.

"Most likely. I think we'll need to find out the details as a priority. But getting back to you, Luis Alberto, what antagonized you, or did antagonize you, with Mojica?"—the detective always corrected herself when she thought she might have strayed from proper Spanish.

"Does the fact that he kidnapped and killed my father seem like nothing to you, Geraldine?" The atmosphere turned tense and silent for a moment, with the ex-president's gaze fixed on the curly-haired woman.

"We didn't know it was Mojica himself who did it," the aforementioned one excused herself.

"Mojica or the movement he led—what difference does it make to you? But that was 38 years ago," he clicked his tongue. "No one can hold onto that much resentment for so long without self-destructing in the process."

"Did you forgive him then?"

"No," the Conservative leader was emphatic. "I was *never* going to forgive him or his henchmen. Who did those Bolsheviks think they were to take my father from me? What happened over time was that I learned to accept, through therapy with a psychologist, that I couldn't do anything to make the Tupamaros pay for the crimes committed during that time, including my father's murder, who poor man did nothing to become their kidnapping and murder victim other than being a wealthy man. And those lazy good-for-nothings, who spent all day scratching their bellies, drinking wine, and trying to overthrow a democracy with two old rifles, basically needed money to avoid working, just like anyone else. Did I forgive them? *Never*! But I knew how to debate in the Senate with those murderers with respect, with dignity, for the good of Uruguay, and not shout 'sons of bitches' at them during the General Assembly when it was their turn to speak." It took a moment for the politician to calm down. "So, you see: I'm one of those who had reasons, yes, to celebrate with champagne that Mojica is dead, but not enough to order his assassination."

"Okay. We understand your position on that, Luis Alberto," Viktor tried to sound conciliatory. "Now tell us, who else besides you had reasons to hate Francisco Mojica?"

"Ugh. The park of geysers I just mentioned? I hope you don't have anything scheduled for today or tomorrow because the list is long. Let's start with Arturi, who is a very cunning political schemer and will try to take the lead in the new presidential ticket of the Front. Then there's Huidó, who, although he was very close friends with Mojica, is a Tupamaro," he said almost with disgust, "and the Tupamaros only look out for themselves. Moreover, today's assassination attempt could have been an internal reprisal within that movement. Let's continue with the former repressors, the military hierarchy during the dictatorship... But if you want to broaden the search, I'd also include the families of the 66 victims that the Tupamaro guerrilla claimed toward the end of the 60s and the beginning of the 70s. Do you understand that there were extortion kidnappings that ended in murder, like my father's, but there were also many more that had no reason to happen? What do you say about the guy who was waiting at a bus stop and died in the gunfire when they tried to take Pando? And the rural worker who found one of their homemade bombs while working in the fields and was killed? And the *dozens* of police and military officers who were murdered just for wearing a military or police uniform? What guilt did those poor officers have, who barely earn a living coming home after an 8-hour shift at the station or barracks, plus an additional 6 hours covering service 222 at a pharmacy to bring a bit more money to their families, and suddenly these filthy hippies, lazy good-for-nothings, fanatical about Bolshevism, come by and one says to the other, 'Look, there's one in a police uniform; let's kill him?' What sense did those murders make in the grand plan to overthrow a democratic government by force? If I were you and wanted to know who was really behind Mojica's murder, I'd ask for a list of those 66 victims and interview them."

"We'll take note of that, of course. Personal motives take precedence over political ones in a country as mild as Uruguay when it comes to murders," Geraldine reasoned aloud.

"Yeah. Look, I'm going to make a confession, and I hope this doesn't leave this room," De La Rúa lowered his voice to a tone of secrecy and waited for both guests in his home to nod. "When you arrived, the investigators I hired were just leaving. You surely recognized some of your colleagues, I mean... like private detectives."

"That thought crossed my mind," Ielicov acknowledged.

"You can understand that, and I apologize to the gentleman present," he joked as the host of the meeting, "I'm *scared to death* that someone wants to kill me too. So, when Mojica died, and two days later they tried to assassinate Huidó with a bullet, I hired them to find out what the hell is going on here. Should I extend the bodyguard service to my son, who was a deputy in this legislature and, if the polling intention is correct, will be a senator for his list, 400, in the next term? Should I cover my wife and my other two children too? What should I do?" The homeowner looked desperate.

"No preventive measures seem excessive if you can afford them in your current situation," Geraldine replied. "When the Decorator's crimes happened, we *all* underestimated the danger we were in, and many died for that, including my father and brother, and there were three attempts on my own life," she recalled bitterly, one of the main reasons she didn't want to set foot in her homeland again.

"President De La Rúa... Luis Alberto," Ielicov reminded him of the suggested address, more concerned that he knew his partner and associate was about to crumble than for any additional information they might obtain from their interviewee. "We appreciate your time." He stood up to shake hands with the short, stocky sixty-something man with dark circles and a prominent double chin.

As they left, Viktor was hugging Geraldine while they walked toward the car when suddenly they saw it. There was a frog stuck with duct tape on the hood of the rental car. It was still alive. It croaked, trapped by the roll of adhesive tape that could be bought at a hardware store for a hundred pesos.

I"What the hell...?" the heavyweight Russian boxer exclaimed, instinctively reaching for the holster where he kept his gun.

A gunshot rang out nearby. The next thing they knew, where the frog had been taped to the hood, there was now a hole big enough for a finger to fit through, and bits of frog had fallen onto their faces.

"DOWN!" Viktor instinctively shouted, grabbing Geraldine as if she were a FedEx package, and both of them threw themselves to the opposite side of the car from where it seemed the shot had come, all guided purely by instinct about the unmistakable sound. He shielded her in his arms behind the rental car, anticipating one, two, a hundred more shots from the attackers, but what followed the bang was utter silence, occasionally broken by crickets and the not-so-distant sounds of engines on Avenida Italia, the street parallel to Pittalluga, one of the main arteries of Montevideo.

The bodyguard from De La Rúa's residence rushed over, gun in hand, taking cover behind the vehicle as well.

"Are you okay?"

"Yes. Yes. We're fine," Viktor responded after the shock. "It seems to have just been a warning."

"We need to call Toro now!" Geraldine decided, shaking off her own shock. "Toro, Toro, answer, damn it! Oh, hi, yes, Toro. Sorry to bother you at this hour, but it turns out we just got *shot* at in front of De La Rúa's house! Can you please come with the Technical Police to see if they can find out anything about the bullet that was fired at us?!"

Aquí tienes la traducción del fragmento al inglés:

CHAPTER 16: TUPAMARO, POLITICIAN, MURDERER, AND TRAITOR?

Belgrano Avenue 1237, Almagro neighborhood, Buenos Aires, September 4, 2005, 6:05 PM.

"Doctor, your 6 PM appointment just called to cancel. It was the last one of the day. Do you need me to stay for any reason?" —came the voice over the intercom.

"No, thank you, Mary. You can go ahead and leave if there are no other doctors," he replied to the secretary at the private hospital's consulting block, the most expensive in the Argentine Republic.

"There are no others. You were the last one. Rest well, Doctor."

"You too."

"Well, another chapter comes to an end," he vocalized his thoughts, the toxicology expert from the Hospital Italiano, now out of range of the intercom.

The son of a woman persecuted by two dictatorships, the Argentine and the Uruguayan, and a Tupamaro traitor responsible for his mother's death, gathered his personal belongings into his backpack: his cup, his thermos, his mate, the fake photo in the frame, his toothbrush and comb in the attached bathroom to his office, took a spray bottle with 70% alcohol, and spent the next half hour diligently erasing any trace that he had ever been there. Fingerprints on the intercom, the phone, the taps on the bathroom sink, the desk, the keyboard, and the mouse. Gone. The same with the toilet lid, the door handle, both the outside and the inside, and the filing cabinet... everything would disappear. He took one last look at his office in the expensive private Argentine hospital, pleased with the result.

He walked, unhurried, toward the director's office, always open by the policy of the occupant of the luxurious office. He knocked the doorframe with a smile.

"Walter, got a minute?"

"Yeah, yeah. Come in, Fer. What brings you to my office?"

"Today's my last day at the hospital, Walter."

"I can't believe it! How the hell did I miss that?! I'm the saddest fool in the world, Fer. I would've thrown you a farewell party. It's the least you deserve for your outstanding service at this hospital."

"Relax, man. I know you've got a lot on your plate," smiled the thirty-something.

"I can't even begin to believe it's been two weeks since you told us you were leaving."

"What can I say?" the doctor shrugged. "Time flies. Listen, I just came to say goodbye and thank you for having me here at the hospital you run for the last four years. Honestly, the experience I gained here was *invaluable*. But I need to take a sabbatical to take care of my mom, you know?"

"Of course. How is she doing?"

"Well, she's got stage 3 cancer. I'm not an oncologist, but I'm the only child she has, so going to Chile and being by her side is the least I can do, right?" he faked a bitter, pained expression in front of his boss.

"Of course, my son!" The director of the private clinic stood up. "I wish you the best, for both you and your mom, okay?"

"Thanks, Walter. It's been a real pleasure working here. Listen, I already sent the email to IT security to revoke my access, and to HR so they can send me my settlement when they can, no rush."

"See you, Fer. Take care!" The director said with an affectionate hug and a pat on the back.

The man who was *not* born with the surname Ortega nor used his name in any of the identities he had assumed during his life as a fugitive, but kept the pattern of starting all his false first names with "F" so he could respond when someone called him, left his magnetic card at the security booth and signed the handover. *More DNA, more fingerprints, and more traces that I won't be able to erase*, he thought bitterly as he hailed the first taxi with the flag up. *But let CSI Miami follow me if they want.*

His mother, Magdalena Schebor, had taught him how to assume new identities when both were fleeing persecution from the Argentine dictatorship. The first step was to secure fake papers, because one can't go through life without documents. Whether for a routine check by the authorities or to rent a room, open a bank account, you *always* needed some kind of identification.

For several years after the dictatorship ended in 1983, Magdalena and her son, whom she affectionately called "Bicho," (Bug), continued to use the last fake name they had adopted. But when the young man finally gained admission to the Faculty of Medicine, they decided it was time to return to their *real* names. For this, they traveled to Uruguay, reported their lost documents at the police station (they certainly wouldn't say they had burned them to prevent the military repression from finding them, right?), and went to the Ministry of the Interior to obtain new ID cards and passports.

However, the place they chose to live was not their homeland, but the Argentine Republic, where the young man enrolled at the University of Buenos Aires, thanks to an agreement between both countries on higher education at public universities. Everything changed when his mother died of cancer, and with the confession she made to him before she passed away.

A deep, *ingrained* hatred was born in the young man, then in his third year of medicine at UBA. When he wasn't studying or working to support himself, being his own financial support, and even *during* those activities, he was planning his revenge on the Tupamaro who had betrayed his own, the one who had planted the seed that led to his mother's cancer. But without the name, who would know who it was?

It took him several years, already working as a medical professional and studying for his master's degree in toxicology, to track down that alleged traitor and confront him, after studying his movements for several weeks in Madrid. He then took a low-paying, tip-based temporary job at Café del Prado, where he had the conversation with Amadeo Píriz. But it turned out that the man everyone pointed to as the traitor was *not* the one. He pointed the finger in two directions: at those who had accused Píriz of being the traitor within their ranks and at the heads of the repression.

But it wasn't him who went to Madrid. He already had the mechanics of obtaining fake documents down to a science.

It took him *years* of further investigation, now working as a professional in his specialty, toxicology, always accumulating more capital, always focused on his revenge, to track down Carlos Falcone, the former head of Uruguay's anti-subversive repression, in Camboriú. But he missed him that time. Months earlier, the former director of the COP had been tracked down by both the press and Uruguayan authorities and had to disappear once more. So, who could possibly know where he was?

The former director of Argentina's SIDE, Oscar Newell, was a pretty solid lead to find Falcone. Fortunately for the toxicologist, Newell had a biographical book with a passing detail that turned out to be *crucial* for locating him. In his book El Gato, named after the nickname Newell was given by his subordinates, by Juan

Carlos Denegri, the military officer suffered from a rare syndrome affecting the immune system: Hyper-IgM Syndrome. This genetic disorder is characterized by a deficiency in the production of IgG and IgA antibodies, though IgM levels are usually elevated. This makes individuals more susceptible to infections.

The key piece of information, though not clarified in the book because it wasn't the focus of the story—rather, it concerned the nefarious way the man operated—was that the treatment for the symptoms required Intravenous Immunoglobulin (IVIG) to help raise antibody levels and reduce infection frequency, prophylactic antibiotics to prevent recurrent bacterial infections, being up to date with vaccinations, and, in severe cases, a bone marrow transplant from a compatible donor.

It was through the intravenous immunoglobulin that he located him, because, of course, it wasn't something you could buy in a pharmacy, and not all hospitals or clinics provided it. By cross-referencing air travel records of the retired officer's children, he also paid a substantial sum to an employee at a travel agency to extract from the Sabre booking system the flight tickets purchased by Newell's children over the past five years.

But the Argentine torturer didn't know who the traitor Tupamaro was either. Only his alias, 2746. However, with the phone number for Falcone in Chile, it was easier to track him down. Again, he had missed him, though only temporarily this time. The neighbors on his street in Pueblo Hundido, located in the Elqui Valley, knew he had gone to spend three weeks at the Sheraton in Caracas. The neighbors were a great source of information, indeed! He found it strange that both Newell and Falcone chose hiding places with a good view of the permanent snow-capped mountain peaks. Maybe the view cleared their minds from the horrors they had caused throughout their lives.

Once at the Sheraton, it was easy for him to steal a beach waiter's uniform from the staff locker room and interrogate Falcone, but he miscalculated the dose. Potassium cyanide wasn't supposed to kill him *that* quickly. It had to be fast enough so he couldn't alert anyone, but not so fast as to prevent him from revealing his father's identity. Still, he managed to extract one key piece of information: that Mojica had had an unacknowledged child with someone named "Anab..." Anabel, no doubt. He recalled an Anabel from the books about the Tupamaros he had read, and it quickly became clear that Mojica's unacknowledged child was Anabel Pulansky's son. He *had* to contact him.

So, that winter morning in late 2005, he left the few belongings he had packed the night before in his suitcase. The night before, he had also carefully cleaned his traces, hairs in the drain, sanitized all the surfaces with 70% alcohol, leaving only his bed and bathroom for the next day. He placed the "Please clean the room" sign on the door handle, left the apartment keys with the doorman, and went to work at the Hospital Italiano as if it were any other day.

In the afternoon, he only entered to ensure that the room had indeed been cleaned by the hotel maids. He took his suitcases while the taxi waited downstairs, then instructed the driver to take him to the Buquebus ferry terminal. He had his tickets and the fake documents he had arranged, including a passport with several (also fake) entry and exit stamps from various countries, and this time he had also had the forger make medical diplomas identical to the ones he had legitimately obtained at the University of Buenos Aires, but with his new identity. He had hired four actors who would speak *wonders* about his work as a toxicology doctor, posing as directors of hospitals in both Argentina and Chile, in case anyone called to verify his references. After all, he needed to make a living while completing his revenge. Plus, some poisons and toxins *are* expensive.

First stop: to get in touch with Facundo, Anabel Pulansky's son and the ex-Tupamaro Francisco "Pancho" Mojica. He thought about this as he boarded the ferry traveling from Puerto Madero on the Argentine coast to Colonia del Sacramento on the Uruguayan coast. Would the young man, who was around his age, know that Mojica was his father? Would they be half-siblings on their father's side? Just because Falcone had known about *one* of Mojica's unacknowledged children didn't mean he was the *only one*, of course.

Kiosk "La Ronda", north side of Cagancha Square, Wednesday, July 22, 2009, 7:03 AM

Horacio had been the owner of the newsstand for 6 years, but the gradual digitalization of the media had made the "accessory" part of his business—the cigarettes, sweets, and soft drinks—become his main product. Still, there were people who enjoyed reading the printed newspaper, and of course, gossip magazines were timeless, as were crossword puzzles and similar games, a classic that never seemed to disappear.

That particular morning, around 5:30 AM, when the dawn was still a faint light to the east against the darkness of the night, the delivery truck for the morning newspapers dropped off *five times* as many copies of 'El País'. He immediately told the deliveryman, "Hey, man, I think you got the quantity wrong," to which the deliveryman replied with a smile, "Oh, yeah? Check the front page. These are on consignment, so if you don't sell them, they get recycled. Trust me, Horacio, you're gonna wish I brought *ten times* more."

All morning, Horacio had seen the same stunned expressions on the faces of early risers in Montevideo, and even some late-night partygoers, who, seeing the cover photo of 'El País' and the headlines in huge print, stopped by the kiosk to catch a preview of the front-page story. Indeed, the deliveryman hadn't been wrong: that day, he was going to make a good sum from the sale of those copies.

But the look on the elegant, curly-haired brunette's face in a navy-blue suit wasn't just one of shock—it was more like...

"Wait, young lady." —As best as he could, he managed to catch the private detective before she collapsed from the shock. "Are you alright?"

"Yes. Yes... I think so. I can't believe this information!" —She pointed to the cover of 'El País'.

"And yet, here it is," —Horacio smiled as, once the thirty-something woman steadied herself, he let go of her. "Are you going to take one?"

"Yes, of course," —Geraldine, now somewhat recovered, picked up a copy of each newspaper, including, of course, 'El País', just as she used to do when she was Head of Press for the National Police of Uruguay. She paid the newsstand owner, walked briskly to the three-star hotel they usually demanded (and often as a maximum, depending on the client), and found Viktor having coffee at the Hotel Emperador's bar.

"Vik, I think we have a problem," —She placed the 'El País' newspaper on the table.

"Don't mess with me!" —The former Russian boxer split the words. "But... and this..."

A text message notification sounded on the detective's phone. While working a case, she silenced non-urgent notifications like WhatsApp or emails, but calls and SMS *had* a ringtone. She checked her phone. The SMS came from a saved number.

Anahí

"Did you see the cover of 'El País', friend? If Shakira sang 'my argument is running out, and the methodology,' then my scenarios and contingency plans are finished. Any comments, or help you could give me, would be super helpful. I feel like a tsunami is coming and I don't even have a surfboard, nor do I know how to surf. I love you, Geral. Kisses."

Geral

"Good morning, Anahí. I *literally* just saw it 6 minutes ago. Viktor and I are about to head to the Parachutists' Battalion 14 in Toledo, but I'll think of something on the way and let you know. Kisses to you too."

"This has De La Rúa's signature and stamp on it, I can assure you," —she said after sending the text.

"Wow. And why is that?" —Her partner asked.

"El País belongs to the Conservative Party. They don't have a direct relationship, but it's *well known* from my days as Head of Press at the police that the newspaper supports the Conservative Party. Come on, darling, I don't think we have time to wait for the car rental place to open to get a replacement car. It's going to have to be a taxi. Using the corporate card Mr. Reno gave us." —She smiled as she showed it to him.

The night before had been long for both of them. Fructuoso Pittalluga, in front of 6412, had quickly become surrounded by police cars, a private car from Toro, another from Di Lorenzo, and the Technical Police mobile unit, in order of arrival. The forensic investigation was quick, and the officers in blue tried to keep the curious away. Even the former president showed up at the scene of the "frog crime," as the police officers started jokingly calling it. By following the trajectory of the bullet entering the rental car's hood, it was determined that the shot had come from the roof of a two-story house that was for sale on the block—that is, it was unoccupied.

It was clearly a warning to the detectives. They were getting too close in their investigation to something the killer didn't want them to know, and perhaps the next shot wouldn't be at a frog taped to the hood, but at their heads...

For safety's sake, they needed to check whether there was another taxi driver in Montevideo, besides the one who had taken them to the new location of the Forensic Technical Institute, who spoke Russian.

"Vy gavoríte pa-rússki?" —Viktor asked.

"Sorry, what did you just say to me?"

"Nothing. I was just asking if you spoke Russian."

"Oh no. I barely speak any Spanish, just enough to get by, and a bit of Portuñol," —The taxi driver smiled through the rearview mirror.

"Well, let's get organized," —Viktor joked in Russian to his partner. Amazingly, or perhaps not so surprisingly, given the times of the 21st century, Viktor and Geraldine had never formalized their relationship. They had never married, which, given that she was an ex-very Orthodox Jew and he was an atheist, would have been unusual, except through a civil ceremony.

"This front-page photo changes everything, don't you agree?"

"First call of the day: De La Rúa" —connecting action to words, as the taxi drove along Bulevar Artigas towards the monument colloquially known by Montevideans as "The Horns of Batlle," but which was, or was intended to be in the minds of their creators, a representation of the raised arms in a V-shape, the classic gesture of greeting to the crowd from the former Uruguayan president. Geraldine took her phone and dialed the mobile of the former president of the Conservative Party, whom they had interviewed just before being "warned" to stay out of the case.

"Good morning, Luis Alberto. I hope I didn't wake you up."

"No way!" —replied the former president and serious contender for a new mandate—. "The old ones wake up early. How can I help you, Geraldine?"

"Well, this morning I went to the kiosk, as I do every day, and I came across a *very peculiar* photo on the cover of 'El País'. By any chance, have you seen it?"

"I don't need to, Geraldine. I was the one who gave them that photo to publish."

For a moment, Viktor was concerned about his partner's state, but then the pale-skinned woman with jet-black eyes regained her composure.

"And I wonder, Cuco" —she recalled the nickname by which everyone knew the Conservative Party's presidential candidate—, "why didn't you mention the existence of that photo yesterday when we were at your house?"

"I thought it wasn't relevant. Besides, 'El País' finishes printing at 6 p.m. What could I know about the assassination attempt that was going to happen at 6:15 against Huidó? It was an unfortunate coincidence, that's all I can say. If I had known they were going to shoot him, of course, I would have held onto that photo to publish it later. What would I gain by putting him in the spotlight while he's fighting for his life in intensive care?"

"So, you admit that you released that photo for electoral campaign purposes, right?"

"Of course! Listen, Geraldine, every candidate does what they can to get votes, right? Those are the rules of the game. Call it dirty campaigning, call it putting someone in their rightful place in history, but I'm playing with the cards that the dealer gave me, okay?"

"But nobody is blaming you for how clean or dirty your campaign is, Luis Alberto. All I want to know is how—you—got—that—photo." —she separated the words with precision, almost five languages in her speech, and "almost" because her Mandarin was probably only good enough for ordering food and asking where certain places were.

"Uuuuh..." —the politician dragged the sound—. "The story is long, but I'll try to summarize it the best I can. In my first year as president, in '91, it was the second democratic term for us after the dictatorship, and the transition of power from Dr. Zanetti to me had been carried out with complete normalcy. But in Argentina, they had already faced two armed uprisings after the return of democracy, and many officers from the dictatorship era held key positions in the armed forces. I had to go over there to show Uruguay's support for the democratic stability of our neighbor."

"I see. And the photo?"

"Well, here's where it gets interesting. One of the people we had to visit with Carlos Saúl... with President Hernem, I mean, was the *most unpleasant* person I've ever met, the Director of Army Intelligence, General Oscar Newell, who had been in that position since before the dictatorship and continued afterward. The meeting was within expectations, meaning: aside from having a torturer and a person responsible for disappearances in front of us who showed no remorse for everything they did and ordered to be done during the dictatorship, he assured us that the SIDE would respect democratic institutions and that he didn't know of any plans to overthrow Hernem's government. But he warned us he would retire the following year, so he couldn't answer for his successor in the position."

"Wow. I suppose that didn't leave you feeling very secure."

"Maybe a 6, let's say, on a scale of 1 to 10. The issue is that as we were leaving, he asked to speak with me privately. In short, he told me that with his military pension and some savings, and I was thinking to myself, 'Some? They stole even *our will to eat* during the dictatorship, those sons of bitches,' he thought he was going to have a good life once he retired, but that he had this photo that might interest me or my party, and he was willing to sell it for a quarter of a million dollars. I told him that, of course, we'd be interested in acquiring the original photo to use it when we saw fit. I asked him who gave it to him, and he said it was his Uruguayan counterpart from that era, Inspector Carlos Falcone. So, I talked it over with the party leadership, we gathered the money, and I was entrusted with the custody of the original Polaroid. Since then, it's been sitting in my safe... until now. Look, Geraldine, what that photo shows is what it shows. And if there's one thing the Law of

Expiry tried to enforce, with more or less success, it's the need to investigate the crimes committed by *both* sides, the military *and* the Tupamaros. Now, if the repeal passes and we can also prosecute the military for crimes against humanity, that's another matter. But this information sheds light on who one of our main opponents in this election was."

"I understand. Thank you for your time, Luis Alberto."

"Anytime, Geraldine." —the former president ended the call.

"Not a single regret, huh? What did he say about how he got the photo?" —Viktor asked, still speaking Russian between them.

"Not at all regretful," —she told him where the photo had come from—. "We need to notify Toro about this."

"I'm with you on that," —Viktor agreed—, "but let me be the one to call Toro." —and he dialed the number on his phone—. "Toro, I hope I didn't wake you up at this hour."

"No. Not at all! I've been awake for a while now. What's going on, Viktor?"

"Have you seen the cover of 'El País' this morning?"

"No. Not at all. I don't read the papers until I get to the Central Police Headquarters at 8."

"Well, here's the thing: There's a photo on the front page, and it shows Senator Huidó in 1971 pointing a gun at the head of 'Vasco' Olavarría, the first Tupamaro detainee-disappeared, even before the dictatorship, and there's a police officer in the frame watching as Huidó was about to execute his Tupamaro comrade."

"What?!" "*Guatafac!*" —as the younger generation now says.

"You're hearing it. The big headline reads: Eleuterio Hernando Huidó: Tupamaro, politician, murderer, and traitor?"

"They're going to lynch him, once he comes out of the coma."

"That's our fear too. Maybe it's wise to relocate him to a hospital where his safety can be guaranteed. I think there's one, the

Military Hospital, which is little more than a fortress, with guards carrying machine guns and all that, right?"

"Yes, that seems the most appropriate. I'll hang up now and start organizing the police escort and everything."

"One more thing, Toro."

"You name it, Viktor."

"Are the full reports on the shooting of Huidó and the frog ready?"

"They must be, I suppose. Yesterday I asked De Paolillo from the Tech Department not to leave until he sent everything to me by email, so I'll open my inbox and if it's not there, Ariel *will be* in trouble."

"Poor Ariel, he must *hate* you."

"No way! He loves me! That guy likes overtime more than milk caramel." —joked the seasoned cop.

"Okay, can you forward it to our email as soon as you can?"

"Sure."

"And one last thing. What we talked about yesterday, if you'll be joining us on the helicopter trip. We're requesting the helicopter to land at Battalion 14 of the Parachutists' in Toledo at 8:30. We have an interview with Menini Ruiz at 8. From there, we'll fly direct to Paysandú. Do you and Di Lorenzo think you'll make it?"

"As if we had any other more important case right now. Ha. Don't worry, we'll make it."

"Last thing, and I won't bother you anymore."

"A *lot* of last things, Viktor. Shoot" —Villa joked, maybe pushing the boundaries of dark humor, closer to charcoal.

"Can you bring us bulletproof vests for Geral and me?"

"Sure. Your size will be tricky, Viktor, but I'll see what I can do."

"Thanks, Toro. See you there, at the battalion." —he ended the call and switched back to Russian to talk to Geraldine. "Do you think half an hour will be enough with the general?"

"I suspect it will be. Also, if the pilot has to wait a little, remember that we asked for the Secretary of the Presidency for the whole morning. How fast do you think that helicopter will go?"

"I'm sure it exceeds 200 km/h. I'd say in less than two hours we'll be in Pulansky's ranch in Paysandú."

"Great. Let me see if Hernández gave me the contact of our pilot." —she searched her WhatsApp—. "Here it is. What efficiency."

"Well, if you think you get to be the Secretary of the President by being careless or forgetful."

"Hello, are you Captain D'Amore?"

"Affirmative." —the martial voice on the other end replied.

"I'm Geraldine Goldman. The Secretary of the Presidency, Gonzalo Hernández, gave me your contact, and I'm sure he already informed you that we'll need your helicopter today."

"Affirmative. Can I know where we're headed?"

"Yes, you may. But please only share it with essential people. First, we'll need you to pick us up at Battalion 14 of the Parachutists in Toledo at 8:30. Then we'll head to Paysandú."

"Paysandú city or the Department?"

"The Department, near the town of Quebracho. I'd say about 3 or 4 kilometers away."

"Do you have a moment to check the map?"

"Yes, of course. Take your time."

"I've got it." —the pilot informed after about a minute and a half—. "The fuel tank is good for a direct flight, and the Paysandú Airport is about 20 or 30 kilometers from there. We'll make it fine, if we fly at cruising speed. But we'll need to refuel in Paysandú for the return."

"No problem with that. Actually, you might even be able to refuel while we're at our delivery point near Quebracho. Do you need to give prior notice to the battalion that you're coming?"

"No need. It's the presidential helicopter. Just a radio announcement when I'm about to land will suffice."

"Better, impossible! Thank you, Captain D'Amore. We'll see you at Battalion 14, at 8:30. Please be punctual."

"Affirmative. D'Amore out."

"D'Amore out?" —Geraldine wondered, after ending the call.

"Professional deformation, I guess." —Viktor shrugged, since the call had been over the phone line, not on a VHF radio.

"Sir, how much longer until we reach our destination?" —Geraldine asked to the taxi driver.

"Five... ten minutes, more or less."

"Thanks." —and she switched from Spanish to Russian—. "I've got time to call Anahí. Poor girl. I wouldn't want to be in her shoes right now."

"I remind you that *you've been there before*, and that time was much worse."

"Well... yes... a little bit, I'll admit it." —she had to concede. "Hello, Anahí. I can imagine what you must be going through. How are you, my friend?" —Geraldine initiated the call.

"Hey, Geral. Well, look: I've had worse days." —replied the current Head of Press at the National Police.

"Really?!"

"No way! I think I was trying to convince myself of that. Look: yesterday when you came to visit me, I was calm, painting my nails, thinking I had everything under control, paying attention to the media fallout from Mojica's death, and suddenly, in the span of... what was it? Twelve hours? They shoot Huidó, who's now in a coma, there's a shootout in front of former President De La Rúa's house..."

"Oh, but you're exaggerating! A shootout? There was *one* shot, and no one was hurt, just a frog and the engine block of a rental car."

"Yeah, sure. Tell that to the neighbors who gave their version to the news crews after you guys left. A little more and they'd have said it was two armies fighting for hours, with mortars and bazookas raining down everywhere. And today, that cover in 'El País', showing Huidó in a color photo executing José 'el Vasco' Olavarría in '71, in collaboration with the cops? I'm at my limit, Geral. *Seriously*. I don't even know where to start, and the press conference is in a bit, at 10."

"Well, that's exactly why I was calling you, Anahí. First: breathe."

"I'm breathing, but I get what you mean. Tell me."

"First things first: separate and conquer. Separate one fact from another, okay?"

"Separate. Got it."

"Mojica? Stick to your initial statement: the autopsy revealed he died from a myocardial infarction, as confirmed by the Forensic Technical Institute."

"Got it."

"Moving along the timeline, Huidó was *indeed* targeted for assassination at the Legislative Palace. It's an ongoing investigation, we can't reveal details, and everything you already know, but we *do have* a ballistic report, and we know where the sniper shot from. The police is deploying sufficient resources to catch the shooter. They'll try to corner you with a loaded question: 'Doesn't it sound like too much of a coincidence that the two top leaders of the Popular Movement, the largest sector within the party with almost 48% voter intent heading into the October presidential election, either died or were targeted for assassination with only a 72-hour gap?' They're trying to create the perception that the National Police is *withholding* information from the public, of course."

"Which, in fact, *it is* the case."

"But the press doesn't have proof, dear. What you answer is, if the question comes from Sergio at Channel 4, you respond: 'A real coincidence would be if the color of your tie, for once in your life, matched the rest of what you're wearing, but I don't judge how people dress,' and then you shrug. And if it's not Sergio asking, you say: 'A real coincidence would've been if Sergio...' Do you follow me? Anyway, you respond seriously after distracting everyone and generating some laughter, saying that if anyone has *any useful information* to provide regarding the investigation into the attempted murder of Huidó, they should do so through the usual channels, either by approaching the police station or calling 911, *including* the press. Oh, and emphasize the "useful," because otherwise you'll just be giving the poor 911 operators a headache with calls like, "My neighbor wasn't home yesterday at 6 PM and he talks badly to me when we cross paths in the hallway," or "My neighbor has a hunting shotgun, and I always told him that weapons are the devil's work," and that sort of thing.

"I got it,"—the one with the metal subcutaneous plate replacing part of her skull wrote frantically.

"As for the famous 'shooting' on Pittalluga Street, it was a neighbor cleaning his gun, who deeply regrets his recklessness and offered to pay for the repairs to the vehicle for the damages caused."

"Wow! Have you ever considered becoming a novelist? You'd be really good. What creativity!"

"Thank you, thank you, *two thousand* thanks"—the Communications and International Relations Licensed, who was almost a Penta lingual... closer to four and a third languages, rephrased and adapted an old sketch by Les Luthiers. "As for the cover of 'El País', that's the easiest part."

"Don't-you-dare!"—separating the words, the current Head of Press exclaimed.

"Wasn't it going to be? Let's assume Huidó *did kill* José Olavarría in 1971, as the photo suggests. It's a common crime, not a crime against humanity, because by definition, what separates one from the other is the seriousness and scope: crimes against humanity are serious human rights violations committed systematically and widely against a civilian population, such as genocide, torture, slavery, or mass killings. Common crimes, on the other hand, usually involve individual or isolated offenses that don't have the same societal impact. Did Huidó kill Olavarría or not? It's a common crime between civilians. It expires after 25 years, meaning it expired 13 years ago. So, here's your golden nugget, which you'll need to coordinate with the 'Toro' from Homicides in advance: you're going to redirect the suspicion towards 'El País' personnel. Ask the journalist they sent how many people in the 'El País' newsroom had access to that photo and information *prior* to the attempt on Senator Huidó's life, and with whom they might have shared it, which could have led someone to commit the assassination attempt. And by the way, let them know that a team from Investigations and Homicides is interrogating *every single staff member* from the paper while you're talking."

"Oh... you're wicked, Geral. That's why the coordination with the 'Toro' from Homicides. Got it. Perfect. Everything's written down. Now I'll put it together. Are *you* alright?"

"Yeah, I'm fine. On my way to meet with General Menini Ruiz. Oh, one more thing: when you talk to Villa, he's going to need to relocate Huidó, even if he's in a coma, to another location. We've suggested the Military Hospital. Remember the distraction we used when we had to move Minister Cortez out of Central Command discreetly?"

"How could I forget? The best over-the-top performance of our lives."

"Great. Offer the same thing to 'Toro', for when they move Huidó out in the ambulance."

"Got it."

"We've arrived"—the taxi driver reported.

CHAPTER 17: GENERAL MENINI RUIZ

14^{*th*} *Parachutists' Battalion, Toledo, Canelones Department, Wednesday, July 22, 2009, 7:57 AM*

The guard at the entrance booth to the battalion took their names, their documents, and indicated that they could wait next to the booth while the morning inspection of the troops was underway. Just over 100 soldiers were lined up in two rows, facing each other in the large front area of the battalion, while a sixty-something man with a severe face and below-average height for a Uruguayan man walked along, inspecting each one individually, very much in the style of Darth Vader—just to clarify, for anyone familiar with the 'Star Wars' analogy.

Ignoring the newcomers next to the booth, the General stopped beside one of his subordinates and grabbed the collar of his shirt.

"This uniform is worn out!" he shouted. "It's a *disgrace* to the military institution! Change it, soldier."

"Yes, General!" the soldier shouted back.

"I never understood why the military yells at each other," Geraldine whispered to her partner.

"I always attributed it to them having bad hearing," he joked, and they both restrained themselves from bursting into laughter, which would have ruined the mood.

The General continued his troop inspection, and one of the soldiers was sweating despite the cold winter weather, feeling how a liquid snot was threatening to escape from his nose and run down to his lip. He had no choice: he couldn't break the "at attention" position or pull out a tissue to blow his nose. So, he opted to "roll" the snot, that is, inhale violently to pull the mucus back into his nostrils.

The sound gave him away.

"Who was that?!"

"Me, General," the soldier admitted regretfully.

"Soldier. Are you sick?"

"I have a bit of a cold, General."

"Then you're going on medical leave immediately! Medical leave. That's an order! I don't want you infecting the rest of the troops!"

"But... they'll deduct the days from my pay," the giant soldier pleaded, reminding his superior that, as in any public or private employment in Uruguay, the first 3 days of certified medical leave are deducted from the employee's salary. The remaining days, if any, are reimbursed later by social security.

"Then let's do this," the General snapped, stepping closer to his face. "You'll go straight to the battalion doctor to get certified, and when you return from your medical leave, you'll sign a one-week unpaid suspension for insubordination, and you'll serve two months of strict weekend detention. Was I clear, soldier?"

"Yes, General!" the enlisted man replied with a salute.

"Good. That's all for today! Rest—NOW!" the order howled, and the soldiers relaxed from their rigid posture to go about their usual duties. Menini Ruiz walked toward the newly arrived private detectives, but instead of greeting them with his hand as usual, he stood a few steps away, eyeing them with what seemed like disdain, and simply said: "Goldman. Ielicov. Come with me." He turned on his heels in front of the stunned visitors, walking at a brisk pace toward the central building of the battalion.

"I think he forgot to finish with 'Please join me,'" Viktor joked, keeping up with the energetic sixty-something's rapid pace.

"What happened to basic host etiquette?" Geraldine agreed.

"He's probably treating us like that in front of the troops so they don't see his leadership as weak," he hypothesized.

"And you think that when we're alone in his office, he becomes a nice guy? I don't think so," she said sarcastically, both whispering, though they could have spoken in a normal tone given the General's lightning-fast stride.

After passing through hallways and stairs, they arrived at a prominent-looking office with a double wooden door, unnecessarily 4.5 meters high. Were they made for giants of the mountains? There was, however, a waiting room before the double doors. The person sitting at the desk stood to greet his superior with a salute.

"Lieutenant Barrios," Menini said after returning the salute. "Seize the cell phones and weapons of these two, frisk them for microphones, and then use the electronic body scanner to check them for bugs."

"Understood, General."

"Hey!" Geraldine protested indignantly.

"They'll either let themselves be searched, or there won't be an interview," the officer glared furiously at her, and entered his office, leaving the right door ajar.

"I have my orders," the personal secretary shrugged with a grimace. "So... do you give me your phones, your weapons, and let yourselves be searched, or are you not going to meet with the General? You decide."

"I can't believe this shit," she muttered to Viktor in Russian, placing her Beretta 9mm and her Nokia N97 on the desk. She waited for Viktor to do the same, then raised her arms to submit to the frisk. "With respect," she warned the army officer in Spanish,

"No buttocks, no pubis, no breasts," and switched to Russian: "Asking for a female officer to frisk me would be too much, wouldn't it?"

"Try to chew and swallow your anger, my love," he replied in Russian. "The information the General might provide could be key to the investigation. Look, it's like the one we have in our bag," Viktor pointed to the electronic bug detector.

"Yes. We need to replace it. There are better ones made in Sweden, at reasonable prices."

"Alright. You can go in," Barrios informed them.

"Close the door," Menini ordered when he saw them enter. His desk was on the right side of the large room with high ceilings, facing the large windows that looked out onto the massive front yard of the battalion, the size of four professional soccer fields.

Viktor couldn't help but notice the thickness of the door, and the fact that the interior was lined with red upholstery, like a cinema's soundproof room. *So, no sounds come out of here*, he thought. *Smart*. He decided to start the interrogation himself to give his partner time to calm down from her indignation.

"Is it just me, or do you have a very high level of paranoia about this meeting?"

"Take a seat," Menini gestured.

"And 'please'?" the former Russian boxer said sarcastically.

"Please take a seat. Happy?"

"Thanks. Now we're good," Viktor replied, and both sat in the armchairs across from the large, old oak desk.

The General, in charge of the battalion, had his lips turned downward, which, for a normal person—though what's normal and what isn't is debatable—would require *a lot* of facial muscle effort. But the soldier seemed to have the corners of his lips pointing downward by nature, and when he spoke, they pointed downward too, giving him the look of a bulldog, making everything he said sound like he was ordering a witch to be burned at the stake.

"It's not paranoia. It's pure common sense and survival instinct. They called me earlier to say you were coming on behalf of Senator Huidó and what topics you'd be discussing, and I don't want *anything* I say here to be saved on any physical or digital medium, and then used against me in the press."

"Is it so important to you what the press knows about what you say or what you know?" Geraldine asked.

"Of course! Do you know the Lodge of the Lieutenants of Artigas?"

"Only by name. Some group of soldiers, or something like that, right?"

"The Lodge of the Lieutenants of Artigas, to which I belong, is the political arm of the Armed Forces. Without being a political force, we have more access and we're more listened to by politicians."

"I see. So that's why you were chosen as the future Commander-in-Chief of the Armed Forces, had Mojica won and Huidó become Minister of Defense. Did I understand that right?" the detective asked. "You're military lobbyists, in other words."

"I don't know what you mean by 'lobbyists.'"

"They're people who negotiate the interests of a power group with politicians, making sure the laws they need or that benefit the group they represent get passed," Ielicov explained.

"Yes, you could say that," the military officer agreed.

"When did you arrive at Battalion 14?" Geraldine continued.

"On November 18th, 1974, I graduated from the Army's School of Arms and Specialties with a degree in History, and I was assigned to Battalion 14."

"You're a historian? Wow, how fascinating, because that's *exactly* what we'll be discussing. But first, I'd like to ask you something: I think I already know the answer before I ask, but I have to ask it anyway, as there seem to be two main schools of thought among those we've interviewed. School number one, which is the majority, claims that in Uruguay there was a coup d'état, a brutal repression against those who thought differently, torture, disappearances, and murders by the state apparatus, mostly carried out by the military and police, a systematic violation of human rights, etc. School number two claims that the only ones who killed were the members of the Tupamaro guerrilla, that the Armed Forces were rightfully called upon by President Borderragui, in accordance with the Constitution, to restore order to the country. Then, the next president, whom no one had voted for, I might add, continued asking them to stay in charge and maintain order, and then the next one, and so on, for twelve years. Which line of thought do you lean toward?"

"Number two, clearly."

"Bingo! I *knew* I was going to get it right even before asking."

"And as a graduate in History, I *have* my reasons. Those who think differently don't."

"And what would those be?"

"History is based on narratives, true, but above all on scientifically verifiable facts. Let me give you three very basic examples that I always used when I was promoted to Sergeant Major and started teaching recruits. Example number one: the Trojan War. If you read the 'Iliad', it's a lovely narrative, but just a narrative in the end. You find gods interacting and fighting among mortals on both sides, the Greeks and the Trojans, love stories, and a bunch of nonsense with *zero* historical value. But if you look at a map, you'll see that the city of Troy controlled the Dardanelles Strait, which connects the Aegean Sea with the Sea of Marmara. This strait was a crucial trade and navigation route in ancient times, allowing access between the Mediterranean and the Black Sea through the Bosphorus. Troy, being located near this strait, held a strategically important position. *That's* why the Greeks wanted it, not because of Helen of Troy, if she ever existed! Example number two: the idea that the indigenous peoples of northern South America and Central America, like the Incas, Mayans, and Aztecs, were cultured and civilized peoples, and that the Europeans who conquered them were barbarians. I don't know where that belief or those stories came from. Now, they were cultured, yes. They had solar clocks that could tell time with a precision of five minutes, *centuries* before mechanical clocks were invented in Europe, and they had a perfect calendar based on lunar cycles and solstices, while in Europe they barely knew if it was winter or summer by the temperature. But in terms of savagery, there's *ample* scientific evidence to prove that they killed each other savagely, sacrificed their enemies in temples, and were capable of genocide in their conquests, long before the Armenian genocide or the Holocaust of the Jewish people. So, to those hippies with long hair who got together to have some wine and smoke a joint on the promenade and invented that the indigenous peoples were cultured *and* civilized, I have *tons* of documentary evidence that yes, they were cultured, but civilized? Not at all. Example number three, and I'll finish with this lesson: There are 66 forensic reports on the victims killed by the Tupamaros, 66 wakes and burials attended by representatives of the Armed Forces and the police to support the families of the victims. Tell me, the ones who constantly talk about what the reinstitutionalization did in this country: how many forensic reports do they have to show?"

"Alright. Thanks for the history lesson," Ielicov smiled. "But in all your service in this battalion, you never witnessed, then, that prisoners were tortured?"

"Tortured? No," the General leaned back in his chair. "Look, there were physical duress. I mean, insurgents *had* to be reformed by any means necessary, and the Armed Forces took care of that."

"I think there's a thin line between physical duress and torture," the Vladivostokian said very seriously. "Let's dig a bit deeper. Beatings? Wet or dry submersion?"

"Physical duress," the General responded firmly.

"Mutilations, rapes?"

"Torture," the high-ranking officer said impassively.

"Got it. I just wanted to be clear on where the line is."

"Look, Ielicov," the General said, his tone taking on a more serious edge. "What happened here was *very* serious. We're talking about a guerrilla group trying to overthrow a democratically elected government to establish a left-wing dictatorship, like in Cuba or Russia."

"I'll take responsibility for that," the muscular man shrugged. "I'm referring to Russia: if you have an election simulation every five years where there's only one presidential candidate, and you cancel out the opposition," he ran his thumb across his neck, "that's in fact a dictatorship."

"Well, I'm glad at least we can agree on that. Those bastards needed to be reformed, and all the measures that modern prisons don't use today were applied: humiliations, physical duress, locking them in a metal cell under the sun with no ventilation in the middle of summer... all of that was done and I have no problem admitting it... to both of you," he pointed alternately at them with his index finger. "That's why the mic check. But everything else... please! Besides, the vast majority of the unionists, communists, and Tupamaros we had here at the battalion were men, and the anus of a man isn't biologically equipped for penetration. So, accusing the supporters of laws of being rapists would not only be accusing them of being torturers, but also of being *disgusting* and *immoral*."

"And the woman's anus, is it prepared for that? Is it biologically ready?" Geraldine raised an eyebrow.

"No... I suppose not either," the question caught the general off guard. "Men and women evolved in anatomy to have one organ that fits into another, and thus conceive life. Everything else is *unnatural*."

Goodbye to whatever was left of the rights agenda with those comments, General, the woman with jet-black eyes thought, but only said:

"I still find it hard to believe, however, that 100% of the prisoners you had in the battalion were this stubborn with their subversive ideologies, as you call them. Were Mojica and Huidó among the slow learners, the stubborn ones, or were they among those who could be reformed?"

For a moment, it seemed like Menini Ruiz had coughed or was choking on a fishbone, but then it became clear that he was trying desperately to suppress a laugh.

"Mojica and Huidó, stubborn in their *coupist* ideals? Please! Those two were the meekest ones. They quickly realized it was stupid to declare war on an entire country, that they'd lost, and they adjusted to their situation. Of course, we couldn't let them go, because the Tupamaros are *very* sly. They could have been telling us yes to everything, and if we had let them go, the first thing they would have done was take up arms again to commit terrorism. But other than that, they were as calm as can be. Sometimes we subjected them, like everyone else, to programmed humiliations—textbook stuff—like making the whole battalion gather to have a barbecue while they stood there, up against the wall, watching us eat. And every now and then we'd throw them a bone from the barbecue, but all of that was done to make them understand that they were on the wrong side of history, and that democracy and institutionalism were on the right side."

"Did you have a chance to see the front page of 'El País' this morning?" Viktor asked. Changing the angle of the conversation during an interrogation was a technique the detective duo had mastered, to gauge the reactions of their interviewees.

"Reading the newspapers is the first thing I do when I get to the battalion at 0700 hours, every day, Monday through Friday. Yes, I saw it."

"What do you think about it? Was Huidó the traitor that the Tupamaros tried to point to as Amadeo Píriz, the one who told the authorities where the other Tupamaros were hiding after escaping from the Punta Carretas prison?"

"Whether Huidó was a traitor among his own, I don't know. That was handled by Army Intelligence and the Police's Political Order Commission."

"And did you ever see Huidó talking to any of them?"

The sexagenarian military man sat silently for a long time, seemingly thinking about his answer, or more precisely, whether he wanted to share a memory that immediately came to mind when he saw the full-color photo of Huidó pointing a gun at the head of "Vasco" Olavarría.

"Once, yes, I saw them," he confessed. "Mojica and Huidó, who were among the most cooperative, the ones who tried to convince their former comrades that they had to face the consequences of their actions and accept that they had been wrong. They dined with us in the officers' dining room. Afterward, Carlos Falcone, the Director of the COP, went out for a cigarette with Huidó. I also went out to smoke after dinner, but I stayed at a distance, because Falcone was a big player in the anti-subversive fight. I don't know exactly what they talked about, but when they were done, Huidó went for interrogation, and the next day, an order was issued for the search and capture of a civilian, Magdalena Schebor, on charges of subversion and attacking the institutions. She was to be considered armed and dangerous. Two plus two is four, right?" the general shrugged. "Obviously, Huidó had kept that information to himself and hadn't handed it over. He trusted it, mentioned it to Falcone, and the next day, all the army units and police stations had her photo."

"Did they manage to catch her?"

"I don't know anything about that. Like I told you, I wasn't directly involved in the anti-subversive struggle. What the hell is that helicopter sound?" the General suddenly reacted, grabbing the phone to speak with his personal secretary. "Who's landing a helicopter without my permission?"

"Oh, never mind. It must be nothing. Maybe it's our taxi," she said, glancing indifferently at her wristwatch. *8:29. Good for you, Captain D'Amore*, she thought. "I wonder why Mojica and Huidó would have considered you, out of all the candidates that must be in the Armed Forces, as the future Commander-in-Chief of the Armed Forces," she asked very seriously.

"Goldman, I think the answer is obvious: whether you agree with me or not, I am a *patriot*, and I love my country. And if the new president was legitimately elected, whether from the left, center, or right, I will obey, and I will make my subordinates obey."

"That puts us at ease, in favor of the continuity of democracy," Goldman smiled. "One more for the road: who was in charge of the battalion during the 'democratic re institutionalization,' as you called it?"

"Commander Alberdi."

"We thank you for your time, General," Viktor stood up to leave, and both shook hands with the member of the 'Logia Tenientes de Artigas' before heading outside. "Did you see, Geral, when I asked you to chew and swallow your anger? We came for one key piece of information, and we left with *several*."

"Huidó was the traitor among the Tupamaros," she began to list.

"Mojica might have been one too."

"Magdalena Schebor must have been important in all this, for there to be a national search for her. We need to find out why, but it's connected to Huidó in some way."

"That Carlos Falcone is the second time he's appeared in the interviews. We need to track him down somehow."

"Oh, Viktor, dear. I'm almost ready to pull the wildcard and call her," she said as they were nearing the helicopter, with the blades already spinning. Captain Gervasio "El Toro" Villa from the Homicide Brigade and Detective Di Lorenzo were waiting for them, already suited up in their bulletproof vests. Each was holding a spare vest in their hand.

"Not yet, Geral, not yet. First, we're going to talk to Anabel Pulansky... and her son."

CHAPTER 18: SIBLINGS

"*The Redemption*" Farm, 3 kilometers along a dirt road from the town of Quebracho, Paysandú Department, Uruguay, March 10, 2006, 7:30 PM.

The newcomer from the capital stopped his Volkswagen Gol next to the farm gate. It was almost dusk, but from a distance, he could see a silhouette approaching from the humble house, perhaps illuminated only by a lantern. When the silhouette got closer, the newcomer could see it had impossible dimensions, and was carrying a long weapon at its side.

"What do you want?" the man from inside the property shot back in a deep, growling voice, holding a double-barreled shotgun.

"I came to talk to you, Facundo," he saw that he had surprised his interlocutor. "But let's rewind and start over. Hello, I'm Fernando, Fernando Schebor, and I came to talk to you, Facundo. Just to talk."

"About what?"

"About who our *real* parents are, what they did, and what they made us into."

"I'm listening," was the surprising response from the mountain of muscle built from hard field labor.

"My father was a Tupamaro, that's all I know, but a Tupamaro who betrayed his movement. He sold out to the military. My mother, when she found out, of course, broke up with him. I must have been about four years old, so I don't remember. She told me on her deathbed."

"Sorry to hear that."

"No problem, Facundo, it was like 15 years ago now. As I was saying, I don't remember my parents being together. What I do remember is that sometimes, on weekends, the doorbell would ring and my mother would send me running to my room, and what followed were violent arguments, blows, things breaking. One day I couldn't take it anymore, I grabbed the gun my mother had and pointed it at the son of a bitch. I told him: get out of here. You're never going to touch my mother again. And he left. I was only 10 years old, and I didn't know that was my father, but we packed our bags right away and left for Argentina. Do you think that a guy who was friends with the military was going to leave us alone in Argentina, which was also under a dictatorship? For almost 4 years we fled from the forces of repression, sleeping under bridges, in tents, in abandoned houses... always armed, always waiting for the fucking cops to find us. My mother died in 1991 of cancer, and what caused her cancer, and I'm telling you this as a doctor, is something that has been studied: keeping such bitterness to yourself, not telling anyone, not even your son, *causes* cancer. I didn't know the story until my mother told it to me on her deathbed, so I'm going to find my father and kill him."

"It seems like he deserves it, doesn't he?" - the giant agreed - "What you still haven't told me is where I come into all this."

"You're also the son of a Tupamaro."

"Of a Tupamara, you mean, right?" - the tenant corrected, although he suspected where this was coming from.

"No. I'm not talking about Anabel Pulansky, your mother. I'm talking about Francisco "Pancho" Mojica, your biological father."

"What?!"

"The former head of Uruguayan repression, Carlos Falcone, confessed it to me after I poisoned him with arsenic and before he died, believing that I would give him the antidote if he told me the whole truth."

"Did you kill him?!"

"Too fast. I screwed up there. But he did tell me that you are the son of Anabel Pulansky and Francisco Mojica, so the father who raised you, I don't know if he was a good father or not, but if you're having breakfast with this news now, at 34 or 35 years old, it's because the two of them never told you. Or am I wrong?"

There was almost no daylight left, but the man on the outside of the door could see the emotional impact that the news had caused in the blunt man.

"Now everything makes sense to me" - he was finally able to articulate -. "Look, I was born and raised in a dungeon."

"I know. I've been taking revenge for 15 years for what those sons of bitches did to both of us, if I'm not Mojica's son too."

"For me, life was like that, you can imagine" - he shrugged his shoulders -. "Life was being in a dungeon, in a barracks, sometimes going out for a walk with my mother through the inner courtyard of the battalion where they had us, shitting and pissing in the toilet in the corner with my mother in the same dungeon, playing soccer with the soldiers sometimes... And my father for me was the soldier who brought us food and stayed a while talking to us. When I was 10, they let me and my mother go, and I didn't understand anything. I mean, could people walk around without people in green uniforms armed with machine guns around them? It was all new to me. The three of us came to live on this farm, and it didn't take me long to realize that "something" was wrong, that the soldier they had told me was my father couldn't be my father. But they always stuck to that version: that I was the son of both of them. My mother tried to send me to school. I was already much older than the others, you can imagine, and school was another torture for me. When they didn't beat me because my mother was a Tupamaro, they beat me because my "father" - he made quotation marks with his fingers - was a soldier. I had to earn respect by beating them, but

I never finished high school. I started working here on the farm and I sent the world to hell."

"No wonder."

"And if we know who our father is, what are you and I doing here talking? Why don't we go and shoot him?"

"Stop, Facundo. It's not that easy. To start with, we have to be sure who our father is, or are. Besides Falcone, I already killed Newell, the head of the Argentine SIDE. And here I am: free as the wind. First I want us to make sure who our biological parents are, who screwed up your and my lives. And when we know, we can come up with a plan between the two of us to make them suffer, but without going to jail. It can be done, but it has to be planned well, or they'll catch us."

"What do you need from me?"

"Two things. The first is a sample of your DNA, to compare with mine" - he extended a tongue to him. The giant opened his mouth to let the medical device that the doctor put in his tube pass through. - "The second is to know how to contact you, because as much as I investigated and investigated during the last few months, I couldn't find your phone number. With great difficulty, asking and asking, I got to your house."

"We don't have a phone here. Only my father has a cell, because he needs it for the deliveries we make here, and sometimes he does hauling too."

"Forget it, Facundo. Can I call you 'Facu', since we might end up being brothers by father, you and I?"

"I mean, right?"

"Facu" – he took out his wallet and handed the other man two hundred-dollar bills. - "When you can, go to a cellphone store and buy one. Here's my number written down for you" – he gave him a white card with a phone number scribbled in pen, but due to the poor lighting, it was hard to read. – "Ask the guy at the store how to activate it, what plans to choose and all that, and then call me. I'll be busy first looking for a lab to compare our DNA, to see if we're half-brothers biologically, then following Mojica and maybe someone else who could be my biological father, the one I pointed the gun at that time in the house we lived in with my mom in Punta Gorda, trying to get DNA samples from them for comparison. Once we're sure who they are, we'll stay in touch by phone to plan our revenge. No texts! No emails! Only calls, OK? Because messages and emails are how they catch amateurs, and you and I are *not* amateurs. Got it? We're in the same boat, Facu? Brothers?"

"Brothers" – the giant hugged him tightly in a campaign-style embrace.

Farm "La Redención," 3 kilometers down the dirt road from Quebracho village, Paysandú department, Uruguay, April 22, 2009, 12:10 PM.

Viktor and Geraldine had to admit to each other—and to the pilot—that flying there so suddenly had been an imprudence... a miscalculation. The only time they had been to the farm where they interviewed Anabel Pulansky the day after arriving from Buenos Aires directly to Termas del Arapey on that same presidential helicopter, they had traveled by land, and an army officer had taken them. From the air, the landmarks were different. They spent half an hour flying over the area looking for something they recognized until Geraldine spotted the blue and yellow tractor she remembered seeing during her previous visit, next to the barn. Then someone who seemed to be Pulansky was visible, very small from up high, by the house with the gable roof, looking up at the sky, shielding her eyes from the sun with her hand, like a visor.

As soon as the helicopter landed, the four of them got out with their bulletproof vests on, the police officers' hands on their holsters. The former orthodox Jewish woman, who was no longer so orthodox, treated herself to a little personal indulgence, turning toward the cockpit and spinning her index finger in the air, signaling the pilot to take off and refuel at Paysandú Airport before he ran out of the little fuel he had left.

"Ah, what a relaxing flight" - said the former Tupamara, as a greeting. - "Never let anyone tell you that you don't know how to arrive in style. You scared all the chickens away."

"Ha. How funny" - retorted Gervasio Villa, nicknamed 'El Toro' among the police, with his deep voice. - "Where's your son Facundo?"

"Gathering the chickens and putting them back in the coop" - the elderly woman replied, as if it were the most obvious thing in the world. - "And why do you want to talk to him?"

"To ask him where he was yesterday between 6 PM and 8 PM" – answered Di Lorenzo.

"And why do you want to know where he was between those hours? I can answer that: he was here at home with us."

"Concealing a crime *is* a crime" – clarified the detective in charge of the homicide case of the candidate from the Popular Movement.

"And what crime would I be concealing, in case Facundo committed one?" – the elderly woman raised an eyebrow, her completely white hair making her appear much older than her 65 years.

"Shooting Senator Huidó when he was entering the Legislative Palace yesterday, and shooting at our car to threaten us and get us to back off the case yesterday too" – Geraldine shot back, trying to break the former Tupamara.

"Look at that" – the interrogated woman nodded, with her head. – "But what good aim my son has, then, to have made those shots from here, from home, 400 kilometers away from Montevideo."

"Don't play dumb with us, Pulansky" – Viktor warned her. – "We *know* Facundo is Mojica's son, and we need to compare his DNA with Mojica's and check his fingers for gunpowder traces. We'll also seize any weapons you have on this property for a ballistic comparison."

"Gunpowder traces on his fingers?" – Anabel laughed sarcastically. – "*Of course*, you'll find them! Around here, we shoot almost every day, kid. Even *I* have gunpowder traces" – she sniffed her index finger. – "Want to smell?"

"And why would you be shooting on the farm every day?" – 'El Toro' Villa asked suspiciously.

"Oh, my son. You guys really show how much you're city folk. When it's not a fox or a weasel trying to eat the chickens, it's a pack of wild dogs trying to eat the sheep, or wild boars eating the pumpkins and potatoes, and when it's not that, it's the parakeets trying to eat the corn. On the farm, you shoot, *period*. Facu shoots more than I do because he's younger and his eyesight's better than mine. But I shoot too, sometimes, and so does my husband. And as for your claim that my son is Mojica's son, where did you come up with that *nonsense*?"

"Does it matter?" – Geraldine asked enigmatically, since Pulansky was right: it had been something Arturi casually threw out, like a rumor, but coming from someone as scheming and devious as the economist, it could mean he was guiding them toward the real person responsible for Mojica's death, someone who also fit the physical description of having locked the lifeguard in the bathroom at the hot springs, and could have drowned Mojica's head while the cardiac accelerants—of which they suspected but had no proof—caused the presidential candidate's heart to explode. – "It's an ongoing investigation, so we don't need to give you the details."

"And of course, it won't bother you if we take a saliva sample from your son to compare it with Mojica's DNA, to see if he is or isn't his son, right?" – Ielicov continued with the cat-and-mouse game.

"Well, it *might* bother me" – the property owner put her hand to her chin as if thinking about it.

"Mrs. Pulansky," – said Captain Villa in a grave tone. – "If you have nothing to hide..."

"No, but it seems *you're the ones* with things to hide, not my son or me."

"Alright. My patience is over." – the veteran mustachioed police officer huffed. – "Di Lorenzo: put on your gloves and grab that axe stuck in the log." – he ordered his subordinate. – "We're sure we can get DNA from it."

"Sure. Take whatever you want, I don't have a problem with it. But first, show me the court order saying you can take it."

"It's an *axe*, for goodness' sake." – 'El Toro' barked.

"It's a *piece of paper* I'm asking for. An axe is worth more than a piece of paper." – The ex-Tupamara shrugged. – "If you left it in the helicopter, we'll wait for it to come back anyway." – she called out toward the inside of the house. – "Gualberto!"

"What?!" – Gualberto's voice could be heard from inside.

"Can you bring me my glasses from the nightstand, and your cellphone?!"

"I'm coming!"

It didn't take long for the retired military veteran, who had met his wife when she was in captivity and he used to bring her food in the barracks, to come back with what she had asked for. Clumsily and unaware of the tense atmosphere between the homeowner and the visitors, he came in, shook hands with the four of them, and took off his beret to do so, as one does in a campaign.

"And? Where's that court order?" – she snapped, putting on her reading glasses. She watched triumphantly as the two police officers and the two private detectives only glared at her fiercely, trying to intimidate her. – "Oh, I see. You didn't bring one, did you? Because I may be a little slow, but I know someone who knows the law. In fact, she works in *making* laws, and maybe she can give me advice." – she dialed her sister's number, Senator and leader of the Popular Movement, Laura Pulansky. – "Hi, Laura, how's it going? Yeah, I'm here on the farm, as usual. You know some people landed here in the front yard? Yeah, they landed in a helicopter, can you believe it? And they came with bulletproof vests, armed, asking about Facundo, the DNA sample, and everything... What do I know about what got into them?" – she waited a moment. – "No, it seems they don't have a court order, hey. Listen, since you're into laws, can you check which law says that if I ask them to leave my property, they have to go? I mean, I *love* having people visit me by helicopter, it's super picturesque, but today I've got to harvest the pumpkins and want to finish before nightfall. Okay, thanks. Send it to Gualberto when you figure out which law it is. Alright, kisses, sweetie." – she handed the cellphone to her husband.

"You'll do what you do, covering up for your son." – Geraldine warned her and turned to leave. The other three followed her example, heading toward the farm's gate.

"Yeah, yeah. I think I know what I'm doing. The ones who don't seem to know are you." – she called after them as they walked away. – "Ha. Getting the truth out of lies from a Tupamara. Amateurs."

Only when she saw them heading down the dirt path, likely waiting for the helicopter, did Facundo stop pointing his rifle at them. He had taken cover behind the seed bags in the barn, making it his trench. He sat down, defeated, with the rifle's stock resting on the floor between his legs, and started banging his forehead on the barrel.

"Idiot. Idiot. Idiot." – he cursed himself. This had to be discussed with his partner, of course. He grabbed the old analog Nokia 1100 cell phone and called the only number in his contacts. – "Hello, Fer. Those two just left here, the ones we tried to scare off with the toad on the car hood."

"Don't mess with me!"

"Yeah, I'm messing with you. They arrived in a helicopter with two more from the police. They were in civilian clothes, so they must be detectives."

"I don't understand how they found you."

"I didn't go out asking them, you can imagine. With how clumsy I am, I might have confessed things I didn't even do. My mom handled scaring them off."

"Your mom's awesome!"

"Yeah, awesome was the lie she kept telling me all my life, that I was my dad's son."

"People lie, little brother. DNA doesn't. Listen: they've got nothing on you or me. Nothing at all. If they had the slightest bit of proof, or witnesses, they would've come with an order to bring you in for questioning at least, and as you can see, that didn't happen. So, don't worry, because they'll still have nothing."

"I hope so." – sighed the big guy with the Herculean physique.

"The... from yesterday, did you send her swimming with the fishes?"

"Yeah, of course. Just like we agreed. Listen: is it safe for us to be talking on the phone?"

"I wouldn't say it's 100% safe. It's safer for us to be talking from analog phones, but to wiretap a line, they need a court order, and if they don't have one to bring you in for questioning, they're less likely to have one to tap a line. Tell me: did they come with bulletproof vests?"

"Yes. How did you know?"

"It's a classic: they think they intimidate a lot with the bulletproof vests. You stay calm, Facu. Normal life, and if you end up having to testify, make sure you have a lawyer around. The one I gave you is really good. He got Amadeo Píriz out of the court like it was nothing, and he's been really sharp in a lot of other high-profile cases, and I'm covering the fees."

"Thanks, brother. Take care."

"Facundo! Facu!" – they called from inside the house, after the sound of the helicopter landing and then taking off.

"I'm coming, Mom!" – Facundo responded. – "Well, looks like things just got complicated."

"I can imagine. Let's talk, but only what's strictly necessary, and in code, okay?"

"Got it. Bye." – he hung the rifle in its place and went out to face the elderly woman, whom he had a head's height advantage over.

"Facundo González Pulansky" – she always used both surnames when she was going to scold him about something, no matter that he was a grown adult. As long as he lived under her roof, there were always limits to be set. – "You haven't been misbehaving, have you? What did you go to Montevideo for yesterday? Is it that new friend of yours who's leading you down the wrong path?"

"Mom. I'm 37 already. Don't you think I'm old enough to choose who I want to hang out with?" – he chose to answer with a question, just one of the three she'd asked him, the easiest one. – "Besides, did they have anything against me, or did they not even have a tiny little bit to lie about in the trick?" – he referred, of course, to the most popular card game in Uruguay, where a "puntita," a one (in gold or cups), a two (that wasn't from the sample), or a three, are cards that win against many others, but are in the middle of the ranking, surpassed by any "mata" or any "muestra" (a type of card in the game).

"No. They had nothing."

"Then they're just fishing in the dark, without a bluff."

"Look at you, with your phrases." – she smiled, the former Tupamara. – "Well, let's leave it at that." – she decided, sensing that her son was hiding something from her, but not feeling entitled to press him for answers, especially considering that she had hidden the truth about his biological father from him his whole life, lived with him in prison for the first 10 years of his life without explaining exactly why they were there or what it was all about, and had never told him what her role had been in the Tupamara guerrilla. "But you better not get into trouble with the wrong crowd, you hear me?"

"Yes, Mom."

CHAPTER 19: NOT AGAIN

"Temporary" Facilities of the Forensic Technical Institute, attached to the Faculty of Sciences, Malvín Norte, Wednesday, July 22, 2009, 5:25 p.m.

Well. Looks like I'm going to leave on time today, she thought to herself, Dr. Lía Regueiro, who was not temporarily but actually in charge of the ITF.

It had been a quiet day. Only one body had been brought to her that morning, and her team had processed it, including the report, before lunchtime. This wasn't surprising in a small country like Uruguay, where the homicide rate is less than one per day. While between 100 and 120 people die in the country, for the ITF to get involved, there must be certainty, or at least a "suspicion," that someone has been murdered.

She took advantage of the rest of the afternoon to catch up on the bureaucracy inherent to her position, because for the director of a state agency, regardless of the field, getting hands-on with a case (in this case, a corpse) was something rather rare. Only in high-profile cases like the Mojica case did she have to be the one, and no one else, to open the body, determine the cause of death, and take care of everything else. Most of her time was spent answering emails, filling out reports, logging overtime for the staff, notifying justifiable absences to be deducted from paychecks, supervising her subordinates, paying small bills like the cleaning service, and handling a myriad of non-medical, and less forensic, tasks.

Then she remembered the toxicological report for Mojica they had sent to Buenos Aires. She didn't think they would have it ready yet. In fact, Friday, in two days, was the expected delivery date, but just in case, she decided to send a follow-up email to the lab in Buenos Aires. She regretted it before hitting send. *No, I'd better call them*, she decided, and dialed her contact's number at Biotech Argentina Lab.

"Hello, Luis. How are you? It's Lía here."

"Hello, Lía!" the Argentine greeted effusivelly. In fact, Argentines were always effusive... effusive, of course, even when the occasion didn't seem to deserve it, for a foreigner who didn't understand their national idiosyncrasies. "What do I owe the pleasure of hearing your voice? Don't tell me you're inviting me to go out this weekend in Buenos Aires. Because, you know, now I have a girlfriend...," the Argentine doctor joked.

"Shut up, you idiot," she smiled. "Listen, I'm calling about the last analysis we sent you. I know you're within the normal timeframe, but if by any chance it's already ready..."

"But I sent it to you yesterday," the Argentine interrupted.

"Wait, let me check," she said, consulting the ITF's email account. "I don't have anything from you yesterday."

"Oh, now *you* are getting me to doubt. Let me check," Luis replied, typing away on his side of the call. "I even think I replied with a receipt confirmation. Something like: Received. Thanks."

A chill ran down the spine of the Uruguayan forensic doctor. There was *no way on Earth* she would have received such an important and expected report like Mojica's and not remember it, let alone respond with just a receipt confirmation. A strong déjà vu hit her. She *had been* in this situation before.

"Here it is," Luis found it. "I have... confirmation of receipt, because we always send them with receipt acknowledgment request, and I have the response 'Received. Thanks,' with your digital signature. Hello... Lía... Are you there?"

"Yes. Yes. Sorry. It must be an issue with the servers," she replied quickly. "Listen, would you be so kind as to forward it to my personal email, the Gmail one? I'll give it to you if you don't have it."

"Let me see... I have it, yes. Forwarded."

"Thanks, Luis. Talk to you soon."

"See you."

"Is everything okay?" Franco's voice came from his office/lab, behind Lía's.

Lía jumped. She turned to speak to him, trying to hide her panic.

"You scared the hell out of me, kid! I thought I was the only one in the office."

"I was a little behind with my investigation, Doctor," the young man stood up. "Do you need help with anything?"

"No. No, no," she stammered, the first bead of sweat running down her forehead. "I'm just dealing with a little IT issue, it seems."

"That's what I figured," smiled Franco, the head of toxicology at ITF for over two years now, standing behind his desk. "If it's an IT issue, I'm pretty good at that."

Lía heard footsteps behind her, down the hallway. She turned to see the cleaning man pushing his cart.

"Gerardo, wait a moment, I need to talk to you!" she blurted, feeling saved by the bell. "Anyway, there's no rush, Franco, we'll look at it tomorrow," she quickly logged off, grabbed her purse, and told the thirty-year-old. "I want to leave on time today, you know how it is. See you tomorrow."

"See you tomorrow, Doctor."

"Look, Gerardo, I wanted to talk to you about something. If you want, you can walk me to the exit and I'll tell you on the way."

"Okay," the cleaner agreed.

"The restrooms, the staff ones..."

Minutes later, Lía was in a taxi, on the verge of tears. She decided not to hold it in anymore and broke down sobbing uncontrollably.

"Are you okay?" the taxi driver asked.

"Yes. Yes. Everything's fine," she lied to him, thinking to herself: *I can't believe this is happening to me... Not **again**!*

She instinctively reached for her phone. In the stressful moment of leaving the ITF and hopping into the first taxi she saw, she had told the driver to head toward Tres Cruces. It seemed like a logical place to start her escape: the largest bus terminal in Uruguay, with connections to every corner of the country and also to neighboring Argentina. But then, now that she felt momentarily safe from immediate danger, she remembered that as a public servant, especially in such a sensitive field as hers, working to figure out how someone died in order to help authorities track down the murderer, she had a *legal*, not just moral or ethical, obligation to report any crime. Report. Okay. But to whom exactly?

She remembered being tied to a chair in the old ITF that exploded and burned down to its foundations, with a homicide detective from the squad she trusted *completely*, pacing in front of her and telling her how she was going to burn in flames and all that she was going to suffer in the process. *What if I trusted the wrong people back then, and almost died because I made the wrong choice of who to trust... who can I trust now?* she wondered. Instinctively, going through her contact list, she called her brother, who worked as a police patrolman, and got the recorded message from his voicemail: "Hi, this is Rodri. If you called and I can't answer, it's probably because I'm at work, but leave me a message..." She hung up before the message finished and before hearing the beep. What was the point of leaving a message in her current predicament? Something like: "Hey Rodri, it's me, your sister. Can you believe I'm in mortal danger again? Anyway. Sending kisses. Take care."

The memories of the last time her life was seriously threatened also brought back another memory: where she had felt safe, at least temporarily. *You still owe me one, you son of a bitch*, she thought, and dialed her ex-boyfriend's number.

"Hell-o"—he answered, just as he used to, the guy who had briefly dated her some time ago, while he was still seeing someone else, keeping it a secret.

"Hey, Wolf. It's Lia"—she just said.

"Lia Regueiro?!"—she heard something fall on the other side of the line, followed by a female voice, somewhere between mezzo-soprano and contralto, asking: "Is everything okay?" to which the man holding the phone replied: "Yeah, Mica. You see how clumsy I am? I dropped the mate. Damn it. How's it going, Lia? You haven't called since the thing with the Decorator. How are you? Please tell me your life isn't in danger again, and that you need my help to hide from the killers and the authorities." -There was a silence on the other end of the line-. "Shit! Tell us where you are and we'll come get you."

"Forget it, Wolf, I probably shouldn't have called you," the forensic doctor sobbed.

"No, Lia. You did the *right thing* calling me. Mica!"—he called his partner, for lack of a better word—"It looks like we have dinner guests tonight!"

"Who is it?"—Mica's mezzo-soprano voice came through the receiver.

"It's Lia. She's in trouble again. I'm going to ask her to come here. Is that okay with you?"

"Of course! But just so you know, it's *your* turn to cook tonight," came the sound of a kiss over the line where the distressed forensic doctor had called.

"If you didn't exist, Wolf, they'd have to invent you"—the director of the Forensic Technical Institute was moved to tears—"I mean you and Mica, of course."

"You get here safe and sound, okay? From there, we've got it covered. I'll send you the address by text."

Helipad at Carrasco International Airport, Canelones Department, Uruguay, Wednesday, July 22, 2009, 3:45 PM

The 4 passengers from the presidential helicopter got off, and Geraldine walked up to the pilot to say, feeling like a bag of wet, smelly rags, such was the defeat she felt, but still maintaining her composure:

"We thank you for your services today, Captain D'Amore. Rest assured that we will thank President Valdez and speak well of your service to the nation."

"Mrs. Goldman, you don't need to thank me," the pilot replied. "I'm just doing my job. Now, would you like to do that thing with your finger that you like to do and watch me take off?"

"Consider it done!" The Jewish woman turned away from the aircraft and made the gesture, pointing her index finger toward the sky and spinning it, while still watching the pilot.

Captain D'Amore of the Uruguayan Air Force responded with a military bow and took off. The three men with Geraldine didn't know how to react. Only her partner and detective business associate was close enough to prevent her from falling.

"What did we do wrong?" she sobbed. "What did we do wrong?"

However, to the surprise of the other three, it was Gervasio "El Toro" Villa who answered the question, which was clearly for herself.

"You didn't do anything wrong, Geraldine. *Nothing*." He emphasized with a gesture. "We ran into an ex-Tupamara with her boots on, sorry for the vulgarity, but with a huge pair, and she knows her rights... and her son's rights. But there's something fishy going on, it's *obvious*! All we need is more evidence next time we go."

"If *there is* a next time." She shot back at the veteran cop's attempt to console her. "You saw her call her sister, who, with

Mojica dead and Huidó in a coma, is the most voted senator from the most popular faction of the most voted party."

"Mmm... yes... and no, at the same time, Geraldine," Villa said ambiguously. "Laura Pulansky isn't a fool: she won't lift a finger to interfere with a murder investigation. So, I'd say you two still have a free pass to investigate."

"Thanks, Toro, for the support," she said, placing a hand on his shoulder, on the verge of tears. "Especially the emotional one."

"Did I ever tell you that when I was young, I was about to become a psychologist?"

"No way!" she said, eyes wide open in disbelief.

"Nah. Just kidding," he smiled, his mustache twitching.

On their way to the car rental place to pick up a new vehicle, the mood had lightened. They offered to drive the police officers to Battalion 14 in Toledo, where they had left their vehicles, and then they dove straight into the first bar they saw open. It was either that or watch Geraldine start gnawing on the car dashboard and seats, or risk delivering a second destroyed rental car in one week, which would surely get them blacklisted from ever renting again.

The bar, a cantina named 'Mojón 24' (an *un*original name since it was located on Route 6, right in front of the marker that indicated kilometer 24, counting from Cagancha Square in downtown Montevideo), still held some of its old charm as when it had been a country bar. It had its tin counter, sturdy wooden chairs, a filter coffee machine, and inverted wine demijohns that dispensed bulk wine, whether to drink on-site or take away. They ordered whatever would come out fastest, which turned out to be breaded beef steaks in two buns.

"Are you sharing one?" the waiter asked.

"No way. One in two buns for each of us, please."

After satisfying their hunger, they realized they had missed a big opportunity by not being able to interrogate or take DNA from Anabel Pulansky's son, their prime suspect.

"Still... there's something that doesn't add up for me," Viktor said, staring absentmindedly at the cars passing by on Route 6.

"Go ahead, dear," she showed interest.

"When we touched on the topic of problems with women, Huidó *also* seemed to lose his soul, for lack of a better term. As if something had happened to *him*, some woman from his past, that had marked him badly. Some pain he thought was buried, and we came to unearth it. Right after, he changed the subject and made it clear that he didn't want to continue talking about it."

"And then we have Menini Ruiz confirming that he saw Huidó talking to the head of the Uruguayan repression, Carlos Falcone, only to see the next day a nationwide search and arrest warrant for a certain Magdalena Schebor. Couldn't it be that this is the woman with whom Huidó had the problem that still bothers him to this day?" Geraldine hypothesized.

"It would be a perfect time for Huidó to wake up from his coma and ask him, but it seems we'll have to investigate from another angle. Let's think about this: Mojica and Huidó were such close friends as young men, such buddies, such party-goers, as Huidó himself told us... could it be that both of them made the same mistake of getting two women pregnant and then abandoning the children?"

"That would generate two children who grew up to become very bitter men towards their biological fathers, especially if, as Arturi suggested, Mojica had asked Anabel Pulansky to abort and she refused. Still... does that seem like enough of a reason to kill them, or at least try?"

"Depends on how that destructive feeling grew, i.e., self-destructive."

"I don't follow you, I think," she said honestly.

"An absent father creates a sense of insecurity in a young person, and I can tell you that because I'm the child of two absentee parents. When Sonya turned 18 and I was still a minor, they left her a couple of thousand euros and took off to travel the world. The feeling you get as a child is that something is wrong with *you*, that you're a defective toy, and that's why your parents didn't want to know about you. Of course, you get angry with them, but then you realize your anger isn't going to make them come back. And in the end, it depends on you and how supportive your environment is—you can cope with that anger and self-anger, and eventually, you understand the reasons. Your parents don't have to be on standby for you your entire life, and they too have their lives to live. In my case, Sonya helped me a lot through that process."

"*Now* I get you. So, should we go look for that hypothetical son of Huidó?"

"Let's go. Where do we start? Maternity records from hospitals that were open 30 years ago or more?"

"Mmm... I don't think so. Plus, with medical record confidentiality, that could take forever. But in Uruguay, by law, it's mandatory to register newborns at the National Directorate of Civil Identification and issue them their first ID card. Back then, the deadline for registration was a bit longer, one or two years, I believe. Now parents have only a week to do it. Furthermore, the Directorate falls under the Ministry of the Interior's jurisdiction. And guess who we've got a free pass to investigate their records?"

"Of course, from the one at the head of that ministry," Ielicov smiled.

"And from his boss, President Valdez," she completed.

"Let's go, partner," he said, getting up and asking the waiter for the bill.

Civil Registry Office, Uruguay Street 933, Montevideo, Wednesday, July 22, 2009, 7:45 PM

Viktor and Geraldine waited what seemed like an eternity, though it had only been 20 or 30 minutes, for the clerk to return from the archives. On their way from Toledo to the capital, they had called Minister Cortez to ensure that there would be someone waiting for them at the National Civil Identification Directorate, the body that issued ID cards in Uruguay, and at the Civil Registry Office, the body responsible for birth certificates. These offices usually closed at 4:30 PM.

Their first stop at Civil Identification took a while. The clerk who had been assigned to them didn't seem very familiar with the computer systems, but somehow, he managed to locate the information for Magdalena Schebor, and then for her son, Fernando Schebor, whose last registered address was on Mar Mediterráneo Street, in the Punta Gorda neighborhood. Although there was a photo on record for both, the clerk explained that digital photos were only introduced in 2001, and these documents were from the 1970s. In 2005, through a budget allocation dedicated to digitizing files from before 2001, they began converting the original documents, but by that time, the photos were over 26 years old and barely recognizable as smudges.

This wasn't a major issue in most cases in Uruguay, of course, because every Uruguayan had to renew their ID at 5, 10, and 15 years of age, and then every 10 years. But the ones they had found were the last ones issued. What was still usable, however, was the fingerprint record. The baby's prints, of course, were tiny. Had the clerk been a bit more tech-savvy, he might have discovered that Magdalena and her son had crossed into Uruguay to report lost documents and get new ones before the young man started university in Argentina. Unfortunately, the forty-year-old clerk only had basic computer skills.

Armed with this information, they made their way to Uruguay Street, where an elderly clerk, Marta, was waiting, sipping tea and eating 'pascualina' while watching the news. She was alone in the huge state office, with only a police officer at the access control. They handed her the name they were primarily searching for, Fernando Schebor, along with his ID. She told them it could take a while because the record needed to be located in the archives and the birth registry file had to be found.

After a long wait, she finally arrived with the file, made a copy of the birth certificate, and handed it over. The document had a pre-printed format in cursive writing, with blank, underlined spaces for the newborn's name, the names of the declared parents, the witnesses, and the Civil Registry official. The detectives exchanged surprised glances when they reached the father's field. The name of Eleuterio Hernando Huidó was written there.

"Excuse me, Marta, but why does the child have the mother's surname and not the father's?" Geraldine asked, knowing that in their country, children born around the same year as hers always carried the father's surname first, followed by the mother's surname.

"Let me check," the elderly clerk put on her reading glasses to examine the document. "Here it is: the parents weren't married." She saw the look on the investigators' faces and quickly added, "At that time, it was mandatory for children to have the father's surname first, followed by the mother's, but only if they were married. If they weren't, it was up to the parents to decide which surname to use for the child. After that, it couldn't be changed, of course. That surprises me too," she continued. "Because it was around that time that women started using their husband's surname after their own, with a 'de' in the middle, marking them as property. It was a patriarchal society." She smiled, clearly amused by the current buzzword. "How I love this new term 'heteropatriarchal.' For example, if someone was named Vázquez and legally married a man named Hernández, she became Fulanita Vázquez *of* Hernández, marking her as her husband's property. The same went for children, with the whole 'father's surname' thing. It seems these two agreed to use the mother's surname only." She shrugged.

"I think I understand why they made that decision," Viktor mused. "What I don't get is why the father would recognize his son. It doesn't make any sense," he commented to his partner.

"I'm drawing a blank, just like you," she replied.

"Look, I know these extra hours have been authorized directly from the minister's office, but if you don't need anything else from me..." Marta gestured meaningfully.

"Of course. Apologies," Ielicov snapped out of his thoughts, momentarily stuck in his internal connections, as both he and Goldman had been frozen in thought, as was commonly said about the old video game machines from the '80s and '90s. "We really appreciate your help today."

The two walked in silence toward the new rental car, not knowing what to say.

"So, Huidó *did* recognize his son, unlike Mojica, who asked Anabel to abort rather than take responsibility," Viktor said from the passenger seat. As per their usual driving rotation, it was Geraldine's turn at the wheel.

"There was love there, Vik, I'll sign it in writing," Geraldine assured, starting the engine.

"That's clear. And I can imagine why they decided *not* to give the child such an unusual surname as Huidó, considering the father was one of the main leaders of the Tupamaros guerrilla. But then... Something must have gone wrong between the two of them for Huidó, ten years later, to use his influence as a collaborator with the Uruguayan repression to organize a nationwide search for his ex-partner, and the mother of his son."

"Do you think we can use our wildcard now, my love?" Geraldine asked, steering the car toward the first pizzeria they could find open on 18 de Julio, the main avenue in the capital. It was already 8 PM, time to eat, compare notes on the case, and sleep. Of course, all of this would have gone according to plan if Geraldine's cellphone hadn't rung. But it did.

"All yours," she handed her partner the phone from her blue blazer pocket.

"Hello," Viktor, the former heavyweight boxer from Russia, answered.

"Hello. Viktor? What a pleasure to talk to you! Paraphrasing the Apollo 13 movie quote, I can say: 'Houston, we have a problem.'"

"What happened, Lobo?" Viktor asked.

"I've got Lía here at the house, scared to death, or as we say in the Río de la Plata: 'shitting herself.'"

"Why?" the Vladivostok detective was surprised.

"Because she thinks she knows the identity of Mojica's killer, and doesn't know who to trust, given her past with the Decorator case. Are you coming over to eat some homemade pizzas at my place tonight? We'll talk it over by the fire, the five of us, reminiscing about old times. What do you think? Great plan, right?"

"Are you at the address you gave us on the card when we met in front of the City Hall?" Viktor exhaled deeply, suspecting that the exact words spoken by the Uruguayan writer had been rehearsed in advance.

"No. It was too risky to keep Lía there. Too many houses, too many neighbors. It's just the three of us, with Micaela, at... well... let's keep that classified, just in case the lines are being monitored.

Do you remember the last time we were all together, when the boat came through the canal?"

"Yes, Lobo. I know *exactly* where you are. We're on our way there now."

"What happened, my love?" Geraldine asked, having only heard half of the conversation from her partner.

"It was Lobo. He and Mica are with Lía Regueiro, who thinks she's figured out who Mojica's killer is. They're waiting for us to have dinner."

"Alright. So where am I driving this vehicle?" Geraldine asked indifferently.

"To the Lupoj Shipyard," Viktor replied, gripping the direction firmly, anticipating his partner's reaction.

"I'm fine. I'm fine," Geraldine reassured him, but more for herself. She gently removed his hand from the wheel. "To the Lupoj Shipyard, then," she signaled right.

CHAPTER 20: COUNCIL BY THE FIRE

Route 1, Km. 22.500, former Lupoj Shipyard, Wednesday, July 22, 2009, 8:40 PM

The thirty-something Uruguayan writer, former classmate of Geraldine Goldman at the French High School, was waiting for the detective duo, smoking a Marlboro. He opened the access gate for them, closed it after their rental car entered, and then got into the vehicle.

"Recreation of the original battle, the first Saturday of each month, except for January and February?" Geraldine reproached him in a bad mood as soon as her former schoolmate got into the sedan, pointing at the giant sign.

"And guided tours every Saturday. Geral, dear. We *had* to monetize this somehow. And by 2005, this property was unsellable. Imagine after a dozen or so neo-Nazis died here trying to kill five civilians. But it's all very well maintained, with special effects and stunt doubles. What can I say? My brother loved the idea of a morbid theme park. They do those tours in the first world: the Texas massacre, the mansions where Charles Manson's crimes took place, that kind of thing... Besides, someone had to cover the maintenance costs for the property... and make a little profit."

"How long has it been since you saw a psychoanalyst, Lobo?"

"Let me think... Never?"

"We accept you as you are, Lobo," Viktor bumped fists with him, much to Geraldine's dismay and reproachful look. "Don't give me that murderous look, Geral. After all, he's *your* old schoolmate."

"That's true," the writer confirmed, and got out of the vehicle. They had reached their short destination after 253 meters of winding road among the eucalyptus trees.

The white-painted brick house had a generous office at the entrance, with a fireplace. Giant posters displayed images of the condition of what had once been the only shipyard in Uruguay that manufactured sports yachts. Later, it fell into disrepair due to a lack of clients who preferred to import ready-made boats. In 2005, during the episodes involving the Decorator and his followers, the neo-Nazi 'Oradores del Sol', this place had been the site of the final battle where the secret sect—connected to the police, the ITF, and even the government—had been eradicated. Their ultimate goal had been to overthrow the first left-wing democratic government of President Valdez.

"So, we're basically in the Disney theme park for ultra-fascist sectorials trying to overthrow a democracy in the 21st century?" Geraldine summarized as she looked around the room, her hands in the pockets of her navy blue jacket, finishing the tour of the advertising posters.

"Give or take," the writer shrugged. "Oh, and there's merchandising too." He opened a cabinet. "For an extra 25 dollars on top of your 100-dollar park entrance fee, you can take home this super-cool t-shirt of the 'Blue Sky' ship blowing up. Or for 2 dollars, you can grab this keychain with the Bonelli family entering the access canal to the shipyard, firing projectiles at the Nazis. And of course, you can buy a copy of 'The Decorator' by A.K. Lupoj for 30 dollars. If he's around, you get it signed and dedicated."

"They should invent a mental disorder to define you, Lobo," the newly arrived detective pondered thoughtfully as he finished the tour of the posters.

"There already is one," intervened a youthful voice came from inside the house, carrying five glasses on a tray. Micaela

Vasconsellos waited for everyone to take their glass, set the tray down, and then went to hug Viktor and Geraldine properly. "It's called compulsive creativity, and it's an OCD. Lobo mostly channels it into his books, but every now and then, his creativity leaks into other areas, and he creates... things like this." She pointed to the posters around them.

"Most of them don't catch on so well," the writer had to admit. "But this one did."

"So, do we know exactly what we're celebrating?" Lía, who had just come from the kitchen after Micaela, asked after greeting the newcomers affectionately.

"That we're alive, for starters," Lupoj raised his glass.

"That this time there doesn't seem to be a neo-Nazi cult trying to kill us," Geraldine added.

"That you seem to have figured out who Mojica's killer is," Viktor smiled at her.

"And that there aren't dozens of neighbors outside with torches, tridents, and machetes trying to burn the witch, which is no small thing," Micaela added, half-joking but also half-serious.

"True," the forensic scientist relented, surrounded by so much collective optimism. "We're not doing as badly as the last time, but I'll only raise my glass because Lobo's homemade grilled pizzas are eatable."

"You offend me," Lobo feigned indignation. They clinked glasses, but Viktor and Geraldine paused, looking at each other before drinking. "Don't worry, no alcohol. We weren't going to give alcohol to the only two people here with weapons, right?"

"Ah, well, okay," the detective agreed and took a sip.

"Shall we head to the barbecue and start the fire for the council by the fire?" The host suggested. In a few minutes, the former scout leader, a passion he shared with Geraldine from their high school days—she was in the Jewish scouts and he in the secular scouts—had the fire going and was setting up the dough bowl, the pre-made sauce, and a tray with 12 different toppings: olives, teriyaki chicken, fried onions, chopped ham, pepperoni slices, and so on.

"Well, how's the case going, Viktor, Geral? Do you mind if you start?" He asked.

The detectives summarized everything they knew up to that point since taking the case: who they had spoken to, the essential parts of the testimonies, their own investigations, and the moment of disillusionment they had felt upon discovering that Huidó 'had acknowledged his son, which separated him from the case of Mojica and his son, who Anabel Pulansky had not recognized. They already had the confidentiality from the other three guaranteed. That didn't need to be discussed.

"And that's where we are," Viktor finished. "I think it's your turn to share what you've found, Lía. How sure are you that you've found the killer?"

"Let's see... between very sure and 'why didn't I call the police right there when I figured it out?' *That* sure." Lía said. "The thing is, it's been over three hours now. The person could be anywhere, even outside the country. I relived the whole Decorator situation right there in the office, just feet away from him. I don't think he didn't realize that I discovered him."

"And what did you find, Lía?" Lupoj asked, who had already placed a couple of pizzas on the grill, but the embers were still not ready. "No one would blame you for not alerting the police immediately. Given how that went last time..." He shrugged.

"Well, the toxicology report we sent to Buenos Aires, and we weren't expecting it back until this Friday, I called the lab, my contact there, and yes, it was ready. But not only that: Luis, my contact at Biotech, told me that he had sent it to me yesterday, and that I replied 'Received. Thanks.' Meaning... there's *no way* that could have happened."

"But he confirmed on his end that he had sent it and that you had replied?" Micaela realized, and the forensic scientist could only nod in response.

"Who has access to that email account?" The man with the unpronounceable name asked seriously, and as such, how unpronounceable the bearer found his name, most people knew him by his nickname, "Lobo."

"Only three people: Dr. Zulamián, Chief of Forensic Pathology, closer to retirement than to the start of his career; Dr. Franco Ortega, the Chief of Toxicology, who you met," she looked at Viktor and Geraldine, "and me. After that, there are the IT people from the Judiciary, of course, but... the Chief of Toxicology hiding a toxicology report from me? It's him! I have *no doubt* about it!"

"But what the hell was that idiot's plan?" Viktor reacted. "Was he going to present a fake report tomorrow, as if it had just come in from the lab in Buenos Aires?"

"What do I know what his plans were?" The forensic scientist snapped. "You can imagine I didn't stick around to ask him. I heard the cleaning guy's footsteps, thought 'This isn't happening again,' and followed him until I got out of the ITF and into a taxi."

"And the report is conclusive?" Vasconsellos, the first refugee from the Oradores del Sol and the authorities whom Lupoj had given asylum during the events of the Decorator, now a trusted ally, asked.

"Completely." Lía's voice was firm. "Mojica had cocaine metabolite levels in his blood higher than Maradona's in his worst days."

"She's killing me," the cook said, literally dropping his jaw.

"What happened, Lobo?" asked his former classmate from the French High School. "Another little contribution from your 'compulsive creativity' that you want to share?"

"No, it's just that I was so caught up in the story that I forgot to rotate the pizzas on the grill. Let's see if they're burnt... Oh, what a fool. I haven't even put the embers under them yet," Lobo replied, quickly getting back to work.

"I imagine that, for a public position like Head of Toxicology at the Forensic Technical Institute, there must have been a prior selection process, right?" the Russian detective asked the forensic scientist.

"Of course there was!" she replied. "Those positions are filled through a competitive exam, and he competed with about 30 or 40 professionals in the field. It's not easy to find expert toxicologists, as you can imagine. He had the academic credentials... his previous clinical references were solid and checked out... but that only counted for 20 points out of 100 in the exam. The other 80 points were based on opposition and merit, and Franco scored 80 out of 80 in that section."

"And there wasn't any background check on his judicial or police record?" Geraldine asked.

"My dear," Viktor chided. "What police or judicial background could they have found on someone who doesn't even use his birth name?"

"Look at me asking the obvious," Geraldine slapped her forehead.

"His name is Fernando Schebor, and he's the illegitimate son of Magdalena Schebor and Eleuterio Hernando Huidó. He was born in 1969, when Huidó was part of the Tupamaro guerrilla, and he was registered under his mother's surname, Schebor, probably to divert attention from the authorities looking for his father."

"Ah, wow," the cook responded. "Then Huidó starts collaborating with the state repression forces, there's the photo of him pointing a gun at 'Vasco' Olavarría's head that 'El País' published this morning, Magdalena finds out somehow, and that ends their relationship," he hypothesized quickly. "What? Don't look at me like that. I'm just the cook today," he shrugged and went to check the pizzas on the grill.

"We suspected something went wrong between them," Viktor confirmed, "but your hypothesis is as good as any other, I think."

"I think it'd be a good idea to bother 'Toro' to get some police info that either supports or disproves that," Geraldine suggested, taking out her phone. "Hi, Toro, am I catching you at a bad time?"

"What? What? No. No-no. Not at all," the veteran's voice sounded agitated.

"Look, if it's a bad time for you, I can call Di Lorenzo instead."

"No, m'hija. Di Lorenzo doesn't get paid to be on call. I do. And that means if my phone rings, I have to answer it. Tell me."

"We think we've got a solid suspect in the Mojica murder, and we need you to access the police database to run a few names."

"Who is it, Toro?" a barely audible female voice was heard in the background at the police housing in Malvín Norte.

"It's work, dear," the veteran confirmed. "Hold on, let me put on my glasses, Geraldine, these laptops are so small for veterans like me. Okay... username and password... Do you want to keep the session open? Yes... go ahead, tell me."

"Magdalena Schebor. The surname is S-C-H-E-B-O-R."

"Got it. Born in 1947, do you need the names of her parents, last registered address, all that?"

"No, no. We assume that if there's any address, it's probably from 30 years ago. Just look for any criminal records."

"Nothing. Wow! There's an arrest warrant for terrorism and sedition from '79. Seems like this woman had an unusual life. Is she the suspect? Because I remember you said 'suspect,' and you don't usually get things wrong when you speak."

"True, I don't," Geraldine smiled. "Now her son, Fernando Schebor."

"Born in 1969, son of... *ARE YOU KIDDING ME*?!"

"No, Toro. I wish it were a joke. *He's* our suspect."

"Nothing after the first ID, when he was born... Oh, wait! He had to get a new ID in 1989 after losing the original one."

"And why didn't they tell us that at the Civil Identification Office when we were there this afternoon?"

"What do I know, m'hija? Depends on which officer you got."

"Okay. Last one, and I think that's it for today. Dr. Franco Ortega, Argentine."

"Police background checks... clean. Argentine ID, I've got it here. Do you need me to send it to you?"

"I don't think it's necessary, but I would appreciate it if you could circulate his photo everywhere because *that's* the face of Mojica's killer."

"Holy shit!" Gervasio "Toro" Villa swore, sitting in his tiny living room in his underwear, a redhead 20 years younger than him stroking his back. "And how did you come to the conclusion that this is the guy?"

"He deliberately hid the toxicology report sent to Buenos Aires, and we've got Dr. Lía Regueiro in custody because she's the one who figured it out. How quickly can you issue an arrest warrant and close the borders for this person?"

"I'm hanging up and issuing it right now. What's the last known location of this guy?"

"Last location, Lía?" the Uruguayan detective asked since her phone didn't have speakerphone.

"5:40 PM at the ITF," the forensic scientist confirmed.

"5:40 PM, Toro, at the ITF."

"So, we can rule out Anabel Pulansky's son?"

"On the contrary, Toro. They might be accomplices."

"Alright. Stay safe. I'll circulate the photo."

"Well, one less problem," Geraldine said. "Now let's just let the police do their thing."

"How are the pizzas coming along, Lobo?"

"Two almost done, two still in progress," the cook confirmed.

"Come on, Geral. You're *dying* to call her!" the former heavyweight boxer turned detective remarked with a smile when he saw her deep in thought, staring at her phone on the table, drumming her fingers.

"I think it's time, don't you?"

"Call who?" Lía asked.

"Remember, Lía, the last time we were here, at this shipyard, who came to our rescue in a zodiac?" Geraldine raised an eyebrow.

"Oh my God!" the forensic scientist understood. "But... but... I wish we had a hands-free phone so all five of us could talk to her."

"Mica, can you bring yours?" asked Lupoj.

"Sure," the twenty-year-old responded. A moment later, she placed a brand new Samsung Galaxy S on the table next to Geraldine.

"Looks like things are going well for you, Lobo," the only doctor at the table smiled.

"What can I say?" the host shrugged. "The royalties from The Decorator are doing fine. Though I'm still rocking my Nokia 1100." He held up his old-fashioned phone. "Clear the table, folks. The first batch of homemade pizzas is ready, 'people trying to catch a killer' style." Everyone quickly moved their glasses and phones to make room on the table, which could easily accommodate twenty people. Alkmer placed the pizzas, fresh from the grill, on round boards, sliced them into eight pieces, and went to check on the next batch.

"Very nice," Geraldine smiled, watching the steaming pizza. "Time to call our savior." She copied the number of the world's most famous French detective from her phone and waited three rings until she answered, now using Micaela's hands-free feature. "Hello, Edith, this is Geraldine Goldman. I hope I'm not catching you in a time zone where it's too early or too late. You're on hands-free. It's me, Viktor, Micaela Vasconsellos, Lobo Lupoj, and Lía Regueiro."

"Hello, Geraldine. The original team, I see?"

"Seems that way, yes," Viktor confirmed. "Where are we finding you today?"

"Hunting illegal hungers," came the reply from the sixty-year-old French detective.

"Hunting illegal hungers?" Lupoj joked, testing if one of the first pizza slices had cooled enough to eat, or if it was still too hot. He decided to wait a bit longer. "Isn't that a metaphor?"

"No-no. Laet and I are actually *hunting* elephant illegal hungers in the Amboseli National Park in Kenya. It's 3:45 AM here. They don't dare to hunt during the day because the rangers are heavily armed. We're camouflaged next to a herd, waiting for them to show up. This is our tenth day, well, night, I guess you'd call it, and still nothing. But no new elephants have been reported killed either."

"You must be scaring the illegal hungers just by being there," Geraldine joked. "Does the reserve have enough money to afford your services? Last time we talked, you were charging $50,000 a day."

"Maybe we gave them a... little discount on our fees, since we love wild life."

"Yes, of course, 'little'!" Another voice was heard from behind Edith. "Ninety percent off!"

"Well, yes. A big discount, maybe," Edith laughed. "So, what case are you working on?"

"We're on the assassination of Francisco 'Pancho' Mojica in Uruguay," Viktor downplayed. "We were contacted by Minister Cortez, but our client is the CSA group, the main financial backer of the Frente Progresista's campaign, the political force that was pushing Mojica for the presidency."

"The Suárez-Artagaveytia Corporation?" the French detective asked.

"You know them?" Geraldine was surprised.

"Bitter memories," Bonelli replied curtly. "But the one running it now is okay. He owes me a few, just in case my name needs to be invoked. So, tell me: how's the case going?"

"We know that they spiked Mojica's whiskey with cocaine, the kind he used to drink in large quantities after sunset," Viktor began. "Then they waited for him to be alone in a public hot spring pool. They may have put a laxative in the swimmer's food beforehand, who then had to leave his position by the pool. They locked him in the toilets for half an hour and forced Mojica's head underwater. Even though he had a strong heart for a 74-year-old, the cocaine accelerated his heart rate, and the fear of dying caused a heart attack."

"Perversely effective," Edith said, professionally. "Good thing the police have you on the case, or it would've passed as natural causes."

"Thanks, Edith. That's an *immense* compliment coming from you," Geraldine blushed. "We think we know who the killers are, or at least one of them. One is Mojica's natural son, born in 1971. He had it with another member of the Tupamaro guerrilla, Anabel Pulansky. Mojica asked her to abort, but she refused. The son grew up thinking Pulansky's current husband, a military man, was his father. This man was respectful and showed her he wasn't responsible for the torments she endured. The other suspect is the son of another Tupamaro leader, Senator Eleuterio Hernando

Huidó, who was shot by a sniper yesterday afternoon and is in a coma. Huidó, from what's been recently revealed, was a traitor to the Tupamaros, and in 1979, his son's mother had a search and capture order for her, possibly initiated by Huidó in complicity with Carlos Falcone, the head of the Uruguayan repression forces at the time. Huidó's son had been working for two years as the Head of Toxicology at the Forensic Technical Institute, and we believe he tried to tamper with the report that would've revealed a high level of cocaine metabolites in Mojica's blood. The police have issued a search and capture order with a border lockdown for Fernando Schebor, but there's no legal basis to arrest Mojica's natural son."

"Jeez. Complicated," Edith pondered for a moment from the Kenyan side of the call. "They've made it pretty hard to trap them, or to prove something."

"What doesn't fit in our theory is the level of violence for revenge, compared to the motive they might have to kill their two parents," Viktor continued. "We've ruled out other suspects, but if you want to check the list..."

"Sure. Let me hear it."

"My favorite by far," Geraldine began, "in case the two main suspects aren't the killers, is the former president and rival of Mojica in the presidential race, Dr. De La Rúa. He has the means to hire hitmen, and the Tupamaros kidnapped and killed his father in 1971. Seeing that according to the polls, an ex-Tupamaro was going to take the presidential seat from him, that might have triggered him."

"Good reasoning," Edith approved.

"Mine is Daniel Arturi, the economist. He was Mojica's rival in the primaries of his party, and he's a very intelligent and scheming individual. In fact, it was him who put us on the track of Mojica's son and Anabel Pulansky as suspects, and he's aware of the police file we're following, although it's being kept absolutely secret."

"I'll continue, but now straying further from the most likely suspects. The repeal of the 'Ley de Caducidad' is up for a vote alongside the presidential elections, Edith, and the polls indicated that the repeal would pass. After that, Mojica was the figurehead for this national consultation. Once the law is gone, the former perpetrators of the dictatorship will be able to be tried for crimes against humanity and imprisoned. Additionally, the shot that left Huidó in a coma was fired from 280 meters at a moving target. He was walking, but still moving. And when we left De La Rúa's house, there was a frog taped to the hood of our rental car."

"Wait. Is my satellite line bad? Did you just say a frog taped to the hood?"

"Yes. When we arrived at the car, we stared at it, then we heard a shot, from the same type of weapon used to shoot Huidó, and the frog exploded. We got splashed in the face." The Jewish woman relived the disgusting memory. "It was a total mess. Clearly, a warning for us to stay away from the case."

"Clearly," the French detective agreed.

"Last one, I think, unless we suspect Mojica's widow, who wouldn't inherit more than being responsible for all the expenses of the farm, right?" Viktor asked his partner.

"Unlikely."

"So, last one. Yesterday, when they shot Huidó entering Parliament, 'El País' had already published a photo on their front page incriminating Huidó as a collaborator with the dictatorship, a man who betrayed his fellow guerrillas to the repressors. It's very likely that this information was leaked, maybe by the Conservative Party candidate, Dr. De La Rúa, to the leadership of the Popular Movement, Mojica's sector, all ex-Tupamaros. Someone within that sector may have sought revenge for their detained and disappeared comrades."

"Not a bad argument either. Let me think. In Uruguay, a political murder is unlikely. Even less so *two* murders, or attempts. Are we sure Huidó is in a coma?"

"As of the last time we checked," Geraldine shrugged. "If it had been Huidó who ordered Mojica's assassination, for example, if he had threatened to expose him as the traitor within the Tupamaros, then he would've hired the worst hitman in the world to shoot him and leave him in a coma, not just grazing his ear, for example."

"Right. I would rule out the repressors, too. The ones who didn't leave the country as soon as the dictatorship ended must be senile and wearing diapers at home by now. It wouldn't change much for them to be wearing them in prison. Let me think...." The sexagenarian former naval fighter paused for a moment. "Let's go back to your main suspects. You said Mojica's unrecognized son, born in '71, mother a Tupamara, and Huidó's son, recognized, born in '69. Then something happened with the mother, and Huidó used his influence as a traitor and collaborator to get her back, or recover his son, in '79, using the dictatorship's repressive apparatus. Are we all agreed so far?"

"Yes," they both replied in unison.

"Good. First, let's look at the son of Mojica and Anabel Pulansky. Was Pulansky imprisoned for the entire dictatorship, or did she get out?"

"Yes, she told us herself, and that she was tortured and raped all that time," confirmed Geraldine.

"And her son?" Edith left a few seconds for her pointed question to land. "It's very likely that he was raised in a cell in a barracks alongside his mother. These things were common during South American dictatorships. There were also babies born from repeated rapes of women who were then given up for adoption to families connected to the dictatorship. Find out when she was released and if her son was indeed raised in a cell with her. That would give you a motive not just heavy, but *crazy*. Then they release them, and depending on when they were freed, the child would be between 10 and 13 years old. If they tried to send him to school, he would've been 4 to 7 years older than his classmates, and being the child of a Tupamara and a soldier, he would've suffered repeated beatings from his schoolmates."

"Shit!" Viktor cursed. "We never thought of that. Thank God we called you, Edith."

"You're welcome, kids. Now the other one, born in '69. His father is a traitor to the guerrilla cause. His mother finds out somehow, breaks with the father, doesn't let him get close to her son, but Huidó has the support of the repressive apparatus, so he's untouchable. He can abuse her, beat her, because he knows the police won't lift a finger against their informant. Something happens in '79, say, she tries to escape with their son, and Huidó uses the dictatorship's repressive apparatus to track them down. What options did she have? No doubt she had to flee and keep fleeing, and the 10-year-old boy was stuck in this situation for at least six years, living hell until Uruguay returned to democracy, or four in '83, if somehow, they managed to escape to Argentina. At some point, his mother probably told him everything, and the young man focuses all his hatred on Huidó. Then, at some point, one of them starts investigating seriously. I imagine it was the toxicologist, Huidó's son, because the other must be a rough, angry person, a fugitive from the world, and they meet, and plan the double murder of their parents. But since they're relatively young, they try not to get caught. That's why the plan is so elaborate."

"See? What did I tell you?" Lupoj chimed in, holding a half-eaten pizza triangle. "Edith, I gave them the *exact same theory* right before you called, and they looked at me like I was crazy."

"Relax, Lupoj. I have 36 years of experience in this profession. It's normal for simpler and more basic reasons to get overlooked in a homicide: my life was miserable, I find someone to blame, and I focus all my anger on that person."

"And how do we make them fall, Edith?" Viktor asked, still astonished, as he often was by the French detective's reasoning.

"There are basically two ways," Edith began. "Number one, I can give you a few contacts to feed your investigation with verifiable data, ones that your suspects won't be able to escape, even if they planned everything down to the last detail. Do you have something to write with?"

"Tell me," Geraldine answered, pulling out her notebook and pen from the inner pocket of her jacket, a remnant from an older, more analog era despite the digital age of telecommunications.

"The first would be Agent Arthur Doyle from Interpol. He's Canadian but has been living in Uruguay for about 15 years. You'll call him and say two things: one, that you're calling on my behalf; the second is that his daughter didn't get herself into trouble. Remember this, because it's important. The poor man lives with his heart in his throat, because his daughter does have a tendency to get herself into tight spots. For the good reasons, don't get me wrong, but she does. He will give you any data Interpol has on the repressors Carlos Falcone and his counterpart in Argentina. I think his last name was Newells, or Nowark."

"Newell. Oscar Newell," Ielicov recalled, remembering who had given the photo to De La Rúa back when he was president in '91.

"That's the one. After the return to democracy and the transitional period, these individuals became internationally wanted criminals, with red alerts and everything. If you could get any of their testimonies, you would have material to pressure the suspects. The second contact I can give you is a truly *despicable* man, I must admit, but I have absolute power over him. He was the Commander of the Parachutists' Battalion 14 in Toledo, and the idiot kept paper records of every detainee he had there. Each prisoner and tortured had their own file. On the release forms of the political prisoners, there was a status indicating where they were sent. PEN meant National Executive Power, meaning they were transferred to ordinary justice after being wrongfully imprisoned and tortured for information leading to the arrest of other rebels, and then released without any possibility of appeal. Another status was AO, which stood for 'Automotoras Orletti', a clandestine detention center in Argentina where they were tortured further, and if they didn't provide any more information, they were killed and disappeared. If this idiot is still alive, referring to Commander Alberdi, with his love of paper records, just mention that it comes from me, the Baroness Krunnenberg, one of my many identities, and he will hand over *everything* he has: files, testimonies—hell, even his *ass* if you ask for it!"

"Mum," Laetitia Bonelli's voice interrupted from behind the Kenyan part of the satellite connection. "I see two jeeps approaching. They must be the ones we're looking for."

"Well, kids. I have to go. Time to hunt illegal hungers." Edith spoke briskly, then added, "Alberdi lived in Andrés Puyol and the Carrasco Rambla back in the '80s. His son was a Catholic priest, and the other one, if he wasn't a lawyer, was a notary. Laetitia will send you the contact for Agent Arthur Doyle from Interpol in a bit. Good luck catching those two, and remember, to catch predators, the most effective method is to set fire to the entrances to their dens, and they'll come running out. Provoking them is the key, then it's just a matter of playing and collecting the prize. Kisses, kids. Laet, night vision on the sights. We're going to play 'duck shooting.'" The leader of the Bonelli Agency switched to French language, signaling her shift to a more military tone. Clearly, the veteran of the Indochina War, who had fought for the French colonial side, had forgotten to hang up the satellite phone.

"Mum, can we agree on *not* to kill them all this time?" Laetitia's voice, still coming through, asked her mother.

"I don't know, Laet, I don't know." Edith's voice took on an enigmatic tone. "Those little elephants are *so* adorable. Plus, I have an appointment with the ophthalmologist next month to adjust my glasses. Maybe I'll aim for a leg or an arm and end up hitting them in the skull instead. Shit happens, darling."

"Mum, you left the line open again," Laetitia scolded her.

"Oh, yes, my bad. Bye, people." Edith cut the connection with a final, clipped tone. "Baroness Krunnenberg, signing off."

"What was all that last part?" Micaela asked, looking at the two of the five who spoke French, since they had gone through bilingual education from kindergarten to high school.

"They were going to kill elephant illegal hungers," Geraldine shrugged and glanced at her former classmate to see if he'd understood the same.

"What can I say? Killing protected species is illegal in African reserves, and the penalty for it is a death sentence for the illegal hungers on site. So... they wouldn't be doing anything illegal... *this* time." The host interjected, offering his own take on the situation. "Well, all this talk of death has made me hungry," Lobo said, taking a slice of pepperoni pizza. "Finally at a temperature that won't burn my mouth." He checked the other two slices on the grill, confirming they were nearly done. "I'll take the embers out from under them, so they don't get too crispy, but I'll leave them on the grill so they don't lose heat."

"Did you just *hear* what you said?" Lía scolded him, taking a slice of ham and mozzarella pizza.

"I think I know where you're going, Lía, and in this case, I'm going to defend my partner," Micaela jumped in, coming to Lupo's rescue. "What brings us closer to life than eating, drinking, and the sexual act—the way Mother Nature designed us to reproduce? To drive away all this death, Akl..." She almost said the author's real name but caught herself just in time. "Lobo's just seeking out those instincts that bring us closer to life. Am I making sense?" She smiled at him. "Out with death, in with life."

"I love you, Mica," Lobo threw her an air kiss.

"I love you too, baby," Micaela blew him a kiss back, a playful moment shared between them.

"Told you, they're made for each other," the doctor chimed in with a resigned smile.

For a moment, the group fell into a comfortable silence, each absorbed in their own thoughts. Then, a notification pinged on Goldman's phone, interrupting the atmosphere.

"It's Villa," she announced, reading the message aloud. "Franco Ortega, or Fernando Huidó, isn't at his house, not at the ITF, and his phone is off. He's definitely on the run." She paused. "Don't worry, you'll find him. Greatly done, Toro," she read aloud, typing quickly. "We're here with the team from the gunfight at the Lupoj shipyard, figuring out how to gather more proof against these two. Good luck with the hunt! Oh, and don't approach Pulansky's son until we come up with a plan." She waited for a response, but all Villa did was react with a thumbs-up emoji. "Ouch, Toro, you really don't know me," she muttered, then smiled. "I *hate* it when they react with just a thumbs-up."

"Ha. And *I'm* the one with the OCD," Lupoj quipped. "Anyway, anyone wants the last piece of pizza with teriyaki chicken and mozzarella? I've got two more to serve."

"Go ahead, I'll end up staying single anyway," the forensic doctor said bitterly, taking the last slice from the two pizzas on the table, referring, of course, to the old saying that whoever takes the last piece of a serving plate will stay single.

"Come on. Go for it, woman," Micaela hugged her affectionately. "You're a bombshell, my dear."

"True, Lia. You're looking stunning," Viktor approved, and immediately glanced at Geraldine, just in case there would be any couple-related retaliation, but he never expected what the pale-skinned woman with round, jet-black eyes would say.

"If I were a lesbian, Lia, you'd be in my top 5 of women I'd like to get intimate with. For sure!"

"Alright, don't exaggerate, guys. I only said it's unlikely I'll ever get married. I never said I was lacking in candidates," she joked, and they all laughed together, sharing a moment of friendship and cooperation in solving a murder case and an attempted homicide.

"Lobo, I think you overdid it with the food," Geraldine noticed the two new pizzas, each half of one flavor and half of another, that her ex-suitor and former high school partner had put and cut on the table. "Though maybe I could eat one with caramelized onions and basil."

"If it's not eaten today, it'll be eaten tomorrow, Geral," Micaela shrugged. "We don't throw food away, you know how it is. And back to the case, how do we get those predators out of their burrows?" she asked, taking a slice of pizza with olives, corn, and mozzarella.

"Edith gave us some additional sources of information a little while ago," Viktor recalled. "Arthur Doyle from Interpol, and former Commander Alberdi, with his printed files from his time in Battalion 14."

Geraldine checked her WhatsApp.

"Laetitia just passed me Doyle's contact. So quick, those hunters must have been dealt with fast. What was it, 10, 15 minutes?" She glanced at the others as she typed. "Should we call him at this hour?" she asked.

"He's Canadian. He's probably asleep, although he's lived in Uruguay for about 15 years," Lobo reasoned. "He might have adapted to local customs."

"Let's call him," Geraldine decided, dialing the number.

The phone rang a few times before a sleepy voice answered.

"Hello?"

"Is this Agent Arthur Doyle from Interpol?" Geraldine asked, her voice calm but authoritative.

"Yes," the voice on the other end confirmed groggily.

"I'm Geraldine Goldman, private investigator. Along with my associate, Viktor Ielicov, we're working on a case of top priority for President Valdez."

"Mhm."

"Edith Bonelli gave us your number. And don't worry, she asked me to reassure you that your daughter isn't in any trouble."

The man chuckled, though it was clear from his tone that he was still in sleep mode.

"Oh, yeah, *that's* Edith. She always does that to make sure I know she gave you my number, and also to remind me that I owe her for keeping my daughter alive. Alright, what can I help you with?"

"Do you have access to Interpol's database?" Geraldine asked, getting straight to the point.

"Yes, give me a second to open my laptop... Okay, what do you need?"

"The last known whereabouts of Carlos Falcone, the head of the Uruguayan repression."

"Carlos Falcone, got it. International arrest warrant in '95... The last lead we had was that he was in Camboriú, Brazil, in '97. But he was tipped off somehow. We found his car and property, but no sign of him. After that, nothing. He was eventually found dead in a lounge chair at the Sheraton Hotel in Caracas. Cause of death: potassium cyanide poisoning. Ouch! They say it's one of the longest minutes of your life. We never figured out who killed him, though. I don't know what other information I can give you... Wait! What are the Bonellis doing in Falcone's file?

"What?!" Viktor reacted.

"The three Bonellis were staying at that hotel. In fact, it says here that it was Edith who tried to revive him, unsuccessfully, when a hotel beach waiter came running in, saying the elderly man was having a heart attack. And then..." –he read a little further–. "Right. The authorities wanted the Bonelli Agency to take the case, but when they found out who Falcone was and what he had done, they declined to take it."

"I see," the Jewish woman thought for a few seconds. "What about Oscar Newell?"

"International arrest warrant in '93. No traces of him until he was found... *Wait a minute!* –Doyle slipped into her native English (well, Canadian actually, for those who understand that language)–. "He was found in April '98, poisoned with Novichok in his house near Wollerau, Switzerland. Something tells me these names you're giving me are *not* a coincidence."

"No. They're not," Viktor confirmed, adding mentally: *though perhaps we would have liked to find them alive so they could contribute to the investigation.* "What about the poisons themselves? Is there an antidote?"

"I'll tell you. It's better if I open another tab for this, in case you want to go back to searching by names. Hmm... we said potassium cyanide, right? It *has* an antidote, but you only have minutes to administer it. As for Novichok... there's *also* an antidote, and you also have minutes to administer it, via injections.

"We understand," Geraldine was trying to make the connections as quickly as possible, so the Interpol agent could continue sleeping. "Let's go back to the name search: Magdalena Schebor."

"She's in the system too" –since the first two names were poisoned, Doyle went straight to the cause of death–. "No, she wasn't poisoned. She died of cancer in '91. She had a son, Fernando Schebor. Wait a second: why did she have the same last name as her mother?"

"Long story, Doyle," Viktor simply said. "I wonder why she would have an international arrest warrant."

"I'll answer that. Oh, of course. I didn't check the dates. It was issued in '79 by the fascist Uruguayan government on charges of sedition and terrorism. She was considered heavily armed and very dangerous. This was to warn those pursuing her that, from the Interpol headquarters, if instead of 'capturing' you kill the person, *no one* will open a file on you or press charges for it. But this... these files were closed as democracy returned to Latin American countries. It was like... did this person *really* commit a crime, or did they just have a Tolstoy book under their bed? These inquiries could take *years* to confirm the dismissal of charges. This file, for example, was closed six years after the return to democracy because Schebor died in Argentina, and the reason for the closure was death, not dismissed charges. Any more information I can provide?"

"No, I think that's all, Agent Doyle," Viktor replied after exchanging a glance with his partner.

"No, I think that will be all, Agent Doyle," Viktor replied after exchanging a look with his partner.

"Well, now it's *my* turn to ask you something. You see, all of our searches in the records are monitored. If someone were to ask me, for example, if these searches I've conducted with my user are related to any ongoing case I'm investigating... if, you know, someone were to ask... what should I say?"

"This is related to the murder of Francisco 'Pancho' Mojica and the attempted murder of Eleuterio Hernando Huidó."

"What the hell?! I heard about Huidó in the newspapers, but Mojica... I just heard the reports: he had a heart attack."

"Maybe someone *helped him* have that heart attack, Agent Doyle," Viktor said very seriously, "and the killer could be the same one involved in the cases of Falcone and Newell."

"I see. A poison expert or something, is that who we're looking for?" Doyle asked, sounding like he was starting to connect the dots.

"Yes, but don't open a file at Interpol yet. Not... *proactively*, I mean. I hope I'm making myself clear."

"Got it. But having that excuse ready will be perfect in case anyone asks."

|"Although maybe," Geraldine thought aloud, "we'll ask you later to correct what seems like a historical mistake: leaving Magdalena Schebor's charges in place from the dictatorship as an excuse to get Interpol's cooperation in her search."

"Change the case closure from 'death' to 'charges dismissed'? I don't see a problem, as long as Interpol in Argentina requests it."

"We'll see if that happens. Rest well, Agent Doyle."

"Thanks for your time," Viktor said after a few moments of silence on the line, realizing that, as with most North Americans, a "bye," "see you later," or "take care" wasn't necessary to end a phone conversation.

"Your turn, Lobo," Geraldine smiled at her ex-classmate and, apparently, the one who had a real knack for grilling those pizzas just right.

"Yeah, that's what I was doing, but after all this talk about poison..."

"Don't tell me you're hungry *again* with all the slices you've eaten!" Lía Regueiro, the forensic expert, and former dater of the alluded, asked in surprise.

"No. That's not it. Not this time," Lobo's eyes weren't on the people at the table; they were focused elsewhere, as if he was looking for a piece of information he thought was *crucial*, but just couldn't recall. Suddenly, his eyes widened. "A coffee with death!" he exclaimed, glancing around at the others as if telepathy existed and they'd followed his reasoning. But apparently, that wasn't the case. "A book by Amadeo Píriz, who was the consensus among the Tupamaros for having betrayed them and handed them over one by one to the authorities, talks about when someone poisoned him while he was living in Madrid, and all they wanted was for him to tell the truth about certain matters. Then the person who poisoned him gave him an antidote, or instructions on how to treat it, and he suffered for a few hours, but eventually the hospital figured out what the substance was, and they treated it. I wish I had that book to be more specific, but I think I traded it for some other used books at the Ruben bookstore in Tristán Narvaja."

"Hm. We might have a copy of that," Geraldine smiled and stood up to retrieve the book from her purse, which was in the trunk of the car.

He handed it to Aklmer (the name that its bearer found almost unpronounceable, and thus preferred to be called by his nickname, "Lobo," based on his surname, though his former high school classmate knew him from when roll call was taken at the French High School). He began to ramble, as was his habit.

"Paperback, matte cover, 75-gram offset paper... list of chapters... Chapter 13: A Coffee with Death," he read out loud, flipping to the indicated page. "Crazy, huh? Chapter 13, marked as unlucky, and in fact, some hotels don't even have that floor— they go from 12 to 14. I mean, I'm an atheist, but I do the same:

I skip from Chapter 12 to 14. No Chapter 13 in my books, but in Píriz's case, it looks like he did it on purpose, because they had poisoned his coffee, at the Café del Prado in Madrid, and the waiter confronted him about it, asking several questions about the recent past of Uruguay— if he was the famous traitor, and all that. I remember thinking this chapter was really interesting, especially since it might have gotten lost among the many books I read, plus the ones I write myself..."

"Is he ever going to stop rambling?" Lía (his former lover) asked quietly to Micael (his current partner).

"When he finds the detail he's looking for."

"Here it is!" the Uruguayan writer exclaimed, finishing the quick read. "The poison in this case was ethylene glycol. It takes hours to act, and if the doctors don't know what they're looking for, they won't treat it in time and the person will die. But the twenty-year-old—" he emphasized, scanning the pages of Chapter 13, "not only gave me the antidote right then, but also recommended I go to a hospital just in case, with the information about what had been used to poison me. And I sat there thinking," he concluded the chapter. "Was I accused of being the traitor among the Tupamaros? Someone went through the trouble of coming to Madrid, following my habits, taking a temporary job as a waiter... all because they wanted information that would lead them to the son of a bitch responsible for the death of his mother? Apparently, the stigma attached to my name had been widely accepted in Uruguayan society. And evidently, the dictatorship hadn't only harmed people through state repression. It had also damaged them through the vile acts of people against one another."

A long silence followed, filled with reflective thought.

"Well, here's my theory about what happened," Lupo said, rubbing his hands together. "They called me to play my part. But Píriz's last point has a lot of truth: we didn't just suffer from the state. We suffered from violence between people, too. That being said, Fernando Schebor is the son of Huidó and Magdalena Schebor. They had him, they wanted him, but then she found out he was a traitor and a collaborator with the repression. She forbade him from seeing his son, but how could she? She's a civilian and he has the whole repressive apparatus behind him. She fled the country to Argentina with her son in '79. The dictatorship was at its peak there, and they collaborated with ours. They were hunted down. The two of them—mother and son—lived through hell for four years while they were being chased, and they kept running. By '83, Argentina returned to democracy. They regained their lives, but in '91, she died of cancer. Very likely, all of what happened played a part in that. He then began the solitary search for those responsible. He first tracks down Píriz in Madrid, so he knows his father, the cause of his pain and the death of his mother, is the traitor among the Tupamaros, but he doesn't have his identity. Píriz clarifies for him—still threatened by death due to the poison in the coffee—that he wasn't the one, and hints that it could have been Mojica, Huidó, or both, but warns him that they wouldn't confess. So, Fernando has to ask the repressors. Following his obsession with finding the truth and then seeking revenge, he locates Newell in Switzerland in '98, interrogates him, poisons him with Novichok, and tells him he has questions to ask before he gives him the antidote that would save his life. Newell gives him the information, but then leaves him to die, because after all, the head of the SIDE was *also* partly responsible for the death of his mother... and of thousands more, of course. He continues with Falcone in Caracas in '99. Same tactic, different poison. He interrogates Falcone, perhaps holding the antidote in his hands in front of the old man. The Uruguayan repressor gives him more information, and this leads him to the son of Mojica and Anabel Pulansky, whom he contacts. He tells him who his parents are, what they did, and together they begin planning their revenge. Two broken, *damaged* people, seeking revenge against the parents who made them what they are. End of the story. Closing credits."

Micaela started clapping, feeling happy that after four years, her partner still managed to surprise her. The others joined in a round of applause.

"I *definitely* have to start reading some of your fiction, Lobo," Geraldine said appreciatively. "I mean, besides 'The Decorator', from which I receive part of the royalties," she joked.

"Thank you. Thank you. *Two thousand* thanks," Lupo quoted the Argentine comedy troupe Les Luthiers, bowing like a ballet dancer in front of the applauding crowd. "Now, besides connecting the dots, do we have any leverage to pressure the children of Huidó and Mojica into confessing?" The question was directed at the private detectives present in the 'Council of the Bonfire'.

"I say, right?" – Ielicov patted his back in acknowledgment, which led to a week of needing painkillers because the writer was stubborn and didn't like to go to the doctor for anything, for example, to see if his shoulder was dislocated. – "We could take the Argentine ID photo of the alias Fernando Huidó used to enter the ITF, Franco Ortega, put it on Píriz's face, and ask him if it was the young man who poisoned him for coercing him into giving him information at Café del Prado in Madrid."

"I can ask the IT experts at the Judiciary to track down which user, Ortega's as we all assume, deleted the emails from the Biotech lab," Dr. Regueiro contributed.

"We can pressure with that, if they find him," – Goldman joined in – "and suggest that we could ask Interpol to reopen the poison homicide cases that he knew and knew how they worked, like Newell's in Switzerland and Falcone's in Caracas."

"Will *that* be enough?" – cut in Micaela Vasconsellos, shutting down the collaborative enthusiasm – "I mean, this is all well planned from the start. And what about Anabel Pulansky and Pancho Mojica's son? How do we get him to make a statement?"

"I have an idea," – said the former heavyweight boxer, his tone enigmatic – "But for that, I need you to listen to me very carefully about a concept that's usually taken for granted: the love between siblings."

CHAPTER 21: MY DAD. MY AUNT.

B*arra del Chuy, border control with Brazil, Thursday, July 23, 2009, 5:45 AM*

Franco Ortega, as he had introduced himself when joining the Forensic Technical Institute, or Francisco Schebor, as his birth name was, waited impatiently behind the barrier in the EGA international passenger bus, for their turn to cross into Brazil. It was *evident* to him that his boss, Dr. Regueiro, had detected him the previous afternoon. She clearly knew everything. To buy the tickets at the Tres Cruces terminal in Montevideo, he had chosen the passport he never used, the one he kept only for emergencies, under the name Fabrizzio López, always picking first names that resembled his own.

The disruption by the customs police on the bus, however, was unexpected. They were holding their cell phones, scrutinizing the passengers' faces one by one. Finally, they stopped at his seat.

"You. Come with us." – the officer snapped.

"But... what did I do?" – the toxicologist from the University of Buenos Aires pretended to be confused.

"You need to come with us for a routine check," – the officer only "informed" him, and placed his hand on his holster.

"Alright, alright. I'll go with you."

Route 1, km 22.500, former Lupoj Shipyards, Thursday, July 23, 2009, 6:30 AM

It was agreed that the two men would sleep together in the only double bed in the house and office, built from white-painted bricks with a gabled roof. In the short time Lupoj had to organize the meeting since Lia called him to her house in Montevideo, until the forensic expert arrived in a taxi, trembling like a leaf, he had gathered inflatable mattresses and blankets in the trunk of his car. He had also bought ingredients for what he had planned to be dinner, though he was missing a few items. They had gone to the former shipyard, now a theme park for morbid curiosity seekers, neo-fascist cult worshipers, and fans of catching neo-Nazi sects. Afterward, they stopped at the Mabel supermarket in the town of Santiago Vázquez, the last place to shop before crossing the bridge over the Santa Lucía River and reaching their refuge and planed destination. What the host hadn't foreseen was that the inflatable mattresses had a weight limit for comfortable sleeping. Beyond that weight, and as one turned, people with a larger frame often end up with a shoulder touching the floor, not to mention the total length of 1.88 meters and a width of 56 centimeters.

So, it was agreed that the heaviest and tallest of the five would sleep in the double bed, and the ladies would take the inflatable mattresses.

As the co-generational group—Lupoj, Goldman, Regueiro, and Ielicov—woke up, all early risers, they tried to make the least noise possible while going to the bathroom, preparing coffee, or getting ready for a run. Yet even that minimal noise woke up the others... the thirty-somethings. Micaela, 22, was still sleeping like a log on her inflatable mattress.

By 6:45, Goldman and Ielicov had started their usual morning routine of going for a run, leaving Lia and Aklmer in the barbecue area, him sipping mate and smoking, her with her coffee, in charge of the detectives' cell phones in case there were any updates.

"You know I *love* the relationship you have with Mica, right?" – the former lover smiled at the writer.

"What can I say?" – Lobo shrugged – "I'm lucky she chose me, when she could have had *anyone* she wanted, man or woman, or even several at once."

"Oh, come on, humble guy," – the doctor patted his arm affectionately. "I'm sure she must have seen something inside you that made her fall in love too."

"Sure, call me ugly indirectly, you too."

"You *know* I'm not referring to that. But to find something valuable in you, one has to dig and dig through layers of cynicism, eccentricity, and delirium, basically. I mean: everything that pushes someone away when choosing a partner. That's what people see in you at first glance."

"Well, apparently Mica *did get* the will to grab the shovel and start digging," – the writer smiled. "Not like others." – He winked.

Geraldine's phone rang on the table between them. The caller ID said "Capt. Gervasio Villa."

"Hell-o," – the host answered. "Toro, right?"

"Who's speaking?"

"It's Lupoj. Geraldine and Viktor stayed with us last night. They went out for a run about... 20 minutes ago, more or less. They should be back in 10 or 20 minutes, according to them, and they left their phones in case there are any updates."

"Oh, OK. Yes, there's news. We caught Fernando Schebor at the border with Brazil, in Chuy. He was trying to cross with a fake passport on an EGA passenger bus. They're bringing him to the Central Headquarters for questioning, but I don't think they'll get here before 11 AM, no matter how fast they're driving."

"We're calm here, Villa. I'll tell you how the morning goes for these two private detectives I have here at the house, according to the plan we put together late last night, based on different possible scenarios... if they caught Fernando Schebor or not, if Senator Huidó woke up from the coma or not... and so on. Geraldine is going to drive to Carrasco to try to recover the documentary files. She'll be the one available in Montevideo at the time of the interrogation when they arrive with Schebor from Chuy. As for Viktor, we'll take him to Carrasco Airport. Are we good so far?"

"Fine. I'll follow your lead," confirmed the Chief of the Homicide Brigade of the Uruguayan National Police.

"Good. We're going to need two helicopters available for the raid on the farm in Paysandú, where we believe Facundo González, the biological son of Francisco Mojica and Anabel Pulansky, is hiding. Why wouldn't he be there, right? Assuming the ones who arrested Schebor at the border have kept him uncommunicated the entire time, right?"

"Look, Lupoj. If they gave the suspect enough time to send a text message to his accomplice saying 'they've caught me,' I *swear to God* I'll blow a fuse. Heads are going to start rolling, and I'll be the one holding the machete!" – the veteran policeman with the mustache threatened, at the mere possibility of such an event.

"How graphic and descriptive, indeed. Alright, let's continue with the raid. Since we know the police don't have their own helicopters, we'll need to borrow two. I've already been told they lent them the presidential helicopter on Tuesday. They can easily ask for it back. The other one will come from the army, or even from the Suárez-Artagaveytia Corporation. They'll figure that out when they get here and start making calls," Lupoj dismissed with a gesture. "Who's going to be on those helicopters? One will carry Ielicov and you, Villa, along with other uniformed officers of your choice, depending on the helicopter's capacity, of course. That'll be the one landing at the farm. Don't forget to bring your bulletproof vests. In the other one, I'll be going with Dr. Regueiro, who's here with me, plus two other civilians. Who? A mystery, a mystery, but the four of us will be taking our own risk of getting shot in the crossfire we expect between the suspect and the authorities. Minimal risk, of course, since we'll be flying, but risk nonetheless."

"I'm not comfortable with having civilians involved, but... they know what they're doing. Also, Geraldine and Viktor, although private detectives, are still civilians."

"They are. And the rest of us, we know and accept the risk, so don't worry. The police cars can easily come from the Paysandú or Salto precincts. I'll leave that up to your discretion, but *know* that we're expecting resistance to the arrest from the suspect, and we know he's armed and has good aim. It was his shot that nearly killed Huidó from a building 280 meters away at a moving target. On the other hand, there's *no way* he won't see us coming, I mean: 2 helicopters, 4 or 5 patrol cars..."

"Yes, of course. I just hope he comes to his senses and surrenders peacefully this time."

"That's what we all hope for. Which reminds me, we're *really* pushing the limits with the documentary and physical evidence needed in this case, but we trust you'll be able to get an order from the judge handling the case to bring the suspect in for questioning."

"I'll figure something out, but it's clear that arresting him without a judge's order would complicate the case even more, given how precarious it is right now."

"That's what we think too. And... I think that's all I can share with you about the plan 2B we put together last night after dinner with the five of us. If Huidó happens to wake up, or if the doctors think he's in a condition to be brought out of his induced coma, even for just a moment, in the morning, we'll move to plan 2C."

"Which is...?" – the veteran policeman grew impatient.

"Which is... that Geraldine, who will be in Montevideo, interrogates Huidó and gets his signed statement, or at least a recorded one. If that happens, we'll need the judge and prosecutor handling the case of the attack on his life to be present as well, so everything is official."

"*Without* talking to his lawyer beforehand or having one present during the interrogation, agreed?"

"*Of course* no one wants that!" – the writer confirmed.

"Alright, it can be arranged," – the police captain considered. "But only if he's being interrogated and testifies as a *witness*. If he's treated as a suspect, we'll have no choice but to have a lawyer present and have him legally advised before giving a statement in the judicial file."

"Rest assured, he'll only be testifying as a witness. If Huidó committed any common crimes before the dictatorship, or even up until 1984, those are already time-barred. But if he slips up, as they say, and confesses to participating in crimes against humanity with the de facto regime, then we'll move to part 3 of the plans, plans 3A, 3B, and 3C."

"No, no, stop. I don't even want to know what those plans involve!" – the police captain interrupted. "Alright, I'll get to work on that. You all stay safe, son."

"We will. Thanks for your cooperation, Captain Villa... Toro."

"Yes. Yes. See you later."

"Goodbye."

Minutes after the call ended, and while Lupoj was telling Dr. Regueiro the part of the conversation she hadn't heard, since Geraldine's Nokia N97 didn't have speakerphone capability, Ielicov and Geraldine came running down the hall, sweating.

"So? Any news?" – Ielicov asked, panting. "Or do we have time to start with the floor exercises?"

"Maybe this time you can skip the floor exercises," the writer wrinkled his nose and flashed a wide smile at them.

Family Alberdi Residence, on the corner of Andrés Puyol and the Carrasco Rambla, Thursday, July 23, 2009, 8:30 AM.

Geraldine parked the rental car on the south side of the rambla, the one closest to the beach, as she had come from the city center after entering via Route 1. Unlike Europe, where "rambla" refers to something else, in Uruguay it was the road along the seafront. The detective was met with an unexpected sight: there was a moving truck in front of the house, and workers from the moving company were slowly loading furniture inside.

"Well, it's not like I was expecting an elderly retired military man in his 80s or 90s to open the door, but a *move*?"

She got out of the vehicle, activated the alarm, and looked both ways across the three lanes in each direction, separated by a wide central median, before crossing. Once on the north sidewalk, she could see up close that what had once seemed like a luxurious two-story residence, about 30 meters along the rambla, now looked rather deteriorated, with graffiti such as "TORTURING MILITARY SON OF A BITCH!" among others. All the windows on the lower floor were bricked up, and the upper floor windows were vandalized with rocks.

A man in his sixties, wearing glasses, supervised the move, dressed in simple yet expensive-looking clothes, taller than he was broad, mostly gray-haired, with frame glasses. As she got closer, the detective noticed a trace of bitterness and sadness in the elderly man's eyes.

"Excuse me, would you mind giving me a moment of your time?" – Geraldine approached the only person not directly involved in the move.

"Oh, hello. Yes, of course. How can I help you?"

"I'm Geraldine Goldman, from the LNB PI detective agency. Here's my card," – she offered it.

"Abelardo Alberdi. Pleased to meet you," – they shook hands.

"Oh, Alberdi. What a coincidence, although I don't think it is. You see, Mr. Alberdi, my partner and I are working with the Uruguayan police on a... delicate case, shall we say, and we understand from sources that this is where the former Commander of the Army, named Alberdi, used to live. I suppose that wouldn't be you, since the Commander Alberdi retired from the army over 25 years ago, and he was already quite old when he did..."

"That was my father."

"Oh... 'was'" – Geraldine repeated. "I'm sorry for your loss."

"No... it's fine... I suppose. It's been 10 years since he passed, after my mom died. Two months apart, the funerals. My brother and I put the house on the market after that, but only *now* were we able to sell it. Neither of us wanted to keep it. Too much maintenance, you know?"

"I can imagine. I wonder why the sale process took so long. Was the property overpriced?"

"No. Not at all! We priced it at market value, but then the graffiti started" – he gestured. "And the rock-throwing, and we had to brick up the windows and reinforce the doors... We had to lower the price, but even then..."

"What do you mean?"

"It was... well, right after my father passed, the news came out in the press saying that my father had ordered tortures during the period of re institutionalization, and that he was a human rights violator... All those 'might have,' 'could have' statements that the press puts out when they don't have anything solid. I don't know... There was never any accusation in court. Well, look at me, I'm saying it too. I'm a lawyer, and you can't judge a dead man, but I mean, *before* his passing, there was never any legal accusation, but some people believed the news and started taking it out on the house. And now that I say 'news,' I'm getting the feeling you're from somewhere. Were you a journalist, or something?" – the lawyer became suspicious.

"I was the Head of Press for the National Police for several years, but since 2005, I've been working on investigations with my partner, Viktor Ielicov."

"Oh, of course! That's why I remember seeing you on TV so often. And how's it going for you now, with private investigations?"

"I can't complain," – Geraldine shrugged with a smile.

"Would you mind if I smoke a cigarette?"

"No, not at all. Please, go ahead." – She didn't really like the smoke, but if it made her interlocutor more comfortable, she could tolerate it.

"It's *not* a case involving human rights violations, is it?"

"Well... no, and yes. That is, there is something *related* to that, but it's not about what your father did or didn't do. It's... *tangential* to the matter. But the case we're assisting the police with is a crime committed now, by people who have *no connection* to your father, ever. I give you my word on that."

"Mmm... okay. Because as a lawyer, I *already* had enough trouble with that rumor in the press. But now it's over," – he waved his hand, holding the cigarette, between puffs. "But it was tough for me to walk around with the label of 'torturer's son,' both in life *and* in court. That's the way things go. News eventually passes, and the focus moves to the next story."

"That's true. No one knows that better than I, as a former Head of Press for the police," – she smiled, seeking complicity with the man, before dropping the bomb. "You see, we understand from sources that your father kept records of the prisoners he held at the 14th Parachutists' Battalion in Toledo during the re institutionalization period. And in those files, which must be quite a few, we're looking for key data for our investigation."

"I... I don't know what you're talking about," – it was clear from the nervousness in the man's voice that he knew *exactly* what she was talking about.

"Look, Dr. Alberdi. Those records are *crucial* for investigating very serious crimes related to the case we're working on. And, as I've already said, they have *nothing to do* with what your father did or didn't do while he was in charge of the battalion. Also, as a lawyer, you know that withholding them would be considered withholding evidence, right? I can make a call, and in no time, the police will be here with a court order."

"All right. All right. Yes, those folders *do exist*," – the man took a couple more puffs from his cigarette to summon the courage to continue. "It was when we sold the house. We tried to sell it with the furniture and everything. It's period furniture, and it was in good condition, but the buyers had other plans. So, there I was, emptying the house. My brother belongs to the Catholic Church. He's a parish priest. It was hard for him too when that news came out. He recommended donating the furniture to charity. I mean, taking it to an auction house and donating the proceeds. I thought it was a good idea," – he shrugged. "But there was a big safe in my father's study. We, my brother and I, knew it was there, but he never told us the combination, so it stayed locked for 10 years."

"I understand." – Geraldine simply said, growing impatient with the long-winded explanation. "Please continue."

"As you might guess, I had to call a locksmith to open it. He couldn't, so we had to break the lock with a drill. Well, it took him several hours, but he managed to open it. What I found inside... my God. I could only take one folder out. I started going through it on the desk. I... I couldn't believe what I was reading... and what that meant for my profession. I burned it immediately. I couldn't even touch the others. I closed the safe door, and those folders are still there, to this day."

"Can I take them? I need to find the information we're looking for for our investigation." – Geraldine pressed. "If it helps you make your decision, the source who revealed the existence of these documents to us, and who that they could still be in your father's possession, also told us that she had your father on her grip. Those were her exact words: 'mention the name by which he knew me, an alias, of course, and Alberdi will give them *whatever* you want. Even his *ass* if you ask for it.' Those were her exact words, so we can infer that she has documentary or testimonial proof, or *both*, that could be very damning against crimes your father committed in the past. And believe me, Dr. Alberdi," – the private detective smiled sardonically. "You *don't want* to anger this person, our source, and have her make public what she has against your father."

"You can take them," – the heir, not only to a house but to a bloody legacy, decided. "In fact, that solves my problem of what to do with that documentation, but remember: I absolutely *don't know* what's in it, and you gave me your word that my father won't be mentioned."

"It's a deal, Dr. Alberdi. I could have found them anywhere else, or gotten them by any other means. Besides, word given, word sacred." – Geraldine shook the lawyer's hand.

"Hey, guys!" – he called to the movers. "Would you mind giving this woman a hand carrying a few folders?"

A few moments later, Geraldine was sitting at the wheel of the rental car. The trunk was nearly full, as it carried their bags with clothes and detective equipment, so the hundreds of folders in different colors had to be distributed among the feet and back seats, and also in the passenger seat, piled up to a height of 30 or 40 centimeters. By instinct or detective curiosity, Geraldine picked up the first folder from the pile on the passenger seat. She began reading it eagerly, understanding right away what it was about... the photos... the accusations... and the abbreviations marking the final fate of the detainees, according to what Edith Bonelli had shared: "PEN", National Executive Power, released. "AO", Automotoras Orletti, executed and disappeared."

She checked the time on her wristwatch. It was just after 9 AM. *I'm going to need help with this*, she thought, and instinctively called Anahí, who had been her second in command when Geraldine was Head of Press. Anahí had since taken over the position after recovering from her injuries in the bloody events of the Decorator case, and now wore a metal plate where part of her skull had been after a gunshot wound to the head.

"Hi, Anahí, are you at the office?"

"Chief. Yes, I've been here for a while. Great to talk to you so soon! Do we know who killed Mojica and shot Huidó?"

"Yes, that's why I'm calling. Viktor and I, along with the police, are racing against time to catch the second suspect and get a confession from the other, but I'm going to need a lot of help processing *tons* of printed documents, summarizing them, and looking for key data to help in the interrogation of the one in custody."

"You got it, Geral. I'm closing the office right now and putting my staff at your disposal. How long until you get here?"

"About 20 minutes, I suppose. You're a rockstar, Anahí!"

"Yeah... I don't know... I hear that often," – Anahí brushed it off. "But I learned from the best." – she returned the compliment.

"Love you. See you soon."

"Me too. Bye-bye."

National Police Press Office, across from the Central Headquarters, meeting room, Thursday, July 23, 2009, 9:25 AM.

The eight Ministry of the Interior officials in this section of the National Police, after unloading the voluminous material, which until now they had no clue about, stared at the folders on the rectangular meeting room table. Geraldine cleared her throat before speaking.

"First of all, good morning, and thank you for helping us with this task, and special thanks to Anahí for lending us her help. I'm Geraldine Goldman, for those of you who don't know me, a private detective, and we're assisting with an ongoing investigation of a sensitive nature, to say the least, for the Ministry of the Interior. Now, what we have in front of us are the famous 'dictatorship files' or at least part of them." – she paused, letting her words sink in. "I don't need to clarify, of course, but just in case, I'm going to mention it again: everyone working here is a sworn official, and given the sensitivity and nature of the information in this office, you *all know* that this cannot leave this room. No girlfriends, no boyfriends, no mothers... no one. Not even to your parish priest or rabbi in confession, or to your psychoanalyst, if what you learn here gives you nightmares later."

"Geral. Relax." – her friend and former second in command, Anahí, gently patted her arm. "My staff knows what confidential information means."

"Good. So, what are we going to look for here?" – she asked rhetorically, pointing to the files. "We're going to need someone who's fast with Excel spreadsheets."

"It's your turn, Beatriz." – Anahí pointed to a staff member for the task.

"The rest of us will open the folders and dictate to Beatriz the full name of the person detained, the entry and exit dates from Battalion 14, and whether there are indications of physical abuse in the file. But please, don't get bogged down in the details, just skim through it: who ordered the arrest, and the key detail is the release code from the battalion's cells – whether it's PEN or AO code. Got it?" – she waited for everyone to nod. "Ah, and whoever finds the folder for detainees Eleuterio Hernando 'el ñato' Huidó, Francisco 'Pancho' Mojica" – Geraldine didn't ask Anahí for permission to use the whiteboard, which she took for granted, and began writing the names. "Amadeo Píriz, Anabel Pulansky, Laura Pulansky, or José 'Vasco' Olavarría, gets an additional prize of $99 (not 100, sorry, can't give an equal or higher amount without declaring why I'm giving it to them)." – She waited for the laughter to subside. "Courtesy of my clients. And in these two columns, we'll tally each PEN or AO code we find, like the points in a card game," – she drew a square and a diagonal. "Got it?" – she waited for everyone to nod. "Let's get to work, people!"

It took the eight of them a record time of 58 minutes to open, study, and analyze the files, dictating the required data to the official on the Excel spreadsheet. Sometimes, they covered their mouths in horror at what they were discovering, other times making clicking sounds, which could only be interpreted as 'I can't believe what I'm reading', with an occasional officer running to vomit into the trash can, wiping his mouth with a napkin, and returning to the task. Geraldine paused for a moment to review the result on the whiteboard. 22 folders for those detained and disappeared during the dictatorship (from 1973 to 1985 in their country), 326 in the column of those who regained their freedom after being tortured by police and military personnel convinced they were doing a great service to their country.

Having completed, among many, the task that would have taken the detective the entire morning and afternoon, well past the deadline—11 AM, the estimated arrival time of Fernando Schebor at the Central Headquarters after his arrest at the Brazilian border in Chuy—Geraldine spoke up.

"Great job, team. Let's give you a round of applause!" – she began, initiating a general round of applause. "So, we have Gerardo with a prize of 198 US dollars for getting to the files of Huidó and Olavarría first, Inés with a prize of 99 dollars for finding Mojica's file, and Cecilia for finding Laura Pulansky's file. Final score. Well, I guess I'm feeling generous today, so I'll add a 50-dollar consolation prize for everyone else for their participation in this exercise of historical and police investigation. Trust me, my employers won't mind. Now, if you'll excuse me, I have three calls to make, and one of them might be... complicated. Beatriz, can you print out three copies of the Excel sheet with the names of those listed as PEN in yellow, and AO (Automotoras Orletti) in a red cell background, before you leave?

"Yending," Beatriz nodded, acknowledging the order, in a mix of 'Yendo' in Spanish and 'going' in English.

"Good luck with those calls, my friend, especially the 'complicated' one," Anahí said, hugging her affectionately, and Geraldine returned the hug.

Once alone in the meeting room, the detective checked her phone and searched for the contact information for Amílcar Fou, the main police news' reporter at Canal 4, whose news program was known for giving considerable space—some would say *exaggerated* space—to police-related news.

"Hello, Amílcar, it's Geraldine Goldman. Do you remember me?" she said, trying to keep her voice steady despite the pressure of the situation.

"Hi Geraldine! Long time no hear. *Of course*, I remember you, and I also remember that you never used the 'vos' form like us. You always addressed us in the 'tú' or 'usted' form, depending on the situation."

"The same as always. And I have an exclusive for your channel, if you're up for the challenge."

"'Exclusive'—that sounds like *music* to my ears. Tell me everything."

"Well, now I'm a private detective, and I've been working on a case here in Uruguay. I can't give you details on the case just yet, but we came across something important during the investigation: files from the dictatorship."

There was a sound on the other end, the unmistakable sound of a man's cellphone screen cracking. "What the hell?" Amílcar cursed in typical Uruguayan fashion. "Another phone screen that breaks. They don't make them like they used to."

"Tell me, Amílcar," Geraldine continued, trying to push through. "As part of the strategy to catch the perpetrators of the attack on Huidó—the sniper—and another crime, which I'm keeping under wraps for now..."

"You're so mean, huh?"

"I must be, and it's called distribution of information based on need to know. It's an old corporate technique. Anyway, part of the strategy involves your channel broadcasting live the police raid where we expect to capture one of the suspects. It doesn't matter where it happens for now, but I need you, one of your cameramen, and maybe one more person, only if necessary, to report to the helipad at Carrasco International Airport as soon as possible. Do you understand?"

"Loud and clear, Geraldine. But I need a detail. You mentioned 'helipad.' Is it far from the capital?"

"Quite a bit. Why?"

"Because, if you're leaving Montevideo, we'll need a satellite truck to retransmit the signal to Canal 4, over in La Aguada."

"Oh, right. How could I forget? While you're heading to Carrasco, your satellite truck should be burning rubber toward

Paysandú—more specifically, to the vicinity of Paysandú Airport. Can you make it in time?"

"You can count on me, Geraldine! And thanks for the exclusive."

"You're welcome, Amílcar. But there's one more thing you should know: at the location where we expect to catch the shooter, shots might be fired. The police will provide bulletproof vests, and the helicopter filming the operation will stay in the air. But..."

"Don't worry, Geraldine. We're police reporters. If we have to sign an agreement that if we catch a stray bullet, we won't file a complaint or sue the police, we'll sign it."

"Thanks, Amílcar, as always, for your cooperation in maintaining public order. I wish you luck with your exclusive of the year. See you soon."

"See you soon, Geraldine. Over and out," he joked, mimicking military radio protocol.

The second of her three calls was a little more complicated, requiring not only planning but also a personal touch.

"Hi, my love, how's it going?"

"Hey, Geral. All set here at Carrasco Airport. I've got the two helicopters ready, one from the president's office, the same one we used last time, piloted by Captain D'Amore, and the other from CSA Group, the one that hired us. We're just waiting for the passengers. How did the review of the files go?"

"Successful, for now. Listen, Amílcar Fou is coming with a crew from Canal 4 to provide aerial coverage. He told me they need to dispatch a satellite truck to retransmit the signal from the helicopter, so they may be a bit delayed in getting there. I'll send you his contact information to your cell. Are Lobo and Lía with you?"

"Yes, of course. Everything's on track according to Plan... what was it again? Plan 2B? We're waiting for the Canal 4 crew, then."

"2B, yes," the detective confirmed. "Take care, and we'll see each other in Montevideo when all this is over."

"I love you, GG."

"And *I* love you," Geraldine closed the call with a soft smile, hearing the warmth in his voice. "Now, it was time for the most complicated call"

She searched her phone for 'Hijos y Familiares de Desaparecidos Uruguay' (sons and mothers of dissapeared in Uruguay), without quotes. The first result was a page with a .org domain, a bit cheaper than the .com ones: desaparecidos.org.uy, belonging to the civil association 'Madres y Familiares de Detenidos Desaparecidos' Mothers and Family of Detained-Disappeared). She tapped the link. Even from the homepage, with its image of a flower missing a petal, her stomach twisted in dread. Gathering her courage, she dialed the number listed, which had an area code from the Aguada neighborhood.

"Madres y Familiares de Detenidos Desaparecidos, my name is Guzmán. How can I help you?"

"Hello, Guzmán. This is Geraldine Goldman. I'm a private detective, and I'm working on a case here in Uruguay. The case itself doesn't matter for now, but during our investigation, we came across files from the dictatorship."

"Go ahead. I'm listening," Guzmán responded, his voice serious, though he was clearly paying attention.

"I need you to cross-reference a series of names I'm going to give you, to see if they match the list you must have—without a doubt—of the disappeared detainees from the military dictatorship."

"Go ahead, Geraldine. I've got the list right here," came the reply, this time with a low, steady voice.

"Amalia Fontana," Geraldine read from the first file in the stack of 22 that had been separated by the National Police Press Office team.
"Detained and disappeared on March 22, 1974."
"Gustavo Ángel Gómez."
"Detained and disappeared on September 30, 1977."
"Magalí Benavídez."
"Detained and disappeared on June 28, 1976."
"Omar Altamirano."
There was a long pause from the other side of the line. Guzmán's voice, thick with emotion, broke the silence.
"My dad," he said, before he started crying quietly.
"I'm sorry, Guzmán. I'm sorry for making you go through this," Geraldine said, unsure how to apologize for the emotional weight of what she had just uncovered.
"No... it's okay..." - the young man from whom the past civil-military dictatorship had taken his father from tried to put his pieces together on the other side of the line. "Detained and Disappeared on January 15, 1977."
"Elsa Altamirano."
"My aunt."
"Okay. Okay. It's okay" - tried to console from a distance the one who had not suffered consequences in her childhood, but who was empathetic enough to understand that others had suffered them - "I don't have to make you go through this, Guzmán. Here's the thing. I had to pay a *very high* price for this documentary material. I had to promise the one who gave it to me that the name of Commander Alberdi, in charge of the 14th Parachutists' Battalion in Toledo, would *not* be published anywhere."
"THAT TORTURER SON OF A BITCH??!!" - Geraldine's interlocutor shouted from the office in La Aguada.

"Guzmán. Please be reasonable," she tried to negotiate. "The civil association you belong to has as its main task to discover what happened to relatives detained and disappeared by fascist regimes. As a *second* task, they have to denounce and arrest those responsible for the disappearances. Alberdi, you should know better than I, has been dead for 10 years. Exposing his name to the press would only cause his children to suffer the repercussions, who may never have known the details of the atrocities committed or ordered by their father. Now tell me, do you want the files or not?"

There was a moment of tense waiting on the line.

"I want them... I mean: we want them... The night they took my father and my aunt, my father's sister, we were eating a barbecue. I was turning 8 and everything was celebrating and enjoying ourselves, until they kicked in the door. There were five of them. All wearing balaclavas, all in civilian clothes... with assault rifles... I was 8 years old, damn it!... and I couldn't... I couldn't do *anything* to stop them from taking my dad and my aunt..." -the young man, who was not so young, because he was around 30 years old, sobbed-. "It was the last time I saw them. I could *never* celebrate a birthday again after that" -he sobbed again-. "When are you going to bring us those files?"

"First we have to use them for the ongoing legal case, but then... can we leave them by the door, during office hours, ring the bell and run away?"

"There's no problem with that, Geraldine -Guzmán" Altamirano continued to suffer-. "Thank you very much for contacting us" -the one who answered the phone at the civil association closed the communication.

Then, it was the time for the former Press Chief of the Uruguayan National Police, and current private detective, to break down, fall to the floor, curled up, and burst into tears.

2 kilometers along a rural road from the "La Redención" farm, Paysandú Department, Thursday, July 23, 2009, 2:15 PM.

Inspector Commissioner Juan Martín Marquez of the Salto Police had faced his share of setbacks in his career. On one occasion, while working in the Investigations Department, he was ordered to follow a suspect and lost her in a miserable way. This had happened in the '80s, during the de facto dictatorship. But then, that same suspect, a French detective, requested that he lead a raid, together with his partner, to thwart a bank robbery attempt by the Fischetti brothers, from the Sicilian Mafia. In a way, a mistake had been covered up by a success, and one moves on.

Marquez, now a Commissioner, had *always* followed the rules. There was an order, and it was obeyed. This time would be no different. He had two years left before retirement, and the call from Central Command found him well-prepared. He gathered his men, loaded them into two police cars and two off-road trucks, and waited for orders on the rural road. The wait was long. They had already been there for two hours when a voice came through the radio.

"To all units of the Salto Police, this is Captain Villa from the Homicide Brigade. Do you copy? Over."

"We copy you, Captain Villa," Marquez responded over the radio. "Units ready and at your disposal. Over."

"The pilot informs us that we'll be arriving in 5 minutes. Are your units ready? Over."

"Ready and moving now. Marquez, over and out." – he stepped out of the police vehicle to give orders to his subordinates. "Let's go, guys! 5 minutes to the meeting point!"

The sound of police sirens was a spectacle that perhaps had never been seen on those rural roads, and perhaps would never be seen again. Why would it be? It was just another farming area in the Oriental Republic of Uruguay. Everything was going smoothly for the Salto Police... until the first shot struck the driver of the vehicle transporting Commissioner Juan Martín Marquez, causing the police car to crash into the fence after crossing the ditch. The career officer, about to retire, gathered the courage to order over the radio:

"Break the gate with the trucks! Fire, fire, fire!"

CHAPTER 22: FIRE... LIKE IN THE OLD SALOON

Military Hospital, 8 de Octubre and Centenario, Thursday, July 23, 2009, 11:40 AM.

It took the police vehicles half an hour to push their way through the angry protesters, who had gathered since the news broke on the front page of El País that Huidó had been the traitor to the Tupamaros' cause, and by extension, to half of the electorate who voted for the Progressive Front, and to the whole country. First, the crowd had gathered in front of the Asociación Española Primera de Socorros Mutuos, where Huidó had undergone surgery after a bullet pierced his left lung on Tuesday afternoon and continued well into the night. But when Ielicov's early call to Captain Villa had triggered the reflexes of the police and the mutualist staff to transfer the comatose patient to the much safer Military Hospital, the news of the transfer was leaked to the press, and the protesters simply walked the 10 or 12 blocks that separated the two health centers.

Essentially, if one paid attention to the banners, signs, and shouts of rage, all they wanted was Huidó's head on a spike. It was that simple. And the decision that had seemed strategic at the time, to secure the comatose patient at the Military Hospital, did nothing to calm tempers. It was *precisely* with the military that Huidó had betrayed the left-wing cause, a very small and marginal movement in his time, but one that made up nearly half of Uruguay's electoral votes by 2009. Soldiers with machine guns guarded the integrity of the walls and gates. Military personnel and their families had the right to receive medical care at that institution. For the latter group, the Cavalry Guard had to organize a safe passage corridor with barriers on the sidewalk along Avenida 8 de Octubre, as there were elderly people going to their geriatric appointments or children going to scheduled visits with the pediatric dermatologist, in addition to a senator in a coma, publicly accused of the most vile and abject betrayal a left-wing voter could imagine from a former Tupamaro leader. One who had conspired with Mojica to point the finger elsewhere, at Amadeo Píriz.

The avenue itself, long at 8 kilometers, until it turned into National Route 8, was heavily congested, with only two lanes in each direction, and one of them, on the southern side, was taken over by the protesters, along with the news vehicles. The news vans parked outside the hospital didn't help the situation. It was as if they were provoking President Valdez to cut their broadcast by decree. The pressure was intense, in that regard, within the Executive Tower. But Valdez had to remind them that the last time such a thing happened, when the state-owned television and radio signals were cut off, was in 1986, when Senator Germán Araújo, elected with votes from his sector, Democracia Avanzada (Advanced Democracy), part of the Progressive Front, and who also had a radio program on his sector's station, CX30 "La Radio," had called for a protest in front of the Legislative Palace against the parliamentary approval of the Law of Expiry, which, three months later, in July 2009, was expected to fall by popular will, according to the polls.

Senator Araújo had lost his parliamentary immunity in '86, with the majority votes of the Conservative and Liberal parties, the radio had lost its state-issued frequency, and now, the Progressive Front could *not* fall into the same trap of censorship, regardless of what was said in the private media outside the Military Hospital, and risk gaining the population's hatred. Especially with the polls so close for the presidential elections in October, with the Mojica-Arturi ticket, and now, with a ticket to be decided next Saturday at the General Assembly of the party.

In any case, Geraldine, aboard one of the patrol cars, remained calm... considering. She managed to regain composure after collapsing out of pure empathy, imagining what it would have been like on her 8th birthday, had people with machine guns and balaclavas kicked down her door to take her father and aunt... and never see them again. Fernando Schebor was already in custody at Central Command, having been captured in Chuy, but the satellite van from Channel 4, which was a key part of the operation in Paysandú, wouldn't arrive before 2 PM, not even if police patrol motorcycles cleared the way with their sirens blaring. And all she could do was wait for the Cavalry Guard to clear a path for them, while the protesters slapped the Hyundai patrol car's bodywork.

They finally accessed the internal grounds of the Military Hospital. Geraldine checked her cell phone once more, hoping to find confirmation that the next step of Plan 2B, which she and Viktor, Lobo, Lía, and Micaela had prepared the previous night, was in motion. The plan would move to phase 2C once it was confirmed that Senator Huidó had woken up. The message from her partner and co-conspirator on WhatsApp was from five minutes ago. "We've taken off, my love, as soon as the Channel 4 team arrived."

It was just a matter of Huidó's statement. Nothing more... and nothing less.

They escorted her to room 302, the intermediate care unit, where two soldiers with machine guns were guarding the entrance. They were about to ask for her ID when they saw General Menini Ruiz walk in behind the private detective. They saluted him, granting her access without further questions. An elderly woman sat in the accompanying area, holding the hand of the man who had been shot less than 48 hours ago. Geraldine glanced at the heart monitor for a few seconds, as if trying to understand the meaning behind the peaks and valleys.

"Mrs. De Melo. My name is Geraldine Goldman, private detective. I need to speak with your husband alone for a moment."

The eyes of the senator, former Tupamaro, and future Minister of Defense in the upcoming government—had his betrayal not become public, not just to his guerrilla faction, but to his party and country—closed his almost transparent eyes (whether due to genetics, cataracts, or both), he blinked and looked at his wife, who nodded and agreed to the request of the newcomer. The woman, who had crossed the sixty-year threshold some time ago, stood up and walked out without a word. General Menini Ruiz closed the door behind her. "We have your son, Fernando Schebor, in custody at Central Command. He's the son you had with Magdalena Schebor in 1969, and we need your help to make sure Fernando's sentence is as light as possible. Most importantly, so that Mojica and Anabel Pulansky's disowned son isn't gunned down by the authorities in a couple of hours." Geraldine threw the "atomic bomb" without waiting for the comatose man, whose nasal tubes were assisting his breathing, to have time to react.

"Is Fernando alive?" The convalescent man managed to ask, overcome with tears as he thought of the only son he had ever had—the one he had last seen pointing a revolver at him in 1979.

"Fernando *is* alive," Geraldine confirmed. "But unless you declare all the mitigating circumstances in his case, he will face between 30 and 35 years in prison, with no chance of sentence reduction for the murder of Francisco Mojica and the attempted murder of yourself."

"*I* made him what he is today," the former Tupamaro said through tears. "Have the notary come in. I will testify to *anything* to make sure Fernando doesn't leave prison at 75, *still* hating me."

The General in charge of the 14th Parachutists' Battalion in Toledo stepped into the hallway. At a wave of his hand, Judge Leguizamo, Prosecutor Ramírez, and a judicial clerk carrying a laptop with an open Word document entered the room. They introduced themselves, and without further delay, began the testimony.

"Please state your full name, your ID number, and your current occupation," Judge Leguizamo requested.

"Eleuterio Hernando Huidó, ID number 738.156-0, Senator of the Oriental Republic of Uruguay."

Presidential Helicopter Bell HU-1, known in the Vietnam War as the "Huey," approaching the "La Redención" farm, Paysandú Department, Thursday, July 23, 2009, 2:22 PM.

The newly arrived personnel at the firefight couldn't believe their eyes. The smoke from the crossfire made it seem as if an elephant stampede had just passed through. Villa grabbed the radio.

"What the hell is going on down there, Commissioner Marquez? Over."

The rule-following officer grabbed the radio, sheltering behind the door of the Hyundai patrol car, which had crashed into the fence after running off the ditch, destroying its front axle. The other three vehicles had managed to enter the property: the first truck broke through the gate with its bumper, and the other truck and patrol car followed behind, though they were in no better position. The police officers were sheltering behind the vehicles, unable to land an effective shot against those holed up inside.

"What's happening down here... is that they have *damn good aim!*" the career officer blurted out. "*That's* what's happening! They shot my driver even before we entered the property. He's hit in the left arm, and whenever one of ours peeks out to shoot toward the house, they get a warning shot. I'm just saying... for the sake of improving the quality of service to the population...Couldn't we have brought a *damn sniper* from the Army??!! Over," he finished with sarcasm, but understandable, given the precarious situation he and the Salto police officers were in.

"Why the hell did they take the M60s off these helicopters, the ones they had in the Vietnam War?" Viktor thought aloud, on a frequency that only those in the helicopter could hear, not the ground personnel.

"Are you serious, Ielicov?" -Captain D'Amore, in charge of the aircraft, replied-. "Imagine President Valdez landing at the Olivos residence for a meeting with the Argentine president, with a soldier in charge of the M60 mounted on the side. This hasn't been a combat helicopter for a long time. It's now a passenger helicopter that can barely fly safely. And let me warn you, it's not an armored helicopter, and we're within shooting range, so I request instructions on where to drop you off and take off again. I may not have a glamorous life, but I *have* one, and I appreciate it. Thank you."

"Drop us where you can, out of shooting range, and we'll manage from there." -decided the former boxer.

"Commissioner Marquez. In your best judgment, are the besieged shooting to kill, or are they just trying to keep us from getting closer? Over." -asked the descendant of Native Americans, at least partially.

"They're trying to keep us from getting closer." -confirmed the man, but at that moment, a bullet cleanly pierced the door behind which he was taking cover, fortunately without injuring him-. "DOORS AREN'T GOOD FOR COVER!" "USE THE ENGINES, OR THE 4X4 BOXES!" -he shouted to his subordinates-. "God damn it. Why the hell didn't the Ministry of the Interior buy Peugeot, instead of these shitty Hyundais?" -he cursed off-air, but then pressed the radio switch again-. "I request instructions, but I'm *not* risking my team's lives for a poorly planned raid. The *army* should be here. Over." -he said very seriously.

"The raid isn't poorly planned, Commissioner Marquez!" -it was Detective Viktor Ielicov who took the radio to speak to the officer on the ground, as Captain D'Amore's helicopter landed at a safe distance-. "This is Viktor Ielicov speaking, private detective, advising the Ministry of the Interior on this matter. The whole point of the raid was to arrest Facundo González, as was communicated to you in advance. If it could be done peacefully, then fine, let it be so. If it was going to be by force, the idea was to create the *perception*, from the Canal 4 cameras in the second helicopter, that the suspect had a *real* chance of dying. Do you understand what I mean? Over."

"But you should have said that earlier, Ielicov! Well, I'll give my instructions to my team. Over and out."

"Bird 1 to Bird 2." -Viktor started the radio communication with the Canal 4 news team aboard the second aircraft, which was much newer than the presidential helicopter. One could almost say... from this year-. "We need confirmation of the time to be live on-air. Over."

"Bird 2 to Bird 1." -Lupoj, in charge of timing on that side, replied-. "I'm consulting with Fou. Over." –there was almost a long minute of waiting, as sporadic gunfire continued-. "5 minutes until the ground vehicle reaches live transmission range, confirmed. Bird 2, over and out."

"Alright. We'll need to buy a little more time." -commented the detective to Captain Villa, who was by his side. The helicopter had already touched touched.

"I'm *not* crawling 100 meters to the police vehicles, not even drunk." -warned the mustachioed veteran.

"I don't think that'll be necessary. First, a quick message to my partner..." -he took out his cell phone and typed: "In 5 minutes live", "now to get some cover fire." -and already over the portable radio in his left hand, while holding his revolver in the right, he asked Marquez-. "Commissioner, we need cover fire to reach your position. Over."

"Cover fire at your discretion!" -ordered his subordinates, and as they could, from beneath the 4x4 chassis, they fired 15 automatic rifles and repeating rifles simultaneously at the house, which was increasingly looking like a sieve.

Viktor, Villa, and the two cuirassiers took the opportunity to run, guns in hand, until they managed to dive into cover behind the police cars.

"You are *not* taking my son!" -Pulansky shouted from inside the house, taking advantage of a brief moment of ceasefire-, followed by another shot from the ex-Tupamaros member at the uniformed officers.

"Is he the only one wounded?" -Ielicov pointed at the officer behind the Hyundai patrol car, who was now lying on the floor, bleeding from the shoulder. Another officer was applying pressure to the wound with what appeared to be the sleeve of his own shirt.

"So far, and because we haven't taken many risks, given the shooting accuracy of those inside the house. The first shot caught us off guard when we were arriving."

"OK. Let me examine the wound, officer." -asked the former Russian boxer, putting his weapon away. "What's your name?" -he asked the man lying on the ground.

"Darwin... Darwin Peláez."

"Listen to me, Darwin. You need to stay conscious until medical help arrives, understand?"

"Yes. Yes-yes."

Sadly, even before teaming up with Geraldine in the private detective business and starting to work seriously at it, Viktor had *already* had experience with gunshot wounds. Only one to himself, fortunately, but many more to his clients, in situations he had been involved in due to his tumultuous past with women, many of them married, and some with jealous husbands, who had the means to hire hitmen. Finally, a year ago, he and his partner had decided to take a break from their activity and attend a 4-day intensive first aid seminar, which included how to treat gunshot wounds and how to suture.

"We're going to need a doctor urgently here. I don't want to scare you, but there is no exit wound, and the bullet is lodged in your shoulder blade. Hang in there, Peláez." -the detective informed the man lying on the floor-. "Bring me the first aid kit from the car, if you can, but don't take any risks." -he asked the one applying pressure to the wound, a task he took over himself while grabbing his portable radio-. "Viktor to Bird 2, copy me? Over."

"Bird 2, we copy you." -Aklmer replied-. "Status on the ground? Over."

"We have an officer shot in the left shoulder blade with severe bleeding. There is no exit wound. We need the surgical medical kit immediately. Over."

There was a moment of radio silence, probably while those in the brand-new CSA Group helicopter were deliberating.

"Lía and I are heading there with the kit. Bird 2, over and out." -reported Lupoj.

"Well, it'll be like the old times." –Dr. Regueiro shrugged.

"Wait, Lía, I think I remember every single one of my outings with you, and none of them involved extracting a bullet while we were being shot at." –Lupoj joked.

"I was referring to the 3 years I spent with the peace forces in Congo, you fool!" -the doctor smiled at him.

"Is it safe to land?" -asked Fou, the lead crime reporter for Channel 4, interrupting a moment of the live coverage he was giving for his channel.

"Relax, Amílcar." -Lupoj patted his arm friendly. "That's why we're all wearing bulletproof vests." –he responded with a half-hearted reply, and then turned to Lía as the ground got closer. "It'll be like the old times for me too, Lía: just stick to my back, and I'll be your human shield." –and then over the radio-. "Viktor, we need you to let the besieged know that we are civilians and that we bring medical help for one of the injured officers. Over."

"Understood, Bird 2. Good luck! Over and out." -Viktor replied, and taking the microphone from the battered patrol car, he spoke to the people inside the house-. "Cease fire! Cease fire, please! We have an injured man who will die without medical help soon. Two civilians are coming, one of them a doctor. Please don't shoot."

"And what does this remind you of, Lobo?" -Lía shouted in Lobo's ear just before landing.

"Rugby." -the writer smiled, and they jumped onto the field, starting to run at full speed towards the patrol car crashed against the fence, with Lía taking cover behind Lupoj, carrying her medical bag.

Everything was going well, until the first shot hit Aklmer Lupoj in the body, throwing him backward onto Lía.

CHAPTER 23: A DIFFICULT INTERROGATION

M*ilitary Hospital, 8 de Octubre and Centenario, Thursday, July 23, 2009, 1:05 PM.*

The Court Clerk handed the three printed copies to Judge Leguizamo, to Prosecutor Martínez, and to the one who had testified, the hospitalized Senator of the Republic Eleuterio Hernando Huidó. It took them less than two minutes to review the statement. Geraldine was once again astonished at how from a Word document on a Judicial laptop, the file had been printed into three copies for the signatures of those involved. For the career military man, General Menini Ruiz, getting something at the hospital was a matter of making two gestures, shouting an order, and it was done.

She paused for a moment to think about why he was helping in the way he was. Perhaps, in the very strict military manner, the soldier was *indeed* sincere in what he had claimed about being a servant dedicated to the nation, regardless of who the democratically elected authority was or what institutions had to be defended. Soon, the three copies were signed by the judge, the prosecutor, the witness who had testified, and the clerk. One was handed to Geraldine.

"Alright. I propose a break for lunch until 2:10 PM." -Geraldine said, checking her wristwatch-. "The meeting point is the interrogation room at the Homicide Division, at the Central Headquarters."

Everyone involved exchanged greetings, and Geraldine was about to leave when she felt the wrinkled hand of Huidó close around her wrist.

"One minute, please," -the witness and convalescent requested.

"Sure. What's the matter?"

"Does your cellphone have one of those things for recording?"

"A voice recorder?"

"Yes, that's it!"

"Yes, of course. What do you want to record?"

"A message for my son. For Fernando."

Geraldine walked out minutes later through the front entrance of the Military Hospital on 8 de Octubre Street, after showing her visitor's pass, covering the word "visitor" and leaving only the hospital logo and name visible. She passed through the fenced security corridor set up by the Cuirassier Guard, as if she were just another patient on her scheduled appointment with the gynecologist or a staff member finishing her shift at the assistance center. She chose not to use the police cars in which she had arrived with the judicial staff for obvious reasons, and besides, no one needed to recognize her face... except that someone did recognize her.

"Geraldine Goldman! What a pleasure to see you again so soon!" -greeted a tall, lanky man with a few hairs in his beard, accompanied by a photographer who had already started taking unsolicited photos of the private detective-. "Figueroa, from El Despertador. I don't know if you remember me, from across the street from the Progressive Front political headquarters."

"You're a hard person to forget, Figueroa. And a very annoying one, too. I suppose you're going to chase me again, asking me questions that I won't answer."

"You're right. Tell me, what do you know about Senator Huidó's health? Has he woken up?" -he was following her with his recorder in hand as she kept walking-. "Has he admitted his involvement in the murder of José 'el Vasco' Olavarría? What's the connection between Mojica's death four days ago and the shot Senator Huidó received?"

"Look, Figueroa," -the detective turned to him once she had passed the security perimeter-. "You want news about an exclusive? Fine! You'll get it. Just buy me a hamburger from a cart and I'll give you information about an exclusive."

"Deal!"

Moments later, the two of them were finishing a complete hamburger with soda from a hot dog and hamburger cart situated in front of another health center, La Médica Uruguaya, just a few meters from the Tres Cruces Terminal. Figueroa had paid, and somehow, he waited for both of them to finish eating, but impatience was eating him up.

"So? What's the exclusive?"

"Oh, right." -She finished wiping her fingers and lips with a paper napkin-. "Tune in in a little while, at 2:00 or 2:10 PM, approximately, on Channel 4, for an exclusive coverage of the case."

"But... but..." -the newsman couldn't believe the trick-. "But you told me you were going to give the exclusive to me!"

"No, Figueroa," -she replied seriously-. "And if you ever want to be a good journalist, learn to pay attention to what the other person is saying. I told you I would give you information about an exclusive. I never said *you* would have the exclusive. So, tune in to Channel 4 at 2:00 or 2:10 PM to see the exclusive news on the case. *Hasta la vista*, baby," -she turned to leave, paraphrasing the famous line from Schwarzenegger in Terminator 2, but then she regretted it, turned back, and placed two 500-peso bills on the table of the astonished El Despertador journalist-. "This covers the meal you paid for, and a nice tip for the guys at the cart."

Feeling grateful to life, she had to admit it, for not having to resort to such devious methods to get a sensational interview to take to the newspaper, one that would also be scandalous and uncover corruption in either the government or the private sector. She first thought about taking a taxi, but then checked her watch, the number of blocks between her and the Central Police Headquarters, and decided to walk instead. It gave her time to prepare for what would perhaps be the most difficult interview of her life.

She was armed with her Beretta 9mm in its holster, a worn folder full of very yellowed papers from the passage of years and decades, with three freshly printed fanfold printer sheets inside, her Nokia N97 cellphone, a notebook, and a pen. Except at the intersections, one couldn't say that Goldman was paying much attention to what was happening around her. She knew that if she kept walking along Avenida 18 de Julio, she would inevitably arrive at the gigantic brick building of the Montevideo City Hall, and just around the corner from it, the massive structure of the Central Police Headquarters, where her next interviewee was waiting, handcuffed. She stopped for just a moment to observe the façade of the old Lycée Français Central, at the corner of 18th Street and Gaboto, where Aklmer and she, along with 80 classmates, had completed their high school education. It no longer belonged to the bilingual educational institution but to another state institution for higher education. However, the original engraving of the building remained: "Lycée Français MCMXXXV," French Lyceum 1935.

She arrived five minutes before 2:00 PM at the interrogation room where Fernando Schebor was being held and saw a tall man with graying hair drinking coffee outside the room. From his outfit, the classic Anglo-Saxon look, and his foreign appearance, she quickly deduced it was none other than Agent Doyle.

"Agent Arthur Doyle, from Interpol, am I correct?" -she extended her hand.

"The same," -the Canadian shook her hand-. "I brought what you requested," -he gave a pat to the two folders in his left hand.

"I hope we won't need to use them. Thanks for coming," -she smiled, knocked on the door to the interrogation room, and opened it without waiting for a response. Inside, she found a radiant Dr. Schebor, or Dr. Ortega, as he had been calling himself in recent years at the Forensic Technical Institute, and a very pale Detective Di Lorenzo from the Homicide Brigade. "Detective, could I speak with you alone for a moment?" -once the detective had closed the door behind him, she whispered-. "You haven't been able to get a word out of him, have you?"

"The number of his criminal defense lawyer. He repeats it over and over again, like a U.S. soldier captured by the Nazis or the Vietnamese, as if all he's been instructed to say in such situations is his name and his badge number."

"Don't worry. Everything's fine. Doyle, can I ask you a favor?"

"Yes, of course."

"When the Judicial officials arrive, let us know by knocking one long and two short on the door. Wait: are you familiar with Morse code?"

"Seriously, Goldman?"

"Okay, one long and two short. Di Lorenzo, how did the lawyer part go with this suspect?"

"The detainee arrived at 11:40. At 12:40, we had no choice but to let him call his lawyer after reading him the charges against him."

"And the lawyer was...?"

"In Punta del Este. I guess we were lucky," -the detective shrugged.

"Or *not* so lucky. Tell me, detective, how likely is it that one of the 16 directors of the Suárez-Artagaveytia Corporation, who frequently hire Dr. Adrián Ojeda, the best and most expensive criminal lawyer in this country, just *happened* to crash his car into an awning last night in Punta del Este, and the alcohol test came back positive?" -the Jewish woman raised a suggestive eyebrow.

"Ha! You two are from another planet," -the detective from the Homicide Brigade marveled.

"Not so much. It's called the Think Tank effect: five reasonably lucid people putting together what they know, sharing the best they can contribute based on their abilities and particularities, and coming up with 12 possible scenarios, which we call plans 1A, 1B, and so on. Each plan has specific actions for each of the five people involved. This interrogation is part of my role in plan 2C. Shall we?" -they both entered the interrogation room and closed the door behind them-. "Well, it seems we finally meet, Dr. Fernando Schebor, graduated from the University of Buenos Aires in November 1992, specializing in Toxicology at the same university in December 1994, not as we were introduced, as Dr. Franco Ortega, with a degree and specialization from the same university at the same time. Tell me: did the fake diplomas with different dates from the originals cost more, and you just wanted to save some money?"

"Ha. Ha. How funny," -Schebor laughed.

"Well, let's leave your stinginess aside as just an anecdotal detail. I'm sure Detective Di Lorenzo has informed you that there are plenty of proven charges against you for document forgery, attempting to cross the border with fake documents, and fraud in the contest that got you into the Forensic Technical Institute."

- "Exonerable, exonerable, and I can lose my job at the ITF, respectively. Big deal," –the suspect mocked.

- "It may be, but I'm sure you understand that the police have more than enough reasons to keep you in preventive detention for those three charges for quite some time. How long do you think, detective? Two or three weeks until the three cases are processed?"

- "At least."

- "Because, of course, someone who's in the habit of changing documents like he changes his underwear (I hope I'm right about the frequency) has a *high chance* of fleeing, so there's no Dr. Ojeda who can stop the police from having *all* that valuable time to uncover *everything* about you: your movements, witnesses who place you at the hot springs, further forensic tests on Mojica's body..."

- "Good luck with that."

- "Yes, good luck and *not* so much luck, because you see, you could have planned it all down to the finest detail, weighed the variables, predicted even the most absurd scenarios that could happen, like the laxative in the lifeguard's meal at the Palm Pool *not* taking effect before 10 AM when he finished his shift... you could have predicted a lot of things, but the perfect crime doesn't exist. What exists are insufficient investigations."

- "If you say so," –the detainee dismissed it lightly–. "Are you going to show your cards, or keep talking?"

- "Maybe. Maybe not. For now, you're only being questioned in the case of Francisco Mojica's murder and Eleuterio Hernando Huidó's attempted murder... your father. Have they taken a DNA sample from him yet, Di Lorenzo?"

- "Affirmative."

- "Good. I just came from speaking with your father, what a coincidence, Fernando. He was glad to know you're alive and that you're... well... detained, but you know what I mean. This is his testimony of everything that happened, his version of the story with your mother and with you, if you want to read it." –she took the copy of the signed statement obtained at the Military Hospital and handed it to the suspect.

- "Just out of curiosity," –clearly, this meant much more to the toxicologist than he was letting on. His features, though trying to remain stoic, sometimes betrayed him with flashes of anger, hatred, and bitterness, which the one who gave him the copy could read on his face.

- "It brings back bitter memories of your childhood, doesn't it?" –she bit her lower lip in false sympathy-. "Don't take too long, we're running out of time," –she checked the time on her cell phone.

- "Why? Do you have an appointment with the pedicurist?"

- "No, with the oncologist."

- "Don't cross the line, Goldman!" –the toxicology specialist warned angrily.

- "But don't be mad at me, Dr. Schebor. If I said 'oncologist,' I could have just as easily said 'physiatrist' or 'hairdresser.'"

- "Yes, sure. Of course, that's why," –the young man was sarcastic. He finished reading the document–. "Pity that none of this is going to land him even a day in prison, right? All of it absolutely unpunished. Great judicial system, the Uruguayan one," –he scoffed.

- "But the point here isn't *him*, it's *you*. Senator Huidó testified as a witness. You, on the other hand, are the one being questioned. Your father's testimony only gives us the context of how you broke down. How you became a broken 40-year-old man capable of planning and executing a murder and an attempted homicide, with full planning."

- "We *all* can kill, right? But not everyone does. Some of us prefer not to, even if we hate the person."

- "Yes, yes. Good luck with that. It could be that the forensic marks found on Mojica's wrist and the back of his head are yours or Facundo González's, your accomplice, who, right now, while we're talking, is having a tough time, but for different reasons. *Another* broken person, like you, who found solace in licking each other's wounds, forming a bond, and finding an objective to channel their anger and frustrations. Their... brokenness, if you will. I'm talking about each of your parents. But let's assume the marks aren't conclusive, what else do we have?" –she pretended to think for a moment–. "Oh, yes, the security cameras and the witnesses who will place both you and González at the Arapey hot springs on Saturday, July 18, and on Tuesday, July 21, they'll place you both at the abandoned building from where the shot was fired at Senator Huidó."

- "All *so* circumstantial," –the toxicologist regained his confidence, shaking his head with a smile.

- "The toxicological exam that the Judicial Informatics Department has already confirmed you deleted from Mojica's blood, the one that was sent to the Biotech lab in Buenos Aires? How do you explain that?"

- "Human error. Oops. I deleted it by accident.

- "And you replied 'Received. Thanks,' also pretending to be Dr. Regueiro by mistake. Sure. But the circumstances just keep *piling* up against you. Then there are the witnesses, of course. Like Amadeo Píriz. Did you know he narrated how you poisoned him with ethylene glycol and then gave him the antidote at the Café del Prado in Madrid, specifically in Chapter 13, which he titled 'A Coffee with Death'?"

- "An old delirious man, as far as I know."

- "The medical records from the hospital where he was treated will say otherwise. And he can recognize you in a lineup, but the facts against you just keep piling up, Fernando. To a judge, they'll be difficult to disprove if you try. Well," –she stood up and walked to the door–. "Agent Doyle, could you come in, please? Agent Doyle, from Interpol, this is the suspect, Dr. Fernando Schebor, toxicologist, the one we talked about. Please explain to the detainee the contents of those folders."

- "They are the files on the murders of former repressors and internationally wanted criminals, Argentine General Oscar Newell, head of the SIDE during the dictatorship in that country, and Major Inspector Carlos Falcone, head of the Political Order Commission, Uruguay's highest repressive body during the previous dictatorship in this country."

- "The first was killed outside Wollerau, Switzerland, in April 1998, and the second at the Sheraton in Caracas in December 1999, I believe. Is that correct?"

- "That's correct."

- "And what are the chances, after so many years, of locating this person" –she pointed to the detainee– "entering Switzerland in '98 or Venezuela in '99? I mean... considering he's an expert in how toxins work in the body, and given that the autopsies of these repressors determined they were poisoned with Novichok and potassium cyanide, respectively... but mostly considering that General Newell was the main person responsible for forcing him and his mother Magdalena Schebor to flee and continue fleeing from Argentina's death squads, and that Major Inspector Falcone was the one who incited the betrayal of his father, which eventually led, in '79, after Huidó and Falcone went out to smoke outside the officers' mess, to an arrest warrant being issued for sedition and terrorism against his mother—an ample reason to want to kill them. Would there be any records that could be tracked to place him in those countries and on those dates, if you had... let's say... 2 or 3 weeks, the time the suspect will remain behind bars?"

- "In Switzerland, almost certainly" –the Interpol agent was emphatic, a father of a young daughter who tended to get into trouble, but for the right reasons– "Europe established the permanent and mandatory registration of everyone's faces entering and leaving the European Community in '97. As for Venezuela, I'm afraid not. Latin America didn't adopt this practice until 2003, and the Sheraton in Caracas probably doesn't keep security footage older than two weeks, I'd guess."

- "What a shame about Venezuela." –Geraldine clicked her tongue, and at that moment, a message with a *very specific* ringtone sounded. She checked the preview "on live 5" from Viktor– "But, oh, now that I think about it... Did you mention, Agent Doyle, that it was the famous French detective Edith Bonelli from the Bonelli Investigation Agency who first tried to revive Falcone, and that when the Venezuelan government tried to hire them to investigate the case, they found out what a human scumbag the victim was and decided to decline the case?"

- "It was her, yes. And you've got a reserved spot in hell with your name on it, Goldman," –the Canadian smiled, sensing where the strategy was headed.

- "Thanks. I hear that often, and I'm Jewish, by the way. What are the chances that I... a humble detective... would have Edith Bonelli among my contacts?" –she took out her cell phone– "Oh, I can't believe my luck!" –she feigned surprise, showing the suspect the contact with the characteristic French +33 country code– "Let's call her, see if she remembers that day. Can you call her, from your satellite phone, Agent Doyle?" –she handed him her phone– "I need to change mine. Someone in my line of work should at least have one with hands-free technology," –she shrugged.

- "Done."

The four in the room waited expectantly as they heard the four beeps before someone picked up on the other end.

"Oui?"

"Hi, Edith. It's Geraldine. I hope I'm not catching you at a bad time."

"In fact, I couldn't be more relaxed in life. I'm here recovering from some bruises in Madagascar, soaking up the sun and enjoying beach massages. Have you still not caught the killer?"

"We caught him, and we have him here detained at the Central Headquarters of the Police."

"Oh, good. That's better. So, why are you calling me?"

"We want to appeal to your memory, which I know is about to be classified as *superhuman*. Do you remember when you were in Venezuela in December 1999?"

"They could never prove anything! It was a drug gang that destroyed another drug gang! Period."

"I wasn't talking about that, silly," –she smiled with her jet-black eyes– "I was talking about when you tried to revive the old man who had been poisoned with potassium cyanide on the beach at the Sheraton in Caracas."

"Oh, yes, the repressor. What's with him?"

"I'm going to send you a photo right now, and you tell me if our suspect looks like the beach waiter who alerted you with his screams, claiming a guest had had a heart attack."

"Let's see..."

The detainee tried to cover himself (a useless gesture, of course, with his hands cuffed to the bar), but Geraldine, while on the satellite phone call with Doyle, had kept her camera on. She sent the photo to Edith via WhatsApp with the skill of a near-native digital user.
"Did it arrive, Edith?"
"Yes. It's him. Those curly red hair and that flattened nose are unmistakable, but look at how he's aged. Must be the redhead genetics. Do you need anything else from me, or can I go surf with my daughter, enjoying the last waves of the day?"
"Good waves, my friend. Talk to you soon."
"Salut." –the call from Madagascar ended.
"And that, Schebor, is what I meant by coincidences and circumstances, and that can *definitely* be defined as bad luck for you. Thank you, Agent Doyle. You may leave."
The Interpol Agent did so, but as soon as he left, there was a knock at the door, followed by a second, then a brief pause, and then a final knock. A long one and two short ones, in Morse code: the Judicial Authorities had arrived... a few minutes past the agreed time.

"The deal is simple, Schebor: you plead guilty to authorship and co-authorship in the non-exonerable crimes of Mojica's murder and Huidó's attempted murder, because the exonerable ones are just the excuse to keep you while we investigate your movements, and the files on the murders of Newell and Falcone will be closed. What do you say? Does it sound like a deal?"

"I think I'll wait for my lawyer," –the detainee reverted to his stubbornness.

"I have one more thing for you to think about, and then I'll give up, okay? It's a recording your father gave me with a message for you about your current predicament." –she searched through her recorder and played it:

"Hello, Fernando. It's me, your father. I *know* you hate me. Big news there. Listen. I truly loved your mother. She was the woman of my life. And I loved you too. But then I screwed up, what am I going to lie about? Falcone offered to let me out of prison with my Tupamaro comrades, that damn 18th of July, 1971, and I accepted like a fool. And then, out of cowardice, I started betraying my own, and I *kept* betraying, so that the consequences of my actions as a guerrilla wouldn't fall on me. Then your mom found out, wouldn't let me see you anymore, and with the backing of the dictatorship, I kept going to your house on Mar Mediterráneo street. I *ruined* my life, and with the photo they took of me aiming at Vasco Olavarría, which was published and now everyone knows... They had me by the balls. But then democracy came back, and everyone saw me as a hero, because besides being a coward, I'm a *damn* liar. I lied saying Píriz was the traitor, and I kept lying about how they tortured me throughout the dictatorship... A whole pile of lies that just kept growing. But now, as you can see, I'm old and the lies have come back to bite me. I ruined my life and I ruined yours and your mom's by *not* being a man, by *not* rising to the occasion when I was pressured. You... don't do that. I love you, son. Oh, and accept the deal Goldman offers. It's for your own good... and for Facundo's. A hug."

Geraldine let a few seconds pass for the recorded audio to sink in.

"Changed your mind about pleading guilty, Dr. Schebor?"

"No."

"Stubborn and hard as a wall. OK. I tried." She turned to the homicide detective, "Di Lorenzo, care to turn on the TV on Channel 4 and see if anything interesting is happening while we wait for the suspect's lawyer to show up?"

"Sure. Why not?" – Detective Di Lorenzo agreed and turned on the TV in the room.

An aerial shot, apparently taken from a helicopter, showed a rural house with a gabled roof, a barn, and several police vehicles. In large letters, the headline read:

"SHOCKING: SUSPECTED SHOOTER WHO INJURED HUIDÓ RESISTS ARREST."

"Live and Direct from Paysandú: INTENSE Gunfire Exchange with Police. *Several* officers injured."

"What did you do, Goldman?" – The mastermind of the criminal duo couldn't believe what he was seeing.

"Me? I didn't do anything, Schebor. This is routine police procedure. When there are two suspects in different locations, they organize the arrests simultaneously so they can't warn each other. You were very cooperative with the customs police; Facundo seems to be resisting being taken in for questioning. Now, do me a favor and shut up, since you didn't want to talk to me about what we need to discuss. Shh. Quiet," – Geraldine, indifferent to the detainee's shock, raised the volume.

"This is a *war zone*, Carolina!" – The reporter on the scene was speaking to someone at the central studio. "It's a *total* war zone! I don't know if the cameras can capture the smoke cloud from dozens of weapons firing, both from the house toward the police vehicles and from the police toward the house!"

"Yes, we can see it, Amílcar. Do we know anything about the ambulances?"

"The ambulances can't get close until the gunfight stops, and the ones holed up inside don't seem to have any plans to surrender, nor do they intend to stop shooting. Carolina... I *fear* for my life," – the reporter's voice cracked. "I've *never* witnessed so much violence in my 30 years as a journalist."

"Stay safe, Amílcar, you and your team."

"Yes. Yes, yes. For now, we're safe in the helicopter... I think. No! Wait! What are they doing?!" – The reporter clearly spoke to someone off-camera, cutting the microphone while the image continued showing a fallen officer beside a police car, close-ups of bullet holes in the patrol cars, the house's walls, and a zoomed-in shot where ambulance lights could be seen waiting.

"I'm being told we're going to land. There's a doctor aboard who worked in war zones, accompanying peace forces in the Congo, and she's going to take the risk of assisting the injured police officers."

"You guys don't risk it, Amílcar. Under *no* circumstances should you get out of the helicopter!" – The reporter in the studio pleaded.

The camera zoomed in on the terrain, then on two people, a man ahead and a doctor in a white coat behind, both wearing bulletproof vests, the doctor carrying a large medical bag. As soon as they descended, the helicopter began to ascend again, but the cameraman followed the two figures, now dozens of meters away from the helicopter, running toward the besieged area. Then the man in front was shot and fell to the ground.

"FUCK!!!" Geraldine shouted, losing her calm, composure, and cynical posture... even the script she had prepared for the interrogation, as she watched her former high school classmate, Aklmer Lupoj, fall. She exhaled sharply and wondered whether throwing the chair she was sitting On would help vent her anger, but she tried to calm herself to continue with Plan 2D, which involved the assistance of Dr. Regueiro on the ground. "DO YOU SEE WHAT YOU'VE DONE, SCHEBOR?! This is all *your* fault!! YOURS!!!"

"They should *never* have cornered Facundo the way they did!! WHAT THE HELL IS WRONG WITH YOU PEOPLE?!"

"Why? Is there a nice way to handle an armed, emotionally unstable suspect? Would you have preferred that we sent the Carmelite Sisters to kindly ask him to come in for questioning, with his overprotective mother and how abrasive Facundo is with society? Do you see what you've caused?" she pointed again to the screen. "You wouldn't have gone looking for him, wouldn't have suggested him to team up to share the pain and seek revenge together in the first place. Do you know how those two are going to leave that house? Huh? I'm talking about Facundo González, who you consider a brother, and his stubborn mother, the ex-Tupamara Anabel Pulansky, who raised him in a dungeon until he was 10 years old. Do you know that? They'll leave there *dead*. Do you understand that? Who do they think they are to declare war on a country? Damn it! We haven't learned *a thing* as a society!" Her eyes were genuinely red, on the verge of tears. "But... you know what? I don't care anymore." She had reached the end of her rope, "I don't care about them, or about justice, or the people who hired me... or you, Schebor. This is where I draw the line. I'm done. I'm *done*..." She slammed her fist on the table. "You can *all* go to hell, Schebor! You, them, the deal I offered you earlier, the one I was going to offer you now, and the damn hell that spawned them! Get out of here, Schebor! Shove your confession up your ass!" She stood up angrily, ready to leave the room.

"Wait. Wait, please!" the handcuffed man pleaded.

"WHAT?!" Geraldine spun around, still holding the doorframe.

"What *second* deal?"

Geraldine took a moment to calm down. "*Damn it! Those acting classes from high school really paid off,*" she thought to herself. "*What an actress I could have been. If only the National Comedy Theatre knew what they were missing. I can even **curse** properly.*"

"Given the massacre that a simple transportation of your accomplice to testify turned into, I was going to offer you one last deal... but I get it... Believe me, I understand. You've already spoken in advance with your expensive lawyer, Dr. Ojeda, and he told you to stick to your story in every scenario presented... and you'll stick to that, so... forget it. I'll have to call my people in Paysandú because I *do have* people I care about there," she pointed at the sensationalist headlines on the TV screen. "I don't think even Ojeda, no matter how good a criminal lawyer he is, would have predicted injured or dead police officers, civilians, like my personal friend who we saw fall just now, or the doctor... dead or injured, your father's complete confession on how he ruined you... I don't think any of that was in his plans, so... you can decide whether you'll be able to sleep at night with Facundo and Anabel's deaths hanging over you." She shrugged and let a tear slip down her cheek. "What I was going to offer you was to let you use your phone one last time." She took out the detained man's phone, still in an evidence bag, from her jacket pocket. "To call your brother and convince him to come out with his hands up. But I understand. You paid for legal advice, and you want to stick to the script, so... let's wait for Dr. Ojeda and see if anyone is left alive by the time he gets here."

"Let them in, Goldman," the toxicologist snapped, but tried to restrain his fury.

"Who?" Geraldine feigned ignorance.

"The judiciary staff, they must be waiting in the hallway. I'll confess everything, but they need to hurry."

"Oh, those. OK." She stepped out to the hallway and signaled for Judge Leguizamo, Prosecutor Martínez, and the clerk with the laptop to enter. She said very seriously to Judge Leguizamo, "We've reached a deal with the detainee. I'll honor my part of the deal, only *if and when* you and the prosecutor agree that his statement is complete, condemning, and—most importantly—verifiable." She walked over to the TV to turn it off. "I'm going to watch the news in the waiting room. Excuse me."

"And no tricks," warned Di Lorenzo, who had witnessed everything leading up to the official and legal statement from the accused.

"Understood. You're declining the presence of your criminal lawyer during the statement, correct?" The judge asked, confirming the situation.

"I decline the presence of my defense lawyer," Schebor sighed heavily.

"Noted." The judge's voice was grave as he confirmed it with a nod to the clerk to record the statement. "Please state your name, ID number, and current occupation for the court."

CHAPTER 24: THIS HAS TO END

"*L*a Redención" *Ranch, Paysandú Department, Thursday, July 23, 2009, 2:45 PM.*
"Wolf!" "WOLF!!" "WAKE UP, DAMN IT!!"
The man who had just been shot in the chest opened his eyes wide and took a huge breath.

"*Damn* this shit," he cursed, he who, like Geraldine for different reasons, rarely swore—she due to her professional deformation as a communicator and her role with the press, and he because he wanted to reach at least Latin American readers, as the "vos" and "che" of the Río de la Plata region were perceived as strange outside of Argentina and Uruguay. "This hurts like hell."

"Well, yeah. The bulletproof vest took it for the wound, but *not* for the impact. What did you expect?"

"At least it met the specifications. It was to be expected that they'd have weapons capable of killing predators, not going through armored cars. So, take advantage and run now, because I hear ours are increasing the fire in retaliation. You're short enough, if you run crouched, they won't hit you. As for me, I'll only have a couple of broken ribs. Last time we were in a situation like this together, I came off *much worse*. But for the cameras of Canal 4, I'll play dead." He winked. "Oh, and please come over for dinner with Mica and me more often—not just when your life's at risk."

"I'll remember, Lobo," she said, stroking his curly hair, now beginning to gray. "I love you, you know?" she added. "As a friend, let's not get confused, but I love you."

"And I love you, too, Lía. Now go, run like the wind, Yee-haw! Giddy up, Bullseye!"

Dr. Regueiro grabbed her large medical kit, which fortunately wasn't as heavy as it looked, and started zigzagging toward the location where Víctor and Toro were crouched behind the police car wreck, next to the wounded officer.

"Gunshot wound with an entry but no exit, probably lodged in the left scapula, heavy bleeding," the ex-boxer Russian said, skipping the pleasantries.

"Alright. Move over, Vik," she asked, while slipping on surgical gloves. "What's the officer's name?"

"Peláez."

"Alright, Officer Peláez. I'm not going to lie to you: this is *going* to hurt, but you have to hang in there, or I won't be able to remove the bullet and stitch you up. You can swear at me, that's fine, but don't move," she said, shooting a significant glance at the detective, who kneeled behind the officer's head, keeping his shoulders pressed firmly to the ground. "Sorry, we don't have time for anesthesia."

Officer Peláez gritted his teeth as Lía began pouring disinfectant over the wound in intermittent spurts, then used forceps to trace the hole left by the bullet, feeling the unmistakable touch of metal against metal as the pin hit the bullet lodged inside.

"Hold on just a bit longer, Peláez," she warned the officer, who was now crying from the pain but nodded obediently to the doctor. Lía eventually pulled the bullet out, throwing it onto the grass along with the forceps before pouring more disinfectant. "That was the worst part, Peláez."

Meanwhile, Villa was keeping a sharp eye on the movements in the house now that the last barrage of police fire had subsided. Something no one had expected happened: the front door with the mosquito net opened, and the ex-tupamara and now small-scale rural producer Anabel Pulansky appeared, shotgun in hand but more or less hanging from her left arm, likely the stronger one, while she gripped her neck with her right hand.

"DON'T SHOOT! DON'T SHOOT!" Toro shouted to the police force.

"You won't take my Facu..." she barely managed to say before collapsing on the porch of her home, which had become a sieve in the crossfire.

"THE OTHER ONE IS ESCAPING TO THE BARN!" a police officer shouted, and the firing resumed, though no one hit the large man, who, despite being at least 50 meters away, was still a considerable target carrying a hunting rifle on his back, along with a holster containing a revolver.

The natural son of Francisco "Pancho" Mojica and Anabel Pulansky dove behind the sacks of grain—the same position where, the last time they came for him, he had aimed his rifle at the two detectives and two police officers who had come down from the helicopter, and his mother had chased them off. *But now, with reinforcements, they **must** know something*, he thought. Still, here, behind the grain sacks, with a perfect view of the cops and boxes of ammunition next to him, he felt safe. This was his personal "Alamo," like they say in the movies. His last stand.

He briefly considered the possibility that they might try to encircle him, but from the police 4x4 on the left to the cover of the house, where he would lose his firing angle, there was a 20-meter gap for anyone daring to try. To the right, from the police car, which had been shot through, to the pigsty, it was at least 40 meters, and the pigsty didn't even offer perfect cover unless someone crawled. *I can stay like this all day, guys*, he thought to himself, engaging mentally with the ones trying to capture him. *But if they've found me, it means they've found you, too, Fer*, he thought about his partner, his accomplice, his brother in pain from the legacy of the brutal military dictatorship, a bond forged in suffering and thirst for revenge. He pulled his analog cellphone from his jacket's front pocket, checking for any missed calls or messages from his accomplice. There were none. He was distracted by a shot near the barn, to which he responded by hitting the police Hyundai's hood from that distance. *I can stay like this all day.*

The Vladivostok private detective, in the other trench, however, saw the opportunity to use Pulansky's wound, macabre as it seemed, to his advantage. He took the police radio connected to the patrol car's loudspeaker, and spoke to the besieged man.

"Facundo. My name is Viktor Ielicov, as you may know, and I am a private detective, hired by the police to advise on this case. Listen to me: it's all over, brother. Turn yourself in. Your mother is dying, can't you see it?"

"My mother *lied* to me all my life!" – was heard faintly from the barn, 40 meters or more away, coming from the entrenched man.

"Yes. I'll admit that part to you" - Ielicov tried to sound compassionate - "but you would also have to admit that she raised you in the worst possible conditions, in a dungeon during the military dictatorship, and then, if that generated in her an overprotective instinct about you... well... parents *also* make mistakes, and I can tell you that, my parents abandoned me when I was 16 because they were more interested in continuing to live their lives on hold while my sister and I grew up than seeing us become adults. Anabel didn't do that with you. She was *always* by your side, friend."

"What exactly are you proposing to me, Ielicov?" - the big guy shouted from the barn.

"Something humanitarian, nothing more: that you leave me and a doctor we have with us, who by the way stabilized the wounds of the police officer you injured, thanks for asking, and can do the same for your mother. What do you say, Facundo? Are you going to let us stabilize your mother while you think about whether to continue shooting at us or turn yourself in so the ambulances can come?"

"There was a tense moment of silence in which neither side fired."

"Just you, Ielicov, and the doctor. Nobody else moves or shoots, or I'll kill you."

"Did you hit your head, Viktor? - Captain Gervasio Villa whispered to him at his side, gun in hand - "It's a trap, that's very clear. You leave the protection of the car and this son of a bitch puts a bullet in your head."

"And what are the options, Toro?" - the former boxer with the aquiline nose and dark curls responded - "Let Pulansky bleed out on the porch of her house?" - he shrugged his shoulders.

"You are crazy... No. No-no" –he looked alternately at Lía and Viktor, both convinced that it was the humane thing to do-. "Crazy, no. What is *after* crazy."

"We are going at our own risk, dear Toro" –the coroner patted the powerful arm of the police captain in charge of the Homicide Squad.

"Well, as "negro" Olmedo said: if we are going to do it, we are going to do it right" –and he shouted to the police-. "Did anyone bring a bulletproof shield that we can borrow?!"

"Here! In the back of the 4x4!" -confirmed a member of the Cuirassier Guard that was part of the ill-fated attack force.

"Throw it over here!" -Villa howled.

A shield with the logo of the Uruguayan National Police, 1.60 meters high and 60 centimeters wide, attached to its back and bent, flew to the position of the patrol car that had crashed before even entering the property, after its driver had received a bullet from the besieged.

The shield landed and slid to end up 6 meters from the Hyundai patrol car.

"Please remind me of *never* play frizbee with your boys, Villa" - Viktor said ironically, and crawled without consequences to his health to the riot shield, with the capacity to deflect low-caliber bullets. He returned with the protection to the patrol car. - "Ready, Lía?"

"I was *born* ready" - the coroner winked, and they began a cautious walk to the position where Anabel Pulansky lay in a pool of her own blood on the porch of her country house. - "She has a pulse" - she reported - "but she's not reacting". -With a flashlight from her medical bag she examined the eyes, after putting on a new pair of sterile gloves. She cleaned the wound with disinfectant and confirmed that the bullet had gone through the right side of the ex-Tupamaran's neck from side to side. She applied compresses to both holes and bandaged her. - "Do you hear me, Facundo?" - she shouted.

"Yes" - the besieged man answered from the barn.

"I don't want to lie to you, Facundo: if we don't attend to her urgently, you're going to lose her. The bullet went through the right side of her neck from side to side, she lost *a lot* of blood and the carotid artery may have been affected. She needs an immediate blood transfusion and to be taken to the nearest surgeon in the ambulance."

"But the ambulances aren't going to come if I don't turn myself in, right? Ha! How funny! Go lie to someone else."

"Think whatever you want, Facundo, but you're *going to* surrender eventually. If not now, it'll be in an hour or two, or when you run out of bullets, or when they come at you with a bazooka—who knows? Do you want to risk losing your mother for a few more hours of playing cowboys with the police? It's your call. Do you even know what blood type your mom is?"

"AB negative. Why?"

"Goddamn it!" – the doctor cursed under her breath. "Are you *sure* it's AB negative?"

"Yes. I'm sure. I go with her to her hospital appointments, when I can convince her to go."

"Alright, here's the deal, Facundo: that blood type is the rarest and the hardest to find a compatible donor for. Let me check if the ambulances have it," – Lía looked meaningfully at the boxer, who unclipped the portable radio from his belt.

"Ielicov to ambulances. Over."

"This is ambulances," – Micaela answered the radio from one of the two units, since in the plans made by the five of them, that was her role: to direct the paramedic efforts, and, above all, to make sure they didn't rush into action recklessly and get trapped in the crossfire. "We hear you, Ielicov. Over."

"We have Anabel Pulansky unconscious. She's lost a lot of blood and needs an urgent transfusion. Her blood type is AB negative. Please check if you have any in the ambulances. Over."

"Negative, Viktor. We don't have it. Over," – Vasconsellos confirmed after a moment.

"Any donor-to-recipient transfusion equipment? Over."

"Yes, they confirm they have it. Over."

"Wait for instructions. Ielicov, over and out." – he spoke loudly so that Facundo could hear. "We have good news and bad news, Facundo," – he raised his voice so it would carry to the barn. "The bad news first: there's no compatible blood in the ambulances. The good news is that I'm O negative, universal donor, and they have transfusion equipment in the ambulance. Now I ask you: are you going to surrender and let us try to save your mother, or do you prefer to stay there until they come for you, dead? I don't mind being the donor. Ha. Like I'm gonna miss one or two liters of blood from this body that God gave me and I trained."

All that came from the barn was silence. The natural son of Francisco Mojica and Anabel Pulansky was deliberating on his options. *They have a point: I don't have a chance of not being killed or captured. If it's not now, it'll be in a little while. Besides... what if they're **not** lying to me?* He gathered the courage and air in his lungs to shout that he was surrendering and that the ambulances could come when something that surprised not only him but the police outside as well, broke the silence of the field: the sound of a cellphone. The besieged man pulled it from the front pocket of his jacket and saw that it was a contact he had saved: "Brother."

"Hello, Fer. You're catching me at a bad time. Can it wait, what you need?" – he answered in his deep voice.

"Hello Facu. I *know* it's a bad time. I've been watching it on TV."

"Oh, yeah. The helicopters," – the worker from the González-Pulansky family farming venture understood.

"Exactly. Listen to me: surrender. They know everything. I don't know how they found us, but they know everything. I already confessed, and Dr. Ojeda should be arriving any minute now to advise me on how the case moves forward. You need to surrender too, but don't say *anything* before speaking to the lawyer, okay?"

"So everything's gone to shit, right?" – Facundo wanted to confirm.

"Exactly. Now what really matters is that you're alright, okay? So surrender without resistance, then talk to Dr. Ojeda, and everything will be fine. We'll be locked up for a while, but I don't think it'll be too long."

"Okay. Anyway, when you called me, I was about to surrender. Mom got shot in the neck. According to that detective, Ielicov, and the doctor who came down from the helicopter, it looks like a bullet went through the right side of her neck. If she doesn't get a transfusion right away, she's gonna die."

"It might be a lie, little brother, but what options do we have? I love you, Facu."

"And *I* love you, Fer. See you in court, like they say in the movies."

"Ha. Hug, bro. Bye."

"I surrender!" – the 130-kilo powerhouse of pure muscle from lifting, harvesting, slaughtering sheep and pigs, and cutting wood shouted to the four winds. "I surrender... unarmed... but *only* to Ielicov."

At the Central Headquarters in Montevideo, Geraldine picked up the phone again, which, though examined, would remain in the evidence room for a long time.

"How did you know?" – was all the detainee wanted to know, the one who had confessed everything before the judge, the prosecutor, and the clerk, just to have the chance to speak to his soul brother, his brother in pain, and ask him to surrender, to avoid them being killed—him and his brother's mother.

"I think I told you this at the beginning of our interview, Fernando: there's *no* perfect crime. What there is are insufficient investigations. They hired us, we investigated, and we found the truth," – the Jewish woman shrugged.

At that moment, a man in his 30s walked in, with black hair and eyes, and clearly more addicted to the gym than video games, wearing a suit and tie and carrying a briefcase.

"What happened here, Franco?" – Dr. Ojeda asked the detainee using his false name.

"It's alright, Adrián," – Schebor brushed it off. "They already know who I am, what I did... they know *everything*."

"But they told me at the entrance that you pled guilty, that you confessed... That *wasn't* the deal we had," – Dr. Ojeda raised an eyebrow in a serious tone.

"I know, but this bitch..."

"Geraldine Goldman, private detective, advising the Ministry of the Interior on the case. Pleasure, Dr. Ojeda," – she extended her hand to the criminal lawyer, who returned the formal handshake.

"They found us, she and her partner, and put me in an impossible dilemma, Adrián. At the same time they were interrogating me, the police had Facundo surrounded in Paysandú. It was either confess everything or lose him, although I guess –" he shrugged, "it was only a matter of time before they found out everything."

"Alright. No problem. You play it my way, Fer," – the lawyer, with his massive pecs, biceps, triceps, quads, and maybe even quintuplets, if there were any, felt confident. "We'll go for the abbreviated trial. The judges *love* that. You negotiate that if it goes to trial, they'll have to spend tons of time and resources proving you're guilty, and our firm proving you're not, so you offer them the deal: I plead guilty to one, save them time, and the sentence will be lower. Plus, with the mitigating circumstances you both have, I'll bet my career on it – put my law degree on the table and tear it up if I'm wrong – you and your brother won't get more than 10 years, for a crime of passion with circumstances that forced you to do it."

"Ojeda," – the private detective patted the lawyer's muscular shoulder. "Stop the cocaine, or the cocaine is going to stop you. Have a good trial, Schebor," – she turned to leave.

"Goldman," – the handcuffed man called out to her, this time for real, as the Jewish woman was about to leave the interrogation room for good.

"What is it?" – she answered.

"How can you sleep at night, after what you did today?"

"Like a baby, Schebor, like a baby. I wish you a nice and peaceful sentence," – she blew him an air kiss and walked out.

Meanwhile, in Paysandú, everything was tense. The police saw the man who had been shooting at them for a long time come out with his hands up, unarmed, from the barn. They all pointed their guns at him, of course. It was the veteran officer, Captain of the Homicide Brigade, who was the first to holster his gun and shout to his subordinates when he realized the danger of "itchy trigger fingers":

"Anyone who shoots now, I'll make them eat a bullet, clear?" – he openly threatened.

Viktor had left the riot shield in Lía's hands and was cautiously approaching the shooter.

"Is your father in the house, pointing a gun at me?" – the detective asked.

"No. Dad's not here. It was just my mom and me shooting," – Facundo replied.

"Alright. Get on your knees, Facundo," – Ielicov requested, now just ten steps from the suspect, taking out the handcuffs from his pocket.

The natural son of Mojica, whom his mother had decided to keep despite the attempts of the then-Tupamaro to have an abortion, complied. Viktor circled around behind the surrendering man and expertly cuffed him.

"Stand up, Facundo. I appreciate that you understood this *had* to end."

"Yeah. What options did I have left? Was what they said about mom's wound true?"

"The honest truth," – Viktor guided him with a hand on his back toward the damaged patrol cars, and with the other, grabbed the portable radio. – "Ielicov to ambulances. They can come. The suspect has surrendered. Confirm. Over."

"Ambulances en route," – Micaela confirmed. "Over and out."

The massive small rural producer allowed himself to be placed in the back seat of the Hyundai patrol car, which had managed to get past the farm gate, but had several bullet holes in its bodywork, and a flat tire. Clearly, it wasn't in a condition to transport the prisoner anywhere, but it would serve temporarily to calm the police until backup patrols arrived.

"It's all over, Carolina," – Amílcar Fou, the lead crime reporter for Channel 4, narrated from the CSA Group helicopter. "Private detective Viktor Ielicov, from the LNB PI agency, advising the Ministry of the Interior," – he read what he had written on his hand with a pen, so he wouldn't get it wrong. "He just handcuffed the suspect and put him in the patrol car. If the camera focuses on the road... Focus there, Tomás," – he pointed to the cameraman. "We'll see the ambulances coming to assist the wounded, including the shooter's mother. All of this is live and direct on Channel 4. Carolina, we'll be landing soon for the interviews from the scene."

"Thank you for your great work, Amílcar. From the central studio, we'll provide continuous coverage of the story, but only land when the police tell you it's safe."

"Yes, yes. Of course. But what a tense moment we've had here!" – his exaggerated tone made the shooting with two injured people seem like the D Day Normandy landing.

Meanwhile, on the ground, Lupoj raised his hand and shouted: "Don't forget about this *other* wounded guy!"

As soon as the ambulances parked at the farm, the one who had been directing the medical assistance operation ran to find her partner.

"Who's forgetting about you, fool?" – she smiled, kneeling next to the one who had pretended to be dead for the Channel 4 cameras.

"Well. It could have been worse," – he touched the hole that, while it hadn't penetrated his vest, had hit him with the force of a sledgehammer from a wall-breaking tool, with 3 kilos of iron on the end. "Can you help me up?" – he offered his hand to his girlfriend, but when he tried to sit up, a sharp pain made him reconsider. "It hurts a lot. I'll wait for the paramedics. Anyway, the day's nice for a field trip," – he smiled.

"Ah, but look at you, Ak, dear, you've turned soft on me," – she reproached him. "You can stay here, but at some point, you'll have to stop playing the human bulletproof shield game."

"Mmm... Well. I promise: last time... I think."

CHAPTER 25: YOU SHALL NOT DRINK FROM THIS WATER

H*otel Emperador, between Colonia and Mercedes, Thursday, July 23, 2009, 8:10 PM.*
Geraldine stepped out of the shower at the three-star hotel, which was the minimum accommodation requirement for their cases, with a towel wrapped around her body and another around her hair. A curtain of steam followed her out of the bathroom. Viktor had already showered when he arrived from Paysandú, and when his partner and fiancée finished her shower late in the afternoon, and after some time at Central Headquarters, she only had enough energy to greet him affectionately, write the final report for the Suárez-Artagaveytia Corporation, and send it by email to Mr. Iván Reno. She had tried calling, sent a WhatsApp... nothing. Email was the only option left.

Viktor was watching the aftermath of the case on the news and refreshing the email server now and then to see if Reno had replied. No news. However, he turned to see his fiancée come out of the suite bathroom dressed like that, through the smoke-like steam.

"Don't let *anyone* tell you that you don't know how to enjoy a shower with continuous hot water when you can," – he joked, but with affection.

"When you can, you can," – she shrugged.

"Did I ever tell you that when we were following the Decorator case together, and I showered for the first time at your place, as a gentleman, I let you shower first, and you didn't leave me *a drop* of hot water?"

"Seriously? But I remember you even sang in Russian while you were showering."

"I sang to avoid grumbling in Aramaic."

They both laughed heartily for a moment before turning their attention back to the news. There was an interview with Minister Cortez about the case, where the highest political figure of the police force dodged questions one after another with evasions, reminding everyone that the details of the case wouldn't be revealed until 7 PM the next day, Friday, July 24. Of course, he let a few minimal details slip, otherwise, the interview wouldn't make sense: the shooter who wounded Senator Huidó had been caught in Paysandú, there were no casualties on either side of the siege, which had been broadcast live in every home and business across the country through Channel 4's cameras, and it was thanks to the external advice from the LNB PI agency and detectives Viktor Ielicov and Geraldine Goldman that the police had managed to identify the perpetrators in record time. It wasn't necessary, as journalist Amílcar Fou had done, to write the names of the detectives on his hand with a pen, since Viktor had been the one to spot the clues that led the investigation in the 2005 case of Uruguay's first serial killer, and Geraldine had been his subordinate for so many years when he was in charge of the National Police's press office.

"Ah, it feels *nice* to be recognized publicly, doesn't it?" – she asked Viktor.

"At some point, it had to happen. Did Minister Cortez give you that check he owed you from that time?"

"I was *not* leaving the building without that check, you can imagine," – she smiled and kissed his muscular shoulder as he sat on the bed in just his underwear. "Oh, I'm exhausted, my love. I know you were in the middle of the gunfire and mud in Paysandú, tending to the wounded, and they took a liter and a half of your blood to save Pulansky on the way to the hospital... But getting Schebor's confession *completely* drained me, physically and mentally. What a tough nut to crack, that bastard!"

"But you did it. And Facundo González too, after he talked to Ojeda."

"Yeah, well, seems like that's been my thing lately. But the rest of the day, I was like an amoeba, running on autopilot, you know, around Jefatura Central. How did the flight back go with the detainee?"

"No problems. My only fear was that he'd jump out of the helicopter, so I asked them to cuff him to the seat too. I trust myself when it comes to restraining a criminal, but that guy was a *beast*, and he had already shown himself to be emotionally unstable."

"But everything turned out fine, both of them confessed, the final case report was written, and now we'll see what the CSA Group says. Vik, darling, I know we have this tradition of what to do when a case ends," – she stroked his chin and kissed him tenderly on the lips, "but I'm wiped out. Don't you want to go get us dinner and, if I'm still alive by the time you get back, we'll make love the way it should be?"

"Sounds tempting," – he smiled and quickly started getting dressed to go find food at a bar on 18 de Julio Avenue, since the Hotel Emperador didn't have room service. They only had a breakfast service that was clearly outsourced to the downstairs dining area.

It hadn't been five minutes since the Vladivostokian had left when Geraldine, still with the towel wrapped around her head, had placed it on the pillow to continue watching the news, which threatened to become a 24-hour broadcast, when she slipped into a deep state of dreaming. And in this state, something of her conscious self, clinging to staying awake, picked up the phone. Few in her circle knew it, but Goldman was a sleepwalker, and could speak in the three languages in which she was most fluent while in this state, and later remember nothing at all.

"Yes?" – she simply said, not even looking at the caller, because that would have required her eyes to be open, and to be awake.

"Hello, Geraldine. This is Iván Reno. I saw your call, I saw your message, but unfortunately, I was in a very long meeting at the port. It's not that I want to assign you another investigation or anything, but they found *four tons* of cocaine in a soy container that the CSA Group was about to ship to the port of Hamburg. Fortunately, we managed to clarify that it was the truck driver who stopped on a rural road, unloaded the four tons of soy into the field, and then camouflaged the same weight of cocaine so it wouldn't show up on the mandatory scales. Then, he managed, with the people who hired him, to tamper with the seal on the container, because otherwise, we would've been in a *serious* bind, as you can imagine. The irony of it all is that the inconsistency was detected by a scanner that CSA itself donated to the port. But, well... now everything is cleared up. The truck driver finally told us where he dumped the soy, it was found, and it still churns my stomach thinking about all that food being wasted out in the middle of the field, with so many people who don't have enough to eat... But... sorry, I don't mean to bore you with the details."

"No, no. It's fine. Go ahead," – she replied automatically, in sleepwalking mode.

"I just read the report. Wow! Who would've thought, right? In the end, what happened with Mojica, and then with Huidó, had *nothing* to do with a political maneuver within his own party, nor from the right-wing or the dictatorship's inner circle, but rather a much simpler and more human drama – two children seeking revenge on their parents for different reasons... or maybe the same ones, but you understand me. From the CSA Group, we are *infinitely* grateful for everything you've done, but since we paid you five days in advance, we'd like, if possible, for you two to meet tomorrow at 10 AM with the Board of Directors of the corporation to go over the case details, at CSA's headquarters, in Colón."

"Yes, of course. No problem. Can you send me the address?"

"I'll send you the location right now on WhatsApp. See you tomorrow, Goldman. Great work! Get some rest."

"Thank you. See you later."

Had it not been for the WhatsApp message she found the next morning, Geraldine would *never* have known that she had an appointment at 10. Viktor found her unconscious, barely, with her cell phone in hand when he arrived with the pizzas and beers. He kissed her on the forehead, she smiled in her sleep, and he prepared to eat alone, watching *whatever else* was on TV that wasn't related to the case.

CSA Group Headquarters, Colón neighborhood, Montevideo, Friday, July 24, 2009, 9:50 AM.

Geraldine at the wheel and Viktor in the passenger seat tried to figure out at the access control of the property, which spanned eight blocks, between the central building, annexes, and parking lot, what was the central office complex. It looked like what it was: a pyramid of glass, 200 meters on each side at its base, rising to several floors in height. A smiling Iván Reno awaited them, after they passed the access control, in the parking lot for clients and guests, wearing a mustard-colored trench coat, always with his wide, perfect smile.

"I'm so glad you managed to arrive on time. The boss has a little issue with punctuality," – he said, speaking rapidly while shaking hands with the newcomers.

"A meeting is a meeting, right?" – replied the detective, who had never known they had been invited, only finding out the morning of that Friday when she saw Reno's message on her phone.

"Follow me, please. The Board is already waiting for you."

Through additional access controls, elevators, and corridors, they were led to what was clearly the boardroom of the directors, located at the very top of the glass pyramid. The impeccably dressed ladies and gentlemen stood up when they arrived, and a round of applause broke out. Everyone except a woman in her early twenties or very early thirties, with long, wavy hair down to her shoulders, gray eyes, and expensive-framed glasses, who remained focused on her laptop.

Around the elliptical black marble table were not only unfamiliar faces: Minister Cortez and President Valdez were also part of the board.

"Well, thank you. Thanks to everyone. It's not such a big deal what we did," Geraldine responded to the applause.

"See what I *always* tell you?" – said a man in his sixties from the head of the table. Behind him hung a portrait of a young woman with a very serious look. From the hairstyle, she seemed to be from the seventies. "Humility, above all, folks."

Darío Suárez, heir to one of the largest fortunes in the country, but also to a tragic legacy that had cost the life of his sister (the one in the portrait, from the seventies), his mother, and had turned his other two younger brothers against their father, waited for the directors to finish laughing at his joke before allowing the group's main lobbyist, Iván Reno, to introduce each of the board members one by one. In each handshake and introduction, there was the customary exchange of business cards, following a tradition that hadn't gone out of style despite the digital age, but had become somewhat of a quaint tradition in the sports world.

In the past, for those who didn't see it, before a sports event of any kind, the captains of each team, or solo players in individual events, would exchange triangular pennants from their federation or club with their rival. The professionalization of sports broadcasting led to the decline of this tradition, and by the end of the 20th century, it was nearly nonexistent. But not so with the "other" pennant exchange—the business card exchange. Each executive gathered there was the head not just of one company, but often of a group of companies, covering *everything* from hotels, real estate, technology, slaughterhouses, banks, and agricultural production.

"Well, young Goldman and Ielicov," – Darío Suárez, CEO of the group, made a broad gesture indicating the board. "As you can see, you have 14 potential new clients among those gathered here. Now, moving on to the matter of the report you presented... In a very intimate and personal way... I have *no trouble at all* understanding the motives of these two, Facundo and Fernando, for wanting to kill their parents."

"Wait," – Viktor interrupted. "So, you are..."

"Then I am..." – Darío Suárez gave him a sharp look. "And I would appreciate it if you kept that to yourself, if you read the book. Every member of this board is strictly *prohibited* from reading that book. I'll *never* understand why Edith Bonelli shared the case details with the writer, but that's her business. I owe her *much more* than just my life, so I can let that one slide."

"I understand. Let's not speak of it again," – the private detective was firm.

"Back to the matter at hand, CSA will cover Dr. Ojeda's expenses, and we'll make sure they get the lightest sentence possible. Poor guys..." – the businessman clicked his tongue.

"It seems that the past Uruguayan dictatorship left more marks than what can be seen on the surface," – Geraldine agreed.

"People are cruel to people, what can I say?" – Suárez shrugged. "Which brings me to consider how airing everything that happened would affect your government, President Valdez, and our group, which has always supported the Progressive Front to govern this country, even before you were in power."

"Well, De La Rúa took care of sinking Huidó with the photo he gave to El País. Huidó's political career is *already* over, and if he knows what's good for him, he'll leave the country soon, like the unjustly accused Amadeo Píriz did in '84. We from the Front *already* removed him from the party, and I have no qualms about giving statements about what legitimately happened: Huidó deceived us all, perhaps *even* Mojica."

"Mojica. Great topic," – the leader of the business group pondered. "Agustina. How does it affect or not affect knowing that Mojica asked Pulansky to have an abortion in '69, when he found out the child was his, and she refused?"

"Are we going to lose the popularity of our rockstar, dad?" – replied the only one who hadn't stood up to applaud when the detectives entered, so focused was she on her laptop. "No, under *no circumstances* can we lose Mojica, even as a martyr. The mathematical models predict that the Progressive Front would drop at least 5% in voter intention," – she pointed at her laptop screen.

The private detectives, seated at the opposite head of the table from the CEO and closer to the girl with wavy hair and gray eyes, behind her expensive glasses, couldn't help but notice the striking resemblance between the young woman and the one in the giant portrait, the one with the '70s hairstyle.

"A 5% drop is *already* absurd," – the father of the one who had analyzed the variables was categorical. "Minister Cortez, what are the chances that this detail, although relevant to the case, might... *not* be related to what Facundo González suffered, growing up with a father who was a leader of the Tupamaros guerrilla, and after enduring the torment of growing up with his mother in a dungeon, channeled that rage toward his father?"

"As far as possibilities go..." – the minister thought for a moment. "There are *always* possibilities, but we can rule it out as a rumor," – he dismissed it with a gesture. "Besides, those would be private and sentimental matters regarding Mojica in the '70s. I don't see how they would contribute or detract from the judicial case. If necessary, we can talk to Judge Leguizamo to have any mention of it removed from the defendant's testimony."

"Good. I would appreciate that. And what about Anabel Pulansky, the shooting in Paysandú, and the fact that she is the twin sister of the first senator from the Popular Movement, after Mojica's death and Huidó's betrayal?"

"That *will* come out, Suárez," – Minister Cortez stated categorically. "There's *no chance* that won't go public. We can tone it down by framing it as just a mother defending her son, one with a very particular and painful personal history..."

"Besides, she's been estranged from her sister, the Senator, for years," – Agustina Suárez, who bore the name of her father's older sister, the one in the portrait, in homage, completed the thought. "A possible drop in voter intention is estimated at only 0.5%, although it could also result in an increase of up to 2% due to empathy for the tragic story."

"Alright. Let it be made public, then," – the businessman decided.

"And what about Arturi?" – Geraldine surprised everyone by looking directly into the eyes of the leader of Uruguay's largest business group, sitting across from her at the elliptical marble table.

"What about Arturi?" – he redirected the question back to her, leaning back in his chair and pinching his lower lip.

"You see, Mr. Suárez. Yesterday afternoon, between Schebor's confession and González's, when we were able to fully mobilize the police resources to gather data, locations, camera recordings, court orders for the list of phone numbers the suspects called, and all that, an interesting detail came up: a recurring number appeared on Schebor's cell phone, that of the personal phone of Economist Daniel Arturi. Oh, what a coincidence! And then, in the visitor logs from the Ministry of Economy and Finance, Dr. Franco Ortega, the name under which Fernando Schebor went by in his daily life, had met with Arturi *eight times* over the past two years. Tell me, what are the chances I, a Uruguayan citizen, could meet with the Minister of Economy eight times?"

"I see where you're going, Goldman, and I must strongly—no, *emphatically*—ask that you desist from continuing that line of investigation."

"And why would that be?" – she raised an eyebrow.

"Economist Arturi, like all of them, is a political animal. What does it add or take away if he saw an opportunity to fan the flames *already* burning in the killer, to fuel the hatred toward his strongest rival within the party? Arturi-Pulansky is the new presidential ticket that will be proposed tomorrow at the Progressive Front's Assembly."

"And why doesn't it surprise me that you *already* know that, *before* the vote?" – Ielicov jumped in to defend his partner.

"Look, folks. What happened here is a human tragedy, okay? I know, *personally*, what someone can do to hurt another. Let's keep politics out of this case, can we agree to that, at least verbally?"

"You shall not drink of this water, right?" – Geraldine quoted from Life is a Dream by Pedro Calderón de la Barca, a classic of Spanish Golden Age theater writer. The phrase is used to express the idea that one should not commit to something that might turn out to be problematic or dangerous in the future.

"One should not drink of this water. I ask this in the name of the Progressive Front and the CSA Group."

For a moment, Viktor and Geraldine exchanged a look, consulting one another wordlessly. Finally, they gave in to the conditions of the person who had ultimately hired them.

"So be it," – Geraldine finally agreed for both of them. "Arturi is off the table."

"Good. I thank you, detectives. Now, let's move on to more pleasant topics," – smiled the financial and technology genius, with his tragic family past. "Iván. I understand you wasted corporate resources, didn't you?"

"That's right, and any additional amount to the prize can be deducted from my salary, Mr. Suárez," – Iván Reno, the group's main lobbyist, smiled broadly, showing his perfect teeth. "When I hired you, at the Arapey hot springs on Monday morning, Goldman proposed an additional prize to your fees: $5,000 if you solved the case in the first week. I raised the bet and told you we'd pay you $10,000 instead of $5,000 if you solved it in the first four days, and you solved it in three and a half. Detectives, here's your check for $10,000," – he handed them a bearer's check.

"Thank you," – Goldman accepted the check, the more disciplined of the two when it came to agency finances.

"The fault is mine, Iván, it's fine," – Darío Suárez waved off with a gesture. "I think I instructed you, if I remember correctly, that this had to be resolved as soon as possible. Your raising the stakes was in line with my instructions."

"Thank you, Mr. Suárez."

"No need to thank me. I was just joking about wasting resources," – Darío Suárez smiled.

"Since we're doing numbers, this is the corporate card you gave me, Mr. Reno," – Geraldine returned the credit card. "And these are the receipts for *almost* everything we spent," – she handed him an envelope with tickets from the car rental, hotel, per diems, and everything else. "There are some... not exceeding a thousand dollars, surely... in 'incentives' that I had to give out yesterday morning to get additional help. And, due to the discretion required by my profession, I'd prefer to withhold the identities of those to whom I gave them," – she was enigmatic, referring to the "bonuses" she'd given to the press office staff to expedite the processing of over 300 files recovered from the dilapidated mansion of Commander Alberdi.

"Nothing to worry about, Geraldine. It's within the expected calculations," – the Afro-descendant man winked.

"Well, if there's nothing else to settle," – the head of the business group rubbed his hands together, "we have one more task to assign you, but this is separate."

"Go ahead," – Viktor replied.

"No. I misspoke. It's not for both of you. It's just for her."

"Oooh, I'm intrigued," – smiled the dark-haired woman with curly hair, pale skin, even freckled, and large jet-black eyes.

"We'll pay you an additional $5,000 if you accept to do a task that will take you just 2 hours to prepare and half an hour to execute... and I suspect you'll simply *love* completing it for us."

Geraldine accepted the new task after learning the details, as the businessman had guessed: she *did love* going back to that place, and it was the most profitable two and a half hours in the history of her detective venture with Viktor. However, President Valdez's hand on her arm stopped her as they were about to leave.

"Goldman... Geraldine," – the oncologist whispered to her. "It was *very sly* of you how you handled the recovery of the files from Commander Alberdi. Giving the documents on the disappeared detainees to the Family Members Association? Seriously?"

"Who, if *not* them, had the right to access information about what happened to their children, their mothers, their fathers? Have a good day, President Valdez," – she shrugged off his grip and walked away.

EPILOGUE: BACK IN THE RING

Press Office of the National Police of Uruguay, San José Street, directly across from the Central Headquarters, Montevideo, Friday, July 24, 2009, 7:00 PM.

That Friday, unlike any other weekday, the prime-time news on channels 4, 10, and 12 would *not* begin with the usual advances for stories to be covered during the next two hours. These were the most-watched programs on Uruguayan television, but on this particular day, they would be even more so because of the previews for the press conference that would be held by the National Police, announcing the details of the death of Francisco "Pancho" Mojica and the attempted assassination of Senator Huidó.

"Good evening, ladies and gentlemen of the press, television viewers, and radio listeners," – Anahí began from the podium. "As you all know, my name is Anahí Velázquez, Head of Press for the National Police of Uruguay, but I will not be the one to provide the details today about the death of Senator Francisco Mojica and the attempted assassination of Senator Eleuterio Hernando Huidó. It will be my predecessor in this role, Graduate Geraldine Goldman, who has been working as a private detective for the past four years alongside her partner Viktor Ielicov, at the LNB PI agency. And before the press interrupts to ask how that's spelled, I'll say it in the International Phonetic Alphabet: Lima November Bravo Papa India, or, easier yet, just look up lnbpi.com on the internet to learn more about them. Detectives Goldman and Ielicov have been advising the National Police on the cases we are addressing, so without further ado: Geraldine Goldman. A big round of applause for her!" – she requested, and the press in the room, though not used to receiving press statements in this format, applauded.

"Thank you. Thank you all," – Geraldine smiled broadly and decided to start with a little joke, just as her predecessor had done, spelling out the agency's initials in international phonetic alphabet.

"Anahí, is it just me or did they increase the brightness of the lights in here?" – she waited for the current Head of Press to nod with a smile. "Wow, I wish I had been told beforehand so I could adjust my makeup accordingly." – some people in the room laughed. "Dear viewers, if I look like a ghost out of a B-horror movie, it's because no one told me the wattage of the lights had been turned up," – another round of laughter from the crowd. "Let's move on to the details of what happened with the murder of Mojica and the attempted assassination of Huidó, as it turned out to be the same case."

"Sorry. *Murder* of Mojica?" – a journalist's voice echoed from the room, after a few seconds of general shock.

"Yes, *murder*," Goldman stated, "but I ask those present, ladies and gentlemen of the press, not to interrupt me, as there will be space for questions and answers later. The Senator and presidential candidate from the Progressive Front, Francisco Mojica, died last Saturday night, July 18, from a myocardial infarction, as confirmed at the time by the Forensic Technical Institute and made public to the population. *However*, further investigations, in which my partner Viktor Ielicov and I advised the police, revealed that Mojica was *assisted* in having a heart attack. How? The criminals with the initials F. G. and F. S. (as everyone knows, primary offenders can only be mentioned by their initials until there is a final conviction, which will take *several* days, if not *weeks*), whose confessions are already on record in the judicial file, put a soluble cocaine derivative into the drink Mojica was having at the Las Palmas Pool at the Termas del Arapey—*Come on, Geraldine, this is when you start to lie and hide things, just try not to make it obvious*, she thought. *After all, what does it add or subtract from the news to mention that what he was drinking were* **industrial** *quantities of whisky?*— "Cocaine, as everyone knows, accelerates the heart rate. At one point, around 9:30 p.m., the lifeguard had to go to the bathroom, leaving Mojica alone in the pool for a moment—*another* concealment, this time by two: what does it add or subtract to mention that they had put a laxative in the municipal official's food, and what difference does it make that they kept the lifeguard in the bathroom for **half an hour?**— "At that moment, the accomplices in this crime took advantage of the opportunity to force Mojica's head under the water. The heart rate, *already* accelerated by the cocaine, combined with the terror of dying in a situation like that, of having one's head held underwater, caused Mojica's death from a myocardial infarction. The murderers left the pool before the municipal lifeguard returned, and despite his attempts at CPR, he was unable to save Mojica. Toxicological tests sent to the prestigious Biotech Argentina laboratory revealed on Wednesday afternoon that Senator Mojica had elevated levels of cocaine metabolites in his blood. The candidate was, therefore, *induced* to have a heart attack, which led to the classification of the crime as homicide for those under investigation. That's all for the details of Mojica's death. We will expand on why he was killed later."

She paused deliberately to take a sip of water in a room full of journalists who could not believe what they were hearing.

"Now, let's move on to Huidó. Not much to say in this case: the accomplices forced their way into a building at the roundabout near the Legislative Palace, waited for Huidó to arrive from the meeting he had just had at the Progressive Front headquarters, and shot him at the entrance with the intent to kill. The suspects with the initials F. G. and F. S. have been charged with attempted homicide for this incident. Senator Huidó was in a coma, but now, as is publicly known, he is stable at the Military Hospital. Both suspects, of course, have also been charged with conspiracy to commit a crime. And we reiterate that both have confessed to their crimes. Now, let's get to know F. G. and F. S. to understand their motives. First, F. G.: in 1971, while Mojica was one of the leaders of the Tupamaro guerrilla, he *also* had a private life. An unusual one, as you can imagine, but he had one. It turned out that a young woman he was dating got pregnant, and the result of that union was F. G. It is unclear—*ha, how could it **not** be?*—whether Mojica knew about this pregnancy. It was a turbulent time, let's remember, before the last military dictatorship, but the mother decided to raise him on her own. Since she was *also* a Tupamara, she was arrested, and anyone with two grams of sensitivity would ask: What about the baby? The baby grew up and lived with her in a dungeon... in a military barracks, until he turned 10. I... *can't even begin* to imagine what it must have been like for the child to grow up in those conditions" – she dramatized a little, but it wasn't without reason. At least *this* part was sincere. – "In a small cell, with a toilet in one corner that he shared with his mother, with no access to medical care or education..." – she clicked her tongue. Everything about the communicator was calculated: every gesture, every word... not like her oversight of not adding makeup, because the lights in the National Police press room had been turned up. She continued. – "She was released in 1981, his mother, and tried to get him into school, as the first thing, but during her time in prison, she had fallen in love with one of the soldiers, and that soldier adopted the child as his own son. Again: how crazy to have your mother in a dungeon and your father outside, bringing food, staying a while to talk. At school, things didn't go much better: while the dictatorship was still in place, he was mocked and beaten by supporters of the regime for being the child of a Tupamara, and when democracy returned, for being the son of a soldier. They moved to the countryside, the three of them, to work the land, and F. G. never finished his secondary education. In fact, he barely started high school. He became surly, isolated from society, protected from it by his mother, and one day he found out that his biological father, Francisco Mojica, had *also* been a Tupamaro, and one of the leaders, and therefore partly responsible for what he had suffered in captivity, and after. There were two significant differences between wanting to love and respect his mother, and hating and wishing death on his father. On one hand, his mother had been a follower, while his father was a leader – *another compliment to highlight Mojica's figure, and I swear I'm going to **puke**,* she thought. *But a job is a job, so do it well.* – "And on the other hand, his mother had actually *been there* for him, and Mojica had not. That was the reason for F. G.'s hatred towards Mojica. Whether he was right or wrong, he blamed his misfortunes on his absent father, though there is no certainty whether Mojica even knew he had a child. Now, let's move on to F. S., the child that Huidó had with a college companion. Like Mojica, Huidó was a fugitive from the authorities, but somehow, he and the baby's mother, who had *nothing to do* with the Tupamaros or even with the left, managed to raise him with all the love the situation allowed. F. S. was born in 1969, but then something happened that changed everything. And this happened on July 18, 1971. Do you see how the dates are starting to make sense? The *same day* Mojica was killed, July 18? On that fateful day, the Director of the Punta Carretas Prison, Chief Inspector Carlos Falcone, called Huidó into his office. While Falcone finished eating a roasted chicken, Huidó had been surviving for months on rice with scraps in the prison, locked up with 148 other Tupamaros and some libertarian guerrillas from other groups. He proposed that Huidó became his partner... that he acted as a mole within the Tupamaro ranks. It was a time of emergency security measures, but these couldn't be sensibly prolonged without a threat that the population believed to be *real*, and with all the subversives locked up, that wouldn't happen. He proposed to Huidó, as the first stage of his cooperation, to allow them to dig a tunnel to escape, while Falcone made sure the officers under his command looked the other way. That was the famous *escape* from Punta Carretas Prison: an agreement between a traitor to his movement, Huidó, and a man convinced he was doing what he did to maintain order in his country. Later, Huidó went in police vehicles, assisting in raid after raid, pointing out the Tupamaros, revealing to the authorities where they lived, where they were hiding... And I'm *not* making this up. As soon as he woke up from his coma, Eleuterio Hernando Huidó confessed everything" – a reporter from El Despertador, with a few hairs on his chin, dropped the microphone he was holding, so shocked was he by the confession. He picked it up and apologized. – "Huidó's testimony is *also* in the case file, and before you ask, the case is under Judge Leguizamo, with Prosecutor Martínez as the accuser, and the defense lawyer for the accused is Dr. Adrián Ojeda. But give them time and space to work, because one thing is for a crime to be known and confessed, and another is the evidence. Just... don't *overwhelm* them, please. Let's go back to Huidó and his pre-fact agreement with the government. Something went wrong during a raid, and José "El Vasco" Olavarría saw him inside the police van. They took Huidó to the back yard of Battalion 14, gave him a weapon, and ordered him to execute Olavarría, because he could identify the traitor within the Tupamaros. It was all a setup. The weapon didn't even have bullets, but they ambushed him and took the Polaroid photo that everyone saw on the cover of El País the next morning" – another pause. – "The pre-coup leadership had Huidó in their grasp. From there, everything went downhill for him: yes, he had some benefits while in prison, but he owed his *absolute* loyalty to the military leadership. At some point, he convinced himself that Amadeo Píriz, who had left the National Liberation Movement – Tupamaros over differences in leadership and goals, was the traitor. Maybe he mentioned it to Mojica and the others, but Píriz was marked from then on as the one who had pointed out to the authorities where the Tupamaros were. Huidó's life from then on was nothing but a downward spiral of lies, always one step closer to hell. But let's go back to the accused F. S., the child growing up with a present mother and a father who tried to be present. One day, when the child was 3 years old, that is, in 1972, she was out strolling with her baby in a stroller when she saw Huidó and Falcone having coffee in a bar in Punta Gorda. Not only was Huidó free, not in prison as everyone believed, but he was sitting there socializing with the top leader of the repression against the subversion. The young mother's world turned upside down. Everything became clear to her in an instant. She didn't tell Huidó, but she informed him that it was over, and that he would *never* see his son again. Tell me now: how can you prevent an ally of the repression forces in a pre-dictatorial country from getting close to your child?" – Geraldine put a hand on her waist. – "Answer: you can't. Almost every weekend, when Huidó was "freed" from his supposed captivity, he would show up drunk at the door of his son's mother. She systematically sent the child to his room, and opened the door to the traitor of his own movement and his country. How could she *not* do it, given who her ex-partner was? Who was she going to call? The police? She tried to confront him at the door, to spare her son the pain, but sometimes she could, and sometimes the exchanges ended in beatings..." – At this point, Geraldine's emotion was genuine, as was the tear that ran down her cheek. – "Sometimes worse. It's *not* necessary to explain what I mean, since we're in a child protection time slot" – she wiped the tear from her cheek with a finger. – "Anyway... eventually the child couldn't take it anymore, he couldn't stand the mistreatment of his mother, so he took the revolver that he knew his mother kept in the bedside table, and went to the door of their house to demand that the man who mistreated his mother leave. That was all the mother of Huidó's child could endure. The next day, she put the house up for sale and fled with her son to Argentina. At that moment, Huidó used his influence with the military repressive leadership to issue a search and capture order for the child's mother, his ex-partner, on charges of sedition and terrorism. F. S. and his mother's flight to Argentina didn't help them, as you can imagine, because they were allied regimes, and between 1979 and 1983, they were *constantly* fleeing, running away, fleeing again, pursued by the repressive forces. Then came 1983, the democratic opening in neighboring Argentina, and finally, mother and son found a brief peace, a chance to *rebuild* their lives. She found work, and he returned to formal education. But by early 1991, now 22 years old, studying medicine at the University of Buenos Aires, she was struck by a sudden, fatal cancer that killed her in a matter of months. On her deathbed, she confessed to her son that his father was the man who knocked on the door every weekend, a traitor to the Tupamaro cause and to the nation itself, but she died before telling him the name, that of Eleuterio Hernando Huidó. And there he was, left alone in life, in a country that wasn't his, accumulating *hatred* towards the one he considered, and perhaps medicine might even support his assumption, not only the cause of all his miseries, but even of his mother's cancer. Because it is *well known* that the pains of the soul, especially those one keeps to oneself to avoid harming loved ones... *cause* cancer. The mind suffers, and the body feels it" – she saw, despite the bright lights, that she wasn't the only one with enough empathy to put herself in the shoes of Fernando Schebor and his mother. – "So, for 20 years, the one I must refer to for protocol as the accused F. S., finished his medical degree, then a doctorate, while *also* investigating by every means who that faceless being was, the one who showed up on weekends, at night, and mistreated his mother. Also, the one who caused them to be fleeing for four years from the death squads in Argentina. Finally, he found him...

he knew it was Huidó... or at least he strongly suspected it was him: it couldn't be anyone else, Huidó or Mojica. At that time, we're talking about just two years ago, he also met, thanks to his investigations, Mojica's son, the accused with the initials F. G., and together they forged an alliance as brothers in pain, brothers in similar and *devastating* life stories, to kill the people they blamed (in one case, clearly so, as in the case of Huidó, in the other, not so much, in Mojica's case), for making them suffer. And then, when they found the opportunity, they killed Mojica in the manner I've described, and tried to do the same with Huidó, failing, but not by much. These are two broken people, two people whom the system failed, whom democratic institutions failed, two individuals with *destroyed* mental and emotional states, whom society could not detect or contain in time for their pathologies. Ladies and gentlemen of the press. I don't know what else to tell you" – she shrugged, wiping away the empathetic tears for those she had helped capture. – "Let's move on to the questions, if that's alright with you. The assistants will circulate among you to bring you a microphone. Please identify yourselves with your name and the media you represent."

There was a moment of expectant silence, until a police reporter from Channel 4, who had narrated the events in Paysandú, was handed the microphone.

"Amílcar Fou, Channel 4: When did the police become certain about the suspects' identities?"

"Wednesday night. Based on interviews with the persons of interest and our own investigations, my partner, Detective Ielicov, and I, along with a task force we formed – *well, as much as a task force as we were... don't exaggerate, Geraldine! We were just five acquaintances with a shared history, eating homemade grilled pizzas* – "We identified the suspects, and immediately notified the police, who issued a search and capture warrant and a border closure.

Suspect F. S. was arrested Thursday morning attempting to enter Brazil by land, and by early afternoon, with the support of the Salto police, we organized a raid at the farm where the other suspect, identified as F. G., was living. We invited you, Amílcar, to witness the event. On behalf of the police, with whom I no longer work, but with whom my partner and I still collaborate, and in pursuit of spreading the truth *without* filters, we thank you and your team for your bravery in being at the scene, despite the risks involved."

"You're welcome, Geraldine."

The journalist thanked her, not only for the acknowledgment of his "bravery" for reporting from a relatively safe location, but also for what it meant for his career in the television industry.

"I want to pause here to clarify what happened yesterday between 2 and 3 PM in Paysandú, which we all saw on television. Imagine this situation. The former Tupamara with the initials A. P., look her up for two minutes or Google her, and you'll *know* who we're talking about." – she raised an eyebrow – "The last time the police came to arrest her was in mid-1971, and what followed were 10 long years of detention without trial, confinement in a cell, and 'physical mistreatment'..." – she made air quotes with her fingers – "to extract information from other dissidents... and now the police was coming for her son. I don't know what more needs to be explained. A mother protecting her son from pain, as she always did. Did A. P. make a mistake by shooting at the police vehicles before they could even show her a summons for her son's testimony? Yes, she *made* a mistake. She didn't distinguish, and in part... once again we can blame the disruption in the democratic continuity for that, and the torments she endured, both during her own arrest in the pre-dictatorship period and her son's during full democracy. She shot first... with the misfortune of injuring a Salto police officer in the first shot, who is fortunately recovering from his injuries, with promising forecasts. What followed... is action and reaction... I shoot, you shoot, *we* shoot... But at one point during the gunfire, the mother of the suspect was severely injured, and her son surrendered without resistance so that the ambulances, which were waiting for the area to be secured, could approach. As an aside, my partner, Detective Viktor Ielicov, offered his arm for a direct transfusion to A. P., mother of F. G. (damn, I *hate* speaking in initials, but the law is the law), or otherwise she wouldn't have made it. She is now recovering at Salto Hospital, in serious condition."

"Omar Paganini, Radio The Witness. Why would the police need external help, like your agency, Goldman, in a homicide case? Is the police force we pay with our taxes failing, perhaps?"

"Thank you for your question, Paganini." – The detective smiled. – "You see, private detectives have other ways of operating, less orthodox, less predictable for criminals. We think *outside* the box, as they say. That Viktor and I reached the killers before the police, however, was only thanks to the *unconditional* support of the Ministry of the Interior, and President Valdez as well, for making the full support of our advisory services available to us. In short: although Viktor and I have a very particular style of investigation, we couldn't have achieved the results we did without the support of the President and the Minister of the Interior. Next question."

"Héctor Durrutia, El País: Goldman, were you the ones who solved the The Decorator case in 2005? Because there are no official mentions on the presidential website, but... then there's that book by writer A. K. Lupoj..." – He shrugged. – "I don't know what to think."

Oh, no, Aklmer, I'm going to get you back for this, Geraldine fumed internally. *You send a journalist to promote your book?* But she only replied:

"Yes. Yes, it was us. I suppose that's why Minister Cortez called us in to advise on this case, but these are topics I'd prefer not to delve into. Last question." – She authorized.

"Will we see you more often in Uruguay, solving high-profile, public interest cases?" – The reporter who had been handed the microphone noticed the disdainful looks from his colleagues and took a moment to interpret his mistake. – "Oh, yes, sorry... Figueroa, for El Despertador."

"You can *bet* on it, Figueroa." – She winked. – "We're back in the game."

THE END

*Montevideo, capital of what happened **not only** due to state terrorism, but also due to violence among the people of Uruguay, September and October 2016. A. K. Lupoj.*

Don't miss out!

Visit the website below and you can sign up to receive emails whenever Marcel Pujol publishes a new book. There's no charge and no obligation.

https://books2read.com/r/B-A-HAMY-ZXVHF

BOOKS 2 READ

Connecting independent readers to independent writers.

Did you love *Lady & Boxer Investigators - Magnicide*? Then you should read *Institute*[1] by Marcel Pujol!

Myra, Senator Lawrence's eldest daughter, committed suicide in a classroom at the SAHISICA Boarding School (Sant Andrews of the Hills Institute for Self-Improvement and Catholic Achievements), of which little is known about its inner workings, except that the graduates are who will lead the United States in the next generation.

Agent Hynreck of the FBI, a former legend of the agency, to the point of having been considered in his time to occupy the Directorship of the Bureau and now fallen into disgrace and alcoholism, will be summoned by an anonymous letter to be the

---

1. https://books2read.com/u/bQezgw

2. https://books2read.com/u/bQezgw

one to unravel the mystery behind that a young woman who seemed to have it all took her life in such a spectacular way.

The young and energetic Special Agent Henshaw in charge of Hynreck as his superior officer and babysitter, faces the double task of trying to unravel if behind the almost impossible death of the Sahisican inmate there is something more to investigate, and if Hynreck has something to do with it.

On the other hand, two sects with the same goals and opposite methodologies, the Corpus Christi and the Templars, dispute the fate of the World Order as if it was on chess board.

Read more at https://marcelpujol9.wordpress.com/marcel-pujol-escritor/.

Also by Marcel Pujol

Crónicas de las Tierras Occidentales
Akarat de Ragoon
Naiara de Gromberg
Belzalith - Emperatriz de Zehiria

Dama y Boxeador Investigadores
Dama y Boxeador Investigadores - El DecOrador
Dama y Boxeador Investigadores - Magnicidio

Diaries of the Forced Time Traveler
Diaries of the Forced Time Traveler - Part 1: Jump Back

Diarios del Viajero Forzado en el Tiempo
Diarios del Viajero Forzado en el Tiempo - Parte 1: Salto Atrás

Edith Bonelli - Detective PrivadA
El Club de lo Prohibido

Juguetes en el Ático
¿Dónde están Clarita y Sebastián?

Edith Bonelli - Détective PrivéE
Le Club de L'interdit

Edith Bonelli - Private Investigator
The Club of the Prohibited

FBI Hynreck and the Montana Fishing Club
Institute

FBI Hynreck y el Club de Pesca de Montana
Internado
Migajas
La Conexión Rossi-Chamorro

Journaux du Voyageur Forcé dans le Temps
Journaux du Voyageur Forcé dans le Temps - Partie 1: Saut en Arrière

Lady & Boxer Investigators
Lady & Boxer Investigators - Magnicide

Los Fuera de Serie

El Libro Que Nunca Se Escribió
Arioco - Señor del Caos y la Destrucción
Verminaard - El Último Dragón
Nudo en la Garganta
Por si pensabas dormir - Vol. 1

Los Raritos

H - Manual Anti-Histeria para Padres
J - Manual Para el Preso Primerizo
S - Manual de las Sectas
Ramillete de Versos Surtidos

Nosotros También Leemos

Nosotros También Leemos - Vol. 1
Dana y Roger Investigadores - El Misterio del Cáliz Celta
Dana y Roger Investigadores - Algo sórdido ocurre en "La Quinta"
Dana y Roger Investigadores - Secuestro en Nueva York

Nous Lissons Aussi

Dana et Roger Investigateurs - Enlèvement à New York

The Out of Series

Verminaard - The Last Dragon

Arioch - Lord of Chaos and Destruction

The Weirdos
Arioch - Lord of Chaos and Destruction (Script Version - Part 1)

We Too Read
Dana and Roger Investigators - Kidnapping in New York

Watch for more at https://marcelpujol9.wordpress.com/marcel-pujol-escritor/.

About the Author

Marcel Pujol escribió entre 2005 y 2007 doce obras de los más variados temas y en diferentes géneros: thrillers, fantasía épica, compilados de cuentos, y también ensayos sobre temas tan serios como la histeria en la paternidad o el sistema carcelario uruguayo. En 2023 vuelve a tomar la pluma creativa y ya lleva escritos 10 nuevos títulos... ¡Y va por más!

A este autor no se le puede identificar con género ninguno, pero sí tiene un estilo muy marcado que atraviesa su obra:- Las tramas son atrapantes- Los diálogos entre los personajes tienen una agilidad y una adrenalina propias del cine de acción - Los personajes principales progresan a través de la obra, y el ser que emerge de la novela puede tener escasos puntos de contacto con quien era al inicio- No hay personajes perfectos. Incluso los principales, van de los antihéroes a personajes con cualidades destacables, quizás, pero imperfectas. Un poco como cada uno de nosotros, ¿no es así?

Read more at https://marcelpujol9.wordpress.com/marcel-pujol-escritor/.

Milton Keynes UK
Ingram Content Group UK Ltd.
UKHW022125251124
451529UK00012B/698